Brought up in the Lincolnshire and Cambridgeshire area, Meg moved to West Yorkshire in 1988. She has a daughter, Emma, and son, Sam, who are both in their thirties. Until becoming self-employed in 2004, Meg worked in property, charity and recruitment.

Much of Meg's inspiration is drawn from the heady heights of the Holme Valley, where she currently lives. Her first publication, *Tarot Teachers*, came on to the market in 2007, and she wrote and directed her first play in 2007, *Memories of To Sir With Love*, which was performed by Turn Again Theatre in Holmfirth.

Since starting to write, Meg has become enamoured with Amateur Dramatics, something she had not been involved in for over 40 years. Smitten, and to enhance her writing and acting, Meg undertook a two-year BTec Performing Arts Course at Huddersfield Technical College. Her favourite roles to date have been Mrs Richardson, in *Fawlty Towers* and Irene, in *The Lady of Letters*. Meg has just been approached to play Kathy in Stephen King's *Misery* in May 2009. Her ambition is to play a cameo role in *Fecundity!*

Meg is a trained Energy Therapist and has a healthy interest in alternative therapies and spirituality. Besides drama and property renovations, Meg is a keen artist, an enthusiastic photographer and loves to cook and bake.

# FECUNDITY!

MEG PLUMMER

FECUNDITY!

AUSTIN MACAULEY

# Essex County Council Libraries

A CIP catalogue record for this title is available from the British Library.

**ISBN 978 1 905609 31 4**

www.austinmacauley.com

First Published (2008)
Austin & Macauley Publishers Ltd.
25 Canada Square
Canary Wharf
London
E14 5LB

Printed & Bound in Great Britain

Dedicated to Emma and Sam, my daughter and son
who are my world and inspiration – I love you so very much.

In memory of my father and grandmother, who felt so near.

# ACKNOWLEDGEMENTS

When I sat at my desk each morning to write this book I would always light a candle for inspiration. I knew the beginning of the story, and the end, but when I set out to write Fecundity! I had no idea how the journey would develop. When I was stuck I would sit and gaze into the candle and would often feel my loved ones, long passed, were there to inspire me. There were times when I was so excited, by the things that evolved from my musings, that when I typed it was like my fingers were being sick on the keyboard – typing to keep up with my thoughts was at times impossible! Emma and Sam were incredibly patient, listening to my endless ideas, and I'm sure must have wondered on numerous occasions if my writing would ever come to anything.

I would like to give my heartfelt thanks to the following, who encouraged, supported or helped develop Fecundity! and dreamt up some of the language that evolved from the story.

My son and daughter Emma and Sam for their patience and contributions
For the photography – Edith Powner-Plested
For modelling – Sean Jagger
Front cover design – Bob Hryndyj

To Jemma Weise, Kate Bedford, Lilian Poultney, Ann Burns, Rowena Short, Darren Stubbs, Peter Barlow, Sheila Szlachcic and Simon Parton
who all believed, encouraged, helped shape and kept me focused

To Beryl Hooley, Irvin Dickinson, Liz Wade, Bev Nichols and Jean Whiteford
and to all the many others who encouraged and helped me along the way

And a special thank you to my neighbour, David Nichols, who inspired me greatly, but is sadly no longer with us

And to those of you who are brave enough to live and feel this book as you read it
I wish you love, light and liberation!

If you once forfeit the confidence
of your fellow citizens,
you can never regain their respect and esteem.

You may fool all of the people
some of the time;
you can even fool some of the people
all the time;
but you can't fool
all of the people all of the time.

*Abraham Lincoln* 1809-1865.
*Sixteenth President of the USA*

2032 found the UK to be a virtually crime free island devoid of criminals – in the main. Those committing offences were, as a rule, quickly detected due to the rigid strictures of the People's Government. Big Brother had taken over!

Portraying itself as an impeccable governing body, for the people and against the criminal, it was predicted crime would be a thing of the past within the next three generations. But all was not as it seemed.

To achieve these aims, restrictions, not always evident, were imposed on UK inhabitants from the day they were born. With meticulous planning the government's objective was to be the exemplary leading country in the WPPL, World Peace & Prosperity Leaders

And all seemed to go according to plan until…
An eventuality, of such unthinkable magnitude,
Out-thwarts the government's plans –
Just one small mistake in mankind and…

# Prologue

## Sunday, 29 February 2032

His menace was hidden by the shadows of the deserted alleyway. Around him lay a variety of rubbish and, just to his side, was a hypodermic, the blood still glistening on its needle.

He'd stalked his prey here many times before. He knew her times of leaving the pub, route home and mocking attitude that she thought made her invincible. But tonight all that was going to change. He was going to teach her the lesson of all lessons, punish her for all her bravado, nonchalant 'couldn't care less' attitude and her mockery. Tonight her future would change, but what he didn't realise was that it would also change his. All he was bothered about, all he could think about, was showing her that she wasn't the impervious Miss Untouchable she liked to portray. Tonight he was going to show her just how vulnerable she was, what a coward and how pathetic she really was when faced with a real man. He was going to enjoy every minute of her torture, just as much as she would hate it, and hate herself afterwards.

His skin prickled with the excitement of expectation. He felt his loins stir as he awaited her approach. He licked his lips in nervous anticipation and unconsciously rubbed his groin, relieved and pleased to feel his growing hardness.

In the distance he saw a light come on at a nearby house. It was near enough to give an outline to the figure that had triggered its brilliance but the shafts of light were too far off to expose his lair. He pulled a padded black ski mask from his anorak pocket and tugged it on over his head. Once on, only his eyes would be exposed and if they could be seen, in the dim light, they would show to be shining brightly with malice and excitement.

As soon as his mask was on he pulled out a crumpled, used and dirty cotton handkerchief that had seen better days. Hardly used nowadays, the rapist still preferred the proper thing, and had done ever since he was a child in his cot and had wrapped one round his hand to use as a comforter whilst going to sleep. Even now, in fact especially now, it gave him comfort but more importantly the confidence he needed to carry out the deed he had set himself.

As he rolled the hanky into a ball in his sweaty palm, he listened to the footsteps of the woman approaching. He straightened himself, positioning his body ready to pounce. As the footsteps drew nearer he could hear her softly singing to herself. He knew that this was the one he waited for; it was her constant singing that really grated on his nerves.

As the footsteps fell in front of him he inhaled deeply and just as her body took one step past him he took an enormous leap throwing his left arm round her neck dragging her backwards to the ground. At the same time he stuffed the filthy hanky into her mouth stifling any scream or noise she might make to summon help. With a practised move he deftly rammed the hanky deeper into her mouth before she could even utter a sound or gather the wit to bite him. With his free hand he grabbed at the front of her coat brutally ripping it open. With a small pop a button flew off and landed silently on the ground among the debris. With her coat open he clumsily grabbed for her breast his enormous hand pinching it hard. She put up her hand to protect herself, trying to fend him off. Without conscious thought of his actions or strength he smashed his forearm into her face breaking her cheek bone and momentarily stunning her.

The weight of her body sagged in his hold giving him the opportunity to let her fall to the ground whilst at the same time giving her another resounding crack, this time with his elbow, causing further damage. In the silent struggle she heard, as much as felt, her nose crack as it broke but in her panic did not feel the sticky warmth as blood gushed from it.

As he threw her down he pinioned her to the ground with his knee, his full body weight upon her. With his other knee he pinned her flailing right arm to the ground to prevent her from striking him. She struck out with her free hand desperately snatching at his mask trying to rip it off to get a look at the bastard's face. She was a brave and plucky young woman and wasn't going to give in to this monster without a fight. *That isn't how Lucy Johnson lives her life,'* she told herself in a bid to bolster her bravery.

He brushed her arm aside, as if it was no more than a fly irritating his skin, and drawing his arm right back punched her cheek with full force. Her head snapped back and her body sank lifelessly into the rubbish as she reeled into black unconsciousness. Unbeknown to her the dirty syringe sank deeply into the flesh of her buttock.

Her attacker took her stillness as the opportunity to tear open her clothing. He tore open her blouse and ripped the cups of her bra apart dragging his long, dirty fingernails down her flesh leaving livid red gouges in her pale skin. He pulled at the hem of her skirt exposing her thighs, clad in flesh-coloured tights. With her still being unconscious he was able to free his other hand, which was holding her down, and instead used it to unzip his flies and pull out his hardened penis.

Pulling at her tights and pants the material ripped open, tearing like tissue paper, the cold night air stirring the woman back into semi-consciousness. Realising what was happening she raised her head in panic as the adrenaline pumped round her body giving her the extra strength she needed to fight him off. Trying to take a deep breath she gagged on the rag in her mouth. She momentarily froze, realising she wouldn't be able to fight him off that easily. Consciously she made the decision to quickly pay attention to her attacker and register what she could about him. Breathing through her nose she could smell her own fear, but could also smell something else. Something that seemed familiar but, in her distressed state, she couldn't quite recognise. Subconsciously, she mentally filed the thought away to think about later. Now she needed all her strength and guile to defend herself and fight off this evil beast. Resolutely she tightened all the muscles in her body as he tried to force himself between her legs. Her body, fit from years of exercise, became as rigid and unyielding as a rock. She heard him grunt in frustration, as he was unable to gain the entry he desired of her body.

He had vowed that this time he would not speak. This time there was a chance he could be recognised. So far he'd been lucky, had never been recognised and not even suspected, yet alone properly questioned. All his previous rapes had been done miles from where he lived and he'd not known any of his previous victims. This time it was different, for he was known to his victim, and she to him. This was the woman who had driven him to become a rapist in the first place. Bitch that she was. It was vitally important he didn't make any mistakes, so she didn't recognise him. For this particular rape he'd carefully and precisely planned the attack so it could be executed quickly and brutally and bring about as much humiliation as possible.

As he couldn't warn her verbally, not to fight or make a noise, he grabbed hold of her nipple and viciously twisted it knowing it would cause her intense pain. In retaliation, not being able to push him off, she started to draw up her leg ready to knee him in the groin. The move was a mistake. It was the move he'd been waiting for and grabbing her leg he pulled it aside whilst at the same time ramming himself into her, grinding himself deeply into her body. Whilst pummelling himself into her he grunted and at the same time grabbed handfuls of breast using them as if they were lumps of dough. The strength of his grip would leave telltale signs of his person, that might later be detrimental to his anonymity, but this was something that didn't even cross his mind.

The woman, realising that she would not be able to fight off this atrocity, and fearing for her life let alone her sanity, closed down all feeling to her mind and body. He may have penetrated her body but he was not going to have the satisfaction of seeing her fight or struggle any more. As far as she was concerned at this moment in time she was dead, maybe not in clinical terms but this moment was just happening – but not to her. It was only happening to the physical but empty shell of the body that she'd just vacated. It was the only way she would ever have the chance of being able to cope with it, if she didn't allow herself to experience it. She locked her feelings deeply inside herself so that no matter how much brutality, humiliation or pain she suffered physically, she was not emotionally present to experience it. At that moment she died within herself and with it part of her died forever.

Her transition to 'death' did not register with him. He continued to grunt and brutally plunge until finally he was spent. He struggled up from her body dragging his clothes together as he rose. Beneath his mask and clothes his body was awash with sweat, his bodily smells mingling with the sour odour of his frenzy.

Having straightened his clothing he looked down at the prostrate body lying at his feet. He leaned over and, forcing the woman's mouth open, pulled the sodden handkerchief out and stuffed it back into his pocket before turning to walk away, strolling confidently and feeling good about himself and what he had done. He pulled off his mask and shoved it back into his pocket, but didn't look round. He didn't even think about the body he'd left there as a woman, or even as a person. The body he'd left behind was the satisfaction of his revenge. A revenge that would stay with him forever – and result in more consequences than he could ever have imagined possible.

~ ~ ~ ~ ~ ~

Daryl, holding a small metal disc between his fingers, placed his hand flat against the black plate secured beside his front door. The palm and iris readings confirmed it was Daryl and transmitted his image onto the internal computer. The actual time was 23.40, but the time on the entry device registered was only 22.40. Automatically the imagery de-activated the locking devices and silently the door glided open, the internal lights in the entry hallway glowed softly in the ceiling. Daryl stepped through the door and onto the mat, which conveyed instructions for the door to shut and secure itself. Slinging the long cylindrical tube from his shoulder, Daryl lovingly ran his hand over the casing before hoisting his much cherished pool cue gently onto the purpose made rack. He allowed himself a brief feeling of triumph, before proceeding through the house.

Daryl stood five foot eleven and a half inches tall, in his unshod feet, and in shoes just a fraction over six foot. He was of medium build with a full head of dark brown hair which, thanks to medical advancements, had not greyed or thinned. His insipid pale blue eyes, which Daryl always kept averted, would have been described as icy, rheumy and cold. But few people had ever seen them properly, as Daryl chose to keep them partially hooded, keeping his head down and never allowing his gaze to meet others. Despite constantly shaving Daryl always sported a five o'clock shadow and had small sideburns, which he thought were smart but were in fact outdated.

His dress sense was old-fashioned, reflecting, he thought, his father's image, which over the years had become markedly distorted. Daryl chose to wear neatly pressed chinos, similar to those worn in the 1990s, short sleeved shirts, usually with a logo on the pocket and a back pleat, and black buckskin Velcro fastening shoes. His outdoor jacket, which he carefully hung up, was made of black leather and lined with a threadbare tartan padding. The jacket itself, cracked and worn, had seen better days and had originally belonged to Daryl's dad, who had died almost thirty years ago. At the turn of the century Daryl's appearance, which he believed was dapper and debonair would have been in fashion, but was totally out of keeping with the fashions of the twenty-thirties. Fashion, however, didn't bother Daryl. Daryl saw himself as his own person, but based that foundation on his missed and much doted on father. The style Daryl sported didn't suit him and certainly wasn't conducive with the current trends, as Daryl had neither the bravado nor the swagger of his father to carry off the style.

Daryl, an individual with very low self-esteem and little, if any, confidence was a sullen individual who portrayed an arrogant, almost surly demeanour in his attempt to emulate how he thought his father had behaved. He still lived at home with his mother who used and abused him. She had utter contempt for Daryl, never had a kind word to say about him or to him, and did her utmost to make his life an abject misery. Daryl on the other hand worshipped his mother, begged her constantly to let him spend time with her and believed that by mimicking his father he would finally win her over. The truth was, though, that his trying to emulate his father was just one of the invisible and unidentified problems between him and his mother, and one of the reasons he was the butt of everyone's jokes and the jibes that were constantly targeted at him.

Daryl, to the world, was a joke. But the Daryl underneath was anything but!

~ ~ ~ ~ ~

Jack and Chloe strolled, hand in hand, along the city street towards the parklands. They walked in quiet unison, deep in their own thoughts. The past few years had been trying and had put them both under terrific strain as they'd undertaken a wide and extensive range of treatments in their bid to have a baby.

Their arduous and emotional journey was now almost concluded, following their final consultation before this next and ultimate stage of the process to become parents. The last of the couples' eggs had been impregnated by Jack's sperm and if successfully fertilised would be implanted in the Brooder's womb tomorrow, 1st March 2032.

Having had extensive talks, consultations and counselling, following a number of abortive attempts to have a child of their own, tomorrow was their last chance to achieve their much sought after ambition to become parents. Tomorrow their fertilised egg would be implanted into the Brooder, who would incubate their baby for the next sixteen weeks. Then on the 21st June the foetus, warmly tucked in its Brooder's womb, would be transplanted into Chloe's body, her own womb being removed only minutes before receiving the transplant. It was then up to Chloe's body to nurture the baby until it was due to be born, something which hadn't happened in previous pregnancies. They prayed that this time a miracle would happen and that around the 6th December they would be blessed with a much longed for son or daughter.

*A new baby just in time for Christmas,* they both pondered separately. However, neither of them dare raise their hopes too much or speak their thoughts out loud, as Chloe's body was not comfortable being pregnant and was inclined to reject incubating babies. The couple and medics involved hoped that, with having a pregnant womb implanted, Chloe's body would accept the pregnancy until at least the thirtieth week, when the baby would be legally entitled to medical intervention. If it didn't then the newborn would be left, medically, for nature to take its course.

Jack, with Chloe's hand warmly clasped in his own, led them both towards the parklands in the crisp coolness of the afternoon. *This is somewhere,* he thought, *that I hope to bring my son or daughter to in the future. Oh! let there be a future,* he silently implored. *Let there be a little Jack or Chloe to make our lives complete, allow me to be a dad and Chloe a mum.*

He wondered what the child would look like, if they were blessed with a child at the end of this long and arduous journey they'd been travelling for the past few years. Would it have Chloe's Latin looks and be petite with her dark hair and eyes and her lovely olive skin? Or would it be like him with mousey-coloured hair and the thin lanky build he was blessed, or was it cursed, with? He was no oil painting, nothing to write home about, but he knew he was blessed with the warm and sunny personality he was loved and liked for. He was always the one his friends turned to if they needed an ear to bend or a sounding board; the one who was invited to all the parties as the life and soul, who gave it the warmth and spark that every party needed to be a memorable occasion. His nephews and nieces, along with their parents, grandparents and other relations, all saw him as the leading light in their slowly growing but strong extended family. The only thing missing from Jack's life was a child to call his own, and missing from his persona was the right to call himself, and be, a daddy. But maybe in nine months time that would change. Wouldn't it? Or would he need to put on hold forever the chance of being a dad?

Jack tightened his grip on Chloe's hand then gently pulled her towards him and letting his arm trail across her shoulders tenderly kissed her hair. In response, Chloe's thoughts and hopes matching his own, they silently sent up beseeching prayers. Tomorrow was the first day of the rest of their lives. Lives that, in a few months time, would see their emotions turning in somersaults, facing feelings they never, in their wildest of dreams, would have expected to encounter.

~ ~ ~ ~ ~

*Today's been a good day,* Liam thought. *In fact excellent in terms of business and… how can I put it? Crumpet? No that couldn't be right, the old term 'crumpet' used to refer to women, if my memory from history lessons serves me well, and my tastes are far wider than that, including men as well as women… as long as they're good company, enjoy a drink and socialising and aren't adverse to a bit of uninhibited sex, well, as long as they enjoy sex I'm happy to work on their inhibitions. In fact I enjoy the challenge.*

Liam, clearing things away at the end of the day enjoyed his work immensely. More importantly he enjoyed the choice of sexual partners his job offered him, unofficially of course, and today had been no exception. Today's group, of some twenty or so people, were all about his age, or a bit older. By midday he'd been hugely flattered by being chatted up by three of the five he'd identified as potential bed partners, and invited out by them all.

He smiled inwardly to himself, knowing he was a popular guy with most enjoying his company, and often wanting more. *I'm not the slimmest of men, in fact,* he reminded himself, *as a government employee I have to set the right standards for the rest of the nation so I've got to address the issue sooner rather than later, even if I'm a long way from being fat. I'm just chunky,* he told himself. Well, he preferred to call it cuddly because he just adored physical contact – with anyone.

Looking at his image in the blank computer screen he appraised his reflection, which showed a blond haired young man, with the strangest blue, almost aqua coloured, eyes. His eyebrows and eyelashes were so pale they were virtually invisible, as was the fine down on the rest of his body; his nose was broad, but not particularly long, and his lips full. He would have loved to be able to say his jaw and chin was strong and square, but had to admit in truth that it was 'loose'. Anyhow, whatever his looks he certainly had no problems getting anyone, male or female, between his sheets.

Being a decisive person, and very focused, he'd decided today to let fate take its course and decide where, and with whom, he spent the night. Just before everyone had left, four of them had arranged to meet up at the Forniclub, where sex was on tap and the imagination could run wild and free. He may end up with one of the group or with someone totally different. Come to that he may just be able to engineer that all four of them end up together and have an orgy. Metaphorically he rubbed his hands in delighted glee at the thought of them all cavorting together naked, either in the club or back at the hotel.

Liam took a sweeping glance around the room to make sure he'd not forgotten anything and readied himself to go back to his hotel for a wonderfully invigorating and arousing shower prior to setting off to see what, and who, he could conquer tonight. He just knew it was going to be a night to pamper each and every one of his sexual whims, of which he had many. Liam, without any inhibitions that he knew of, or had discovered so far, loved sex, with women, and men, either singularly or in a group. Sex was his weakness, in any format, and he loved it and lived for it. He craved the anticipation of setting off on a sexual adventure, which at twenty-one he'd experienced a wide variety. Ever since his first encounter, with a woman old enough to be his mother, he'd loved every aspect of sex.

Tonight would be as good as he could make it, and would be just one in a long line of many nights to come, not only for now but over the next few years. Or so he thought. Leaving the building with those happy thoughts and anticipations in mind no one could have foreseen that in a few months time his extraordinary love of sex would be his ultimate downfall, and would change his life and attitude forever.

~ ~ ~ ~ ~

Jed, who was just fifteen, lay on his slumber-pit. He was a dark haired lad with a sallow complexion, deep set very dark brown eyes and eyebrows that met in the middle, almost resting on the bridge of his nose. He was a tall lanky lad still growing and with a lot of filling out to do before he reached his full masculine peak.

Jed hated his bedroom with a passion. It may have a state-of-the-art entertainment system, with a large plasma screen where he watched his films, played games and accessed the internet, but it was a room for a boy much younger than himself. Jed constantly harped on to his parents about updating it and making it more conducive to the individual he believed he was. His parents though were always 'too busy' or dismissive of his claims believing 'most lads of his age would be pleased with a room like his'. Jed was not. He was so embarrassed by his room that he never brought his friends home, not even his best friend Ben, whom he'd known all his life.

The house he lived in was a government property, signed over to his parents just before Jed had been born. Prior to his birth Jed's parents had lived in a very trendy and pleasant area, overlooking the river in the then much sought after 'professional sector' of Cambridge. However, it had not been the sort of property that lent itself to bringing up children nor did it afford the room for a child so, just before Jed had been conceived in 2016, his parents had applied, as a married couple, to have an approved child. Their application, and the subsequent conception and birth of Jed, had qualified them for the house they now lived in.

They'd remained in the same house and township, since Jed was born, on the outskirts of Cambridge city centre, which had everything a young family could want, or need, from being born to leaving home. With schools and colleges, golf courses through to cinemas and safe areas for children of all ages, the residents were well provided for, and closely monitored by Big Brother.

The township was just close enough to the city to make an easy transition from home to work. Sadly though Jed's parents weren't just working people, they were career people who lived and breathed work and expected Jed to fall into their working pattern without causing a ripple. Life, though, wasn't quite like that and Jed had very set ideas about what he did and didn't want in his life, and knew how to go about it without his parents being too aware, despite the Wristlet he was forced to wear.

Jed was a sullen, spoilt individual with a tendency to disparage his fellow pupils. At school he ran a SwapNet scam along with his partner in crime, Ben. The SwapNet was an official school site allowing pupils to advertise and negotiate the swapping, selling or buying of goods that they either desired or no longer needed. By sheer fluke Jed and Ben had somehow hit upon a way of infiltrating punters; commandeering the goods and using the items for their own gain. In general the transactions were peaceable, but it was not unknown for Jed and Ben to use bullyboy tactics to get the benefit of a transaction exclusively for themselves. In effect they skirted on the borders of being bullies.

Although only fifteen Jed had been sexually active for a couple of years now, and saw himself as a 'man of the moment' and was not adverse to using sex as a means to an end. Typical of a young person brought up in a loveless home, Jed was not a naturally tactile person or familiar with the finer feelings of intimacy. He could see no wrong in using sex for what he wanted and his 'intimacies' were not laced with feelings. As a 'hardened man' Jed could not have foreseen the emotional roller-coaster his sexual activities would force him to face in the next twelve months.

# First Trimester

## March – May 2032

Two hours after the attack, Lucy's unconscious body was found and within minutes the area had become a serious crime scene, with medics working skilfully on the inert body. As the administered drugs took effect it was evident the girl was slipping into a much deeper and more relaxed state. Scanning her body it was obvious she'd suffered multiple fractures to her head, face and body, and there was massive bruising over her entire body. From the extensive injuries it was obvious to the medics the attacker had a vicious streak of brutality.

Not only was the scanner identifying injuries but picking up patterning of fists and boots, with amazing clarity. In fact from the patterns being picked up it looked as though the perpetrator had deliberately fallen on her with his full weight causing immense damage to her and exacerbating the damage incurred where she'd obviously had her legs wrenched apart.

Whilst the medics did their work the police were simultaneously carrying out a number of tasks. Technology had advanced so much, since the turn of the century, there was little evidence likely to escape their notice. From DNA to indentations, chemicals to smells left behind by the attacker, they would be picked out and identified by the scanner being used on the victim's body.

As soon as Lucy was admitted to the Crimedical Centre she was attached to the Subliminal Voyeur and within a short space of time the machine had established a wide array of information about the attack. Amongst the initial findings they were able to determine she'd been gagged with a wadding of material pushed far back into her mouth. Samples taken from Lucy's mouth alone would enable them to identity a whole array of information about the rapist's behaviour and lifestyle, from traces left by the gag. Results would be ready almost instantaneously and activate a whole host of other programmes within the Crimedical systems.

Within minutes the analysis had established the gag to be an old-fashioned material handkerchief with DNA from two other people, besides Lucy's. One sample would of course be the rapist's, the other, at this moment in time no one knew. As the information was fed through to the investigation team it also activated other systems, which would search for matching DNA and crimes logged with the same characteristics. It would only be a matter of time before other crimes, with similar and same characteristics and data, would be matched and fed back to the investigator. The handkerchief was likely to be a major breakthrough in this case, with few people possessing them nowadays, it was just a pity they didn't have the actual article. Within an hour of the swabs being taken it was discovered the third sample of DNA belonged to a previous rape victim, but from an incident in Inverness, nearly four hundred miles away and of little use as information at this moment in time.

Lucy's condition was not good and for the first forty-eight hours she'd be kept heavily sedated and linked into the Subliminal Voyeur, which would run several memory programmes and tap deep into her subconscious for information on the attack her conscious memory may not recall. If they were lucky it would pick up clear images of the perpetrator, which would show his facial features along with other small details, which would help identify him. The smaller details were often ones blocked by a victim, like mannerisms or smells, blanked by the conscious mind. With the Subliminal Voyeur the only time a perpetrator's image was unlikely to be seen was if a mask was worn, but even then the extremely advanced and sophisticated reconstruction programmes would be able to scan facial contours beneath the covering, unless of course it was a moulded mask.

Just two hours after the swabs had been taken, it was established the attacker's DNA did not link with any known criminal and was not on the Government DNA Database, a misdemeanour in itself. National Crime Control had identified five other rapes with the same DNA, and behavioural patterns, so they knew their attacker was the serial rapist and the case would take priority, otherwise the Government would be in breach of national and WPPL rulings.

As a specialist Crimedical Inspector DDI Froud had a combined criminal and medical background and was one of the topmost personnel involved in the Crimedical Scheme. His research and programmes of innovation were envied and emulated throughout the UK and only the exceptionally talented were lucky enough for a place on his team. Froud was immensely proud of the Crimedical Sector's achievements since being established, and the part he'd played from inception, yet displayed no characteristics of smugness or superiority. The man was an inspiration to his staff and very much a vehicle to their progression if they were lucky enough to be chosen for a case, which they jostled for enthusiastically.

As was protocol, a senior female officer was assigned to the rape case and with the sensitivity of the case Melanie Roberts was chosen. At thirty-three she was a popular, well respected Specialist Sergeant and the first government protégé ever recruited to the newly formed Crimedical Sector. Melanie wasn't exactly ugly, but was a long way from being called pretty, or even attractive. At five foot two, and thin to the point of being scrawny, she had short, clean but un-styled hair and a pasty, slightly pocked-marked skin. However, what Melanie lacked in the looks department, she made up for in intelligence and determination. If anyone was to get to the bottom of this case it would be Melanie, who'd met the scrupulous entry criteria for recruitment and undergone extensive training, primarily as a doctor and then as an investigator, before completing several years' apprenticeship and qualifying for her current senior post.

Melanie had been heavily involved in the development and introduction of the Subliminal Voyeur, which probed deeply into the subconscious mind and produced film quality pictures of those images. It was one step beyond mind reading and when originally perfected, in the mid twenty-twenties, had also created a major marketing coup of less sophisticated 'Dream Machines', which were launched to fund the continual development of Subliminal Voyeurs. One of the programmes incorporated into the Subliminal Voyeur was a system which totally eradicated memories from victim's mind, but were retrievable should the need ever arise. The victim always had the choice of viewing their memories of the incident but few chose this option and re-programming, after a major trauma, enabled them to cope with life as if the incident hadn't happened.

The invention had created an immediate impact in Crimedicology and was now the most successful investigation technique used. Justifiably proud of her contribution to its development Melanie had one other attribute she'd brought with her; an extensive and enviable database of every investigation technique she'd ever read from fact and fiction publications. In her teens when she'd originally started it, each time she'd finished a book she'd record the crime, techniques, findings and other aspects meticulously recording them with book title, page and line information for ease of future reference. Although a large proportion of it was based on fictional books it had become a constant source of reference in the department and several had added to it over the years.

~ ~ ~ ~ ~

Daryl woke at 06.30 exactly, took an invigorating shower then dressed carefully and put one of his dad's old handkerchiefs in his pocket. He preened in front of the mirror proud of his appearance, especially his full head of hair, silently blessing modern science for overcoming the issue of baldness. Despite everything Daryl had great pride and was meticulous in his dress, oblivious to the fact he wore totally the wrong type of clothing. He'd no idea his pristine appearance invited ridicule and his clothes were outdated and smacked of who he wanted to be – a mummy's boy. Daryl tried to mimic his father's style, which was partly the cause of his mother's animosity towards him, not that either of them were aware of this fact.

Finally satisfied with his appearance Daryl made his way downstairs and walked into the kitchen, the image of 'real' toast quickly fading from his mind as he entered the sterile perfection of the room. Consuming two breakfast pearls, instead of toast, his mood immediately blackened and he became annoyed with himself for being so spineless where his Mam was concerned. As much as he loved real food he loved his Mam more, worshipped her in fact, and it was more than thought could bear for him to upset her. He'd only worry and agonise, wondering if he'd spoilt her day, then arrive home to have even more of her scorn and hatred poured over him again.

At 07.43 exactly Daryl left the house and set off to work, the metaphorical black cloud hanging more heavily as he neared the factory. He'd arrive at precisely 07.52, never a minute before or after, so precise were his actions. It was a standing joke; the entire production process could be set against him as he always took his breaks at the same time and if ever he had to stand in on a line the production rate never differed. His precision and timekeeping was uncanny, adding fuel to his tormentors' fire, the weird thing being he never wore a timepiece.

His feeling of dread increased and he started sweating as he entered the factory. He looked round anxiously to see who was about, seeing the usual faces, with the exception of his main antagonists Angela, Sadie, Lucy and Amanda who collectively made everyone's life a misery. Daryl was usually their prime target, his gullibility and fixation on his Mam being the main butt of their jokes, but he'd never understood why. He cringed inwardly as he remembered some of the jokes made at his expense; the merciless ribbing about his lack of girlfriends, the way he dressed, how particular he was with his appearance, and anything else they could find to ridicule him with.

*Today won't be any different*, he thought his heart sinking. Then he remembered the events of the night before and smirked inwardly, which created a feeling of euphoria and replaced his normal mood of despondency. *I'd better make sure I don't look too happy and I'm not behaving different, otherwise it'll probably draw attention,* he cautioned himself silently. *But it feels different in here today,* he mused. *Bit more relaxed, or is it me?* By the time Daryl had donned his overalls and collected his toolbox, at two minutes to eight, no one had spoken to him, let alone mocked him, which was unusual.

Daryl was anyone's and everybody's victim. He was an odd character totally devoid of any social graces and regarded locally as a colourless simpleton, which he wasn't by any stretch of the imagination. He had no conversation, no friends and had never had a girlfriend. When he was younger he'd been picked on and bullied at school, despite doing everything possible to become accepted by some, or even just one, of his fellow pupils. He'd tried to run with the wild ones but always ended up as the butt of their jokes and taking the blame, so was constantly being disciplined, taking it as a lamb, meekly and without fight or even argument. Whatever he tried he seemed to fail at, which intensified his misery. He'd been an only child and was as lonely as he was only, a sad pathetic little boy – who later became a sad and lonely man.

By the time he'd reached adulthood Daryl had accepted he wasn't meant to share his life with anyone. His Mam, he knew, had nothing but contempt for him and used him as a verbal punch bag, and as a means of not having to go out to work. Whilst ever Daryl was earning and living at home she could just sit in her Vibro Centre and spend the day, evening, and often late into the night, watching interactive soaps on her entertainment centre. Her acidic tongue cut Daryl to the quick and he knew she couldn't bear the sight of him, and was constantly telling him so. As a child he'd been brought up on real food but now his Mam refused to cook for him and hated him going into her kitchen, as he was never able to clear up enough to satisfy her, receiving an acerbic tongue lashing which always compounded his unhappiness. Now, when he was at home he lived on food pearls, which contained everything nourishing but satisfied nothing.

Over the years Daryl had given his Mam money, bought her every upgrade of entertainment centre, the very best slumber-pit, paid for her Vibro Centre, along with her clothes and holidays, but all to no avail. She never changed her tone or attitude towards him, both of which were foul. So damaged was Daryl's psyche that if anyone spoke to him they were lucky to get a grunt in response, which always portrayed him as being surly and unintelligible, or was it moronic? However, it was not an effective way of communicating. In fact he seemed incapable of any real form of communication.

Despite the fact Daryl came across as slow he did actually have a latent intelligence. Although being constantly in trouble at school he'd managed to achieve respectable exam results enabling him to get an apprenticeship at NapPals, a factory manufacturing nappies and baby bottles. He'd found the job easy, having a naturally analytical mind, and the studying and qualifications he was obliged to undertake were of some interest, but never really captured his imagination.

College, like school, had been a painful experience. He didn't fit in with the other students, being one of those individuals who were embarrassing to be with, and anyone seen with him took a lot of ribbing for talking to him. His three years of college had been as painful and lonely as school had been; he'd made no friends, or enemies, but become the brunt of everyone's jokes and the general laughing stock.

At NapPals it was no better, in fact if anything it was worse. None of his colleagues in any of the departments befriended him, but didn't ignore him either. They did worse, constantly and mercilessly tormenting him and making his life hell. The stooped stance Daryl had first adopted in his teens became more and more pronounced as he got older. It seemed that for each year's ribbing he lost another degree in his upright stance and the cloud of doom, which appeared to hang over him, became more evident. Or so it felt to him.

Daryl, though, had one talent no one rubbished and that was playing pool. If he'd had character and determination there was little doubt he could have played professionally. However, he'd never dreamed of it and didn't dream of it now. All he wanted to do was play pool and manipulate the balls into their relevant pockets. Whom he played with he didn't care, as long as he got a game most days. Anyone complimenting him on his playing was shrugged off dismissively, so damaged was his confidence, and whilst he'd no friends to play pool with there was never a shortage of anyone to challenge him. His reputation in the town was that he was a force on the table to be reckoned with and had to be taken on and beaten, although few ever did. This in itself could have been the making of Daryl but he was totally unaware and blind to it. Whilst everyone was eager to take him on, no one was prepared to befriend him. Mostly that was Daryl's fault; he never mocked, coached or guided his opponents, certainly never talked to them, but merely grunted. Over the years it seemed as if he was turning in on himself and his reputation from school, as a colourless simpleton, followed him like the grim reaper.

There was one other skill Daryl had besides playing pool. It was a talent no one really knew the extent of, and something Daryl kept quiet about. Daryl was a highly accomplished electronics and programming expert, self taught but effective all the same. He'd learnt it to kill time when he'd been banished to his room, which still happened despite him being in his thirties. A diligent and thorough worker he thought nothing of spending hours developing bits and pieces. The trouble was he'd had no one to discuss or share it with, so it remained an unknown talent to all but himself. He was glad now of this isolated knowledge, as he'd found an outlet for his talent which created cover for him. He may not have had any devious or calculating friends but through his programming he could create cast iron and indisputable alibis for himself, which he did – time and time again.

When Daryl thought about his isolation and unhappiness he could never decide whether it was the home or work situation he found the most difficult. He desperately loved his Mam, sometimes just begging to be in the same room as her, but to no avail. Work wasn't much better either, as he had to stay on the premises and work at whatever he was doing, so had no option but to stay put, which left him wide open to being taunted and unable to get away.

Worst of all were the four women he'd known since school days. They knew too many of his weaknesses and played on them cruelly and mercilessly. If he thought his Mam's tongue was bad then it was nothing compared to theirs. As far as the bitches in the factory knew he was still a virgin and disputed he even had any tackle, subjecting him to being debagged on more than one occasion. The fear and humiliation of those encounters had made his manhood shrivel into his body, causing even further jokes and taunting.

At thirty-two years old Daryl had never plucked up the courage to ask anyone out and had only had a fumbling kiss and grope many years ago in a dark corner of a nightclub when he was in his teens. It had been a disaster, as the girl who'd cornered him knew exactly what she'd been doing and, despite the fact they'd not even touched intimately, he'd come quickly and profusely causing a dark stain to spread boldly on the crotch of his pale coloured trousers. The girl had pointed it out mockingly to the rest of their group and Daryl had hurried home, shame faced and with the ring of everyone's laughter stinging his ears. The incident had earned him the nickname of 'Squirter', which he hated and the feeling of inadequacy that went with it. Since then he'd never approached another girl for a date, and made sure he avoided physical contact with anyone. The memory of that night still haunted him and was made worse by the women at work, who'd been there at the time, and frequently tormented him about it, making him constantly revisit the stress and trauma of his shame.

*Well? Could he call himself a man?* he'd often asked himself, and until recently had never believed he could. The only way he'd survived the years had been by withdrawing into himself to maintain his sanity. Even so, he clung to it tentatively, afraid one day he'd not survive all the animosity aimed at him.

Then one day, a couple of years ago, Daryl had been pushed right to the brink. It was as if the worm had turned and from that day on a malicious streak emerged in Daryl, which had probably lain dormant for years. Worse than that Daryl had cunningly managed to keep it hidden, cultivating an air of innocence about him, which added an extra element of menace to this new side of him.

It was mid morning when Daryl went back into the recreation room for his break. Amanda, Sadie and Angela were huddled together in one of the quiet annexes, with a woman in a navy suit. They were more subdued than usual and as Daryl watched surreptitiously he saw Angela burst into tears and Sadie gather her in her arms. Amanda stood with her mouth agape, a look of incredulity on her face. Her gaze was partially focused on another young woman, in a similar suit, who was over in one of the other annexes talking to another group of workers.

Daryl eased himself across the room to get himself some refreshments, near to where the women were sitting. Waiting in the queue he pretended to be busy making his selection, when in fact he was leaning back as far as he dare, without being too obvious, to see if he could hear what the group was so upset about. It was unusual for them to be sitting in isolation, and even more unusual for one of them to be crying. In fact the idea of any of them having any human emotions fascinated him. He'd never considered that before, not after their merciless treatment of him over the years.

Whilst he was getting his drink one of his fellow maintenance men came up to him and said in hushed tones

'You heard the gossip Daryl? Somebody attacked and raped Lucy last night. Down that alleyway near where she lives. She wasn't found until this morning,' he informed Daryl. 'When the Crimedics arrived they scanned the area, knocked her out and took her off to hospital. She's in a pretty bad way and they reckon she'll be unconscious for a few days before she's brought round. They're going to interview her whilst she's unconscious and then erase the memory. Clever that ain't it? Being questioned and giving a full account of what happened without even realising it. Always amazes me that it's impossible to tell lies when yer in that state of limbo and reveal more than if yer awake,' he intoned. 'Hate to think what my partner would find out about me if she got hold of one of them machines. Know what I mean?' he grinned digging Daryl in the ribs. 'Still a pity it happened to the lass even if she is a gobby cow,' he finished, before picking up his drink and walking off.

Daryl grimaced at the thought of anyone probing his mind without him having any control over it. He was such a private person and the thought of that sort of intrusion made his skin crawl, especially if they replayed some of his dreams.

*As for Lucy, she'd only got what she'd deserved and it would create a buzz round the factory for the next few weeks whilst they all speculated about who'd done it,* he thought maliciously. *Then the media will build it up, and drop it when something else happens. Wonder if any of the others are bothered about it happening to them?* he wandered idly. *Each and every one deserved it and more besides,* he thought as he walked away, a wry grin on his face. He sidled past the group of women and Sadie looked up catching the expression on his face, but it didn't register with her and she was quickly distracted by a fresh outbreak of sobs from Angela.

Daryl walked through to his work area with a smug feeling of satisfaction. It had pleased him to see the women upset and one of their friends done for. *That'll teach the bitches to make me life a misery,* he thought nastily, and looked back over his shoulder for a long hard look at the group huddled together. He almost felt delight at their misery, and would have given a hop, skip and jump if it hadn't drawn attention to him. He quickly settled down his gleeful thoughts and made himself walk glumly and doggedly back to his work area. *Christ!* he thought with a jolt, *I'm getting a fucking hard on at their misery,* and part of him felt a further kick of enjoyment whilst the sober side of him felt a pang of anxiety. Come what may he didn't want to draw any attention to himself, especially with the police around.

There was a black side to Daryl that had developed over the past couple of years and been kept carefully hidden. His Mam had no idea it existed, nor did the women in the factory who taunted him. No one could have even dreamt there was another side to Daryl, he came over as so monotonous and boring. If the girls had seen this secret side to Daryl they'd never have persisted with their brutal, persistent mockery. It was their constant taunting, references to his unsuccessful manhood and his Mam's scorn that had created the blacker side of his character.

His Mam was constantly contemptuous in comparing him to his dad, which drove him mad and the years of her ruthlessly harping on about his lack of character and abilities had taken its toll. Finally two years ago he'd been driven to such distraction, anger and revenge that he'd driven out of the area one night and raped his first victim. He'd left the scene satiated and satisfied, knowing he'd finally proved he could overpower a woman, perform and take what he wanted. His first victim, and every victim after that, had been the ones to pay the price for his tormentors. With each successive rape he'd felt a growing sense of pride and retribution as he'd left the scene.

His first attack had happened at random, when he'd attacked and raped without any thought of the consequences. It had happened in a remote area of parkland on the outskirts of a small town in Lancashire. He'd spotted the woman crossing the park, stealthily followed her then dragged her off the pathway and into the bushes. At that stage he'd probably been as surprised as she was, as he'd never intended, imagined or even believed what was happening. He'd overpowered her, tormenting her with cruel menacing words, his spittle spraying her face as he spat out the guttural abuse, and with it he released so much venom he'd found himself sexually aroused. He'd started beating her, and each time his fists met her body he became more aroused. Finally she'd lost consciousness, her body falling onto the damp grass and quickly Daryl had torn off her trousers and ripped away her pants. Next thing he found himself with his trousers undone and his virgin penis stiff and hard. He'd wrenched the woman's legs apart and after some difficulty had finally rammed his weapon of delight and punishment, as he saw it, roughly between her legs, and oh what bliss! He'd thrust with all his might, probably only half a dozen times, until he'd come inside her, his weight falling on top of her as he grunted out his orgasm. He'd felt triumphant in his achievement, this his first time. He was no longer a virgin and no longer felt guilty of any of the things the women at work taunted him about.

Fortunately, for him, he'd been so heavy-handed with the woman she'd still been unconscious on the ground as he'd looked down at her sprawled body laughing as he'd tidied his clothes, spitting at her that she was *'a daft bitch and someone had to pay.'* Then drawing back his leg he'd kicked her repeatedly finally leaving her bleeding, broken and near to death. It had been a frenzied and violent rape, and Daryl was surprised when the woman was found and actually survived the brutality of his attack. For a few days he'd been terrified the police would swoop on him, but when they didn't he had such a feeling of achievement and respect for himself it was like he was on cloud nine.

The girl, who only just survived, could tell nothing of the man who'd attacked her and despite the fact there was DNA in abundance at the scene, there were no matches on any files. As a fit and healthy man Daryl had not attended the doctor's or dentists for years so there were no medical, police or public records in existence that could be used to trace him back to his attack.

*Good job I'm in my thirties*, he thought to himself. *'Any younger and my DNA would have been on file from birth and I'd never have got away with something like this, and got away with it six times!'* he crowed to himself. *Good job I'm never ill or have accidents either, or on the list for annual check-ups. Yet another scheme I've managed to escape. I'll just have to stay fit, healthy and safe to keep avoiding the system. Should be easy enough. Long may it continue*, he congratulated himself. No one in their right minds would ever have associated Daryl, the quiet harmless simpleton, with the scheming, malicious monster that was the other side of his nature.

When the fear of being discovered by the police had subsided, and he realised what he'd done, he was shocked, almost stunned and mentally struggled against raping again. His groin though had other ideas and told him 'yes'. The feeling of power and revenge he'd felt had been so intense, when he'd fucked the woman, he knew he would do it again, would enjoy it and it would help him cope with all the mockery he was being dealt. They may mock that he was still a virgin but he knew differently, and each and every time they mocked and took the piss out of him his anger took on a different guise to before. Now his thoughts turned to plotting and making another stupid bitch pay.

*Yes he'd show the fucking bitches he was as good as his dad had been, not that he could ever tell his Mam*, he thought inwardly, as he continued to watch the huddled group from a distance.

Lucy's friends were indignant, angry and upset all at the same time. Angela, in fact, was so upset that by late morning she was sent home, being incapable of doing her job properly due to the state she was in. Daryl kept out of their way, as was his wont, but he couldn't help allowing himself the luxury of a smirk every so often. There was no way anyone would even think it was him, let alone accuse him of it, not with his reputation, the girls had seen to that with all the torment and humiliation they'd targeted at him over the years. He'd finally got the better of them.

When Daryl arrived home late that evening, after a few games of pool, Sharon, his mother, was sitting in the Vibro Centre wearing the entertainment helmet when, to her annoyance, a light began to flash warning her someone was at the front door. Pressing a remote control button Daryl's image flashed onto the security system. She snorted derisively, the contempt she felt for her only child almost tangible. She watched as he came in, her dislike for him rising like bile.

*Spineless little shit,* she seethed inwardly. *Pity he's got no backbone or personality 'cos then he'd be able to catch a bitch that'd take him out of my hair,* she thought spitefully. At thirty-two Sharon reckoned Daryl was still a virgin, because he'd certainly never had a girlfriend, and she didn't believe he'd had a man either. She snorted in her frustration at him.

*He's nothing like his dad,* she thought wistfully. *His dad had been dynamic, sexy and a bit of a wide boy.* She smiled as she remembered some of their good times together back in the nineties. *On the town trawling the clubs in Leeds, each one with their own theme, prices and attractions on drinks. Many had their own drug attractions too,* she remembered, *and me and my old man tried them all, hash, coke, crack, heroin and ecstasy.* She chuckled inwardly as she remembered one particular weekend they'd tried the designer drug Viagiant. *God we'd been as randy as hell all weekend and at it like rabbits.* She chortled aloud at this memory. *We hardly slept all weekend but just screwed and screwed not able to get enough of each other, going on for what seemed like forever. By the time the drug had worn off we were both knackered and could hardly walk. When we'd gone into work on the Monday we'd been the butt of everyone's joke. The 'Shag Twins' they called us, when we walked in on legs that felt as if they were made of jelly, so bandied they were. The state we were in caused grins and wisecracks for the rest of the week.* It wasn't long after that she'd found out she was pregnant and although she'd resented not finding out sooner, in time to get rid of it, Darren had at least done the decent thing and married her. Unheard of in those days.

Her reminiscences were quickly brought to an abrupt halt as Daryl came into the room, her temper quickly beginning to rise. She harboured an evil attitude when it came to her only son, with her cunning and wiliness the only things maintaining her freedom. If she'd behaved outside, as she did behind closed doors, her freedom would have been curtailed many years before. She'd have been whisked away for re-programming pronto, no questions asked or time given for explanations. As it was she appeared to all and sundry as any other person, even tempered and considerate. Had anyone ever seen or heard the real Sharon though it would have been a completely different picture. How she'd managed to maintain her duplicity for so long was anyone's guess, but she must have used every modicum of the intelligence she possessed to maintain the deceit.

'Hello Mam,' he said, in his whiney voice. 'What you got on? Can I watch it with you?'

'Shut up Daryl and piss off,' she spat, not taking off her entertainment helmet. 'Sod off and go to your room you useless lump. Leave me in peace,' she intoned, dismissing the son who irritated her so much.

'Oh go on Mam, let me stay,' he whinged. 'Let me come and sit with yer'.

Sharon, irrationally irritated by her son's intrusion whipped open her helmet and snarled, 'For fuck's sake Daryl bog off. Why would I want to talk to you? You little shit. What have you got to tell me, huh? How many babies bottles were made at the factory today or how you got the perfect angle on the red ball?' she mocked in mimicry. 'Give us a break yer fucking little tosser and get a life. You've nothing to tell me and never will. You're the most boring shit I've ever come across and you bore me to hell. Just fuck off.' Seeing Daryl's crestfallen face she added cruelly, 'Can't believe you bloody came out of me and yer dad's loins. Now there was a man,' she intoned setting off on one of her long memory-laced tangents, which were always dressed with an odd combination of love and bitterness. Love for the man she'd worshipped and bitterness for the fact he'd been so cruelly snatched from her when he'd been murdered.

She'd always thought he was a stupid bastard to open his trap as he had to brag. Being a gobby bastard was one of his weaknesses, and he'd bragged to all and sundry about a gang bang he and his mates had done. The police never found out who'd done it, despite extensive investigations and all sorts of media coverage, but what she knew, and the police didn't, was that each and every one of the gang bangers, all eight of them, had died within a couple of years of it happening. She'd been terrified her Darren would be found out, when he'd admitted to her after the first two murders he was one of the gang bangers. She was terrified he'd be the next victim, and their fear had deepened with each death. Finally it was his turn and he'd died, killed in a hit and run, as victim number seven. Sharon knew it had been no accident but couldn't do anything about it. She'd been left by herself with Daryl when he was only a toddler and her resentment towards him had deepened as the years passed by. Gradually it became a twisted bitterness aimed at her son, who she saw as an insipid leech on her life.

Right from the day he was born she'd had little affection for him, and any modicum of feeling she'd had had gone out of the window years ago. If he'd got a bit of backbone or colour in his life it might have been different and they, as son and mother, might have got on better. As it was he was always trying to ingratiate himself to her, bowing and fawning at her feet and demanding her attention. The more he whinged and whined the deeper her loathing grew. As a kid it had been annoying enough but at thirty-two... she felt the bitter bile of resentment rise in her throat and ripping off her helmet altogether leapt from her chair screaming abuse at him moving towards him with menace and waving her fists threateningly.

Daryl, recognising he'd angered his mother again, made a hasty retreat, his heart heavy and beating fast in the fear his mother would come after him and give him a walloping. He ambled along to the kitchen and looked round at the gleaming room. His Mam may have a quick and evil tongue but she always kept everything in pristine condition, something else that caused Daryl grief. He opened a cupboard with the thought of a good old-fashioned sandwich in mind. Then suddenly stopped, thinking of the mess he'd make that no matter how diligently he cleaned up was never good enough for her, and would just cause an atmosphere and tongue lashings for days. Reluctantly, with an even heavier heart, he put the things away and reached for a food pearl, popping it into his mouth to suck and chew on it for as long as he could. As much as they satisfied his hunger and calorific needs they were nowhere near as good as the real thing, the only advantages being the cleanliness of them, and protection from his Mam's tongue.

He left the kitchen and made his way upstairs. Undressing carefully he bundled his clothes into a laundry processor and stepped into his cleansing unit, dialled in a sleep programme and stood, his hands laced behind his head, whilst he was soaped, scrubbed and dried. By the end of the programme gel pummellers kneaded his body gently, a light scent of lavender and camomile permeating the cabinet, soothing his mind and increasing his drowsiness. Finally he stepped out, pulled on his pyjamas and climbed into his slumber-pit. As soon as his head hit the pillow the bed slowly undulated, lulling him into a deep and peaceful sleep. *It was madness anyone not sleeping,* he thought just before he dropped off. Modern technology now meant insomnia and back problems were a thing of the past now gel slumber-pits were available. The technology sensitive beds were programmable to the occupant, the bed's movements ensuring the occupier slept soundly, waking up at the time required. Daryl's bed was programmable for dreams too and as he drifted off to sleep his pre-recorded life-long dream, of him and his mother getting along brilliantly, began to play in his mind. Daryl often thought that if he didn't have that dream he'd have killed himself long ago, all he needed to do was ensure his mother never found out about it, because if she did she'd destroy it and with it the small modicum of pleasure he received.

Over the next few days the police continued to come in and out of the factory, pulling different people to one side to talk to them, Daryl being no exception. Lucy was still under heavy sedation and there was concern about some of her injuries. In addition, despite the fact they'd managed to interview her subliminally, they'd not come up with anything constructive to help with their enquiries, which was odd. They knew from talking to her colleagues Lucy tended to be a bit of a 'ring leader', but more on the lines of humour and practical jokes than anything malicious, or so they believed. No one seemed to have a bad word to say about or hold a grudge against her, including Daryl.

Daryl, as planned, had come across as slow, almost retarded, and without backbone when he'd been interviewed. In his favour, with the interviews not being formal, he'd not been asked for an alibi, and even if they had Daryl would have been able to provide 'indisputable' cover, just as talking to his Mam would've verified his homecoming at the earlier, rather than the actual time registered on her entertainment helmet and house security system. Everything was looking favourable for him and by the end of the week each and every employee had been interviewed before the police finally turned their attention elsewhere. Daryl felt safe, his saving grace being that the other rapes had all been carried out in different parts of England. That red herring meant their investigations seemed to indicate someone who travelled with their work, rather than someone static like Daryl.

Daryl hadn't been at all perturbed by the police interviewing him. When he'd committed his first rape something in him had awakened, and a dormant intelligence emerged. That same astute deviousness was now being used for planning other assaults, and helping Daryl keep his 'simple' image intact. What he concentrated on now was ensuring his attacks weren't interrupted, and only ever leaving behind his DNA; after

43

all the police had plenty of that already. It was becoming more difficult though keeping up the pretence of still being as thick and boring as before, the hardest thing being to keep his eyes blank and face expressionless. It had been natural before but since unearthing these new depths, and Daryl knowing he could get the better of someone, maintaining his blankness was becoming increasingly difficult.

Since his first encounter with sex Daryl often thought about having a girlfriend and a normal sex life, but the thought of the humiliation still haunted him and at least with rape he didn't have to talk, be pleasant or even introduce himself. Added to that there was no way any of his victims would mock him, he was the one scoffing now. In fact he always laughed at them, silently as he slipped away from the scenes of his crime.

Daryl's life these days was more mapped out than ever before; he had a sex life, which he'd never dreamt possible before; anonymity, via his 'colourless and boring' character, and he had one over on the female population. Life was good and would stay that way, because there was no way, unless he was forced to provide a DNA sample, he could be caught. As long as he stayed fit and healthy, chose his victims carefully and took care to leave no clues then life would continue to be good.

~ ~ ~ ~ ~

Jack had met Chloe just over ten years ago in 2022 through internet dating. Jack had tried the old-fashioned manner of meeting people first, at random in nightclubs and pubs, but it just wasn't for him. He enjoyed socialising and nights out with his mates but wasn't the most confident with the opposite sex, despite the fact he was an incurable romantic. He'd wanted to meet someone in the old style his parents had met, way back in 1999 so on many occasions he'd spruced himself up; dressed himself down; gone to nightclubs, pubs and all the places his parents talked about but none of it had been for him. The modern man in him finally triumphed over the idealist and he bowed to convention and registered on a few dating sites and… well the rest was history. He'd had one or two false starts and met his ideal partner, but that hadn't been Chloe. He happened upon Chloe some two years after Jinni's demise.

Tragically, at the height of their relationship and out of the blue, Jinni had been hit by a car and killed outright. It had really knocked the wind out of Jack, as by the time they'd got medical aid to her she'd been dead too long to do anything. If they'd managed to get to her before she'd been dead six minutes they could have put her into animated suspension and rebuilt her wrecked body and re-programmed her brain with emotion and mood probes until they had replicated her original looks, character and personality. What medical techniques couldn't do these days was nobody's business, but her life and their life together had been cruelly torn away. Without modern re-programming it would have taken Jack years to come to terms with his loss and singledom again. As it was, science had advanced so much in emotional trauma and psyche damage that it had been only a matter of weeks, rather than years, before he'd recovered from her death. It had been worth paying for the re-programming treatment, as the one thing Jack was sure of was that, above all else, he wanted to be a father.

After Jinni had died and he'd completed his re-programming, Jack had resumed the search for his perfect partner on the internet. It wasn't too long before Chloe's details had come up and Jack's breath was taken away by her looks. She had those finely honed, almost haughty looks of an Italian descendant and moved with the grace and delicacy that reminded Jack of a gazelle. He was entranced and smitten by her from the start; she was so light and delicate and yet had the hardiness and resilience of a lion, with a mane of hair to match.

Whereas Jinni had been his heart's desire, Chloe was the woman of his dreams and their profiles matched perfectly. Not with the hundred percent score that everyone aimed for but with enough of a margin left for them both to preserve their individuality and maintain an element of surprise that would keep their relationship and respect for each other alive in coming years. He and Chloe let their relationship develop naturally and took naked delight in getting to know each other, much like a gourmet banquet where everything had to be savoured. Chloe, the same age as Jack, had somehow gained a greater understanding of life and human needs than he had, despite his disappointments in romance and life to date.

His relationship with Jinni he'd believed to be nigh on perfect, but he could instantly see that with Chloe there was an element between them they'd only dreamed of in the past. Theirs was one of those elusive exclusive relationships that only a handful of the human race encountered, and they had been two of the lucky chosen few. Their romance from day one had been magical and they were so certain of their feelings together that they skipped the cyber sex and met in person, much sooner than they normally would have done. They'd very quickly applied to have their chemistry ratings done and been delighted at the results, both rating highly on the romantic side. The only area that caused any concern was Chloe's family's conception rating, which was so miniscule as to be inconsequential.

Chloe, the middle daughter of three, had herself been conceived with the aid of fertility treatment; her sisters hadn't, neither had her mother. Chloe's older sister, Zoe, had two children, conceived naturally and without problem, so neither Jack nor Chloe or either of their families gave the matter any credence and it was swept under the carpet. In fact Cassie, Chloe's sister, had fallen pregnant almost as soon as she'd decided to try for children. So that area didn't really cause too much concern for them.

It did cause concern, though, when they had applied for their marriage licence. Since 2020 the English law, which was no longer under the influence of the EC, had revised its marital regime. There had been a steady reversal in trends towards marriage since 2015, when there were enhanced tax and other benefits to being married. Prior to 2015 the ruling bodies had never looked at how easy marriage and divorce was, which the government realised made a mockery of the marital laws, tax and social status of married couples. So in 2020 it had been decided that to get the equation of marriage right, divorce would be abolished for any couples marrying after the change in law and applications to marry would become more stringent. It had been addressed very cleverly, but very humanely. Some very thorough and searching research had been done and several referendums held regarding the topic of marriage. The only individuals benefiting from marriage and divorce previously were solicitors, who'd easily lined their pockets; with the real victims being any children of the divorce. The government came up with several new marriage proposals, satisfying most couples' needs without having to outlaw common law marriages or compromise anyone's choice. Those granted marriage certificates, at whatever level, were given enhanced tax and social status, bequeathed medical and property rights but were outlawed from divorce.

The government had hit on just the right prescription. It had been a masterpiece and the government's main coup of the century. No other legislation had exceeded its success or been accepted as readily by the nation and gave those who did not want or agree with marriage the option to stay single or live with their partner, whatever their sex. The many tiered levels of marriage gave different benefits for each category and could be applied for by opposite and same sex couples.

Gone were the days when the mention of marriage was a taboo subject between couples. Marriage was an acclaimed and sought after status and both Jack and Chloe's aim had been to get married and have children. The topic had been discussed before they'd even met up. After all, it would have been pointless to pursue the relationship unless they'd both wanted the same outcome, and were prepared to work long and hard together to achieve that cherished status. That was certainly what the government had been striving for when it had implemented the matrimony laws.

Two years after meeting, Jack and Chloe applied successfully for their marriage application and, despite the fact that no one could ever foretell what questions they would be asked, their marriage application went through relatively smoothly. The panel had really liked the couple, there being such affinity between them as to be almost tangible. The only part of the process, which had caused concern, was when they got to the final interview process where questions about their family's Crimedical records were delved into. Although these presented no real problem there was some concern over Chloe's own conception, which could threaten their application for a life-long marriage licence. What impressed the panel, when they were interviewed separately and together, was the couple wanting to work carefully on creating their 'extended families', which the government was keen to promote. It was also obvious they both desperately wanted to become parents and had similar views on conception and bringing up a family. If it had been any different they wouldn't even have been considered for a life-long marriage application, let alone obtaining it.

Jack and Chloe were deemed suitable material, for the government's future breeding programme and by the end of that day they had been granted their two-year trial marriage certificate. Whilst the topic of procreation had been thrashed out satisfactorily not all the panel were convinced the couple shared the same beliefs on procreation, should Chloe not be able to have children herself. With some concerns, about Chloe's ability to conceive, medical tests would clarify her suitability, the results later proving satisfactory. The decision as to the type of marriage licence they'd be granted would be made at the end of a successful trial period. As it was, they achieved the highest marital status, which entitled them to various social benefits, unlimited medical treatments, but would preclude them from having a full surrogacy or adopted child.

The commencement of their acclaimed life-long marriage allowed them to start the process of conception, it having been a forbidden element of their sexual relationship during the two-year trial period. It came as a great surprise to Jack and Chloe when they didn't conceive immediately. Protocol dictated they'd have to wait a year before applying for medical assistance, but once the twelve month period had passed there was no limit as to how much assistance and finance the government would invest for them to achieve not just conception but also full-term pregnancies. The couple would be allowed two full-term pregnancies that produced healthy babies, before they were sterilised.

At the end of the year, with no pregnancy on the horizon, both Jack and Chloe were booked in for extensive testing. Jack's tests came out fine, but he was given a course of chemical intervention to strengthen the resilience of his sperm anyway. Chloe's tests, however, despite the ones done before being granted their marriage license, now showed that there may be a problem with conception and possibly carrying a child to full-term. With this knowledge at their fingertips the couple left the clinic somewhat daunted but still confident it was not an insurmountable problem, especially with the government's unlimited funds for helping them produce offspring.

Over the next few years they underwent numerous treatments, firstly using Chloe's eggs, then Brooder's and finally virgin eggs, all fertilised by Jack's or a Sire's sperm. The next stage in their treatments was for Chloe to have developed foetuses implanted at six, eight and twelve weeks maturity, which Chloe's body always rejected within weeks and sometimes only days. The number of failed pregnancies Chloe had undertaken was well into the double figures and had it not been for modern re-programming and medical advancements, she would not have been able to cope with the trauma, either physically or emotionally.

During the early 2010s medical advancements had finally devised a very simple and practical device called a skzip, which virtually abolished the need for stitches and obliterated wound infection once the device was fitted. Operating on a similar basis to a clothing zip, but without the tag, it was opened by scanning, in the same manner as goods going through a supermarket checkout at the turn of the century. Programmed with a patient's data it was through this device that Chloe had had her Babypouch fitted, which enabled her to have all her treatments with the minimum of physical trauma. The subliminal programming, which was available for all manner of emotional issues, enabled them to take the loss of their babies in their stride.

When Chloe's Babypouch was fitted they'd also implanted the first of her matured foetuses. It was hoped with the foetus being several weeks developed that Chloe's body would not reject it. Sadly this was not the case, with this or any of the other pregnancies that followed. After further testing and counselling Jack and Chloe were finally ready for the final and conclusive stage of their journey.

Years previously there had been a 'glass womb' developed, which hadn't been a total success. Babies born from these glass wombs were sickly and did not survive past infancy. The trauma and grief this caused, not just to the parents but the nation as a whole when deaths were reported, had resulted in the government outlawing them until such time as they became fully developed, allowing a baby to be born that was genetically as strong and healthy as a humanly born child. Prior to glass wombs being abolished the government had looked at various alternatives and created the position of 'Brooders'. This role, in terms of prestige, was of extremely high standing and one of the highest accolades a woman could achieve in society. A Brooder had incubation potential for twenty years, developing foetuses for the government, but not giving birth to them. Foetuses, developed as full surrogate babies, were birthed by 'Birthing Brooders', with a Brooder's final pregnancy always resulted in their womb, complete with an intact mid-term baby, being transplanted into the body of its true mother. This was the final stage of modern day fertility treatment, and the process Jack and Chloe were to undertake.

When it had become evident that Chloe's body was rejecting undeveloped foetuses it was decided to move onto the treatment of a 'piggy-back' pregnancy, where a fourteen-week foetus, still nestled inside

49

its Brooder's womb, would be piggy-backed onto Chloe's womb. Normally a couple would have been at their wit's end by this stage but through the counselling they were compelled to undertake, to allow them to continue their treatments, their spirits remained buoyant and the strain on their relationship kept to a minimum. The one thing they continued to be grateful for was that they had managed to achieve a life-long marriage, which entitled them to unlimited treatment, unlike any of the other marital statuses. However, at this stage they now had to face considering life without children, if this next series of treatment were not successful.

Chloe had remained optimistic on the surface, dismissing all of Jack's worries and doubts. She'd never allow herself the luxury of even contemplating a life without children and not achieving a full-term pregnancy. If determination could have achieved a successful pregnancy then there was no doubt Chloe would have accomplished it. Jack, trying his best to match Chloe's optimism, hung onto hope, but deep down he was not as confident as he seemed to be.

In April 2031 their baby, nurtured by their Brooder for the past sixteen weeks, was transplanted, in the Brooder's womb, into Chloe's carefully prepared body and conjoined to her own womb, where it was hoped Chloe's body would continue to nurture it until it was mature enough to be born. This method, which was showing an enormous success rate, had originally been inspired by Dr Christian Barnard's experiments back in the sixties, where 'piggy-backing' hearts in human surgery had later led to the full heart transplant techniques.

Whilst they'd never met their Brooder personally, she'd been more than happy for them to be linked in remotely to the views of her womb. 'Wombs with a View', as Babypouches were affectionately regarded, gave couples peace of mind and enabled the bonding process to start even before they were implanted into the mother's own womb. Jack and Chloe had watched the minute cells develop until clear details of the body's little limbs, ears, eyes and sexual organs were clearly defined. They'd watched fascinated as the foetus grew in size and strength inside the Brooder's womb and later watched the baby move healthily and energetically within Chloe. It had intrigued them and given them great hope, and they'd named their baby Joey.

Tragically, Chloe lost the baby only a month after having the pregnant womb conjoined to her own. It had been a major blow to the couple, as this time it had been a real life lost, the pregnancy being advanced enough for them to see and feel the baby's movements until finally he'd given up the fight… and was no more. Joey had represented so many dreams for them and the loss of Joey was yet another stage they had to cope with. They also had to face the fact that it was unlikely Chloe would be able to carry a baby to full-term, and there was now only one chance left before they had to give up forever their hope of becoming parents.

Having waited the prescribed six months, and having undergoing the mandatory counselling and re-programming, they were finally ready for the last and ultimate stage of their treatments. If that was unsuccessful then they would have no choice but to accept they had a barren marriage and there was no future chance of ever becoming parents, a thought neither of them could face let alone come to terms with.

Now here they were several years down the line and having to face what they'd always dreaded, and prayed they'd not have to. The ultimate procedure would be personally intrusive and conducted with a great deal of monitoring, not just physically but emotionally too. Very few couples actually got to this stage, as most achieved success earlier. If this next pregnancy failed it would not only mean the loss of their baby but also their very last chance of ever having a son or daughter.

Their allocated Brooder had no trouble carrying and nurturing foetuses, and both Jack and Chloe wished she could carry their child to full-term. However this was the one aspect a life-long marriage precluded them from – a full surrogacy child. If they had known then what they knew now… but any child of the marriage had to born of Chloe's body. It was a strict rule and one that there was no way of overcoming and a real bone of contention to couples who were unable to carry a baby full-term. It was what the referendums had decided, despite groups lobbying, campaigning and demonstrating to get it changed before and after the results, and something the government had no right to alter for the next twenty years. Full-term surrogacy was completely and totally outlawed in life-long marriages. There was no rationale or logic behind the decision and it had caused sorrow and untold anguish to many couples in the past as it would in the future.

Both Jack and Chloe were extremely apprehensive about this final stage. If this failed the only way they'd ever become parents was if one of the children they were guardians to became orphaned. Something neither of them would ever want to happen, despite their desperation to become parents. Determined this final attempt would result in the delivery of a healthy child, they approached the final fertilisation positively but realistically, well aware that the odds were stacked against them. Whilst Chloe's womb did not nurture foetuses they hoped this time, with her womb being removed and replaced with the Brooder's womb along with their own baby, things would be different. The Brooder, who would be retired soon after and never need to earn money again, would be on hand until the birth of the baby, should any transfusions be required.

During the sixteen weeks, whilst they waited for their baby to mature, Chloe's womb would be expanded to accommodate the Brooder's womb and matured foetus. It was with some relief they heard that their unborn child was a girl as the constant monitoring, carried out during her pregnancies, showed Chloe's body had a higher tolerance to pregnancy when carrying a female child.

As with Joey they'd watched each stage of their baby's development, observing the tiny buds transform into minute legs and arms and watched the minute fingers and toes develop and saw for themselves what sex the baby would be. They had not chosen what sex they wanted their child to be, although they had always been given that choice. Irrationally, or superstitiously, they had always believed that if they specified the sex their chances of a successful pregnancy would be reduced. There was no rationale behind their thinking but both had felt the same way and had decided to follow this instinct. After all they wanted nothing more than a healthy baby who had a chance of surviving. What more could they ask for or want?

~ ~ ~ ~ ~

The rape of Lucy Johnson was a puzzling case and it was evident from DNA samples she'd been attacked by the same rapist who'd committed a number of vicious rapes over the past two years, their brutality increasing with each attack. Whilst the rapist struck frequently none of the attacks were in the same vicinity and there was no correlating resemblance between his victims. The only common denominator, his signature, was the use of a cotton handkerchief, of a type no longer manufactured.

From the scans taken onsite, and from previous crime scenes, it was established he was approximately six foot tall, wore a size forty-five shoe and weighed about ninety-seven kilograms in weight. He had fine dark wavy hair, which he dressed with a long established hair gel, and ate a mix of both traditional and pearlised foods. There were no distinguishing irregularities identified healthwise, but there was a slight peculiarity in his DNA, which to date no one had been able to analyse. The other worrying factor they'd been able to establish was he had unacceptably high levels of anger, which would be the ruin of other women if they weren't his own downfall first.

Geographically there appeared to be no pattern in the attacks or the type of area he sought his prey in. There was nothing evident to the electronic process or human brain which allowed them to calculate where the next attack was likely to be. What they needed was for the attacker to make a mistake, although this was deemed unlikely as, apart from the first attack, he appeared to be a meticulous planner and must be aware one fatal mistake would now lead to his arrest, incarceration, castration and deportment from the UK.

Causing further confusion was the timing of the rapes, always done late at night but sometimes midweek, other times weekends. Did this mean he was in a transient occupation and how did he get to the sites? There were never any vehicle tracks in the areas which couldn't be identified and accounted for, and footsteps traced by the Pathway Tracker always ended up on a busy street, if they weren't lost en route, despite the device's sophistication. Not once had they led to or from a pub, so the perpetrator obviously didn't need Dutch courage.

There was no evident pattern in his choice of victims either. To date they'd ranged from a young girl of nineteen through to a much older woman of fifty-five; dark haired, blonde, a redhead, some with long, and others short hair. Their heights and weights varied too, but at least from that information they'd established he was over six-foot tall. He obviously didn't have an archetypal victim though, and this was hampering their investigation. Where was his rationale and patterning in these attacks?

Although little made sense, what had really thrown everyone was the victims' total lack of conscious and subconscious memory. None of his victims were able to recall much detail of their attack or attacker, despite the use of the Subliminal Voyeur. So why was there so little memory recall? Nothing had shown up in tests to indicate he'd used any substance for memory loss. The whole series of rapes and lack of comparable facts remained an enigma defying logic.

The only certainty they knew of their attacker, apart from having his DNA, was he'd not received any medical attention, legitimately, for at least fifteen years, otherwise his samples would have been registered on the Government DNA Database and they'd have been able to identify him immediately. The attacker was obviously fit and healthy, either that or he'd access to underground medical treatment. As Melanie checked the file she noted each of the forces involved in the past rape investigations had submitted '*Urgent confirmation of newly registered adult males across the UK,*' which meant anyone seeking medical treatment who weren't already registered, or were arrested for any reason, 'would automatically have their DNA and other data input onto the database. The only way to speed up total UK residents' DNA registration would be to organise a mass scheme, which would take some considerable time to execute.

Looking at the computer generated list of medical record statistics, Melanie was horrified to note over twenty-three percent of adults aged over twenty-two did not have their DNA registered on the Government DNA Database. Despite a healthier nation she was certain only a handful of these wouldn't have needed medical or dental treatment in recent years, so how come there was such a high number unregistered? Appalled at the lack of integrity of the government, Melanie could see why the nation and WPPL had little faith in the UK systems and why their membership to WPPL was being questioned. Maybe a mass registration scheme was the answer to solving this and other crimes, and for the restoration of everyone's faith.

~ ~ ~ ~ ~

It was nearly two months before Lucy returned to work. The verbal attacks Daryl had experienced, prior to the rape, were no longer as scathing and there was now a brittle bitterness and edginess about Lucy that amused Daryl. Many a time he'd stealthily crept up on her making her jump, then pretended to look surprised at her tirade of abuse, making out to be in a world of his own with a blank look on his face. It was a little game the darker side of Daryl had invented, when in truth he was really sneering at her, remembering the night she'd been at his mercy and impaled on the end of his dick. It entertained him and distracted him from his current predicament, which was his health.

Daryl hadn't been feeling too well in the past few weeks and despite his concerns he wasn't able to go to the doctors for fear of his criminal activities being discovered. He constantly felt nauseous and on a couple of occasions had actually vomited; just eating and drinking seemed to make him feel worse, so now he ate virtually nothing but food pearls. Coffee in particular upset his stomach, which he put that down to his Mam buying a different brand and scrimping on the decent stuff. It was a problem he wasn't sure how to handle knowing he couldn't go to the doctor. If he knew where to find an underground doctor it would be different, but he'd no idea how to go about finding one.

His ill health came to a head one night when he was in his bedroom, well out of the way of his mother. He'd been wondering how to find an underground medic and was contemplating whether or not he dare look on the internet, knowing any activity over the airwaves was probably being tracked by the powers that be. It was an aspect of modern technology no one seemed able to overcome, and if they did it was only temporary. Too many people had been traced and charged with trying to block surveillance. Daryl was loath to risk it. He'd switched his computer on and was playing games as he contemplated where and how he should look, if he was to look at all. So far he'd been clever, managing to create cast iron alibis and leaving no tracks or evidence, apart from his DNA. If he went onto the net and his activities happened to be traced then he was a goner but if he didn't, and his illness was something sinister, was it the beginning of the end for him anyway? He continued to ponder on this whilst he played his games listening to the booming music playing at full volume in his sound-proofed room.

All of a sudden he got an overwhelming urge to eat some food, real food, but he didn't know what. So strong was the yearning that it took him down to his Mam's pristine kitchen and within minutes he found himself rooting through her cupboards. As he scouted the shelves, frantically searching his mind trying to work out what he fancied, he suddenly spotted it. There, at the back, was a tin of the sardines he'd loved to eat as a child. He took it out, licking his lips in anticipation. It was one of those old-fashioned tins with a ring pull so he quickly opened it exposing the shiny smelly fish that lay side by side in their oily bed. He plunged his fingers into their slimy mass stuffing one greedily into his mouth, the oil trickling down his chin. He'd eaten a couple more fingerfuls before he realised he needed something to go with it. He set down the tin and again searched the cupboard, luckily spotting what he wanted straight away – blackcurrant jam!

Unscrewing the jar he thrust his fish smeared fingers into the depth of the purple blackness hooking out as much jam as possible. Putting the combined fish and jam into his mouth he sighed in satisfaction as the mingled flavours hit his taste buds. It was just what he needed and a feeling of blissful contentment settled over him. He shook a large quantity of the jam over the remaining fish, mixing it together and stuffing it into his mouth as quickly as he could. It seemed only seconds before the tin was empty, with only the purple streaked oil and tiny fish bits remaining. Pulling the tin lid off completely he lapped the remnants out of the container like a dog.

Having scoured the tin completely he realised he wanted more, and quickly got down on his hunkers to get a better look, searching frantically but finding no more. He got up feeling disappointed, unaware he'd left the unit in disarray. Without thinking he left the kitchen, leaving the empty containers discarded on his mother's work surfaces, regardless of the consequences should she find them.

Daryl grabbed his jacket and quickly made his way to the local food hall inputting jam and fish onto the information board. As soon as it indicated their location he stepped onto the walkway and strode forward purposefully, following the electronic indicators. Reaching the designated areas Daryl picked up a tin of sardines and a jar of jam. He was just about to pay for them when he decided to get several more of each, so grabbing a basket loaded in several tins of sardines and a variety of jams before paying and walking home, his mind a complete blank as his internal auto-pilot took over.

As he went through the normal hand and iris recognition ritual and stepped through the doorway he was greeted by his mother's banshee like wailing.

'Daryl? Is that you? You dirty little shit bag. Get your arse in this kitchen now.' Daryl cringed inwardly, bracing himself for his mother's onslaught, the penny having dropped that he'd left the remains of his feast abandoned in her kitchen.

'You fucking little shit bag,' his mother bellowed, as he went into the kitchen. 'What the fuck do you think you're doing eating my food and leaving yer rubbish about. Who bleddy said yer could have any of my food? What's wrong wiv getting yer own? I get food pearls in fer yer to eat so don't start messing about with my food yer bleddy gret slob. I'm not here to clean up after yer so get this shit cleaned up,' she screeched, then quickly shut up as she spied the carrier in his hand.

'What's that you got there?' she asked, snatching the bag out of his hand and up-ending it onto the counter. 'More bloody fish and jam? What yer playing at Daryl? What yer got all this shit for eh?'

Thinking quickly, Daryl told her he'd been out to get replacements for the ones he'd eaten.

'Eight tins?' she screamed at him 'eight tins o' the bloody stuff and four jars of jam? What doya think I want all this lot for, or are yer planning a party or summat?' she asked aggressively. 'Well this is what yer can do with yer fucking tins and jars,' she told him nastily, and pulling down a door swept the goods and empty containers into the refuse discarder. Daryl stood rooted to the spot, annoyed with himself for not clearing up and mortified by the loss of his much coveted food.

'Sorry Ma,' he answered in a small, frightened voice. 'I'll clear it up shall I? I didn't mean to leave a mess I just… just,' he hesitated, frantically trying to work out a string of words that made sense.

'Too fucking right you'll clean up,' shouted his mother. 'Don't you dare go nicking my stuff again or you'll know what for,' she warned him, and although he was taller than her she looked down her nose at him. Feeling totally worthless he hung his head dejectedly as his mother pushed past him roughly and stormed back to her beloved soaps.

Having cleaned the work surfaces, Daryl stood anxiously in the doorway listening to hear if his Mam had settled or was likely to come back. Once satisfied she wasn't he opened the refuse discarder and gingerly probed about in its dark depths, trying to locate the tins and jars his mother had pitched in. As he scrabbled about, fishing out the jars and tins, he suddenly caught his hand on a shard of jagged glass. Taking a sharp intake of breath he quickly withdrew his hand, again catching his cut on the same piece of glass. Automatically he put his hand to his mouth sucking hard on the cut, wincing, his stomach turning at the thought of seeing his own blood. Reluctantly he held out his shaking hand to inspect the damage and was dismayed to see a dirty ragged cut between his thumb and index finger. Feeling queasy he looked more carefully and saw the cut was deep and had sliced right into the webbed area, which was bleeding profusely. He swooned slightly, contemplating what to do. Did it need attention or would it heal without stitches? He realised with horror it was quite a bad cut and really needed proper medical attention, which he couldn't get. What was he to do?

As these thoughts swam in and out of his head he forced himself not to faint as the blood dripped steadily onto the floor.

*Me Mam'll do her nut,* he thought desperately, *if she sees how much mess I'm making.* He grabbed a tea towel and wrapped it tightly round his hand, then frantically tried to mop up the blood, making things worse rather than better. In a few moments he knew he'd have to wring out the cleaning cloth, but his hand was throbbing so much he knew he wouldn't be able to grip it tightly enough. Panic began to seep in, he didn't want another of his Mam's tongue lashings so decided the only thing he could do was ditch his cleaning attempt, which was making things worse rather than better. Clumsily picking up his pile of much coveted trophies, he made his way upstairs.

When he'd dumped the booty down he steeled himself to unwrap his hand, to see how bad the damage really was. Tentatively he unravelled the towel and to his dismay saw his hand was still bleeding copiously. He quickly rebound it, collapsing into his chair to think long and hard about how to stop it bleeding without having to resort to medical treatment. Inwardly he was panicking and at a loss what to do.

*What if it should bleed at work and someone stole a sample of me blood and I'm shopped?* he asked himself. *Stop it!* His inner voice answered back. *Who in their right mind would want your blood? You're being paranoid,* and the internal dialogue continued to race disjointedly through his panicked mind. He got up off his chair feeling somewhat light-headed, from panic and his dislike of blood rather than actual loss. Pacing up and down, his swaddled hand cradled in his other arm, his face was a mask of worry. Suddenly remembering there was a first-aid kit in the car he was galvanised into action. He walked purposefully down the stairs and was just about to open the door when the raucous tones of his mother trilled out.

'Daryl! Daryl I thought I told you to clear up this shit in here but it's worse than before. Get your fucking arse in here now,' she commanded shrilly.

Reluctantly, but obediently, Daryl once again made his way into the kitchen carefully nursing his hand and realising to his horror, it was wrapped in one of her tea towels.

'Sorry Mam. I'm really sorry Mam,' he whined, 'I didn't mean to…' he trailed off as he saw his Mam's look of horror as she spotted the tea towel.

'What the fuck yer doing with that tea towel yer great lummox,' she screamed at him. 'What yer done now you useless, spineless git,' she bawled, snatching at Daryl's hand and roughly tearing the wrapping from it.

Sharon, seeing him wince, peered closely at his hand telling him none too gently to 'stop being such a fucking wimp.' She prised the edges of the cut apart examining it as best she could through the freely flowing blood. She felt, rather than saw, Daryl begin to sway and roughly pushed his head down so he was bent double.

'Stupid fucking twat,' she spat at him, dragging him over to the sink and turning the tap on then shoving his hand under the flow of water.

'Keep it there whilst I go and get summat for it,' she commanded, and left him feeling sick and miserable as the flow of the water stung him. Despite feeling sorry for himself Daryl was relieved his Mam was looking after him, maybe he could get away without stitches after all.

She returned a few minutes later with an ancient green plastic box, which she slammed onto the work surface and thrust the blood-stained tea towel back at Daryl instructing him to dry his hand.

'Give us yer hand,' she said gruffly, and held her hand out to receive it. 'This'll sting,' she warned, opening an old green bottle and letting the thick clear liquid drip over the cut.

Daryl let out a loud 'Aaaghh Mam' in protest, then quickly bit down hard on his lip to prevent himself making any further noise or crying, which he knew would just anger his mother further. When he looked at his Mam he saw a smug expression on her face, as if pleased at his discomfort. Seeing this smugness Daryl found a little bit of his inner self curl up and die within him.

*Why can't me Mam be nice to me and care just a little?* he asked himself, only too aware this was never likely to happen. He found his core of self pity turning to one of anger as his mother continued to prod and poke his hand. He felt resentful towards her coldness, and at that precise moment decided to go and seek out his next victim and get his own back – once his hand had healed.

His mother, having finally stopped the bleeding, forced his hand into a glove type plaster and turned her back on him dismissively.

'Thanks Mam,' Daryl said quietly through gritted teeth, hovering in the doorway hoping she'd offer a bit of comfort and support. He idly picked up the small green bottle and read the label.

'Mam,' he gasped with horror. 'This here bottle says its best by date is 2003. That's nearly thirty years out of date,' he informed her, a note of hysteria in his voice.

'So?' she challenged. 'Stopped yer bleeding didn't it, yer ungrateful little shit. Yer didn't even need stitches so yer should be bloody grateful.' Catching hold of his sleeve she propelled him out of the kitchen and out of her sight.

Daryl made his way to his bedroom feeling sorry for himself, sad at his Mam's indifference. He was sure she'd felt pleasure hurting him, and the thought made him feel doubly sorry for himself. As he entered his room he found himself drawn to the fish and jam again, and made his way towards it with the idea of another feast to cheer himself up. Then, changing his mind, he shoved them out of sight and into one of the drawers when he realised he wouldn't be able to open them.

Deciding to take a shower instead, Daryl found undressing and putting on his night clothes almost impossible. Sorting out his clothes for the next day he wondered how he'd cope with the cumbersome dressing, and worried how he'd be able to do his work and avoid a visit to the company medic at the same time. As he finally got into bed, his hand smarting and the feeling of sickness still lurking in the back of his mind, he decided he wasn't going to let the sickness or pain get the better of him. To occupy his mind he began plotting where he'd make his next strike and what type of woman he fancied raping next. He was due to go off on a works course soon, somewhere in the Lake District, where he'd not attacked before. As he settled to sleep he decided to make the best of it by scouting the area to see what sort of prey he could find. He wouldn't attack anyone whilst he was there, that would be too risky, but he'd suss out the lay of the land to plan his next attack. Not surprisingly Daryl found these thoughts sexually arousing, but dare not masturbate for the fear of hurting his hand. It was some time before he finally drifted off into a disturbed and troubled sleep.

When the slumber-pit's wake-up programme woke Daryl the next morning he lay un-rested in bed, desperate to go to the toilet. As he swung his legs out of bed and his feet hit the floor an intense wave of nausea washed over him. Greedily gulping in breaths of air, trying to combat the sickness, he staggered to the toilet his good hand clasped over his mouth, the other throbbing violently. He fell in front of the toilet and retched, emptying the contents of his stomach.

*Damn it,* he thought. *Me hand's so bad it's making me ill. Unless… Christ what if that stuff me Mam put on me has poisoned it and it's infected? That's what'll be making me sick,* he thought panic-stricken, the fear of having to get medical attention foremost in his mind. He made his way back to his slumber-pit and hung his head between his legs, willing the feeling of sickness to pass.

A few minutes later, still feeling sick and shaky, he ventured into the shower setting the programme to progress from a gentle wake-up to an invigorating finish, with the hope it would freshen and make him feel better than he did at present. After a few minutes of forcing himself to stand under the shower the body buffers sprang into action and began to gently massage his body with his favourite smelling lather. As soon as he smelt the lather he knew without a doubt he was going to be sick again and clutching his hand to his mouth staggered, wet and naked, to the toilet and fell onto his knees, his stomach straining with dry retching wanting to empty its non-existent contents. Clutching the rim, as the waves of nausea eased, he realised with misery that his hand had started bleeding again and was throbbing with a vengeance.

*This is no good,* he thought. *I've either picked something up or there's an infection in my cut. No way can I go to work today,* he told himself. *I can't go in being sick everywhere. They'll send me off to the medics, I'll just have to stay home and ride it out.* Having made the decision he staggered back to the shower cubicle resetting it for a refresher rinse and dry, feelings of self-pity overwhelming him as the unit washed and dried him.

Finally his ablutions complete he crawled back to bed, the feeling of nausea still threatening to overtake him. Pulling the covers over his body he set the slumber-pit to the illness programme and slept until midday. He woke, mortified to see the time, realising he'd not informed work of his illness.

*Before I do anything though,* he thought, *I'll have to see how I feel. Am I still feeling sick and is my hand still agony?* Instinctively he'd not moved it yet, nor had he lifted his head from the pillow. Thankfully he realised he no longer felt sick, as he hated feeling sick and vomiting actually panicked him. Tentatively he sat up, a sudden memory vivid in his mind of a time when he was little and his dad had stood with him, gently rubbing his back whilst he was ill. The memory brought a lump to his throat and he was reminded it was always his dad who'd looked after him before he'd died; even then his Mam had only done things grudgingly for him. The provoked memory reminded him of his Mam's smirk the night before, when she'd poured the liquid over his cut.

She *probably poisoned me deliberately,* he thought bitterly, suddenly thinking about the liquid being thirty years out of date. *If it has they'll be no antidote for it,* he panicked. *Christ. What am I going to do? How am I going to get the poison out of me body? What will it do to me?* His mind was in total turmoil as these thoughts bombarded him all at once.

Fighting to control his panic, he struggled to get up but as soon as his feet hit the floor he realised his head was throbbing, his entire body was clammy and awash with sweat and he began to swoon. He let himself fall backwards onto his slumber-pit just as a powerful wave of nausea threatened to overtake him. Shaking violently he burst into noisy sobs of fear and self-pity.

*Am I going to die of blood poisoning or summat just as hideous?'* he asked himself. The thoughts running through his head terrified him and even though he knew his Mam was somewhere downstairs the realisation struck him he was isolated in the house. Tears of self-pity rolled down his face as the jumbled thoughts, all of and for himself, ran through his mind. All he could think about was how the poison would be truly imbedded in his wound and invading his body and there was unlikely to be a remedy for it. He was doomed to die, but not without a fight, he decided.

After a while it dawned on him how thirsty he was, and simultaneously realised he was desperately hungry too.

*It's as if the sardines and jam are calling to me,* he thought as he made his way tentatively across the room. *Well, if I'm going to die,* he told himself, *I won't die hungry!',* and with that thought in mind he reached into his hidden stash of food pulling out the first tin and jar he came across. Struggling to open the containers the pain shot up his arm, but he was quickly compensated by the oily mass of fish he stuffed into his mouth. As soon as he started sucking the oily wetness the feeling of sickness began to abate, not that he was aware. Hooking out another fish and adding a huge blob of jam to it he crammed it into his mouth, the glistening flakes of fish laced with the sweetness of purple jam. Greedily he continued to eat his bizarre snack, the succulent morsels obliterating all thoughts of sickness, poisoning and dying from his mind.

Suddenly feeling better, and realising his Mam probably didn't even realise he was still in the house, Daryl picked up his remote control and strengthened the density of the sound-proofing in the room turning his music to near full volume, before helping himself to another tin of sardines and dancing clumsily round the room as he ate.

*Things will work out,* he told himself. *After all I can't really be dying if I feel like this. Can I?* And on that reassuring note he raised the music to full volume, relishing the freedom of an extra day away from work and the bitches.

*This will give me time to decide where to go and stay to find a new bitch for me pleasure,* he told himself gaily as he helped himself to a third tin of fish. *Some little beauty's going to be coming my way and I'm going to teach her that men are to be held in awe and not be mocked,'* and with those thoughts held firmly in his mind he crossed over to his work bench and turned on his computer, where for the next few hours he would cast his net to see what crimes had been committed and where. They would no doubt give him inspiration and undoubtedly highlight some new form of humiliation he could add to his little attacks that would pleasure him – if not his ladies.

Daryl stayed off work over the next few days after waking each morning feeling sick and with his hand throbbing. He was still convinced he was to die, especially as an angry purple patch was now spreading up his arm. Finally plucking up courage Daryl had taken the putrid plaster off, horrified by the stench of yellow pus, which oozed from the cut as soon as it was released from its wrapping. Despite its pain and ugliness Daryl dare not seek medical advice so finally made a trip to the chemist, where he bought antibiotics and a powerful antiseptic solution to bathe and dress his hand with. Advised to seek doctor's advice Daryl had nodded as if agreeing, but with mounting panic. From then on he meticulously bathed and dressed the wound, spending astronomical sums on all the items he needed for it, each time buying them from a different chemist. He also continued to buy copious tins of sardines and jars of jam, which he hid away obsessively, irrational when no one could enter his room.

Daryl continued to feel sick and generally unwell and at the weekend, as was usual, his Mam demanded he get out and leave her in peace. Surprising them both Daryl put his foot down refusing point blank to leave the house whilst his hand was still troubling him. He also accused her of giving him blood poisoning, from the bottle of gunk she'd poured over his cut. This didn't go down at all well but what mortified Daryl most was the way she'd grinned when he'd told her, before quickly turning it into a grimace. She refused to accept the liquid skin was the cause of his malady, or that she was in any way responsible for his cut not healing. She also told him in no uncertain terms he was pathetic, a baby and no way a man.

*Well nothing new there* Daryl told himself as he trudged back upstairs, her acidic tongue still ranting on from below.

By the Monday Daryl was back at work, still struggling with his sickness and injured hand, and the first place he visited was the toilets, where he stood willing his heaving stomach to still itself. A couple of lads, hearing his retching, started to tease him about not being able to hold his drink, but Daryl, shaking his head miserably, tried to explain it was his cut and the drugs he was taking. With knowing nods and winks the two lads advised Daryl to get back to his doctor for an alternative remedy, rather than get hauled into the medic here, who had the reputation of a butcher.

'No point,' Daryl replied. 'Only two more days and the drugs'll be finished so I might as well persevere before I go back…' but before he could finish the sentence he found himself emptying his scant breakfast into the pan.

Two weeks later, Daryl having finished a second course of antibiotics, little had changed. He continued to re-dress his hand with scrupulous care, which fortunately had stopped smelling foul despite the festering cut. His sickness though had not abated and now the skin on his chest hurt, his nipples in particular being hyper-sensitive and sore, which he put down to side effects from the medication. He was also finding certain smells or tastes set off his nausea, particularly coffee and bitter, and he missed his early morning cuppa, which immediately turned his stomach. His body really did seem to be out of sync, and yet oddly he felt generally healthy.

Finding his hand a hindrance at work there were several jobs he'd had to pass on to others, which did nothing for his popularity. The restrictions from his injury, and continual sickness, finally made his manager instruct him to visit the factory medic. Daryl, for once thinking on his feet, immediately replied he was already having treatment and he wasn't about to submit to someone else messing about with his hand, which could potentially set it off again just as it was healing.

'Well lad,' his manager had responded, 'I reckon you should go along to the medic and get a swab taken just to make sure it's ok. Last thing we need is to be sending out contaminated baby bottles and have a law suit on our hands.'

Daryl, irrationally incensed, almost shouted his own doctor had already done a swab so what was the point of having another when the results weren't even back yet? To his intense relief, a potential disaster averted, this was reluctantly accepted but accompanied by the warning that the manager would be keeping an eye on things.

~ ~ ~ ~ ~

Liam rolled over on to his back with a satisfied grunt and a huge grin on his face. He was twenty-one years old, extremely successful in his work and even more of a success between the sheets. He stood, when he wasn't on his back, at five foot nine inches tall. His body, which had never been finely honed, was beginning to thicken with a soft pliable layer of fat, which was thanks to the fine style of living he enjoyed. He was now at the stage when, if he didn't do something about his weight, the government would do something for him. *I'll just have to have more sex and work it off that way* he thought, rolling onto his side to look appraisingly at the woman beside him. She was a petite brunette with the most amazing breasts, tipped with sweet, neat, rose-coloured nipples. Her waist was slender with a nicely rounded stomach, and she had the most amazing curvy hips and slender, beautifully toned legs.

*Now she looks after herself,* Liam thought with admiration. *Not like Cassy from last night with an excess of soft fat clinging to her body. We'll both be hauled in for the enforced government weight plan soon if things don't change quickly,* he mused cringing inwardly. *Now Tanya here is in a completely different class* he thought and immediately began to feel his loins stir again appreciatively.

Trailing her fingers down his body the young woman had propped herself up on an elbow to watch his face in the aftermath of their just completed sex session. Tanya, as a ripe twenty-two year old, was one of his stars. She had incredible social skills and was a dream in bed. She was the only woman he ever slept with regularly and he loved her gentle, yet intelligent and challenging manner, and her incredible sexiness between the sheets. She had amazing agility, an incredible tongue and was open to try anything and everything he'd ever suggested, and suggested even more herself. There was something about her that kept drawing him back to her, which was more than just the physical aspect, it was almost as if she could read his mind and anticipate his needs, sexually and intellectually. It was uncanny and whilst he enjoyed this unique communication it also unnerved him somewhat.

*Of all the men and women I've ever slept with, and there've been scores of them, Tanya's the only one I'd consider as a permanent partner, if ever I'm to think of settling down,* he told himself. *I'd miss the variety of different and new sex partners I enjoy now, but then why should that stop? Tanya's even more sexually free than I am! Anyway, I'm not anywhere near ready to settle down yet and it'll be a long time before I'll forgo the variety of sexual pleasures I enjoy at the moment. If I do decide to settle then I'll have to give my all to the relationship,* he told himself unconvincingly, as that was the type of guy he was.

Liam wasn't totally convinced he could actually tie Tanya down. *Hell, listen at me. Tie her down? Where the hell has that thought snuck from?* He wondered.

Liam had tried all sorts to test Tanya's feelings towards him but hadn't actually been aware that this was what he was doing. It was odd really because there was a true link between them which was somehow indefinable, but also elusive. He fell into a reverie as to some of the things that had happened between them in the past. *On one occasion I made some really special arrangements to take her to one of our exclusive government parties we hold twice a year for select and chosen stars,* he remembered. *Then the day before, on the flimsiest of excuses, I cancelled her going with me and damn it! She didn't utter one complaint and then when I arrived at the party, with another date on my arm, she was there with Robbie, my biggest bloody rival! On another occasion I invited her over here for sex and invited another woman along to join us in bed. I thought she'd be angry and show her true feelings for me but instead we spent the night playing sex games and the two women almost excluded me they were so happy together! Un... bloody... believable! I'd planned to do it with another man as well, but somehow I couldn't face the thought of being excluded again.*

*I've tried treating her like royalty, bringing her gifts and flowers, treated her to some of the most amazing experiences I could only get through my work connections. I've deliberately treated her she was like shit, ignored her, not contacted her, flaunted other women in front of her just hoping she'd show some emotions or a reaction at least, and what's happened? Sweet nothing! She's behaved towards me, and whoever was with me, as if we were just people she knew. Not dismissively but courteously and still with a degree of warmth. If anything I was the one who felt dismissed and ignored so the whole lot's just backfired on me big time. Where am I going wrong?*

Yet once again here she was gracing his bed, back between his loins sharing with him the most fantastic and amazingly erotic sex. She knew that tonight he'd be entertaining somebody else in his bed, and he also knew that she would be opening her legs for someone else. Now he found that really hard to stomach, but she seemed not in the least bit bothered by it.

*The whole thing's an enigma. I've met some amazing women, and come to that some pretty spectacular men. I've had sex with an amazing variety of individuals; some good, some bad and some unbelievably, amazingly brilliant! But nothing and no one has been anything like, or as good as, Tanya,* he thought.

'Hey big boy,' she crooned, running her hand down to his groin nudging him out of his dreams, and making him groan in pleasure. 'Tell me what you're thinking. Share it with mamma, baby.'

He turned his head and kissed her on her luscious glistening lips. He pondered whether he should tell her what he was really thinking, or give her some throw away line that might just provoke a reaction in her. He decided on the latter.

'Well,' he drooled with sharp intakes of breath, as his arousal heightened. 'Just wondering what sweet piece of ass I shall find at today's session to entertain tonight. Just wondering if I should have a guy for a change or maybe even a guy and a gal together. What do you reckon?'

She smiled sweetly at him, a glint of mischief gleaming in her eye. *Damn it,* he thought as he saw the impish sparkle. *It's bloody genuine* he realised, and immediately felt gutted. Once again he'd made the wrong choice. *Why did he never get it right?* he challenged himself.

'Oh,' she replied wistfully. 'I think you should do what I'm planning to do tonight.'

'Oh yes? What's that?' he asked hoping she might invite him along, whatever she was planning.

'Well,' she replied, drawing out the words to tease him and wrench up his emotions just a notch more. 'I'm entertaining two guys tonight. Out to dinner first, on to a club and then back to mine for a major sex session. And...' she continued. 'I'm not planning on inviting anyone else along to share in them 'cos they're going to be all mine. All mine for the duration of the night. I can do with them – and will do with them – whatever I damn well like and plan to make it a banquet of sexual delights not to be forgotten.'

Liam tried to close down the expressions on his face so she wouldn't be able to read his thoughts or feelings, or be able to see his disappointment. He yawned, trying to look nonchalant, stretched and rolled off the bed and onto his feet.

'Well sweet-cakes, if that's what you want then you go for it,' he told her, looking down at her elegant body sprawled on the bed. 'You've got the looks, the brains and you certainly got the sex that any red-hot and panting for it guy would die for,' he said in a light tone, trying to mask the mix of emotions he was feeling. 'As for me I'm off for a shower and then I'm heading off for today's session. Thank god I'm not travelling today 'cos I'm knackered after you kept me up all night,' he finished with a grin and picking her silk underwear up from the floor he threw it casually across the bed so that it landed on her face. 'So get your sweet ass out of there and into the shower with me 'cos then I'm kicking you out to get on with the day.' With that he strode into his bathroom his slightly bulbous and soft stomach overshadowing his semi flaccid manhood, which made him look less well endowed than he actually was.

Tanya looked over at him fondly and jumping energetically from the bed tossed back. 'No time Tubs. You'll have to wash your own tackle today. Just follow the centre line until you hit the hairy bit and then you'll know you've found it. You'll not find it by looking 'cos that overhang of a belly's blocking your line of vision,' she instructed laughingly. 'I'm off down to the steamer, gotta be extra clean and smelling sweet for my boys tonight. Don't want to leave any of you down there to put them off now, do I?'

Liam hated 'Tubs' her pet name for him, but this morning it had gone totally over his head, her words of dismissal stinging him. He was momentarily at a loss. *How do her words make me feel?* he asked himself silently. *If only I could identify the way she makes me feel. Is it loss? Rejection? Jealousy? Christ I don't know,'* and before he allowed his thoughts to drift off in that direction he bade her a false cheery goodbye and made his way into the shower, knowing she would be gone by the time he was finished. As these thoughts ran through his head Tanya was watching him, noting the slight stoop that had appeared in his stance. Mentally she shrugged her shoulders, then collected her clothes and departed for the steamer.

*Sod her,* Liam thought morosely, as he heard the door shut behind her. *I'll find my own form of entertainment tonight.* With that final defiant thought he switched his thinking to the day ahead, and got on with his ablutions.

~ ~ ~ ~ ~

Four weeks later and Daryl was still not himself. His hand, although healing, continued to sport a purplish tinge and although the wound itself appeared to be healing the edges were raised and livid. Intensely bored with his own company Daryl had finally ventured out for a game of pool, but had found the position he needed to use his hand in pulled at the wound. Within a couple of shots the cut was throbbing intensely and Daryl felt sick, although unbeknown to him it was the smell of the beer rather than the cut causing this. The visit to the pub though had been quite an eye opener for him. He'd never realised, until his absence, just how much in demand he was with his fellow players, but not in the way he'd have liked. Nobody locally could normally play pool to the same high standard as Daryl and his first night back had seen him beaten twice, out of the three games he'd played. The pub had been delighted at his demise, which had angered Daryl even more, knowing he'd only been missed as someone everyone wanted to beat, and not as someone people wanted to spend time with.

It was a painful lesson, and not just in terms of his injured hand. He'd stormed home, a man with pent up anger, and had anyone got in his path, namely a woman, it would not have taken much to push him over edge he was in such an ugly mood.

Work wasn't much better either. Whilst he didn't have to pass work over any more he was still resented by his colleagues for the extra load he'd burdened them with, despite the fact he'd taken on some of their lighter tasks in exchange. The women constantly mimicked him too, talking to him as if he were a baby, hiding his mug and replacing it with one of the millions of baby bottles produced in the factory. They imitated him too, by holding a hand across their chests with pained expressions pretending to whimper and cry with pain. Despite doing his best to ignore them Daryl's anger was mounting and his inward promises of revenge, for their treating him that way, becoming louder and more violent in his head. He could see no reason why they should treat him like this but they'd regret it and he'd get his revenge in the end. He'd already taught one of them a lesson, and he couldn't wait to get the other bitches too.

*Thank God I'll soon be out of here and on that course*, he told himself. *At least when I get back I'll be out of their way and one up on them.* It was this internal dialogue he used to console and bolster himself as he forced himself through his daily house of hell.

~ ~ ~ ~ ~

*If I'm to get my hands on Adsexlent,* Jed thought, *I'm going to have to screw Fiona Middleton. But whatever the price it's going to be worth it 'cos I've got to have that game.* Jed had tried to persuade his parents the night before to let him have the extra credits he needed to buy it, but they'd refused not approving of his choice. *And as cash no longer exists I can't borrow any money or tap into anyone else's pocket cards. Big Brother's really put the kibosh on that!* he thought angrily. *Now cash is abolished how am I supposed to get hold of things when I need my parent's consent for just about everything I buy? It must have been so much easier for people years ago when there was cash. At least then I could have got some through bullying, or even nicked some.* Which was exactly the reason cash had been abolished, and replaced by recipient responsive pocket cards.

Funding, or rather the lack of it, was the problem Jed found himself pondering as he luxuriated in being lathered, massaged and dried by the gel buffers in the cleansing unit. He always found it the best place for uninterrupted thinking and making decisions, no matter how poor the outcomes often were.

*If I hurry and get to school early I can catch up with Ben, then we can go off and do some filming to use with the blocking devices for our wristlets,* he calculated. *It'll only take a couple of hours then we can knuckle down to our schoolwork. Then we'll have some sort of freedom without the constant thought of interruptions from the parents. Damn Big Brother for restricting our activities through those bastard Wristlets!* he thought violently. *All these fucking restrictions make life shit! But nothing and no one is going to stand in the way of what I want,* he concluded arrogantly. If only he'd known then how those thoughts would impact on his future.

By just after three that afternoon Jed and Ben had done enough filming to give them a few hours freedom; completed sufficient school work to meet their targets for payment, and had a leisurely lunch with a group of other lads. They walked out of the school together, having carefully set their Wristlet blockers, Jed to meet Fiona and Ben to go and meet a contact he'd found to buy chemicals from. If either had any problem, with parents checking in on them through the Wristlets, it was agreed they would contact the other and each would stand by their pre-arranged alibi. The lads parted ways with Ben's mocking words ringing in Jed's ears, as to the lengths he was prepared to go to to get hold of his much coveted game.

It wasn't long before Jed met up with Fiona, who was dressed in smart but non-descript clothing. Her shoulder length mousey-coloured hair was brushed back off her face, and whilst it looked clean it had little shape or imagination in its styling, very much like the clothes she was wearing. On her shoulder she carried a brightly-coloured bag, bulging with goodness knows what. He hoped it contained, amongst other things, the game he so desperately wanted.

She smiled as he came into the area; inwardly Jed cringed. She wasn't at all attractive, but if he needed to have physical contact with her, even sex, he would, but he didn't relish the idea at all. He noticed her blush violently, looking as awkward with the situation as he felt.

'So you made it then?' she observed somewhat nervously, a less confident Fiona than Jed was used to. Looking challengingly at him she passed him a book with a small piece of paper poking out from its pages.

'Do you read books?' she asked. 'I mean I'm sure you read e-books but there's just something about an old-fashioned book that's so rewarding isn't there?'

Jed gave her a scathing look as she continued, 'It just feels good to hold one in your hand and turn the pages instead of scrolling down a screen. Don't you think? Do you have any books at home?' Initially Jed had thought this was Fiona being obtuse but quickly realised it was a coded conversation so reached out and accepted the book.

'It's a very old book from the end of the last century,' she intoned. 'Well, from the nineties anyway. There was a whole series of them. I could lend them to you if you wanted,' she told him, flicking the loose piece of paper so he couldn't fail to notice its presence.

Removing the note Jed read in Fiona's very large scrawled handwriting, '*Have you blocked your wristlet?*' He looked straight into her eyes with almost a glare.

'Yes,' he said, 'and I presume from this you have too?'

'Of course,' she nodded. 'But if you want we can go somewhere where I can block signals altogether so you won't have to waste your film, I presume that's how you're blocking,' she surmised. 'You coming or not?' she called over her shoulder as she walked away. She strode forward, more confidently now, with Jed taking long loping strides to catch up with her.

*Obviously she likes to be in control of things,* he thought, a wry grin now on his face. Suddenly he realised he quite liked her style – *Fiona Middleton was not all she seemed to be!*

As they walked along their conversation was somewhat stilted.

'Are you really into old books?' he asked. 'Or was that just a ploy?'

'Both,' she replied, 'I do like books but used it as a ploy. It's an innocent topic of conversation our parents wouldn't think to question it if they happened to look in and you weren't logged out. Anyway I'm far more interested in the business we're here to deal with, aren't you?'

'Er, what business exactly?' he asked, hoping it was about the game and not her virginity. She threw a disdainful look over her shoulder but didn't actually answer. Instead she tilted her head to the left indicating they'd be turning down a driveway. A few yards on, hidden behind the high hedges, stood a tall, imposing house and parked in front was a vintage Jaguar XJ6, in immaculate condition.

'Wow!' gasped Jed, impressed with the sight in front of him. 'Nice car! That your dad's?'

'No,' Fiona chuckled delightedly. 'It's mine actually. A christening present that's been kept in immaculate condition for when I'm old enough to drive. Well next year I am, so I'm learning to drive on the track behind the house. Come on we need to check in with the security system otherwise we won't get into the house.' With that Fiona laid her hand flat against a black panel, next to the impressive front door, and looked into an optic. As her hand print was recognised she pressed a small panel at the side then instructed Jed to do the same.

'Just pass me the book will you Jed?' she asked in a level tone, and taking it from him turned over the paper and handed the book back to Jed with a knowing glance.

*Don't say anything about why we're meeting today until we're in my den,* it stated. Jed acknowledged this with an almost indiscernible nod.

Entering the house they made their way across a spacious hallway to a large, old-fashioned kitchen, and Fiona walked over to the corner where a tall, bright blue fridge stood, which she opened. Inside was a whole range of bottles and boxes along with taps set at different levels. She called back over her shoulder

'What do you fancy? A juice or there's even a coke.'

'Coke?' he asked amazed, knowing it had once been one of the world's favourite drinks.

'Yep. Coke and it's the real thing,' she told him with a grin, taking two out of the fridge. 'Ice cold like it should be. Ever had it before?'

'Only once,' he said. 'I loved it but can't understand why they stopped mass producing it.'

'Purely because other products came on the market and the tastes of the nation changed, or were made to change.' she added. 'You want ice with it?' He nodded and took the proffered glass from her.

'Ready?' she asked, collecting more coke and walking out to a small annexe, where she placed her hand on another security panel.

*This family has some serious money,* Jed thought looking round appreciatively. He particularly liked the furnishings that were obviously quality and probably antique too.

As the security measures were followed and the door opened, activating the lighting, Jed stood in the doorway and stared round in wonder. The room held a dozen or more computers, all of which were turned on and showed different images of the house. Fiona walked over to a long electronic panel and began to quickly lay her palm on the different insets, in what was obviously a very practised pattern. Jed watched fascinated, noticing how graceful and confident her movements were. As Fiona continued the ritual the screen images began to change finally becoming a line of electric static with a messaged displayed that read:

*'Private Alarms Activated – Input Time Allowance'*

Fiona keyed in an instruction and turned, in a relaxed but very commanding stance, to Jed and said, 'Right. We've got privacy now. Warning systems on and no parental or guardian angels watching over us. Impressed or what?'

Jed, not wanting to show he was too impressed shrugged and responded nonchalantly. 'So how long have we got and how have you blocked it all?'

'S'easy,' she replied. 'A lot of the equipment in here's quite ancient. My parents gave it to me to 'play with'. I've spent the last few years learning how to programme and now I'm pretty much a wiz at it. The monitor over there,' she indicated one at the far end of the bench, 'will warn us if anyone arrives at the gate. But if my mom and dad are on the way back it'll pick up a signal a couple of miles away. It gives me freedom should I want it, and doesn't raise any alarms or warnings with my parents, giving me time to stop doing anything they'd raise objections to and lets them think their goody-two-shoes daughter is quietly sitting at home playing with her electronics.'

Jed was impressed and it now showed clearly on his face.

'I also created an interference which blocks signals to our wristlets without it activating a warning but at the same time,' Fiona continued, 'gives false body function readings, whatever I'm doing. So you can turn your blocker off now as you're safe in here,' she finished blushing prettily.

*If what Fiona says is right she's an electronic genius,* Jed mused finding his dislike of her quickly diminishing.

'Neat,' he said. 'Who taught you about electronics?'

'My uncle who used to live with us. I used to spend hours watching him strip them down, rebuild and programme them. He taught me the basics of programming and how to build the devices to run them with. So, since I was about ten I've just developed things myself. When he came to visit last year, he was pretty impressed with what I'd developed. We've discussed the possibility of me going to work for him when I've finished my education and he's talked about sending me over to NASA to learn a few more of the in-depth things that I can't learn here.' She finished trailing off, mortified she might be sounding big-headed.

Jed was impressed not only with her talent but the fact that she'd kept quiet about it at school. She always came across as studious and boring, but it was obvious she had hidden depths and didn't broadcast them and he liked that. He glanced over at her, and found himself looking properly at her for the first time.

*If she wore different clothes and changed her hair,* he thought, *she could be quite an attractive girl. She's got a good figure too and could be a goldmine into the bargain,* he thought thinking of all the outlets he and Ben could find to sell her gismos, given half a chance. *Yep!* he reckoned. *She could be quite a catch!* As she'd worked on the panels Jed had become almost mesmerised by her and was surprised at how comfortable and relaxed she was to be with. She had a hypnotic voice and beautiful hands, he'd noticed, with long slender fingers that moved with quick deft movements as she worked.

Satisfied that everything was in order they went over and flung themselves onto the large bulbous sofa, where they sat uncomfortably sipping their cokes. After a few awkward minutes Fiona picked up a remote control and started pointing it in different directions round the room. As she pointed music came alive, lights dimmed and then globes of colour appeared. The brightly-coloured orbs hung in the air, pulsating in time to the music and creating an atmosphere that held promises of wonderment and anticipation.

There *must be six or seven different colours,* Jed thought in wonder. As if able to read his thoughts Fiona told him. 'They represent the different colours of the rainbow,' she explained, seeing Jed's fascination. 'What colour do you see yourself as?'

Jed gave her a funny look. 'What do you mean what colour do I see myself as?'

'Well at the moment I see myself as red, because I'm full of energy and ideas for the future. Very positive. Look.' She picked up a piece of equipment, which was like a glass tube with moving colour inside.

Pressing buttons on the control she ran the tube over the outline of her head and body, not actually letting the gadget touch her.

'Watch the red shape in the ceiling,' she instructed, and as Jed watched the shape suspended above them began to reform, taking on Fiona's shape and features.

'So what colour do you want to be?' she asked Jed.

'Er, blue,' he finally decided and watched the blue globe take on his own shape as Fiona programmed it. He moved tentatively, watching the blue imitation above mimic his movements. It was fascinating and as he gained confidence he moved more energetically, captivated by his blue self emulating him.

'Wow! They're awesome. What the hell are they? They're bloody amazing!' he exclaimed in wonder.

She smiled with a look of enormous pride on her face.

'It's one of my inventions, but I've still a long way to go with their development yet,' she added modestly. 'I call them my Colorbs. Here watch this. I'm going to programme the rest of them into the music. Do you like the Beatles or ever heard of them or any of their stuff?'

'Don't know much of it,' he said, 'but my grandpa was really into them so I've heard them a few times. What are you going to do?'

'Just tune a colour into each of the Beatles and their instruments. Know how to twist?' she asked with a mischievous grin. ''Cos that's what we're going to do.'

'No. You'll have to show me,' he said, watching the remaining Colorbs become imitations of the long gone Beatles playing their instruments. Within minutes the room was pulsating with colour and rhythm the Colorbs gyrating in time to the music like living objects. Swirling round the room Jed could almost imagine a person inside the shape fighting to get out. It was incredible, if not a little spooky.

Fiona walked over to him and, taking hold of his hand, told him, 'Watch the colour of our shapes.' Looking up Jed saw that where their hands were touching their images had become a vibrant purple.

'Wow!' he responded and touched her cheek, whilst watching her image's cheek turn almost cerise pink.

'Why…' he started, and when he turned to look at her saw she was blushing.

'Oh!' he responded quickly pulling his hand away, but not before he'd noticed his own image's face had turned an electric blue, and realised he too was blushing.

Fiona pulled him into the centre of the room and to the sounds of 'Twist and Shout' was showing him how to twist, or how she thought one twisted. Together they danced, carefully keeping contact to a minimum and watched the images above emulate their actions. They found themselves laughing delightedly, just for the sheer fun of it.

As the music continued a slow number came on and Jed, without thinking, pulled her towards him.

'My grandpa always told me how he and my grandma used to do a 'smooch' to this record,' he told her, taking hold of her hands and placing them round his neck, whilst he wrapped his arms low round her waist.

*Christ!* he thought. *Am I actually doing this? What the hell is going on here?* But he pulled her closer to him anyway, enjoying the unusual experience.

'Look!' she giggled, indicating their floating images. Looking up he saw that between them there was a lot of purple but at their groin areas the colours were vibrant and pulsing quite madly, almost indigo in colour. He suddenly realised how aroused he was, and almost at once realised that Fiona was too. Without thinking he started to kiss her. It seemed the most natural thing in the world to do, but felt surreal and he experienced a fleeting moment of anxiety as he remembered that if this went any further it would be her first time.

*Do I want it to go further?* he asked himself, and with a jolt realised he did.

'You've not had sex before have you?' he asked bluntly. Fiona shook her head. He lifted her face up with his hand, surprisingly gentle for him, and asked, 'Do you want to?'

She shrugged her shoulders and in a quiet, husky voice told him uncertainly, 'I think so.' Without saying anything more he pulled her closer and looking up saw their images change shape and colour.

They continued to smooch, his hands roaming over her body feeling her tense and relax as his hands travelled tentatively over her clothing. Still kissing he led her back to the sofa and slowly began to undo her buttons, slipping his hand inside her top. He could feel her quiver in anticipation and all of a sudden realised how much he wanted to have sex with her, but not just for the taking, this time he wanted to savour the experience, unlike past times.

Once undressed and naked beneath him he stopped and looked down at her. She had a beautiful body and he imagined quite pale in normal light, as it was her body was multi-coloured with the reflections from the coloured globes undulating above them. He looked up at their images, still amazed at how incredible they were, and realised they were quite a turn on too.

Promising Fiona he would be gentle, he quickly stripped off the remainder of his clothing, before lowering himself to lie down beside her. He let his hand trail over and explore her body until finally he gently lay on top of her and slowly penetrated her tense yet eager body. At the moment of penetration he looked up at the images floating above them and saw the colours blend together in an evocative manner. As their hands eagerly explored each other they kept catching glimpses of the colours pulsating above them, their shades strengthening as the youngsters' passion increased. At the moment of climax Jed threw back his head and was amazed to see millions of tiny stars implode in the images above them. The whole experience had taken only a couple of minutes and as he looked down at Fiona he felt a rush of intense emotion wash over him.

'You ok?' he panted, his breath still coming fast.

'Yes,' she said hesitantly. 'Is that it?' she asked in a small, slightly disappointed voice.

'Yeah! Great isn't it?' he crowed, not realising there was an edge of disappointment in her voice. 'We'll have to do that again,' he finished rolling off her and planting a kiss on her lips.

'Christ!' she exclaimed. 'Look at the time. My mother'll be back soon. You've gotta go.'

Jumping off the sofa and grabbing her clothes she clumsily began to pull them back on. The images above them were now losing the intensity of their colour, toning down as their pulse rates settled back to normal.

'Gotta kick you out now,' she told him, as she started to move amongst the equipment adjusting this knob and flicking that switch. 'I've got things to do and my parents will be back soon so you gotta go. They'll know you've been here by the security system but not for how long or what we've been doing.'

'Do I have to go?' he asked, in a voice that sounded almost like a whine. 'Can't I stay for a while and watch you work?' he asked, finding himself deflating as the music quietened and the floating colours reverted to spheres and fading until finally they disappeared. He found himself feeling quite bereft of their presence.

'No,' she responded, with a flicker of annoyance. She had no idea why she felt irritated, but she did. 'You have to go. Now,' she responded strongly. 'I've re-activated your Wristlet so you can't stay now.'

'I can put my blocker back on,' he told her hopefully, but she was already gathering up his things and pushing him towards the door.

'Wait,' he told her, putting the things back down again. He drew her into his arms, with the view of pulling her close and just holding her, but she just gave him a chaste kiss and pushed him away.

'Time to go,' she told him firmly. And with a feeling of complete rejection he realised she meant it.

'Can we meet again? Soon?' he asked, in what he thought was a sexy voice.

'Maybe,' she replied, walking towards the door and pulling it open. He followed her meekly and just as they got to the door he stopped in his tracks.

'The Adsexlent,' he said. 'You haven't given me the Adsexlent which was the deal.'

'Oh yes!' she responded with a grin, and pulled open a drawer, which was full of them. 'How many do you want?' she asked, and he saw to his annoyance that there were several copies.

He looked at her questioningly. 'How come....' he started and before he'd finished his question she'd quickly jumped in with, 'They're one of my uncle's developments. I've already got the next version but this is the one you wanted isn't it?' and she handed him a copy and made to walk out of the door again.

Jed took the box with an incredulous expression on his face. 'But I thought ...can I see you again?'

'Perhaps,' she told him glibly. And feeling almost humiliated Jed realised, for the first time, how many of his past conquests must have felt.

Despite contacting her over the next few days Fiona wouldn't agree to meet up with Jed and didn't turn up at school again until the following week. Jed was still marvelling at the brilliance of Fiona's Colorbs, and trying to sort out his confused feelings. He really wanted to see Fiona again, despite Ben laughing at him and warning him to watch his street cred, as she wasn't the prettiest girl on the block. Well his street cred was important to him, but then he'd like Fiona to be as well. All weekend he'd asked himself if he should ask her out again and turn a deaf ear to any comments his mates made. However, he had no more idea of how he felt or what he should do, when he woke up on the Monday morning, than he'd had the week before.

As it was he needn't have worried as the decision was taken out of his hands over the weekend. When Fiona arrived at school on the Monday morning it was obvious she'd been busy in the past few days. She was no longer the ugly duckling but now a beautiful swan and every boy wanted to ask her out – and several did. Her hair had been styled and coloured to a lovely honey blonde, and her clothes were as modern as anyone else's. What she had though, that other girls her age lacked, was the poise and confidence he'd watched as she'd worked on her machines, which was now evident in the way she moved and interacted with the other kids. Now she attracted males to her like a bee to a honey pot, and although Jed was worried she'd not want anything to do with him, now she had the pick of the bunch, he couldn't have been more wrong. From then on, in Jed's mind, they were a couple, but to Fiona, with her new found freedom, they weren't, but she did spend more time with Jed than with any other lad.

Over the next few weeks Jed and Fiona spent more time together and Ben started going out with Jade, Fiona's best friend. It was natural they all go out in a foursome and a few weeks later it was decided to introduce the girls to skateboarding. The skateboarding park, where Ben and Jed were members, was open to traditional and computerised boarders but they wanted the girls to try the traditional boarding they followed.

The girls were as different on the boards as they were in looks, taking to the sport in totally different ways. Jade had a natural grace and balance that really suited boarding and rapidly mastered the basic skills. It wasn't long before she was gracefully negotiating the ground level course, having skilfully learnt how to manipulate and steer her board. It was obvious she had a natural leaning for the sport and was thoroughly enjoying herself.

Fiona on the other hand was not doing anywhere near as well. Not being a physically active person, like Jade, she found difficulty in even being able to decide which foot to use on the board. The ease and grace that Jed had noted when she was working on her computers was certainly not evident in this activity. However, she certainly wasn't faint hearted or afraid to give something a go, and doggedly persisted until she could finally negotiate a straight line and mild bend without falling off, only occasionally losing the board from under her. By the end of the session she was able to do a full circuit, be it somewhat clumsily, without either losing contact with the board or falling over. Jed admired her determination if not her poise.

They all went off to the eaterie, Jed and Ben waxing lyrical about the chips. The only reason the club were allowed to sell chips, they explained, was because it was a centre for physical activities and they were licensed to sell chips and other calorie laden foods. Opting out from traditional fayre Jade chose food pearls, whilst the others ordered the strictly controlled foods that were only available in this type of centre. Their food selected they made their way to a table overlooking the club's display team, where several of the team members were practising. Despite Ben's disparaging attitude towards Fiona previously, the four of them were comfortable together and settled to their lunch whilst watching the team practise and execute some spectacular moves. Ben outlined how determined he was to get onto the team.

'What about you Jed? Do you want to get onto the team too?' Fiona asked Jed.

'No. I'm nowhere near as good as Ben and never will be. I love the sport but know I'm not good enough for competitions, but my dad used to be the county champion twenty years ago,' he added.

'Really? Does he ever board now?' Jade asked with interest.

'Nope. He had a car accident years ago and his leg got smashed. He's not been on a board since and reckons he never will because he's lost his agility.'

'But he follows you in the sport doesn't he?' asked Fiona innocently.

Jed, blushing beetroot, looked at Ben as if seeking help. Then answered honestly, 'Nah. My dad and I don't really hit it off. He's still got all his boarding stuff but it's packed away. He won't even let me see it let alone borrow it,' he told them uncomfortably, and a hushed silence fell round the table.

'At least you've got your parents to yourself,' Jade jumped in quickly to cover the awkwardness. 'I have to share mine with three brothers and sisters,' she explained.

'Three?' Jed exclaimed surprised. 'How come? I didn't think families were allowed to have more than two children,' he questioned.

'No it's not two children but two *pregnancies*,' Jade explained. 'And my mother had triplets when I was two years old. A throw-back to previous generations, which wasn't picked up in the marriage application process,' she chortled.

'Must be brilliant having all those brothers and sisters,' Jed responded wistfully. 'I suppose your mum's a full time parent as well isn't she? I'm lucky if I get to see my parents during the week and sometimes I see neither, except on screen,' he added morosely.

The young group continued talking about their families with the conversation interspersed by Ben, every so often, pointing out a particularly good boarder and explaining the stunt being practised. The activities outside and conversation round the table kept the four of them occupied for some time, and it felt as if the four of them had been friends for years rather than just weeks. Because the atmosphere was so comfortable, Ben decided to take a gamble and tell the others about an opportunity he'd been offered.

'A mate of mine, who works for a big drugs company round here, has just concocted a new recreational drug and offered me some to try out for him. What do you reckon? You lot interested?'

'What sort of drug?' Jed asked bluntly.

'Well you remember back about thirty years ago a designer drug call Viagiant?' Ben asked. Jed laughed and responded sarcastically that he remembered it as if it were yesterday. Ignoring the sarcasm Ben continued.

'No come on mate, this is serious stuff. Do you know the drug I mean?'

'Course I do,' Jed laughed. 'In fact I happen to know that my dad played around with it before I was born. In fact I reckon I was conceived when he was on it,' he scoffed, 'Can you imagine that? My stiff upper lipped and serious father actually messing about with something like that. Perish the thought,' he said, mimicking a posh and pompous tone of disapproval. 'Where he got it from and the fact that he knew what it was for is a wheeze in itself, not that I'm supposed to know any of this of course. The old man'd flip if he knew I know. I only found out by chance when he had a few friends round and I was listening in. They'd been drinking and were reminiscing about 'before they had children' and they teased him something cruel about having a hard on for days that he couldn't get rid of. They were really laughing about it and taking the piss. Anyway, he reckoned that no matter how much he screwed my mum he just couldn't get rid of it and reckons I was the result. Just think of it mate. If he'd not had that then I probably wouldn't be here,' he finished laughing. 'Nice to know he was human once upon a time even if he's not now,' he added wistfully. 'Anyway what's this got to do with these drugs?'

'Well this bloke reckons this concoction is amazing. It's got the same properties as high volume alcohol along with the power of Viagiant; plus it gives heightened imagination and overrides inhibitions. It's in little seeds that pop and explode when you put them on your tongue. Reckons it lasts a couple of hours.'

'Yeah but how safe is? Not wanting to seem wet mate, but I do want to live a bit longer.'

'No it's sound. He's tried it out and run tests on it in the laboratory he works in. It checks out big time,' he nudged Jed, a leering grin on his face. 'I know Jed'll be up for it but what about you girls? Are you game?' he asked cocking his head to one side as if it might make them answer more favourably.

The four of them tossed and argued the idea until it was finally time to leave, with still no clear indication as to whether or not they were willing to give it a go. Walking the girls back to Fiona's, and leaving both girls there after a couple of cokes, Ben and Jed walked home speculating as to their ultimate reply.

'Hey you reckon the girls could get sweet with each other too?' Ben leered, giving Jed a jarring jab of his elbow. 'You know what I mean,' he winked and together the lads fantasised about the two girls together before turning off in different directions to go home.

A few days later Jed and Ben were at the skateboarding park working on a particular stunt Jed was having trouble with. It was as they were working on it Jed told Ben his latest news.

'Hey, do you remember I told you my dad used to skateboard and was a real whiz at it? Well the other night he got out some videos of his, you know of the competitions and things? Well some of the tricks they did were pretty awesome and he was fucking fantastic, into all sorts of stunts and things. I was really amazed,' he told Ben.

'What for real and you were impressed? Bloody hell he must have been good,' Ben replied to Jed's nodded responses. 'Do you reckon he'd let me have a look at them sometime?' Ben asked. 'I mean I know I'm not his favourite person but if you could get hold of them I could come round one night if you wanted.'

'No,' Jed responded faster than need be, thinking how much Ben would laugh if he saw his babyish room, which he'd visited before but not for many years. 'I'll sneak them out one day and we can watch them at yours, ok? When dad showed them to me I thought he was softening, 'cos he was quite civil. Hah! Fat chance of that happening, within half an hour he was biting my head off and telling me I should do this and that. He's got no fucking idea what's going on today and resents the interruptions he gets through the Wristlet. The only use I've been is them getting the house and other social trimmings they got when mum became pregnant. That was my purpose. Full stop,' he finished bitterly. 'When we were watching the film I asked him if he'd come and do some boarding or even just coach me but he reckons that since smashing his knee there's no chance. And he kept rubbishing my board,' he finished indignantly, as if it was the ultimate insult his dad could throw at him. 'Reckons its crap compared to the one he used to have but when I asked if I could borrow it he told me there was no chance 'cos it's got sentimental value. I mean,' he continued his voice rising, 'how pathetic is that?'

'Shit, man, it must be tough having a dad like that, especially when he's so strict. My dad's just as strict but at least he's interested in what I do. Too interested sometimes. Anyway enough of that let's just try that stunt again then I've got to get off. You follow me and I'll tell you what I'm going to do and you can copy. Ok?' he shouted over his shoulder as he set off. Together they worked at the stunt until finally Jed could execute it with perfection. Leaving the park Ben went off to see when he'd be able to get hold of some of the drugs he'd told the others about, and Jed went off to see Fiona.

Jed had never planned on having a steady girlfriend, which was how he saw Fiona, but it seemed she was having a positive influence on him, although he wasn't aware of this. There had been subtle changes in Jed's behaviour and attitudes and he was now buckling down to work at school. His father had also been pleasantly surprised when Jed showed willing to do jobs about the house and garden. He was even more surprised at Jed's competence and enjoyment in the tasks he undertook, but not as surprised as Jed was. It had become apparent to Jed, since meeting Fiona, that she was very competent when it came to computers, and he'd discovered Jade had an enviable talent too, when it came to art. Even Ben had something he was interested in that he could follow as a career path, through his knowledge and fascination for chemicals, but Jed had nothing.

Compared to the others Jed had always felt lacking in that department. Now he felt he'd found a natural talent when it came to doing practical tasks in the house and garden, something he'd not done before, willingly or not. In addition to the enjoyment Jed got from doing the different jobs he also liked the extra credits it gave him to spend. Always on the look out for new opportunities, Jed had seen a way these newly discovered talents could be used very much to his advantage – and get his bedroom done into the bargain!

~ ~ ~ ~ ~

# Second Trimester

## June – August 2032

Daryl arrived at the hotel in the centre of Kendall just after 6.30 on the evening of Monday 17th May feeling tense and nervous, but excited. He was looking forward to exploring the town and also staying in a better class hotel than he usually enjoyed on his weekend jaunts. He was anxious about meeting the others, knowing he wasn't a good mixer, but determined to contribute to the course and be taken at face value and accepted as one of them, rather than be dogged by his normal reputation.

He carefully unpacked and took a long and invigorating shower, preparing himself to go down to meet the others. The shower was a different system to the one he had at home, and working out his cleansing preferences distracted him from the task ahead. Mentally he prepared his voice and things to say as he went through the shower's cleansing ritual. By the time the warm jets of air had dried him he felt almost over-confident, but still found himself shaking slightly as he dressed.

The information he'd received for the course had instructed participants to meet in the hotel bar at eight for drinks and a meal, where they'd receive their briefing for the next four days. Daryl knew there'd be a choice of food pearls or traditional food and had carefully considered what he could eat during his stay. His stomach still had a tendency towards queasiness, although it wasn't as virulent as it had been before, and he reckoned it would be safe to choose traditional foods, as long as they weren't too rich or spicy. Since injuring his hand he'd barely eaten anything except food pearls, with the exception of his sardines and jam, just managing to keep his sickness under control following his bout of what he believed had been blood poisoning.

The thought of his strange yearning suddenly gave him a craving for the food but he'd not brought any with him and was kicking himself for not thinking of it. Trying to abandon his desire for them, he left the room to go and find the others; the thought of his jam and sardines, though, was to plague him throughout the evening.

Daryl went down to the bar area and as he made his way there the tag he'd been given to wear, allowing him access to the different facilities, lit arrows along his route. Reaching the bar area he stopped to read the optical screen, which informed him where to go and who'd already arrived from his party. Lingering to read the screen, for longer than was really necessary, he felt a small moustache of sweat form on his upper lip, and steeled himself to go and join the group. Killing time, and half-heartedly reading the notices, he spotted a small announcement about a Knockout Pool Tournament due to be held in the hotel. Daryl's spirits both soared and plummeted at the same time. He was just contemplating whether to enter when the tag he was wearing vibrated, alerting him to another member of his group passing the Identifier he was standing by. Daryl turned quickly to see a small rotund lady, who he assessed to be in her mid-forties, looking anxious and uncertain. Daryl, much to his surprise, quickly addressed the woman and introduced himself, receiving in return a beaming smile as a look of relief swept over the woman's rather plain features. Without forethought Daryl muttered something about looking at the notices and about the pool tournament which was going to be held the day after next.

'Oh, are you a keen player then?' asked the woman, and without thinking Daryl started to launch into one of his boring dialogues of his love and skill at the game. To his delight the woman appeared to hang on his every word, listening intently, an animated expression on her face. When he'd finished she almost squeaked.

'Brilliant! That means I'll be one of your opponents because I must enter myself. I've been playing for years and have won…' and she began to recount a list of cups and tournaments she'd won over the years.

Daryl was astounded, and not knowing how to react suggested they move into the bar to join the others, giving him time to work out how he should respond. He didn't know whether to be pleased or mortified, as she was a woman and may well beat him. Before he could work out how to answer he found himself in a group of strangers and a round of introductions, which he found highly confusing. No two people came from the same companies, or knew anyone else, which made Daryl feel a little more confident, but he was sure everyone else was more used to these courses than him. When the last two finally arrived Daryl looked round assessing the group. *A motley crew*, he thought, *and several looking as uncomfortable as I feel.*

As their drinks arrived, via the table planner, the conversation slowly and hesitantly started to buzz round the table. Daryl felt really tense, concerned no one would talk to him, yet there were three people who seemed to be making a real effort to include him in the group, making him feel relieved and flattered. Gradually the talk turned to the meal, and with them all being well over thirty, it was decided they'd partake in the old-fashioned restaurant, which served traditional foods.

The meal was excellent, a superb example of how UK produced GM free meat, fruit and vegetables should be served and taste. Daryl, who was enjoying the company as well as the food, had chosen a starter of Grilled Sardines, to appease his yearning for his fish, and finished up with a jam pudding for his desert, which everyone else had found amusing. Daryl quickly explained that whilst he still lived at home he'd no culinary skills and his mother refused to cook. As jam pudding was a long forgotten childhood favourite he couldn't see the point of passing up the opportunity of tasting it again. Much to his delight several others threw caution to the wind and ordered old favourites themselves. It set off a whole topic of conversation, based round traditional versus pearl food, with emphasise on their favourite dishes and how youngsters were missing out on all the wonderful tastes real food had to offer. At the same time it temporarily satiated Daryl's desire for his bizarre food tastes.

They were just rounding off the meal with coffees, which Daryl avoided knowing without doubt it would set off his sickness, when conversation turned to the next four nights' activities. Sonia, the woman, he'd initially met up with, quickly piped up there was to be a knockout pool tournament she and Daryl were thinking of entering. The group immediately turned their attention to Daryl asking if this was the case. With the heat on him Daryl reverted back to type and found himself mumbling and sweating again. One of Daryl's very many social problems was his tendency to mumble when he was put on the spot, speaking as though trying to keep the words in his mouth and making it difficult for others to hear what he was saying. As he answered questions about his pool playing skills he was constantly asked to repeat his answers. Suddenly he'd had enough of his own inadequacies and, about to lose everyone's attention, drew a deep breath and announced in a crystal clear voice, which surprised him more than anyone else, he'd been playing for over fifteen years and would enter the knockout if he could get hold of a decent cue, as he'd not got his own with him. Still shocked at this new side of himself he was somewhat flummoxed when one of the guys told him there was always a sale of cues before a tournament.

*If that's the case,* Daryl thought, *then there's no choice but to take part in the game,* which he wasn't at all certain he wanted to do. His uncertainty was further compounded when Sonia started to enlightened the group with her extensive list of wins, which ended up with the group opening a book as to which of the two would win. The thought of a book being run on him and against a woman totally floored Daryl, who immediately started to make excuses about not being able to compete. However the others would hear nothing of it and a general feeling of camaraderie settled comfortably on the group, with Sonia lapping it up and Daryl squirming in his seat. Frantically wracking his brains for excuses not to enter, he instantly hit on the idea of using his partially healed hand to get himself excluded. But as the thought hit him a conflicting little voice at the back of his head was telling him how good it was to be the centre of attention and for such good reasons. He realised he'd have to think very carefully before committing himself either way, and decided to sleep on it.

Daryl had a pretty restless night, partly due to being in a strange place but mainly because he was worried about entering the Pool Tournament, and he was worried about how he'd fare on the course and what the others thought of him. Whilst he wasn't used to socialising he'd actually enjoying the evening, which surprised him. The idea of buying a new cue quite appealed too, as he'd been promising himself one for some time and had plenty of credits to buy a really good one. He had two main worries though, clouding his thinking. Firstly he was uncertain how his hand would hold up but more importantly Sonia sounded as if she was pretty good, and he couldn't bear the thought of losing to a woman. The thought made him shudder. He didn't like women; in fact he had a deep rooted contempt for them, but there was something about Sonia he found endearing. She was obviously older than him and had a 'mumsy' feel about her, but she seemed full of energy too, which for some unfathomable reason he found amusing. The thought of her beating him though really bothered him, as it would make him look stupid in front of everyone else.

Arriving downstairs for breakfast, his mind still not made up, Daryl was mortified to see his name already on the tournament list. When he asked, as casually as he could, who'd added his name he was informed it had been a 'team decision' as they thought he had a good chance of winning. Daryl was quite elated by this, and the fact they'd obviously been speaking of him in friendly terms, rather than the contempt he usually encountered.

The day's course went well and Daryl was relieved he'd no problems keeping up with everyone else. Having spent the past couple of weeks studying the language and writing several small programmes he felt inordinately proud of his understanding, which not everyone had. He'd even chipped in with how he'd overcome a problem at work outlining the add-on which could have prevented it happening in the first place. When he'd finished speaking he'd been horrified by the collective and ominous silence, expecting them to pour contempt and scorn over him.

However, to his delight one of the guys ruffling his hands through his hair, as if checking things inside his skull said, 'Shit. That's such an obvious solution. Why the hell didn't I think of that when we had exactly the same problem with our system?' Daryl blushed pink with pleasure, but still squirmed uncomfortably in his seat, so unused to praise was he.

At the end of the session the only thing marring Daryl's day was his constant craving for sardines and jam, and he berated himself for not bringing any with him. He decided he'd have to find a shop and stock up, but not until after he'd had a nap, he was completely exhausted.

Having settled for a doze Daryl was horrified when he woke up, much later than planned, giving him no time for shopping. Going down to the restaurant, desperately hoping there was something fishy on the menu, he felt obliged to go along with everyone else's decision to share a Mexican banquet, a decision he was to later regret. The spicy food gave him the most terrible indigestion during the night and he'd tossed and turned for several hours, he finally decided to get up and go in search of sardines and jam, which he was convinced would settle his stomach along with the exercise.

Having dressed and left the hotel he strolled round the unfamiliar streets towards the direction of a park, indicated by the digital signs suspended on lamp-posts. He found the night air calming and the exercise eventually seemed to be settling his stomach. Finally arriving at the park he walked along the garden paths which wove in and out of a coppice, playground and around an area of seating and eateries. Strolling leisurely along he unexpectedly spotted a lone woman sitting on one of the seats. She hadn't spotted him and looking more carefully Daryl saw her to be in her mid-thirties and, like himself, was dressed all in black.

Without realising what he was doing Daryl began to stalk his way round the paths, so he was behind her, hidden from her sight. He settled quietly in the bushes watching her intensely, listening at the same time to make sure no one else was about. The park was silent and Daryl positioned himself, ready to pounce. All of a sudden the woman sneezed, and Daryl froze. The sneeze, whilst a common function of the human body, had somehow alerted Daryl to his intended actions. He was horrified to realise he'd been about to grab and rape the woman without even thinking about the consequences. He'd been totally unaware of his actions.

*How stupid would that have been?* he admonished himself. *My details are on the hotel register along with my real name, address and work details. If police checked the rooms of people visiting the town they'd take DNA samples and be able to trace me. It would only have been a matter of hours before they'd identified me and matched it to the other attacks then my freedom would have been curtailed permanently,* Daryl thought irrationally. Daryl shuddered at what a near miss he'd had and how out of control his attacks were becoming. An icy cold film of sweat coated his body and he found himself shaking. Fortunately the woman was still unaware of his presence and totally oblivious to the fact she'd been watched with the view of being raped. Daryl stood stock still, willing his thumping heart and heaving stomach to still themselves, but it was another ten minutes before he'd calmed himself enough to get back to the hotel.

Those minutes seemed an eternity as the woman continued to sit there, Daryl willing her to go. Finally he realised he desperately needed a pee and had no option but to leave his lair before he had an accident. Stealthily he moved back to the pathway, casting a quick glance to see if he'd been spotted. Thankfully the woman seemed to be overcome by a spasm of coughing, and was completely oblivious of his presence.

At five-thirty in the morning, as the world outside was on the verge of waking, Daryl finally gave up trying to sleep and got up, feeling incredibly sick. Having showered and dressed he made his way out again to the shop for his much craved fish and jam, finding himself taking almost gulping breathes of fresh air in a bid to appease his sickness. He bought half a dozen cans of sardines and a jar of blackcurrant jam and making his way back to the hotel wondered idly how many he'd bought in the past few weeks, the question dismissed before he'd even answered himself. All he wanted to do was get his head down for a few hours sleep, which he knew wasn't going to be possible, especially if he had the tournament this evening.

Daryl only ate a light snack that evening, having consumed more than half the morning's shopping before meeting the others for supper. The meal over, Sonia and he went down to examine the merchandise on offer, each buying a new cue. With just enough time for a quick drink before the tournament started they made their way back to the bar to join the others, who were already there with drinks in hand. To Daryl's surprise more than sixty contenders had registered to play and were beginning to arrive. Daryl hadn't realised it was such a big tournament, so went early to register his presence on the optical screen, waiting until it identified his partner and the table he'd be playing on.

Having received his instructions, and identified his first opponent, he made his way to the tables to watch the games just started. There were five tables in all and he decided to watch the game on table four, where the winner would be his opponent in the next round. The players were nothing special to speak of but obviously enjoyed their game and the younger of the two obviously believed he was better than he actually was, judging by the way he strutted round the table. Daryl could feel a well of contempt rise inside him and hoped to god he won the game so Daryl could wipe the floor with him in the next round.

Bored with the poor state of play Daryl went back to the optics board to view the results. Sonia, he noted, had won her game, which Daryl believed would be her last. He needed to assess how she played though, just in case he ended up playing against her, which he thought highly unlikely. Those thoughts were quickly changing though, as each time he won his way into the next round so did Sonia.

It didn't seem long before they were into the semi-finals and Daryl happened to hear one of his colleagues say, 'Well the next round will sort the wheat from the chaff. You reckon it's going to be Daryl or

Sonia taking the cup?' Hearing the comment Daryl felt a momentary wave of panic wash over him.

*What if Sonia does win her game and I have to play against her? What if she beats me? I'll never live it down,* a panic-stricken voice in his head challenged. *And I've not even had a chance to see how she plays yet,* he panicked. Suddenly Daryl was desperate for the loo, but for more than just a pee. Daryl had just hit upon the idea of sabotaging his hand so he had an excuse if he lost, reckoning it'd save face, if he happened to lose. As he reached the gents he checked his scar to see how it was faring. Although it was beginning to heal it still looked inflamed, and unconsciously he began to massage it.

'That looks like a nasty cut,' Patrick, one of the guys from the group acknowledged as he came into the room. 'How did you do it?' he asked.

'Cut it on an empty jar a few weeks back,' Daryl explained. 'Me Mam put this stuff on but it was years out-of-date and I ended up with blood poisoning,' he continued, believing what he said. 'Still a bit sore but at least it's healing now,' he told Patrick, as he meticulously washed his hands.

'You reckon it'll hold out the night?' Patrick asked. 'Only it looks pretty inflamed to me. Does it hurt? He asked.

'Yeah, just a bit,' Daryl admitted, glad Patrick had spotted his 'weakness'. Still I've only one more round 'til the final so it should hold out,' Daryl replied in a tone he hoped emphasised his doubt.

'Well from what I've seen it looks like you'll be up against Sonia. No idea which of you will win. The book on you both is pretty balanced.'

Daryl winced but didn't reply and playing for time feigned a coughing fit telling Patrick, between splutters, he'd meet him back in the bar. As soon as Patrick left the room Daryl started to maul the cut so the edges, which were only just starting to knit together, were pulled slightly apart. It hurt like hell but as far as Daryl was concerned he didn't care. He just didn't want to look an idiot if he lost.

Daryl was to play his semi first and with some difficulty managed to win, although he struggled with one or two of his shots. Having won the game he downed a pint then went off to the gents to again manipulate his scar so it would open up completely. He was panic stricken about playing against Sonia and hoped his hand would bleed and cause the match to be halted and the game declared a draw. Having damaged his hand, to the point of it bleeding slightly, Daryl went back to the tables to watch Sonia play.

The game was almost over with just three balls left on the table; a red, a yellow and the black. It was Sonia's shot and she was snookered. Daryl watched as Sonia walked slowly round the table, calculating where she'd be best taking the shot from. Whilst she surveyed the table Daryl silently chanted and prayed she'd balls the shot up and lose the game. After what seemed like an eternity, she took her shot, Daryl sending up another prayer for failure. Sonia hit but didn't pocket the ball. Daryl very nearly let out a whoop he was so pleased, but he'd not looked at her shot properly. She'd done to her partner exactly what he'd done to her and left him with a very tight, almost impossible shot. Daryl held his breath praying the guy would pocket his shot, although it looked unlikely. He was almost muttering his incantation aloud when the shot was taken and a groan went up from the crowd.

*Damn it*, Daryl muttered to himself. *He's missed the shot which means two shots to fucking Sonia.* The last shot, having been played badly, had left a clean sweep for Sonia to clear the table, which she did, executed with grace and dexterity. So, as Patrick had predicted, both he and Sonia were through to the final, their party buzzing with anticipation at two of their group going head-to-head in the ultimate game. Once again Daryl found the need to visit the gents, whether through nerves or too much liquid he didn't know or care, but it gave him a further chance to do more damage to his hand.

As he walked back to his group, with more bravado than he felt, he was pulled aside by Patrick.

'Daryl,' Patrick said quietly. 'Is your hand going to hold out for the last game?' he said indicating the injury. Daryl looked down and pretended to be dismayed at seeing the cut open again and very inflamed. It hurt like hell too, which he didn't try to hide, as it would just add to the sympathy he'd get. He lifted his hand as if to inspect it carefully, gave it a long look, a prod and poke and then told Patrick reassuringly it should just about hold out, but what was going through his head was something totally different.

*If my hand starts to bleed*, he thought, *there's no way I'll be allowed to continue to play in case I soil the table.* So he stuffed his hand in his pocket, as if to protect it, and secretly worked it knowing it was weakening the scar even more.

A few minutes before the game was due to start Daryl and Sonia made their way over to the umpire who publicly regaled the rules and announced the details of each player to the listening, but somewhat noisy, audience. The atmosphere was electric, as over the evening's event it had become evident there was a real battle raging between the two of them. Part of the audience wanted Daryl as the male player to win, but he hadn't curried any favours with his monotonous yet arrogant manner. The rest of the spectators wanted Sonia to win, even if it was only to take Daryl down a peg or two and show him he wasn't invincible, whether against a man or a woman.

The toss was taken and Daryl lost the call leaving Sonia to take the break. She broke the mass of balls superbly, potting three balls before leaving the table for Daryl to play. Her shot though had left the white ball surrounded, with very little opening for him to take his shot without incurring a penalty. Daryl, unperturbed, took a very slow walk round the table looking at every angle available to him or not. Finally he placed his injured hand on the rim of the table arching his hand and spreading his fingers wide to support the cue. It hurt like hell but holding his cue at an acute angle he slowly and carefully took his shot, the white ball trickling through the red to very gently kiss the nearest yellow ball. As the shot was shown on the optic screens round the room a collective sigh rippled through the audience, whether it was one of relief or disappointment Daryl didn't try to work out. He was just relieved not to have lost a shot, even if he hadn't pocketed anything. Sonia looked at him and grinned, she knew she had the advantage.

She took her next shot, again pocketing a red ball, and with her next shot set up Daryl's ball so he'd experience the maximum of difficulty.

Again Daryl approached the table walking round it clockwise then anti-clockwise. Having finally decided on his shot he leaned over the length of the table, positioned his hand to cradle the cue and then…

'Stop,' came a loud and commanding voice. 'Please remove yourself from the table sir.' In mock surprise Daryl straightened up looking round to see who'd spoken. It was of course the umpire. The room now had a very peculiar atmosphere, a silent hush hanging in the air with spectators trying to establish what was happening. Sonia also looked puzzled.

'Sir,' the umpire said. 'I can't allow you to take a shot as your hand is bleeding and about to soil the table. I'm sorry Sir but you'll have to have it dressed before the game can continue.'

Daryl looked down at his hand, as if surprised, and was relieved to see his hand bleeding profusely, actually dripping blood on the floor. He quickly pulled his handkerchief from his pocket and carefully wrapped his hand in it before following a steward into a side room. As he made his way out he could hear the umpire explaining to the puzzled crowd what had happened to suspend the game.

A few minutes later Daryl arrived back at the table sporting a broad plaster on his hand. He'd not allowed anyone to touch the wound but put on the dressing himself. He offered his hand up for inspection and it was given approval, despite the fact Daryl knew it wouldn't hold out for very long.

Again he prowled the table sizing up his options before settling back to where he'd originally been going to take the shot from. Placing his hand gently on the table he arched the palm and spread his fingers, wriggling them as if trying to get comfortable before resting the cue in the crook between his thumb and forefinger atop the dressing. Making a show of wincing he took his shot carefully, pocketing a yellow. He was about to take a second shot when once again the umpire stopped him, having seen a trickle of blood run down his thumb about to deposit a stain on the table.

Daryl was again taken aside and the umpire called Sonia over, explaining to them both that under the rules of the game, and in respect to the hotel's property, they couldn't allow the game to continue. He then explained to the crowd what was happening and that a decision would be taken with advice from the UK Pool Board in conjunction with Hotel Management and they'd come to a decision, as to the outcome of the game, within the next few minutes. Daryl, convinced he'd saved himself, quickly turned his expression of triumph to one of a grimace and was immediately astonished to hear Sonia say, in a very quiet whisper, 'Have you done that deliberately to stop being beaten by me and save your face?'

Daryl was so taken aback by the accusation, and the way in which it had been said, that he looked directly at her giving her the filthiest look he could muster and said, 'I'll ignore that,' he said warningly, 'but I'm quite happy to continue the match. It's not my decision to stop the game.'

'Isn't it?' intoned Sonia, so quietly Daryl wasn't sure exactly what he'd heard. They both made their way back to their group to await the decision, Daryl quietly confident the match would be declared a draw.

Some ten minutes later the umpire came back and beckoned the two players to join him, which they did, Daryl nursing his bleeding hand.

'Having taken advise from the UK Pool Board and Hotel Management,' he began, 'it's been decided the game will not proceed and,' he paused waiting for the audience to settle, 'that the winner will be Sonia Morrison.' The room erupted with a mix of groans and applause, whilst Daryl stood looking stunned and was about to protest when the umpire continued, 'On the grounds that of the three shots taken by each player, Ms Morrison had potted four of the balls whilst Mr Payne had only potted one,' he finished.

Daryl was not going to take this. He grabbed the sleeve of the umpire and protested, 'That's not fair nor is it in the rules the game should go to Ms Morrison. I'd not finished my shot so there's nothing to say or show I wouldn't have caught up with her.'

'I'm sorry sir, but that's the decision of the Board and Hotel Management, who are both the hosts and sponsors of this match. Their decision is final.'

'That's bang out of order,' protested Daryl angrily and loudly. 'The match should have been declared a draw.'

'In addition sir,' continued the umpire loudly, unperturbed, 'we took into account the number of shots taken by Ms Morrison and number of opponent's balls left on the table at the end of each game. Ms Morrison took six shots less than yourself but left nine more of her opponent's balls on the table in total, than you did in your own games, Sir. For that reason the match is being declared in her favour.' He immediately relayed the same information to the crowd once again announcing Sonia the winner and asking the hotel manager to come forward to present the winnings.

Daryl was incensed, and not at all appeased by the reasons given, although deep down he knew they made sense. With barely any grace he offered his good hand to Sonia and gruffly congratulated her, whilst in his mind promising himself revenge. Sonia did at least have the grace to say she'd have preferred to have won the match by playing to the end, not that it helped Daryl.

'Well you wouldn't have won,' Daryl growled walking away with his head hung, bright red in the face. As he left the room Patrick quickly followed him saying, 'Hey mate, that was rotten luck.'

'Thanks,' Daryl muttered dejectedly. 'But I'm off to bed now and to see to this,' he said lifting his hand to show the mess it was in. 'See you tomorrow right?' And before Patrick could invite him to join them for a drink, he'd turned on his heel and was gone, leaving Patrick to go back to the group, who were all talking animatedly amongst themselves about the outcome.

Yet again Daryl encountered a disturbed night. This time though it wasn't because of food craving, as he'd eaten his fill earlier on returning to his room. His restlessness was caused by pure anger and humiliation. He was incensed.

*The tournament's been snatched away from me and by a woman!* he seethed. *That fucking bitch Sonia. The ruling was completely out of order; I hadn't finished my last shot and had the same opportunity as Sonia. As for the decision based on the number of shots she'd taken throughout the tournament and the number of opponent's balls I left on the table at the end of each game – well what a load of fucking rubbish that was.* He could not accept it was anything other than unfair.

Throughout the night Daryl had paced the room, repeating over and over again to himself how unfair it was, convincing himself a great disservice had been done to him and his treatment was unfair and bang out of order. He couldn't and wouldn't accept the fact she was a better player and, anyway, he told himself, he'd been hindered throughout the game by his injured hand, which had taken such a hammering the cut had opened up again, completely forgetting the fact he'd deliberately re-opened the cut himself.

Daryl, having had little sleep, woke convinced he'd been cheated out of the cup. His thoughts were so irrational, and at odds with reality, he couldn't believe the group's reaction at breakfast where he found them all congratulating Sonia on her 'superb play' and reassuring her the judge's decision had been right. Then in the next breath they were commiserating with Daryl on him not being able to finish his game and telling him, absurdly, the final decision had been fair.

'Fair,' Daryl almost yelled. 'What do you mean, fair? It's a load of crap and I've never heard of that ruling before,' he stormed aggressively.

'Daryl,' Sonia started in a warning tone 'I won the tournament fair and square. Even if you'd been able to finish the game you wouldn't have beaten me. You don't have the finesse to get out of trouble or really put your opponent into jeopardy. I left you a shot yesterday you only just managed to get out of and you didn't even see how you could use it to jeopardise my next one, so you would've lost anyway,' she finished dismissively.

Daryl could feel his hackles rise and his face darken with anger.

'Yes well the only reason you won was because you used your feminine wiles to distract your opponents and seduce the judges. You're like all women. You're a tart and use your fanny to get what you want, you slut,' he spat contemptuously, oblivious of everyone round the table.

'Daryl for god's sake get a grip on yourself,' Patrick warned with embarrassment. 'You're bang out of order. Sonia played a fair game using her skills and nothing else. I actually rated you as decent and honest but listening to you now I think the least you can do is apologise to Sonia,' he said heatedly, indicating Sonia who now sat white-faced and looking ready to burst into tears.

'Apologise?' growled Daryl, glaring at Patrick. 'Apologise to that cheating little cow? No way. I'll wait until hell freezes over before I apologise to a cheating little slut like her.' And with that he stormed out of the dining room and back up to his room.

Arriving in his room Daryl threw himself down on the slumber-pit, suddenly mortified at the way he'd behaved, knowing it was wrong.

*Why the fuck should I apologise for the truth? The fucking little tart needed to be told. She's nothing but trouble and knows I'm right. It was obvious she was strutting her stuff,* he told himself, not sure whether or not he really believed it.

He paced the room again, like a caged wild animal, his anger at such a pitch he finally threw himself down on his bed and, dropping his head in his hands, cried great wrenching sobs of temper, self-pity and everything else he'd ever felt. Then, as if nothing had happened, the tears finished as quickly as they'd started, and getting up he hurriedly breakfasted on the sardines and jam, before hurrying down to the course.

99

Arriving at the team room, his appearance pristine with no trace of tears, Daryl was greeted by an icy wall of silence. The tutor, well aware of what had gone on, turned to Daryl and said without preamble, or expression on his face, 'Daryl, a word outside please.' Daryl, wondering what on earth was going on but carefully keeping his face straight, followed Martin, the tutor, into the corridor. Daryl quite liked Martin, who'd taken the time to listen to Daryl's suggestions with as much respect as he'd given anyone else. Daryl respected him as well, as he had as much experience with engineering as with computers. It was important Martin's opinion of him wasn't altered in any way, not that Daryl was aware of this.

'Daryl,' Martin started, 'I understand you didn't win the tournament last night due to the fact the game was halted because of an injury. And that,' he held up his hand to silence Daryl, 'you didn't take the news particularly well. I also understand that when you joined the group for breakfast you were surly, rude and, according to some, aggressive and verbally attacked Sonia.'

Daryl, who'd opened his mouth to speak, was again halted by Martin's hand signal.

'Please let me finish what I have to say Daryl and then you may answer,' he continued commandingly, a small sheen of sweat now visible on his top lip.

'What you said, and the manner in which it was said, was totally unacceptable. Do you realise we should report your behaviour to the Justice and Social Behaviour Unit?'

Daryl's eyes widened in shock, he hadn't realised his outburst could warrant him being reported.

'What I suggest Daryl, is for you go into the room and make a full and sincere apology. Not just to Sonia but the entire group. If you do, and the group accepts your apology, then no more will be said about this morning's outburst. Otherwise Daryl, I'm going to have to take this matter further and it wouldn't surprise me if some of your colleagues did too. They'd be perfectly within their rights.'

Daryl by this time felt like a schoolboy being reprimanded and could feel his hackles rise and his face darken as his temper threatened to surface again.

'What do you mean you'll take it further?' asked Daryl in a cold voice.

'I mean you won't be allowed back into the course and your employers, who've paid for it, will be informed why and will no doubt take further action over it back at your place of employment,' Martin said with a slight tremor in his voice, uncomfortable with this unpleasant task. 'In addition we will need to contact the UK Pool Board to report your unsportsmanlike behaviour. It will be up to them to decide if you're banned from future tournaments and whether or not they'll want the incident reported to the authorities.

'Are you prepared to go in and apologise to the group Daryl?' he asked, beads of sweat now clearly visible on his brow. Martin wasn't actually surprised Daryl had come out as such a surly and unpleasant character. Right from meeting him, and seeing the way he interacted with the group, there'd been warning bells going off in his mind since the start. Martin believed Daryl was now showing his true colours and hoped he'd refuse to apologise and could be sent packing, then it'd be out of his hands and he'd only have to submit reports on the incident.

'What will be reported to my employers?' Daryl asked belligerently.

'First of all,' Martin responded, feeling sweat break out under his arms, 'the confrontation at breakfast; the accusations made about Sonia and her supposed behaviour and your unsociable behaviour on the results being announced last night.'

'Does that mean,' asked Daryl, feeling close to tears, 'the fact Sonia took the cup away from me will have to be reported too?'

'Sonia did not take the cup from you Daryl,' Martin told him in clipped tones, 'she won it in a fair and publicly witnessed series of games, which you should acknowledge.'

'Sonia accused me of deliberately sabotaging myself. That was out of order,' Daryl said defensively, completely in denial it was exactly what he'd done.

'Did anyone else hear her say that?' asked the tutor wondering how he should handle the situation.

'Not that I know of,' grunted Daryl. 'She's far too clever to let anyone overhear something like that,' he said, an edge of menace creeping back into his voice. 'Would work have to know about me losing the game?' he asked in a more hopeful voice, sounding almost like a child.

'I don't see how it can be avoided as it's the cause of all this, do you? In addition several other guests have complained to the hotel about this morning's outburst so the hotel may be obliged to report the incident if the complainants insist.'

'What does that mean?' asked Daryl, seriously worried now how this could impact on him. If he was reported to the Justice and Social Behaviour Unit then all they had to do was check the Government DNA Database to find his details weren't registered. Then he'd be forced to give DNA and other identity samples and would be revealed as the serial rapist they were hunting. Daryl's head was spinning trying to compute this all at once, desperately wondering what he should do, but not wanting to lose face.

Unconsciously Daryl had been massaging his hand, which was now throbbing, and Daryl felt himself near to tears and almost light headed. The colour drained from his face and he began to sway, about to fall over. Martin put out his hand to steady him and asked in a firm voice, 'Are you alright Daryl?' To which Daryl nodded miserably, knowing he'd no option now but to apologise, knowing it would crucify him.

'Yeah I'm alright,' he reassured Martin. 'Just me hand playing me up. It's not long since I got over blood poisoning.' Martin looked down at the poorly dressed hand and without preamble advised Daryl, 'I suggest during the midday break you get yourself to the local hospital to have it properly dressed.'

'No, no,' Daryl responded over-quickly. 'I've got dressings in my room and can get my doctor to sort it out when I get back. He knows what he's doing with it,' he said, in what he hoped was a convincing voice. 'It'll be alright, I promise. S'pose I better apologise,' he added sulkily.

'Well in that case let me warn you if there are any further repercussions or I hear you've upset anyone else or been unpleasant in any way I'll have no option but to report you to your employers, the Pool Board and the Justice and Social Behaviour Unit. I also suggest you find someone from the hotel management and make your apologies to them too. Do I make myself clear Daryl? I'm not to be messed about and won't tolerate any repeat performances like this morning's. You've been a good student up until all this happened and made some valuable contributions to the programme. I hope that will continue but I'll warn you of one last thing – it's your fellow colleagues who'll decide if you stay or go so when you apologise you had better make sure you mean it. Ok?'

Daryl nodded miserably, with memories of being chastised like this at school foremost in his mind. The thought of having to face the group and apologise really stuck in his craw, and he genuinely wanted to be sick. But if he didn't apologise and was sent home he'd be the laughing stock; be ostracised from future pool tournaments and undoubtedly end up being investigated by the Justice and Social Behaviour Unit. If that happened he knew he'd have to submit DNA and would end up being arrested, castrated and deported for being a rapist. Swallowing hard he sullenly followed Martin into the room, feeling resentful and belligerent. He looked up to be confronted by a sea of faces with a mix of different expressions; it frightened him. Some looked like thunder, others with expressions of contempt and some had looks of confusion and compassion on their faces.

He stood for a moment, shocked, as a sudden thought assaulted his mind.

*These people have treated you well in the last few days,* said the voice of rationale inside his head. *They've listened to you and been impressed with the things you've had to say. Do you really want to alienate them?* it asked him internally. *Do you really want to upset them more than you did this morning? Think about it. These people could be your friends.*

Suddenly Daryl realised how much he'd enjoyed their company and support. He also began to, inwardly, acknowledge Sonia's game had been played skilfully and she'd deserved to win. Then, to his utter horror, as he stood in front of them hanging his head and shuffling his feet, he felt an overwhelming feeling of self-sorrow sweep over him. He was terrified he'd end up crying, and took a deep breath to help gather his thoughts and get himself in control. He didn't want them to see him cry, as it would just add to his humiliation.

Shuffling his feet a bit more, his head still hanging, he shot a quick glance at Sonia and mumbled, 'I'm sorry for what I said this morning Sonia. You did play a good game.' Then he looked round the rest of the group and, still shuffling, muttered 'I'm sorry for behaving like that. I shouldn't have said what I did… and, and I hope we can forget it. Please?'

'What Daryl? What did you say? You're mumbling,' said Patrick. Daryl looked up expecting to see Patrick mocking him and was surprised to see a look of compassion on his face.

'I... I was just ap-apologising t-t-to you all,' he stuttered, and to his horror realised there were tears rolling down his face. He dashed them away with his hand, as if swatting flies, his head still lowered and his feet shuffling.

'Daryl,' Patrick invited. 'Come and sit down here for a minute.' Then, turning to Martin, he asked, 'Can we have five minutes to sort this please Martin?' Martin nodded and quietly left the room as Patrick pulled out a chair for Daryl to sit down on. Although the group had only met a few days ago and despite Daryl's behaviour, there was still a feeling of camaraderie and support between them. All had felt an enormous sense of shock and pity when they'd seen Daryl's tears. He was the last person they'd have expected to be emotional.

As Daryl sat down they could see him struggling to pull himself together. He looked up at Sonia, who had a look of horror crossed with compassion on her face. He realised the look of horror wasn't one of disgust, but of shock. Looking her in the eye he took a deep breath, gulped and just said, 'S-s-sorry Sonia. You played a bloody good game and... and... I...I.'

'Hey mate,' said Patrick, patting him on the shoulder. 'What's all this about? Look you're amongst friends here so why not share your problems with us?' he suggested quietly.

'You... you won't w-want to know,' stuttered Daryl. 'It's... it's p-pathetic,' he stuttered, trying desperately not to lose total control of his emotions. No one had ever been this nice to him before and it was tempting to spill the beans on everything, even though he knew he couldn't. Then turning his attention to Sonia he started, 'I... I was j-jealous of how w- well you were playing. I knew th-that I m-might not be able to b-beat you and... and... and that you... you might laugh at me,' he explained stiltingly, battling to keep his sobs at bay.

'I... I... had to... to be horrible to... to you so... so that you wouldn't laugh at... at me like everyone else,' he continued haltingly. Then suddenly he blurted out, 'I'm sorry, I'm really sorry Mam I... I,' and all of a sudden the realisation of what he'd just said hit him, and everyone sitting in the room. Panicking Daryl looked round, an expression of abject horror on his face. Seeing the expressions of shock

104

and pity he could no longer hold back and letting his head fall into his hands the flood gate of tears, and all the years of emotions, came gushing to the fore. Great rasping sobs shook his body, he'd finally lost it.

Almost immediately, to his disbelief, he felt Sonia's warm arms wrapped round him and he could smell her perfume. For a split second he believed it was his Mam, and rested his poor head onto her bosom feeling her arms wrap more tightly round him. Momentarily he abandoned himself to his wrought emotions and into her comforting warmth when, suddenly... suddenly he realised with dismay this wasn't who he thought or hoped it was. He looked up and realised, with horror, it wasn't his Mam who'd wrapped him in her arms, as he'd yearned for all these years. He was being held in the arms of a stranger and was in a room of other strangers.

In panic he flung his arms out knocking Sonia out of his way. Leaping to his feet he blindly looked round trying to work out where he was. Spotting the door he flung himself away from Patrick and Sonia, who'd both put out their arms to reassure him, and, pushing them both aside wrenched open the door and ran into the corridor, just as Martin was making his way back in.

'Daryl,' he vaguely heard Martin say. 'Daryl what the hell is going on?' Daryl didn't hear Patrick's response as he flew up to the sanctuary of his room and out of earshot.

Once inside his room Daryl banged the door shut and fell back against it. Great racking sobs came from his huge bulk as he slid down the door into a crumpled heap, abandoning himself to the past feelings of hurt and rejection he'd suffered over the years. After a while he somehow managed to get to his feet, despite the fact it felt there was no substance to his bones or energy in his body. He felt as weak and pathetic as a little kitten, but somehow he made it to the slumber-pit, falling across it before deep rasping sobs heaved up from the depths of his soul.

The realisation of what he'd done had finally dawned on him.

*I called Sonia 'Mam' and I mouthed off at her this morning in public,* he thought with panic and self-pity. *I'll never be able to face the group again so my only option is to go home. Everyone downstairs will be laughing at me crying and if it gets out at work about me losing to a woman, I'll be the laughing stock. My life's over, even though I've apologised I know they'll report me. Then it won't be long before the Justice and Social Behaviour Unit come to see me and then they'll find me DNA ain't on the Government DNA Database and once they've got a sample it'll only be hours before my secret identity's exposed. Then I'll be arrested and detained, not even in Armley; then investigated and tried; and when they find me guilty, which I'm not 'cos they were all up for it, I'll be sentenced, castrated and deported. My life will be over. I'll never see me Mam again, she'll disown me totally, and I'll never see England again. I'll spend the rest of my life living on an island of criminals.* The thought terrified him as the swirl of emotions continued to bombard his panic-stricken mind.

As these thoughts raced through his mind there was a gentle knock on the door. For one awful moment Daryl thought it was someone from the Justice and Social Behaviour Unit who'd come to get him. Then he heard a small voice, muffled by the thickness of the door, say.

'Daryl? Daryl? It's me Sonia. Please will you let me in?' Daryl was stunned she'd bothered to come upstairs, but sure she'd come to mock and taunt him, even though her voice had sounded gentle.

'Daryl? Daryl love, come on, let me in so's we can sort this out. It can't be as bad as all that surely? Come on, open the door and let me in,' she cajoled. Slowly, realising she could be a nice woman and genuinely not want to hurt and humiliate him; he eased himself off the bed and leaned against the door, his ear tight against the wood.

'Sonia?' he asked tentatively. 'Sonia is it really you? he asked in a small voice, his breath still ragged from crying.

'Yes Daryl, just me and no one else. Let me in Daryl. Please?' Daryl looked through the spy-hole and seeing only Sonia made the decision to let her in. After all what had he to lose?

Cautiously he opened the door, his head bent to hide his tear-streaked cheeks. If Sonia was shocked by his appearance she didn't show it, and, picking this up, Daryl appreciated it. For some odd and obscure reason he felt comfortable with Sonia, which wasn't logical after the humiliation of losing to her and then calling her 'Mam'.

Sonia came in and stood quietly looking at Daryl with a kindly, patient expression on her face. Daryl was thankful she didn't rush at him clucking sympathy, or look at him with pity or smugness etched on her face. A myriad of these thoughts flew through his mind as he wondered how to behave or what to say. After all it was only last night he'd been planning his revenge and yet now here she was looking as if she really cared and wanted to help.

'S-S-Sonia,' he stuttered. 'I... I... I'm so sorry for all... all... the... the awful things I s-s-said to you and about... about you,' he struggled to say, still fighting the sobs that caught his breath. 'It... it was tot... totally un-uncalled for and you... you didn't de-deserve them and I... I... I'm so, so sorry for... for saying them. Will you... will you forgive me...p-p-please?' he said looking at her with appealing eyes, about to call her Mam again but stopping himself just in time.

'It's alright Daryl. I'm here as a friend to see if I can help you sort this out. Come over here and sit down,' Sonia said indicating the couch.

Unbeknown to Daryl, Patrick was standing outside listening intently, unsure how Daryl would react. He'd agreed he and Sonia would go up together but only Sonia would go into the room. Patrick would stand outside and listen, until he was sure Daryl wasn't going to be abusive or aggressive, then he was going to wait along the corridor and give them twenty minutes or so to talk. If Sonia was in trouble she'd activate her telephone alarm, which they'd programmed before going upstairs. If she did use it Patrick was to force his way into the room alerting security beforehand. Why they'd planned all this he wasn't sure, except they knew how volatile Daryl's temper was.

Inside the room Daryl and Sonia sat on the couch unsure of how to react to each other. Sonia felt incredibly nervous, her stomach in a knot. Daryl, for his part, had never sat this close to a woman before and the emotions buzzing round his head seemed to be bombarding his senses with conflicting feelings. Part of him felt like hitting out at Sonia, for what she'd done to him, whilst the other side of him wanted to be taken in her arms and cuddled against her ample chest again. Subconsciously he wanted her to be his mother, to put his thumb in his mouth, lean against her and have her stroke his hair until he fell asleep. However, the conscious part of his mind prodded him into behaving differently so he sat quietly, afraid he'd give in to his instincts and make an even bigger fool of himself than he already had.

'Daryl, whatever happened to make you so unhappy?' asked Sonia, in a quiet voice.

'What do you mean what happened? What makes you think I'm unhappy?' asked Daryl almost belligerently.

'Well it could be something to do with the way you've behaved in the past few days, always on the defensive,' Sonia answered, 'and the fact you can be very surly. In fact even aggressive,' she added tentatively. 'That's usually a pretty good indication of unhappiness isn't it? Is that because of your Mum?' she asked gently.

'Why should it be anything to do with me Mam?' Daryl asked sharply.

'Well you called me Mam as if you wanted to please and not upset her,' she told him gently, carefully watching for his reaction. 'Is it your Mam Daryl?' Daryl nodded, and once again big fat tears ran silently down his face.

'She hates me,' he said, 'and blames me for me Dad,' he added in a small childlike voice.

'What happened to your Dad then?' Sonia asked gently and slowly, Daryl told his sad tale of his Dad's death and how his Mam was always carping on about how disappointed he'd have been with Daryl. As Daryl told his story the tears continued to trickle down his face and he rocked himself backwards and forwards, as if for comfort.

'But it's not your fault your Dad's not here Daryl,' explained Sonia. 'You didn't kill him or send him away, and it sounds like your Mum's very unhappy and perhaps', she paused at this point, 'perhaps bitter about him dying and takes her unhappiness out on you as you're the only one around. She probably doesn't even know she's doing it,' she tried to explain. 'It sounds as though she's never got over losing your father,' she added tentatively.

'So why does she always take it out on me?' Daryl asked in a whiney voice. 'She's... she's always t-telling me how useless I... I am. She's... she's h-hateful to me,' he said, astonishing himself with what he'd just said, realising for the first time it was true.

'I... I try so h-hard to make her l-like me. And... and,' he added the sobs finally getting the better of him, 'she... she never does and... and I d-don't th-think she ever will,' he finally managed to get out.

Sonia, her arm round his shoulders and holding his hand, drew him gently towards her, nestling his head into her body, stroking his hair and making soothing noises, as he'd always wanted his Mam to do. They sat there silently neither moving until, after what seemed like an eternity, Sonia asked him if he wanted to talk to her about his Mam.

Daryl had never talked to anyone about his Mam before. He'd never had the luxury of someone listening to him and the idea quite appealed.

'I've never talked to anyone about me Mam before,' he told Sonia.

'Well maybe now's the time,' Sonia coaxed. 'So how about I send a message down to the group saying we'll join them later?' she suggested and without waiting for an answer got up and went to the door telling Daryl she'd let the rest of the group know what was happening.

Having spoken to Patrick, to tell him what was going on, Sonia went back into the room to find Daryl still sitting on the couch, his head in his hands. For some inexplicable reason Sonia felt a sense of dread pass over her as she stood watching Daryl, who was totally unaware she'd come back into the room. Steeling herself to follow through on her promise to Daryl she went and sat next to him, unconsciously mimicking the position he was in. Talking quietly and reassuringly Sonia finally got Daryl to open up, and emotionally he began to tell her about his childhood and adult years at home.

Sonia, appalled at some of the things Daryl's mother had subjected him to, which had wrecked any sense of self-worth and confidence he may have had, felt an intense dislike for the woman and knew physical abuse may have been easier for a child to cope with than what Daryl had just described. At that precise moment Sonia would cheerfully have given the woman a piece of her mind and taste of her own medicine, had she been in the room. She'd heard some horror stories of upbringing in the past but nothing compared to this woman's evil tongue and her cold, callous behaviour towards her son. What really angered her was the way she'd used her son's desperate generosity, which he'd hoped would win her round, to feather her own nest and idleness. That really incensed Sonia and her heart went out to Daryl.

Having listened to his story Sonia shuddered at the thought of having to live with the knowledge his father had been murdered, the murderer never having been found, and held as an emotional hostage by his mother ever since.

*What sort of damage had it done to this poor man?* she asked herself, and although she felt genuine sorrow for him she still felt there was something not quite right, which made her uneasy.

Having told his story, and feeling no better emotionally, Daryl unexpectedly felt an overwhelming surge of anger towards his mother at how unfairly and irrationally she'd treated him. She'd undermined him all this time so he stayed at home, allowing her to live in the lap of comfort without doing anything in return. She'd the nerve to take his money, gifts and freedom but still banish him from the house. Suddenly he saw her for the cold, calculating, heartless bitch she really was. He leapt up from the couch only just managing to keep the roar of his temper, bitterness and hurt silently within himself.

As he leapt up Sonia gave a small cry, and for a split second, Daryl saw her as the wanton woman he now realised his mother was. Seeing red he almost lashed out at her, believing her to be his mother, but stopped himself just in time when he saw an expression of abject terror on her face. Instead of recoiling, or lashing out verbally or physically as he was expecting, Sonia tentatively reached out her hand and lay it courageously on his arm, saying, 'Daryl, Daryl. It's all right love. It's me, Sonia. Calm down love. You're ok. All that's happened is you've just let out an enormous river of feelings and confusion and seen things differently. That's all. Come and sit back down,' she said bravely, shaking like a leaf. For a moment Daryl had looked and behaved like a wild, trapped animal but now, once again, looked like a lost little boy desperate for a modicum of love and understanding. When Daryl had erupted she'd instinctively been tempted to activate the panic call, but was now relieved she hadn't.

After pacing the floor aggressively for a few minutes, which to Sonia seemed like hours, Daryl finally quietened down and sat down again, next to Sonia. Dropping his head in his hands he shook his head from side to side, as if he'd finally realised what a fool he'd been taken for and couldn't believe how he'd been used.

'She's used me hasn't she?' he asked, not expecting Sonia to answer. 'She's used me all these years to get what she wanted without having to pay. Everything I've done for her and given her, it's like she's made me pay over and over again for her having to bring me up. She's told me time and again it was my fault me dad died. But it wasn't anything to do with me was it? Was it?' he almost shouted at Sonia, as if demanding she tell him the truth.

'The fucking bitch's made my life a fucking misery,' he wailed. 'She made me believe it was my fault he was dead. It might just as well have been me who pulled the trigger the way she's gone on about it all these years. The bitch. The fucking, fucking bitch. What's she done to me and

110

what have I done to deserve it?' he asked in hurt and bewildered puzzlement.

Sonia sat silently, more than a little worried and glad she'd got a panic link to Patrick. She was shocked at how quickly realisation had hit Daryl and by his reaction. He'd obviously not talked about this before and saying it out loud had finally made the penny drop. She looked at him, alternately shaking his head, as if to get rid of something inside it, and wringing his hands. She supposed he was in shock, because it had seemed to hit him so hard and cruelly.

Finally Daryl seemed to stir, and turning to Sonia, said, 'I'm sorry. I didn't mean to frighten you. It was just awful when I realised how much she hated me.'

'I don't think she hates you Daryl,' Sonia reassured, 'but she does sound a very sad and bitter lady, who's taken out her frustrations on the nearest thing to her, which is you.'

Daryl nodded his understanding, even though none of it made any sense to him.

'I thought mothers were supposed to love their children but it seems as though I'm her object of hate.'

'You mustn't think like that Daryl. Maybe she needs help and if that's the case then it's a pity someone didn't recognise it years ago. Maybe you should feel sorry for her.'

'I do feel sorry for her,' Daryl responded quietly, 'but at the moment I hate her. Really hate her. If she was here now I think I'd want to kill her. But you know what really confuses me?' he asked. 'Despite everything I still love her after all these years of hurt and misery and I still want her to love me. Is that crazy?' he asked. Sonia shook her head, having heard not just his words but the tones he'd used, which had chilled her. Suddenly she very much wanted to be back in the company of the others.

'Look Daryl. Why don't you take a shower and have a nap then come down to the course?' she suggested tentatively. 'You've got loads to think about and maybe it'll be easier without me around. I'm going down to join the group now so why don't you ring down when you're ready and either Patrick or I will come up to meet you to go in with you? How does that sound?' she asked, half afraid he'd not let her leave.

Daryl gave her a long, hard, calculating stare trying to work out in his mind what she was thinking. Suddenly, the realisation hit him and he said very quickly, 'You're frightened of me Sonia aren't you? You're frightened of me now I've told you I want to kill me Mam,' he accused her, his tone rising.

'No. No of course I'm not Daryl. I think anyone would have said the same. I know you didn't mean it and anyway,' she started to add desperately, 'you told me you still loved her so I know your words were empty. About killing her I mean,' she added lamely, hoping the fear she felt hadn't reached her voice.

'Sonia, Sonia,' he said urgently. 'You won't tell anyone what we've talked about will you? You won't will you? Promise me?' he begged, relieved when Sonia promptly agreed she wouldn't. She'd have promised anything at that particular moment, as something inside her felt uneasy and she could feel panic rising, even though it seemed illogical.

'No Daryl of course I won't tell anyone. Why should I? What you've told me is just between us. Ok?' she told him, desperately hoping he wouldn't question her any more.

'Do you really promise Sonia?' he asked with a blankness in his eyes and a flat tone in his voice that chilled her. 'And Sonia?' he added. She looked up trying hard not to look him in the eye. 'I'm really sorry for all the things I said to you. You know I'm sorry. Don't you Sonia?'

Sonia nodded eagerly, now feeling so panicked she felt almost claustrophobic and desperately needed to get out of the room as quickly as possible.

'I'll see you downstairs Daryl. Ok?' she said in a squeaky voice, her shaking hand reaching for the door handle, and before he could stop her she was out of the door and down the corridor in a flash.

Getting into the lift Sonia realised she was shaking from head to foot, and it took all her energy to remain upright and not to sink to the floor, so exhausted did she feel. When the lift doors opened she saw Patrick walking across the foyer and on spotting her, he immediately recognised her distress and rushed over to her.

'Sonia! Sonia!' he said loudly, catching hold of her arm to steady her, as she looked about to keel over. 'What the hell's the matter? What's he done to you?' he demanded. 'I knew I shouldn't have left you alone with him,' he told her looking round to see if Daryl had pursued her downstairs.

'Nothing, nothing,' Sonia responded, realising that he'd taken her look of distress as the aftermath of an attack. He didn't do anything Patrick. He just.... he's just... Patrick he's really weird. He really frightened me,' she added, fighting back her tears.

'Just wait till I get my hands on the little shit,' Patrick raged.

'No Patrick. No. He didn't do anything. Really he didn't. We just talked and I think he shocked himself as much as he shocked me. It's just that... that,' Sonia tried to explain as she and Patrick sat in the chairs nearest to them. 'It wasn't what he did or said,' she tried to explain, 'it was the way he said it and the look on his face. It was almost as if he meant everything he said. I... I almost felt as though he was dangerous Patrick. I felt so trapped and panicked but he's not done anything. Nothing at all,' she finished in a pleading voice seeing the look on Patrick's face, which seemed ready to refute everything she was saying.

'I can't tell you the details Patrick,' she told him, 'as I promised Daryl I'd keep everything confidential and I can't break that promise, but he really frightened me Patrick. I don't know why because he didn't threaten me it's just... just that... oh god I was so frightened at one point, I thought he wasn't going to let me go?'

'What do you mean you thought he wasn't going to let you go?' asked Patrick confused. 'Did he do or say anything to make you believe that?'

'No, no that's the stupid thing,' Sonia tried to explain, 'he didn't do or say anything to threaten me, it's just the way he made me feel. It's all so irrational,' and she shuddered violently, the thoughts so disturbing goose pimples popped up on her arms. 'He didn't do anything Patrick. Nothing at all,' and although she left her statement there, Patrick could see the haunted look in her eyes, which conveyed to him that the reaction in a woman like this wasn't in her imagination.

'Patrick. I've never seen anyone so upset before. When he realised how his mother felt about him, it was as if all the stuffing had been knocked out of him. He was just so, so upset, as if all the pieces of a jigsaw had suddenly fallen into place and the picture wasn't what he'd been expecting.' Patrick sat listening to her as she described what had happened and how he'd reacted. Part of him was shocked, although another part wasn't really surprised as the characteristics Daryl had displayed showed Daryl to be a man of unrealistic beliefs. The reactions just described correlated perfectly with his irrational behaviour towards Sonia when he'd lost the game.

'Do you reckon he'll be ok or should we go up to him?' Patrick asked, partly out of concern for Daryl, but mainly due to the fact he wanted Sonia to see he believed everything she'd had to say.

'No I think we should give him some time to get his head round it. If he's not down by lunchtime we'll go and see him but at the moment I think its better we leave him. Thing is though, Patrick, this has been such a shock to him he's going to need some support. Otherwise I think he'll do something stupid.'

'Stupid?' asked Patrick. 'How do you mean stupid? You don't think he'd try and harm himself or someone else do you?'

Sonia shook her head tiredly. 'No he wouldn't do anything like that. To be honest I don't think he'd hurt a fly but I do think he may go home and lambaste his mother to the point of no return. His anger and hurt is so intense. It was almost tangible,' she explained shuddering, as she recalled how much negative energy had washed over her from his outburst.

'Do you know what the saddest thing of all is, Patrick?' Patrick cocked his head to one side to listen.

'I don't think Daryl's ever had a friend. So not only has he got the mother from hell and a father who was murdered, I don't think he's ever told anyone what a goddamned awful life he's led.'

'Poor bastard,' Patrick said with feeling. 'No wonder he feels the world is against him. Whilst I don't particularly like the guy I do think it would be worthwhile keeping in touch with him after this course, even if it's just to help him through this rough patch.'

Sonia looked at him appraisingly. After witnessing Daryl's devastation it was a refreshing change to hear such heart-warming thoughts coming from another man, and she agreed to his suggestion without hesitation. It was just then they saw Daryl across the foyer, looking pale and miserable. He came over and plonked himself down in a chair opposite them. Without preamble he said in a low but determined voice, 'Thanks for sticking by me and listening Sonia. I don't think I've ever talked to anyone like that before and, well,' he hesitated, not sure how to go on. 'Well it helped me sort it out in me head a bit. It's been a bit of a roller coaster these past couple of days and I've learnt more than I can handle really, but can I ask just one thing?' Sonia and Patrick raised their eyebrows as if in question. 'Do you mind not saying anything about any of this to the others? Please?'

Both Patrick and Sonia nodded their agreement and then, as if to lighten the atmosphere Sonia said with a wink, 'I'll keep quiet Daryl as long as you get us all a coffee and come and join us.'

To which Daryl, surprised at first, then, picking up the humorous intonation of her voice responded pleasantly with, 'It would be my pleasure Sonia. Coffee for you too Patrick?' before walking away for the drinks with more purpose in his step than he'd felt in a long time.

~ ~ ~ ~ ~

It was a bright and sunny day, on Monday 5th July, when Jack took Chloe to become pregnant for the last time. They'd stayed overnight in the beautiful clinic, which lay in extensive grounds with wonderful views over the surrounding area. When they'd woken the sun had been strong from the moment of the brightly hued sunrise, the wind still and temperature just right. They'd lain in bed cocooned in each other's arms, hugging each other tightly and calling upon their own invisible gods to keep this baby safe. Jack and Chloe already knew the features of their tiny daughter, just as they had with Joey, but to date, once nestled within Chloe's warmth, there had been as much protection for their babies as if they'd been left on a bench outside.

Only hours later, although familiar with the staff and procedures, they were still nervously waiting for the treatment to commence. As Chloe lay on the baby couch tightly clutching Jack's hand, their baby, cradled in the Brooder's womb, was gently carried through from the adjoining room. Within minutes it would be transferred into the warm, and hopefully welcoming, confines of Chloe's body. Only time would tell if the baby would survive, a time that would be fraught with worry for Jack and Chloe.

The implant went well and an hour later Chloe was connected to a myriad of monitors and instruments she'd stay attached to for the next forty-eight hours at least. The same equipment was attached to the Brooder, in the adjacent room, and fluids would be passed mechanically between the two women, in a bid to take the strain off the transplant and give the pregnancy the best possible chance of survival.

Whilst Chloe lay there, with prayers and dreams for the future reeling in her head, the Brooder next door would be undergoing intensive re-programming, now her days as a government incubator were over. This couple may need her to come back within the next few weeks but otherwise she had many years of retirement to enjoy, and would never need to work again, her womb already having earned its salary for the years ahead.

As monitors were checked and mother and baby's progress was seen to be going to plan gradually, one by one, the team disappeared. Jack and Chloe sat silently with no need for words in this precious moment. Within half an hour of the baby being cocooned inside Chloe's body she saw and felt the first fluttery movement of their daughter. The high resolution monitors clearly showed the baby and tracked the responses between mother and baby. Through the screen's clear pictures they watched in delight as their baby settled in Chloe's body. Emotionally exhausted, but exhilarated at the same time, Jack laid his head on the pillow next to Chloe's and listened to the steady rhythm of their baby's heart, which finally lulled him into a peaceful sleep.

After two days, with the transplant still going according to plan, Chloe was gradually disconnected from the various pieces of equipment until the medics were certain the baby was surviving without external help. On day five, Chloe was finally allowed to go home, where equipment had already been installed, which would allow the clinic to monitor the pregnancy remotely. Wherever Chloe was in the house her pregnancy would be electronically scrutinised and whilst it meant her being housebound, in the initial stages, gradually she'd be able to leave the house for longer and longer periods as the medics' confidence in the pregnancy grew.

Things progressed well during the first three weeks. Anxiety still visited Jack and Chloe occasionally, but the counsellors allocated to them helped keep this to a minimum. However, by the end of the fourth week the hospital had identified a couple of hiccoughs, which they'd been able to deal with remotely, but were still giving some cause for concern.

By the fifth week, when the foetus was twenty-three weeks old, Chloe was finally readmitted back into the clinic when the monitoring showed levels of stress to the baby, which could jeopardise the pregnancy's survival. After various tests had been carried out Chloe was put back onto the machines and linked back to the Brooder. Within hours of this being done it looked as if things were going to re-stabilise, much to the relief of Jack, Chloe and the medical team, but they were still not out of the woods by a long chalk. The next forty-eight hours would be critical for this baby to survive, so Chloe was to remain hooked up to the Brooder for at least a couple of days.

Their optimism was short lived and once again the baby began to deteriorate. Jack and Chloe spent an emotional night praying their baby would survive and that Chloe's body would not reject it, as it had in previous pregnancies. Another seven weeks and their baby would be legally entitled to medical intervention if she was born early. Delivered before then and the only chance she'd have was if she survived unaided, which they knew was impossible.

By the morning the picture was not looking good and further treatments were given to nurture the foetus and the drugs increased to reduce the chances of Chloe rejecting the baby. By the thirty-third day it was beginning to look almost certain the pregnancy would not thrive. The baby's heartbeat was irregular and the movements weak and less frequent. Jack had been taught how to massage the baby, through the Babypouch, using only the lightest of finger contact to stimulate the unborn babe. With infinite care he'd stroked the tiny form willing his daughter, who lay weakly within, to fight and survive against the odds.

*The crucial date for their baby was 27th September. If only she could survive in the womb until then the doctors would be able to help her,* he intoned silently. *Any less time and the medics legally and ethically wouldn't be able to intervene. It was so unfair.* Again and again Jack cursed the individuals who'd voted in the referendum for life-long couples only to be allowed babies from the wife's womb. If the law had been different this little one, who they both wanted so very much, would have been safely nurtured, and survived, in the Brooder's womb to full-term. The chances of her surviving now were almost negligible and the child they'd yearned for would never happen.

At 05.45 on the morning of Wednesday 11th August 2032 little Jenny finally gave up her efforts to live. Desperately the couple had watched her final struggle, the monitor gradually fading and dying along with their daughter. The morning was grey and overcast, reflecting the couple's feelings, just as the morning of the implant had reflected optimism. When the womb containing their beautiful tiny dead daughter had been removed their last chances of being parents were taken as well. This had been their last hope and chance of ever having a baby of their own. All their hopes and dreams, and those of the government for them, had been dashed, destroyed and at this moment in time replaced by a festering bitterness. Not only devastated by the loss of their baby they both harboured feelings of guilt for other reasons. Chloe, because she'd insisted she was capable of bearing Jack's child, and had argued long and hard they should aim for the life-long marriage; and Jack, angry and resentful for the lives they'd lost over the years and for his weakness in agreeing to Chloe's arguments and logic, despite never having fully agreed with them. Counselling and re-programming would lessen their pain and loss and would help them come to terms with each other and what had happened, but they'd never forget the tiny son and daughter and all their other unborn babies they'd longed for but lost.

After the baby had been taken away, and the Babypouch temporarily resealed, the grieving couple had finally gone home, not wanting to stay in the clinic a minute longer. Little was said as they'd journeyed home and once back in their flat Chloe, with a tear streaked face and looking utterly devastated, had opted to go to bed. There was still medical treatment she'd need and discussions scheduled with the doctors to find out what had happened, but none of that had any bearing at the moment. All Chloe wanted was to be left alone to grieve, away from Jack who she felt she'd cheated so badly, as well as herself.

Jack, unable to settle in the apartment, could not sit still. He needed to be active, to get out and think, so left Chloe to sleep and went out. As he aimlessly pounded the near empty streets, in the balmy night air, he felt as though he'd never be able to cope with the feelings of grief and desolation engulfing him. For Jack wasn't just devastated he felt incredibly cheated, because now he'd never have the opportunity of having a child of his own, or anyone else's. The thought was unbearable. He felt angry, cheated and grief stricken, not just for his lost daughter and son but for the loss of fatherhood too.

*Why oh why did I let Chloe convince me a lifelong marriage, with all the free medical intervention, was the best for us? It may have been the best thing for her but not for me,* he argued with himself. *I'd happily have taken on another woman's child; adopted or better still had our own child through surrogacy, but that can't happen now. I should have thought it through properly and been stronger and spoken out about what I wanted,* he berated himself. He needed to be a father.

*If we'd taken the silver marriage we wouldn't have had all the treatment but Chloe could still have had an implanted baby and felt it growing within her. And when we'd found out she couldn't carry full-term we'd have been entitled to have our own baby through surrogacy which would have been truly ours and been fit, healthy and alive. Or we could have adopted. So why oh why didn't I insist on taking that option?* he asked himself again and again. *Chloe's so ambitious, so keen to be one of the best, the elite and I've been carried along on the wave because of the intense love and belief I have for her. I should have been stronger. For me, Chloe and for our babies.*

Heartbroken and devastated beyond rationale thought, at this moment in time, he almost hated Chloe and didn't know if his love for her was enough anymore, or if it could even take him through this period of blackness let alone the rest of his life. He knew these thoughts and feelings would become manageable again, after re-programming, but here and now at this moment in time he didn't know what to do or where to go. He didn't want to be with Chloe and he didn't want to be at home. He needed something but he didn't know what.

Tears were very close to the surface and his pain almost tangible as he walked along the semi-deserted streets. He didn't see anyone, notice anything or even know where he was, so deep was his pain. He walked aimlessly, weaving in and out of the city streets placing one foot in front of the other without thought of direction or destination. Finally he turned into a large fronted pub, sat on a bar stool and ordered a large drink, unaware of where he was or the type of place he was in.

He sat nursing his drink, his misery having withdrawn him from the world, unaware he was being closely watched. Unbeknown to Jack, he'd entered a Fornipub and the Sexlasses had spotted his anguish and were giving him space before approaching him. The men and women, employed as Sexperts by the government to work in Fornipubs, had more than just sexual skills to offer, each had specialist skills as counsellors and were trained to spot potential problems, whether they were to the individual or could pose a threat to the public, as part of the anti-crime campaign.

As Jack sat at the bar, staring morosely into his drink, the different women around the lounge watched him, quietly discussing who'd be best to approach him. It was obvious there was something profound upsetting him, as he looked very close to tears. Whether it was a death, argument or whatever no one knew, and wouldn't until someone went to talk to him. Between them they decided Zoe would be the best one. Zoe, who was about five foot six, with shoulder length brunette hair, was regarded as 'ordinary', not having any particular services to offer. Having allowed him some space in time she finally walked over to where Jack was sitting and signalled to the barman to set up drinks for them.

Sitting on the high bar stool, next to Jack, she elegantly crossed her legs exposing their perfect shape to attract his attention. Jack looked at the woman, and then looked around the bar. He stared into his drink again and then quickly scanned the bar a second time a look of horror crossing his face as he suddenly realised where he'd ended up, mortified to find himself sitting in a Fornipub; respectable or not! Making as if to leave Zoe put out a restraining hand, indicating there was no need for him to depart.

'Hey love,' she said gently, 'there's no need to disappear. You obviously need someone to talk to so you've come to the right place.'

'But, but,' he stuttered in embarrassment. 'This is a Fornipub. I don't need a woman. I don't need anyone. I just want a drink.'

'Well you look as if you could do with a friendly ear,' Zoe responded. 'People do come in here just for someone to talk to you know. It's not just for sex people visit. Something subconscious must have guided you here,' she surmised.

'No. No I was just wandering along and ended up here. I didn't even look,' he paused, looking desperately round the room as if for an escape.

'To be honest I don't even know which part of Cambridge I'm in. I was just walking, needed to think to get my head straight and my feet just led me here.'

'Well it's as good a place as any to find someone impartial to talk to,' Zoe replied gently. 'So how about telling me what's upsetting you so much? It must be pretty bad because you look, if you don't mind me saying so, awful.'

'It's…' he started, wondering if he should actually tell her. 'I… I lost my baby today, a little girl, she was born too soon to be resuscitated. She was only twenty-two weeks mature so legally they couldn't save her. What a goddamn awful law that is. It's so barbaric and she... she was just so perfect. So tiny and so, so beautiful,' he finished in a hushed manner as large tears rolled down his face splashing onto the bar.

'Oh! I'm sorry, how awful. Is there a chance you can have another at some stage?' she asked kindly laying her hand gently on his arm to show a small modicum of human warmth.

Slowly, Jack shook his head. 'No. She was our last hope of becoming parents. I shall never be a father,' he told her looking beseechingly into her eyes, begging understanding and silently asking her to understand his pain.

'Are you a life-long marriage partner then?' she asked quietly. Jack nodded slowly, dropping his head into his hands, his elbows on the bar as his body slumped on the stool.

After a while Jack pulled himself together and began to watch the people about him, many arriving or leaving. The room was large and luxurious, without being ostentatious, and filled with men and women of a wide range of ages, shapes and sizes. Whenever someone entered the room seemed to stand still, as the entrant's eyes swept the room as if searching for something special. It was like watching kids at a sweet shop window. As they searched they were watched by the various men and women already there. Jack took all this in, as the woman beside him sat quietly, waiting for a reaction or comment from him.

All of a sudden the true realisation hit Jack, of where he was, the impact of his surroundings fully penetrating his consciousness. Zoe was watching with a wry expression on her face noting his changing expressions. Once again she stretched out her slender hand, as if to reassure him when he looked as if he was about to take flight.

'Don't run away,' she told him in a low tone. 'Don't you think sometimes your instincts lead you to where you need to be? Maybe tonight you need some solace and time to adjust to your situation with some warmth and comfort. Perhaps I can help you there. I'm a Gobi, can't have children and I'm a government Sexpert so if you want some fun or comfort you'd not be breaking any of the marital laws. We could go to my room,' she told him gently, 'and you know as well as I do that sex can be very therapeutic, almost healing. Otherwise we can just talk,' she told him, 'in private.'

*I've money in my pocket, a hole in my heart and maybe some love and nurturing wouldn't hurt later, so why shouldn't I stay?* he thought. *As a Gobi it'd be acceptable to society and Chloe couldn't object, although she might feel betrayed, especially tonight,* he warned himself. *As it is I need to look at my own needs to be able to deal with hers later, and at the moment I need a drink and maybe more,* he told himself. He thought about the past few years, and the way he'd been expected to perform mechanically at the flick of a switch. The thought of going to bed for recreation, instead of procreation, suddenly appealed to him and appealed very much. *Maybe later,* he thought, and signalled to the bartender for another round of drinks.

'We've not introduced ourselves,' the attractive woman purred. 'I'm Zoe.'

'Jack.' he responded. 'Your drink,' he offered, using as few words as possible and passing her the glass. For the first time in a long time he smiled, a warm glow of anticipation stirring within him. He realised it had been some time since he'd felt a sexual thrill, and taking a long swallow from his drink looked over the rim of his glass into the woman's eyes. He noticed she was watching him intently, and it made him feel good, like a man again. Relaxing he looked round the room again, this time with more curiosity and interest than before, watching the busy room buzz. Anyone coming in, presumably looking for someone to have sex with, but appearing to flounder, were approached by one of the Sexperts, obviously keen for the business.

Zoe watched him take in the room's activities.

'I'll never tire of watching people,' she offered. 'You can almost predict how people will behave when they come in here. Look. Do you see that man over there? The one with blond hair who's quite short and chubby? He'll be looking for a Sexlass but I bet you anything you like one of the Sexlads will go over and chat him up. You know what'll happen next? He'll end up in a corner talking to both a man and woman but he won't end up with a woman. It'll be the man he spends his time with tonight, and it'll be the first time of many, although he'll still go to bed with women, but not as happily as before.'

Jack listened fascinated watching the man look carefully round the room with a worried expression. He approached the bar next to a Sexlass and within minutes a Sexlad went and stood at the other side of him. Having ordered his drink the man turned towards the woman and made to approach her. The Sexlad nodded almost imperceptibly and spoke to the man before he'd managed to utter a word. Now he had no choice but to talk to both of them or appear rude. Zoe smiled as the three of them started talking.

'That's how they work the room,' Zoe explained. 'He showed indecision and now he's been approached he no longer needs to deal with the decisions himself. It'll all work out quite naturally now and once he's on the road to discovering the other side of his sexuality Gary there, who's trained for such situations, will help talk him through it so he can accept it without guilt.'

'Now if he'd gone to one of the private Whoretels he'd still have been approached, but wouldn't have got the counselling to help him cope with it,' she continued to tell him. 'You have to be one of the very best to get into the Government Fornipubs and clubs. Most of us start out in the private sector but there's an unwritten agreement the private sector will feed potential members through to the government payroll and get paid well for the referral into the bargain. We get the training and accolade and the punters who come in here get the best.'

Once again she called for another round of drinks, knowing Jack needed the time to relax and acclimatise to the situation he'd found himself in. If she rushed him she knew he'd just run away, when what he really needed was to relax, talk and, she suspected, find the fun side of sex again. No doubt the relationship with his wife would've been mechanical, whilst trying for a baby, and if they'd not been re-programmed yet she'd be able to help him readjust with just a little bit more warmth and enjoyment than he'd encounter on the NHS circuit.

'Do you see the woman who's just walked through the door?' she asked pointing out a smartly dressed woman. 'She'll make a direct line for the big tanned guy over in the far corner. She's been coming in here for years. Never has another man and if Jamal isn't about she'll just go off. She's a really successful business woman and won loads of awards. She's employed thousands over the years and I'm told is a very fair boss. Anyway because she's so caught up in her business she won't have a proper relationship. Says it would take up too much of her time and thoughts if she got emotionally entangled with someone, she's saving that for a later date, probably for retirement, which she reckons'll be when she's about fifty,' she carried on explaining. 'Anyway she and Jamal always get together. Sometimes she just has a drink with him and a few others, others times they disappear upstairs. She's a lovely woman and doesn't care who knows she comes here because she reckons it's her salvation and coming here keeps her sane. She says sex is the best way of getting rid of frustration and aggression without offending anyone.'

Jack watched the woman walk across the room. Her posture, style and clothing were superb. She held her head high and carried herself gracefully, walking with a subtle sway of her hips. Reaching Jamal, she bent down and they greeted each other with air kisses. Then acknowledging the other people in Jamal's group immediately started up a conversation with one of the women sitting in the gathering.

Jack turned his attention back to Zoe and looked at her questioningly.

'So what made you come into the game?' he asked. She guffawed at the way he'd framed the question throwing back her head and laughing in delight at the awkward way he'd asked his question.

'Darling,' she laughed. 'You sound like someone out of the dark ages. This is no longer a job that's hidden and disapproved of. It may be the oldest profession in the books but it's a much respected and sought after position.' She grinned at the word she'd deliberately used.

'I pity the poor women who were exploited in the past. Sex was a means of money whether it was used to keep body and soul together or to keep them fixed with drugs. Whatever, it must have been a pretty miserable existence, especially if they were made to work for pimps. Now it's quite different. Since the government acknowledged it's a required and desired service they've made it into a respectable profession. Whilst they provide a safe and respectable means of having sex they're reducing the exploitation of women and number of rapes, not that rapists exist as such anymore. It's all to the good and,' she added, a mischievous glint to her eye, 'we only do it because we enjoy sex and want to make life enjoyable in other ways too. Hence our counselling skills,' she explained in a more serious tone. 'That goes for men as well as women. The numbers of each sex employed are pretty equal now as we get just as many female customers as men. It's not unusual or frowned upon for group sex either or to try something different. Nothing and no one surprises the nation today. People can do what they want and do it safely without causing offence,' she explained to him. 'This is one of the approved and safe places and no one coming here can have their visit used against them. In fact they're admired as they're addressing a need and no longer denying it, women as well as men. It's certainly stopped all the blackmail that went on at the beginning of the century. There were forever MPs being dragged out from the political governments and hung out to dry for their sexual orientations or activities. Pathetic really.'

As they continued to chat, the drinks relaxing Jack, Zoe reckoned he was comfortable enough to be led off without questions, yet know exactly where he'd be going. She finally slid from her stool and beckoned him to follow. She'd been right. Jack followed her meekly, yet eagerly, up the impressive staircase leading to the private annexes.

The room they went into wasn't like the seedy backstreet brothels from the turn of the century he'd read about, nor did it have the air of discomfort and disgrace men must have felt when trawling the backstreets to find anonymous sex. This was far more comfortable and personalised and seemed perfectly natural.

Zoe sat on the sofa crossing her long slender legs and patting the seat next to her, inviting Jack to join her. He threw himself down, determined to enjoy himself and surrender to her ministrations. She reached across and gently stroked his cheek. The small gesture took him completely by surprise and he suddenly found himself with tears pouring down his face, as the dam gates of grief opened. Zoe cradled his head against her, crooning and stroking his hair to comfort him. He sobbed as if he'd never stop, unleashing the tears of pain he'd held back through all the pregnancies. As his sobs eased he became aware of his face being nestled in the wonderfully scented warmth of Zoe's bosom.

Finally his weeping ceased and Zoe gently dried his tears, which Jack found strangely erotic. Before he knew it he found himself kissing her, deeply and passionately, unleashing all of the feelings he'd been holding back from Chloe, although until this moment in time he hadn't realised he'd been restraining his emotions with her. Fleetingly he remembered hazy day of passion he and Chloe had shared, before the traumas of procreation had overtaken them. Passions they'd explored but been deprived of now for too long.

Zoe was stoking the nape of his neck as he nuzzled her bare shoulder. His hand slid down the front of her blouse and clumsily he unfastened her buttons. He was shaking with an urgency he'd not experienced for a long time and when they were both semi-naked Zoe led them to the bedroom beyond, where they basked in each other's bodies and sexuality.

The sex between them was strong and passionate, yet strangely gentle. They sated each other's needs and when Zoe threw back her head, the sounds of orgasm rising from her throat, Jack found himself responding, climaxing in a powerful wave of sensation. He was touched by the intimacy of the sex they'd just shared. It was so different to the sex he'd had with Chloe over recent years, which had been all about having a baby. It hadn't recognised or honoured their love for each other but had become sex of hope and desperation. The sex he'd just enjoyed with this stranger had been different, sweet and gentle and, he searched his mind for the emotion he was looking for and suddenly realised what it was. Fun! It had been sheer delight and he felt hedonistic with the pleasure he'd just enjoyed, which had been missing in recent years.

'I'd forgotten how much pleasure and fun sex could be;' he told Zoe. 'For years it's just been about babies and procreation and our desperation to have a child. We were both terrified we'd fail, which we have,' he finished, his voice trailing away and a look of pain clouding his eyes.

'Yes but tonight it was fun and fulfilling as it will be again in the future for you and your wife. And just to prove that…' and she pushed him off her body and rolled him expertly onto his stomach and sat astride him. Expertly she began to massage his back, using her strong fingers to pummel the muscles along his spine. Under her expert administrations Jack felt himself relax, listening and answering the questions she asked, the responses she gave appeasing him.

Gradually the massage became erotic, and they found themselves making love again, revelling in each other's sexuality; enjoying the sweet wetness of each other until they climaxed, with an almost perfect synchronicity.

Afterwards, they talked of hopes and dreams and disappointments, of Jack's shattered dreams and how he would deal with his complete and bitter disappointment. They chatted about their pasts and childhoods sharing stories told by their parents and, in Jack's case, grandparents.

They discussed the use of sex-enhancing drugs, and how worthwhile they'd be in helping Jack and Chloe revert from procreation to true recreation. Jack told Zoe the story of when his mum and dad had experimented with sex-enhancers, when they'd been young, and tales his mum and dad regaled with hilarity once the stigma of sex had ceased to exist. Although it had never been confirmed, but intimated on many occasions, Jack believed he was a much wanted result of his dad using Viagiant. He laughed as he recalled the story his dad had told him and together he and Zoe scoffed at the subterfuge their parents' generation had had to go through, to experience the drugs which were now openly available along with a variety of other sex-enhancing drugs.

It was almost midnight before Jack got up to leave. He'd been absent for several hours but felt, as he made his way home, better able to cope now. Chloe would understand his need, and hopefully welcome the lightness he now felt. He felt no guilt, no anger and no longer felt cheated. Somehow he felt different, and deep inside lay a quiet contentment he couldn't quite fathom, nor did he want to. It just was.

What Jack wasn't aware of was that as from now his life would change beyond recognition. What had happened today, 19th August 2032, would alter his and Chloe's life forever. When he'd left home tonight he'd thought his hopes and dreams were at an end. If he did but know it they were just beginning. He was now in a world unvisited and if he could have a caption floating over his head it would read 'Watch this space'!

~ ~ ~ ~ ~

Liam arrived back at his penthouse, unusual for him midweek, feeling decidedly blue, unloved and very lost. Several people had talked to him during the day but he'd been distant and vague. Of the forty or so people, in today's group, he must have slept with at least five of them in the past, but couldn't be bothered to single them out or to seek a new partner. One of the men and two of the women, who'd been his sexual partners previously, had suggested they go along to the Forniclub for a drink and finish off what they'd started on their last session, but he'd declined them all.

He looked round his suite without enthusiasm. It was allocated to him by the government with shares in the property coming under his ownership for each year of employment, a privilege envied by many and yet tonight it meant nothing to him. He'd an inkling what his problem was, Tanya! Tanya, like him, loved sex and they often fornicated together alone, and with others, both taking advantage of the sexual freedom afforded them in a taboo-free society. His confusion with Tanya though was he wanted more than she was prepared to give; yet at the same time knew that what he wanted wouldn't satisfy him. Tanya, he knew wasn't enough by herself, as he wasn't for her. They'd discussed it many a time and despite their feelings for each other both had the insight to acknowledge there was something missing between them, but neither knew what.

He was just considering whether or not to ring Tanya when his tiny communications transmitter activated. The automated voice informed him the incoming call was from Tanya, which really surprised him as she rarely called him, it being Liam who usually did the calling.

'Hiya baby,' she drooled, in her educated but sexy voice. 'How ya doing? You ok?' His hopes soared on hearing her voice, especially as he'd been thinking about her.

'I'm fine,' he said. 'You?'

'Wonderful,' she intoned sexily, and then without preamble. 'Liam who've you got lined up for tonight? Anyone important or can you make yourself free? I was all lined up for a threesome, but one of the guys can't make it, so I wondered if you'd like to join us? This guy is delectable; you'll love him so how about joining us?'

'Is he into men as well as women, or am I going to be like a spare prick at a wedding?' he asked in a level but joking tone. 'I mean is it someone new and juicy or someone I've enjoyed before?'

'No. Fresh guy tonight and new to the area too. He's an up and coming government bod and very delectable. In fact he's based in the same building as you. Tall, slender and black as they come. A total contrast to you darling.'

'Not my cup of tea then?' he laughed, flattered that Tanya wanted him to join them.

*Dare I ask her to forget him and spend the night with me,* he wondered?

'What about kicking him in touch and just the two of us being together?' he suggested tentatively.

'Nice try big boy,' she responded, 'but this is one guy whose piece of meat I want to taste. But hey honey, I really fancy a threesome so say you'll come,' and she giggled deliciously at the innuendo. Liam quickly ran a few scenarios through his head.

*Do I want a bit of black dick myself? To share Tanya with someone else? Or should I persuade Tanya to ditch the other guy and somehow commandeer her all to myself?* The thoughts and variations whirled through his mind at a million miles per hour. Finally he agreed to make up the threesome and they made arrangements to meet up later.

'You want a Viagiant to help you keep up? I'm told he's a bit of a goer,' she laughed good-naturedly.

'Hey baby! Remember me? I don't need any help for donkey dick here, even if this other guy does. All you get from me – is me!' he added enigmatically. 'See you at nine,' he finished, and severed the connection chuckling quietly to himself.

Having finished the call he noted a funny sensation in his stomach. It was like a tight ball of excitement, but was tinged with a feeling of something he couldn't quite fathom.

*I don't know this guy,* he thought, *nor does Tanya; and I don't know how he'll perform or if I'll be able to keep up with him. The last thing I want is to end up on the sidelines watching the other two fuck each others brains out, whilst I try and keep my end up. Shit. There's a lot at stake here so maybe this once I'd better take a Viagiant, ' cos I'll not lose Tanya to him. I'll show this guy a thing or two and make his mind, balls and cock buzz, as well as getting Tanya's luscious juices flowing,* he told himself decisively.

By nine o'clock he'd arrived at the Forniclub, which was buzzing. He'd not taken a Viagiant in the end but a Supa-Sexed instead. It would keep his thinking crystal clear but heighten his imagination, and would also keep an erection no matter how many times he ejaculated. It didn't matter either if he didn't get any sleep, as it wouldn't have any repercussions on his performance at work the following day. He knew it was the right choice as he'd popped one in his mouth before setting off.

The Forniclub they'd agreed to meet in was a fetish club, of the type created in the early 2000's, but with fewer inhibitions. This one though was the business, a retrograde club where everyone was up for a good time and everyone attending obliged to wear club garb, and club garb meant dressing for the part.

As he entered the bar area, Liam congratulated himself on how he looked and would appear to others. He was wearing a traditional black leather sex suit, which was tight without being uncomfortable. It slimmed down his physique but left his crotch exposed. He looked down at his engorged penis, which stood proud and erect, the exposed glans glistening with a small drop of semen, enhancing the attraction of his manhood.

He looked round at other men, openly appraising their penises. There was a real selection; big, small, erect and flaccid and some adorned with make-up or tattoos. He loved this openness of sexuality and nudity and still marvelled that it hadn't always been like this. With the current climate no one gave a second thought to recreational nudity, although work and towns still followed the old traditional dress code during work hours. It was nothing to work with someone during the day then meet them out socially, either naked or wearing fetish clothing. Most people wore coats out on the public footways but now having 'nothing to wear' meant just that. He couldn't imagine what it was like to be forever restricted by clothing, but supposed a lot of it was to do with the climate, which was now clement all year round. Adverse weather was a thing of a past, he mused, although if it did occur it arrived with a vengeance, as if making up for its lack of frequency.

Liam looked round the bar for Tanya and, scanning the room, noted several people who appealed to him and also saw several looking appreciatively his way. He instinctively stood taller, jutting his hips forward provocatively. He was just beginning to think they weren't going to show when he spotted Tanya, with a very tall, broadly built black man by her side. As the couple strolled across the room Liam looked appraisingly at Tanya. Barely casting a glance at the guy who walked by her side Liam wanted to watch them as long as possible, before either of them became aware. They stopped midway across the huge room, to talk to a small group of people, and it was whilst they were talking Tanya finally spotted him, a huge smile lighting her face, her pupils dilating at the pleasure of seeing him.

Tanya touched the elbow of her partner, to catch his attention, and discreetly pointed Liam out to him. The guy looked across and seeing Liam nodded his acknowledgment, openly evaluating him from a distance. His glance finally stopped at Liam's crotch and a smile of approval crossed his face. Tanya, watching both men's reactions, smiled with satisfaction.

*Liam was obviously impressed,* she thought watching his hardness respond. Apparently wanting to make his mark on the proceedings the black guy, not taking his eyes off Liam, trailed his hand across Tanya's naked breast and over her leather clad stomach, until it brushed lightly against her pubic hair. Then still smiling broadly, he leaned down to whisper something in Tanya's ear and as he straightened, gave Liam an almost imperceptible nod. Liam, feeling his penis stiffen in response, knew he was going to enjoy himself tonight.

Tanya strolled across the room, her seductive sway catching the eye of several men and women. Liam, who was watching appreciatively also kept an eye on the other guy, to see what effect it was having on him.

*How could a woman be so sexy, seductive yet as elusive as Tanya?* he wondered. *And how much of a threat was this guy? Was he a good performer? Better than him or on a par? He certainly had the tackle to do the business with,* he decided, reassessing the black manhood.

Reaching Liam, Tanya threw her arms round his neck and kissed him long and hard, her tongue slipping warmly into his mouth. She ground her crotch against his rampant member, and Liam couldn't help but notice the hot moistness between her thighs.

*Christ!* he thought as the sexual tension soared from groin to brain. *If I'm not careful I'm going to end up screwing her right here,* which of course was against club rules, with the bar reception being for pick up and conversation only.

Tanya giggled deliciously, acknowledging his unspoken response. She turned towards the black man and letting her hand slip down to cup Liam's balls, told him huskily, 'Liam, this is Crawford, our partner for the night and Crawford this here is Liam, a long-time buddy of mine, who'll give us all a good time. Well does my choice meet with your approval big boy?' she asked Liam. 'Reckon you can take him on as well as me?' she asked, lightly running her hand down his thigh and up along the length of his shaft.

'Try me,' Liam managed to respond, rolling his cold glass across the exposed flesh of Tanya's back. The cold contact made her jut forward, which pushed her exposed breasts already straining against the cut-outs of her leather tunic, push further forward. Liam got his first opportunity to really appraise the guy close up. He reckoned he was a few years older than him, definitely taller and certainly fitter. He'd liked the way he'd made his way across the room, with his thick black erection leading the way.

*Yes,* he thought. *Tonight's going to be a good night.*

Crawford stuck out his hand, as if to shake hands with Liam, but instead took Liam's cock in his hand, grasping it gently but firmly. As he did this, he looked directly into Liam's eyes, holding his gaze steadfastly and drawled, 'Nice to meet you. Very nice,' and Liam, in response, felt a surge of sexual tension race through his body.

'And you,' Liam responded, looking directly and openly down at the black erect member in front of him. 'And you,' he repeated again more quietly, as if speaking directly to the rampant penis.

The two men fell easily into conversation outlining the roles they both played within the government strategy, surprised to learn they worked in such close proximity to one another. They were deep in conversation, and very aware of a mutual attraction, when Tanya came back with drinks. Approaching she appraised the men and body language between them, smiling to see the obvious magnetism between them.

Putting the drinks down on their station Tanya listened to Crawford telling Liam he was in the 'Social Liaisons Department' dealing with the government health plan to be delivered in the London area.

Butting in with a chuckle Tanya told Crawford good-naturedly, 'Liam'll probably be one of your not-too-far-in-the-distant clients,' she said playfully patting Liam's belly, which, Liam thought thankfully, was nicely contained by the tight leather of his outfit.

Not wanting Liam to feel thwarted by Tanya's remark, no matter how playful she may have thought it was, Crawford quickly went into rescue mode telling him, 'Don't wait to get onto my list officially, I'd love to workout with you any time,' delivering the invitation with a look of warning to Tanya.

'Liam,' she responded, deliberately ignoring Crawford's warning glance. 'Go for it. I know you'll have a lot of fun under Crawford.' Thankfully the cheeky riposte made them all laugh, the innuendo dispelling any awkwardness. 'Anyway, enough of work because tonight we're going to party, have some real fun doing a bit of watching, lots of playing and loads and loads of sex.' She took a delicate sip of her drink looking coquettishly over the rim of her glass at the two men, who simultaneously raised their glasses in response as if saluting Tanya's proposal.

Looking round the room, and pointing out different costumes and people, they were impressed by the array of outfits, some of which were quite astonishing and others sheer luxury. Period costume was one of Tanya's hobbies and she collected authentic outfits, for something just like this evening's entertainment. Her main collection was twentieth century school uniforms, from various schools across the UK. All were authentic, as she only ever bought from schools still in existence. Watching a group nearby she smiled as two women, both in school uniform, raised their uniform skirts to reveal hideous school knickers. One woman's were navy and the other's grey. Hideous things to wear on a day-to-day basis, but pretty good for a night like tonight. Tanya knew they wouldn't be worn for long and turning to her two companions pointed the women out to them, suggesting they go along to the school section to watch them at play.

'I've seen them in here before,' she explained, 'and once they get going they're quite something to watch. Might even be fun to join in for a while, unless of course you two have a better suggestion?' she added raising her eyebrows suggestively.

'Yeah,' responded Crawford. 'Not been to the school section before so it might be a bit of an eye-opener. I fancy a bit of bondage too. How about you two? Does that fit in with your tastes?' he asked his gaze flitting from one to the other as he spoke.

'Sounds good to me,' responded Liam. 'I certainly fancy a bit of bondage, but school first sounds good to me. That ok with you Crawford?' he asked getting an eager nod in response.

Tanya took the two men by the hand and led them to the school section as if their leader, which in effect she was. She'd instigated this meeting, picked her partners and had brought them together in this club, which was merely a meeting place and somewhere to whet their appetites. Tanya had other plans for the three of them later and, assessing the men, was pretty sure they were both tanked up on Viagiant or something similar. She smiled at the thought. There was nothing like bringing two men together, who'd not met before, for a session of sex. Neither knew how the other would perform and she knew, from past experience, they'd both be looking to outperform the other. She smiled to herself, knowing what Liam was like in bed and having a pretty good inkling Crawford would be as good, if not better. It would be interesting to see how the night developed, and reckoned she'd be in for an exceedingly interesting time.

The threesome made their way to the school section, where they watched with delight as if everyone was involved in a play. One chap had appointed and dressed himself as the headmaster, complete with cape, mortar and cane, over a tight black rubber tunic, which hugged his body but exposed and seemed to enlarge his genitals. He was rampantly hard and took great delight in administering punishments to the various pupils. It amused them to note he always made the 'girls' pull their pants down to their knees, and stick their bottoms high in the air, whilst he made the 'boys' drop their trousers and fondle themselves as he lightly thrashed them with his cane.

The teacher, who was shouting at the top of his voice as he sent various 'pupils' along to the headmaster for punishment, was watching eagerly obviously aroused as he made sure they were properly chastised.

'God knows what novels he's read,' Liam told Crawford. 'Certainly wasn't Jennings.'

The various pupils of different ages, builds and nationalities played their parts with great gusto. Friendly fights broke out, with boys tussling on the floor and two girls pulling each others hair, whilst others fawned over the various teachers. Two of the 'girls' went into the stock cupboard and the trio stood outside the glass sided cupboard fondling each other as they watched the intimate lesbian antics get frantic between the girls.

'Remember your first time?' Crawford asked Liam as he joined them.

'Do I ever!' Liam replied. 'I was expertly broken in by an older woman with superb tits and a lot of experience. Didn't last a full minute the first time but it wasn't long before I was ready again and it was fucking brilliant! What about you?'

Before Crawford could respond Tanya was leading them away telling them it was time for a bit of bondage. The two men looked at each other, grinned and simultaneously tucked a hand under each of Tanya's arms hoisting her off the ground and carrying her between them.

'Baby, for you – anything. Can't wait to see you securely tied to a feather soft mattress unable to do anything but enjoy yourself,' Crawford told her, and Tanya threw back her head and laughed in delight.

Having had a pretty raunchy session in the bondage box, looked on by a handful of others, they decided it was time to go back to Tanya's for some real fun. Collecting their outdoor clothing they bid goodnight to their fellow players and made their way back to Tanya's.

Arriving at Tanya's they helped themselves to drinks and made their way into her boudoir. Not having been before, Crawford was bowled over by what he saw. This was obviously not just a place for sleeping but a place for sex. He knew Tanya took sex seriously but, damn it all, this was one of the best places in a private pad he'd ever seen. The room was enormous and from the ceiling and walls hung electronically controlled mirrors, programmed to follow the occupants' activities. On one wall were rails and rails of Tanya's fantasy outfits; school uniforms, waitresses' outfits, nurses' uniforms and a variety of others, each in immaculate condition. On another her extensive collection of lingerie; pants, bras, stockings, suspenders and tights of all colours, fashions and eras adorned the walls on purpose-made displays.

There were men's outfits for doctors, policemen, firemen and servicemen, from current and earlier periods; a whole area sporting a variety of whips, chains and other accessories for bondage and discipline, whilst in another area were feathers, silk scarves and the biggest range of vibrators and sex toys outside the museums Crawford had ever seen.

'Hey baby,' Crawford said. 'You really take this sex stuff seriously don't you?' To which Tanya nodded with a smile, appreciating Crawford's admiration of her extensive collection.

'Doesn't everyone?' she replied, taking down a number of silk scarves and tossing them to the guys. 'What do you want me to wear? Something or nothing?' The two men scanned the walls then together strolled over to the display of underwear. Consulting each other quietly they picked out a half cup, finely ribbed corset, to show off her beautiful breasts, a pair of minute lacy black knickers, suspenders and silk stockings. To complete the picture they selected a pearl coated choker with a large tear shaped pearl hanging from the centre, which would point its way to her cleavage. Their selection complete they turned to see Tanya holding two identical black leather outfits complete with studded chokers, similar to old-fashioned dog collars.

'Before we dress for the kill,' she drooled, indicating a huge transparent cubicle, 'we shower.' As the men eagerly began to undress Tanya stopped them, instructing that from this moment forward none of them did anything for themselves. Crawford was to undress her, Liam to undress Crawford, and she was to undress Liam. They all complied enthusiastically, lacing her instructions with kissing and suggestive comments, touching and taunting the person they were undressing, before finally making their way into the pre-programmed shower.

The shower was huge with adjustable seating and a variety of nozzles and attachments to excite, as well as cleanse them. Tanya indicated where they should all position themselves, and then the fun began. An hour later, with every crevice of their bodies caressed and scrubbed clean by the shower and each other, they emerged dried and moisturised, their bodies glistening with oil and glowing from the heat and exertions.

Picking up their allocated partners' minute outfits, they set about dressing each other. The Super-Sexed was still doing its work and by this time both men, and to their delight Tanya as well, admitted to having popped a pill prior to meeting. Crawford, his penis once again erect and swollen rigid, encountered some difficulty having it eased into his costume but Liam, in charge of dressing him, resolved the situation by applying some lubrication with his mouth. He found himself really turned on by the huge erect black penis in his mouth, and took great delight in savouring the length and head of the enormous shaft, licking the clean shaven balls. On the brink of climax, Crawford pulled away and pulling Liam towards him kissed him hard, thrusting his tongue deep into Liam's mouth as he took Liam's penis in his hand. Tanya, who was watching the two guys pleasure each other, was pleasuring herself enthusiastically but before her men climaxed she pulled them apart, demanding they dress her in the scanty items they'd selected.

There was already an uncanny understanding between Crawford and Liam, who looked at each other and grinned. Between them they picked Tanya up and carried her to the bed. They'd seen how much Tanya had enjoyed watching them, and laying her on the bed spread her legs apart. Whilst Liam gently spread her sex and entered her Crawford knelt beside them sticking his huge tongue out and spread it flat to stimulate both Tanya and Liam together. Moaning together with intense pleasure, Crawford felt their sex gliding in and out as Tanya fondled his swollen black cock, holding it tightly and pumping her hand up and down, until one after the other, each came in a noisy climax, finally collapsing in a heap of spent sexual energy.

For the next few hours they cavorted round the bed interchanging positions, caressing, kissing and penetrating each and every orifice and generally going all out for as many sexual experiences as they could discover. By the early hours of the morning they'd all climaxed several times, knew each other intimately and were peacefully dozing together, still entwined.

Tanya was woken from her light sleep by the birdsong and the sounds of London waking up. She looked over at her two men fondly, realising there was still time before work to have another, if somewhat shorter, session of sex. Disentangling herself she left the slumber-pit making just enough noise and movement to rouse the men. Crawford watched her as she donned the clothes they'd selected the night before, and getting up to help her dress they kissed and caressed one another intimately. Liam was now awake watching the antics from where he lay, his hand on his awakening appendage.

*Tanya looks like a tantalising seductress*, he thought as Crawford helped her dress, carefully arranging her breasts so they balanced neatly on their delicate platforms, licking her nipples to make them glisten in the subtle morning light.

*Together*, Liam thought, *they look incredible. Like ebony and ivory embellished with leather and laced with sexuality.* Hugely aroused now, he played with his throbbing manhood watching, as Tanya bent over, her legs straight and shapely in silk stockings as Crawford took her from behind. One hand cupped a breast, his thumb tweaking the nipple whilst the other played expertly with her clitoris, quickly bringing her to a noisy orgasm. No longer wanting to just watch, but be involved again, Liam got off the bed masturbating furiously. He stood to the side of Crawford and thrust his free hand between Crawford's legs to cup his balls, which were now silky with Tanya's wetness. At Liam's touch Crawford's pace increased and, then as if pre-orchestrated, they all changed places. Liam stood sandwiched between Tanya and Crawford and entered Tanya whilst at the same time Crawford penetrated him. Within seconds Liam came, his sperm pumping out in strong spurts, quickly followed by Crawford just as Tanya came to yet another noisy climax. In unison they shuddered in ecstasy, their noise gradually becoming groans of deep contentment, a resonance of sound they'd mentally replay for weeks to come.

Once again sated, and with time running out, the three entered the shower cubicle and together showered and made ready for work. Having clad themselves in office garb they made arrangements to meet again and together Crawford and Liam left to make their way to their respective offices.

~ ~ ~ ~ ~

Jed devised a plan he hoped would persuade his parents to finally remodel his outdated bedroom. His idea, he'd painstakingly designed and drawn up, was to totally refashion the garden. He reckoned the design wouldn't just look good but would need little maintenance too. It may only be a pocket-sized garden, but it took a lot of maintenance with its fussy layout and for years his father had moaned about it, threatening to have it totally revamped, but never getting round to it.

Presenting the plan to his parents, they'd been openly impressed by the design and the amount of thought and work he'd put into it. When Jed offered to do the work himself, in exchange for having his room done his father, sceptical at first, had finally seen his son's serious offer and slapped him on the back laughing long and hard. When he'd finally finished laughing enough to wipe away his tears, and was able to speak coherently again, he proudly told Jed how they'd make a businessman of him yet. Jed, more than a little startled at his father's response, had decided to milk the situation for all it was worth. By the end of the evening they'd struck up a deal neither of them would have previously thought possible. From that day on the distance, between Jed and his father, quickly began to diminish.

A couple of weeks later Jed's dad told him he'd set aside the following Saturday to go with Jed to buy materials for the decorator his dad was insisting upon. Then, much to Jed's surprise, he suggested they visit the skate park, en-route for lunch, so he could see how Jed was faring at the sport. Jed, although thrilled, was in two minds about this. Firstly he'd already arranged to go to the park with the others and secondly he was pretty convinced his father's tastes, when it came to decorating his room, would be totally different to his own. On the other hand his dad was offering to spend time with him, which was something Jed had always yearned, so he wasn't about to turn down the opportunity and decided the others would more than likely understand. Anyway it would give him an opportunity to introduce Fiona to him, as he hadn't taken her home yet for fear she'd laugh at his bedroom.

His mother, with sympathy for her son, and aware of the fragility of this new turn in the father-son relationship, decided to intervene, with the choice of bedroom scheme. She knew Jed's heart was set on something totally outrageous, which would cause havoc between her two men, so set about persuading Jed to have his room decorated with Image-Receptive Gel, which was accepted with amazing gusto. Jed couldn't believe his luck, as it was still a relatively new concept and trendy enough to be envied by his friends; Jed in particular wanted to impress Fiona. It would cost more than they'd budgeted for, his mum told him, but she'd argue with his dad they'd be saving money long term, as they'd be able to project different images, rather than redecorating, if anyone came to stay when he went to do his National Service.

Recognising how devious her husband and son could both be, she also knew how to manipulate them to everyone's advantage. Knowing how desperate Jed was for his father's approval, she just hoped they'd both get up in reasonable, rational moods for their first day together, and Jed wouldn't let them down in the summer by not doing the promised work. Whatever happened, it was destined to be either a disaster or a roaring success.

When Saturday dawned Jed, as expected, had woken with boundless energy. His dad though wasn't as exuberant, although he wasn't in his usual grouchy mood, and much to his wife's relief had been in favour of the Imaging Gel scheme, liking the idea of ever changing themes. Jed and his friends couldn't wait to try out the different images, and Ben promised to get hold of some of the more 'imaginative' ones, he knew Jed's parents would never approve.

They'd left the house and were down at the park by ten, where Jed had taken his dad into the eaterie to watch in comfort, with a drink. The rest of the gang weren't due for another hour, when Jed was planning on introducing the girls to him, so took his time putting on his gear, feeling nervous about boarding in front of his father. Therefore it came as a surprise to Jed when his dad came out after ten minutes and started to coach him, suggesting different ways he could execute the tricks he'd been doing. They'd been at it half an hour, his dad teaching him a new trick which he was quickly able to master, when the others arrived. They'd stood back watching from a distance as Jed did a simple, but neat, trick they'd not seen done before. Having heard Jed's dad instructing, and knowing how important this time with his dad was, they decided to go and do their own thing and set off round the track to warm up. It was some time before Jed spotted them, so absorbed was he in what he was doing.

When he finally spotted them he beckoned them to come over and meet his dad, introducing them proudly. Jade immediately started twittering about the stunt Jed had been doing and asked if he'd show them too. Before long all of them were giving it a go, amazingly under the instruction of Jed's dad. Jed had never felt prouder in his life.

It was lunchtime before Jed and his dad called it a day and retired to the eaterie for a meal. The conversation between them was animated, as it'd never been before, and Jed felt for the first time he was really connecting with his dad.

'That dark haired girl is a natural on the board,' Jed's dad commented. 'Has she been boarding long? She executes those tricks with a quite exquisite grace,' he commented knowledgably. 'And as for you Jed, well you're pretty good. What made you want to do traditional boarding instead of the computerised one though? I'd have thought you'd have achieved far more with it all programmed in,' he finished.

Jed, delighted his father seemed genuinely interested replied. 'Tried the computerised boarding, Dad, but apart from keeping your balance and listening to instructions there's not much to it. Anyone can do that. But traditional boarding is something else. You've to get your own speed and maintain it as well as controlling the board and I really like the challenge of trying out new tricks and mastering them, no matter how long it takes. I've been working weeks on doing the One-eighty Pop Shove and I still can't master it,' he continued, 'but I will soon,' he added determinedly.

'As for Jade, she's the dark haired lass, she's only been doing it a few weeks and I can't believe how much she's learnt in that time. Fiona though, she's a different matter. She's not got the balance and grace on a board Jade has, but I'll give her her dues,' he added generously, 'she's not faint-hearted and still keeps coming along despite the fact she's always falling off.'

'Well probably got a soft spot for either you or Ben,' his dad said knowingly.

'Well, actually we've been going out a few weeks now, and Ben's going out with Jade. She and Fiona are best friends,' he added trying to gauge what his dad's response would be.

'They both seem nice lasses,' his dad told him. 'Is that why you're so keen to have your room done then?' he added, laughing softly as he saw Jed's crestfallen look. Covering the awkwardness he quickly covered it with, 'She important to you then son?'

'She's pretty amazing dad,' he started. 'You should see some of the things she's invented. She's developed these amazing Colorbs,' he continued, and outlined what they did and the plans Fiona had for them in the future. His dad listened attentively and Jed couldn't remember the last time they'd sat and talked like this before, if ever.

Then his dad almost spoilt it all by rubbing his hand across his slightly bristly chin, always a warning sign for Jed and said, 'I have to agree, son, it sounds like she's got a lot of talent and will go far. She's very focused by the sounds of it and I can see why she attracts you. She's pretty as well, and obviously has quite a lot to talk about. Just don't go getting too involved lad. Just remember you're only fifteen and you'll be off to camp in a couple of year's time. Just spread your net, get lots of dates, at least until you've done your service,' he advised. 'And talking of futures have you any idea what you want to do after camp?'

Jed shuffled in his seat. He did have a few ideas but didn't want to commit or tie himself to any of them just yet.

'Well,' he started hesitantly, 'I did want to go into business, you know buying and selling, but then Fiona suggested I might as well get a degree in business or marketing which quite appeals,' he continued.

'Aah,' his dad interrupted, 'she has influence on you.' Jed looked at his dad and decided not to upset the apple cart by retorting.

'But then I reckon that when I go to camp, I may just come across something I'm really good at, I've actually enjoyed doing those jobs in the house and garden and reckon I could be quite good with my hands. So I've not really got anything in mind yet, just a few ideas.'

His dad looked at him appraisingly. 'Jed, lad,' he started, 'I reckon that's the best answer you could have given me. I was pushed into doing architecture to follow in my father's and grandfather's footsteps. I didn't want to do it, but I'm good at it; not that I've ever enjoyed it, which is probably why I'm so grouchy all the time,' he confessed. 'What I really wanted to do was to work with animals. You know big animals on a farm? I've never done it and probably wouldn't have been any good but I'd have liked to have given it a go to find out.' There was a sadness in his face Jed hadn't noticed before, and he felt that if he spoke now he'd break the spell.

'What I'd like for you is to do something you enjoy and can really put your heart into. It's obvious you're not set on just one track and for that I'm pleased. I reckon when you go to camp and try all the different skills you might just hit on one and come out on top of it. So you see, Jed,' his dad paused, 'the fact you're not too focused, but seem to know your own mind, is good news to me.'

Jed was amazed to hear this compassionate person that was his dad. He'd never had a man-to-man discussion with him before or, come to that, any real conversation either. What he'd have liked just then was for his dad to clamp his arm round his shoulders, but knew that was expecting too much.

As if on cue, to save the day, the rest of the gang trouped in full of laughter and energy. They came over asking Jed and his dad how they thought they were doing. Jed, relieved his dad was being civil, almost fell off his chair in astonishment when his dad offered to do a bit of occasional coaching with them all. The others readily accepted, and Jed suddenly realised that this wasn't the father he'd talked to the others about recently. Dismissing the thought quickly, Jed was further surprised when he went and bought everyone drinks and sat telling them all about the competitions and teams he'd been involved in years before.

By the end of the day, the Imagery materials bought, along with several other items for the room, Jed and his father's rapport seemed to have found a new level. From that day on, there was a firm footing to their relationship, one of maturity, which in a few month's time was to be the only saving grace in Jed's life.

~ ~ ~ ~ ~

In an amazingly short space of time, Melanie had successfully argued her case, and the Crimedical Department had instigated a major DNA registration campaign. Within three months of Lucy being raped, only eighteen percent of those unregistered had failed to come forward. The threatened penalty, of failing to register, had obviously paid off and the assumption was the remaining unregistered adults, or majority of them, must have something to hide. With just under a million unregistered there was still a phenomenal number to eliminate but it could be done. Each and every man, woman and child living in the UK was listed, even if their DNA wasn't currently on the Government DNA Database. This task in hand wouldn't just match the rapist with his crimes but several other criminals and their misdemeanours, major and minor.

In the time the registration campaign was being put into practice, Melanie was working on the next part of her campaign which, only after intense persuasion and sound argument, Froud had finally sanctioned. Melanie knew the announcement wouldn't be greeted with enthusiasm by her colleagues, and was apprehensive when facing the team to tell them.

Of the twenty-seven strong team only one person looked happy when she outlined the plan to incorporate traditional policing methods into their investigations. Apart from Alan Foster, everyone else received the news with groans, rolled eyes and criticism. Melanie had expected this reaction, and was relieved one person approved the plan. She wasn't surprised it was Alan, an 'old school copper' with over twenty-five years service in the force who'd started his career when the old traditional policing methods were still in use. He was often mocked by his colleagues, when he suggested the old methods be used with the new, but now the tables were turned and he sat with a triumphant expression on his face delighted by Melanie's announcement. He wasn't surprised at his colleagues' reaction and offering his support to Melanie his colleagues had groaned good-naturedly. He glanced from one person to another, trying to calculate how many had used traditional policing methods in the past and calculated it was less than half. As much as he saw credence in modern policing he'd always believed the modern procedures should be supported more by the old methods. The Government DNA Registration Scheme was a perfect example; useless in its unfinished state and would only become a valid tool when the task was completed, as he suspected Melanie was going to announce as their next task. Alan was going to offer as much support to Melanie as he could. He knew she'd studied the old methods over the years and incorporated them whenever she could, which Alan respected her for. Despite Melanie having a reputation as 'Miss Starchy Knickers' he'd always held the belief there was more to Melanie than met the eye, and welcomed this new opportunity of getting to find out who she was.

Melanie, aware of Alan's approval and the chagrin and intrigue from the others, started to outline the case, forces involved and the achievements to date with the DNA campaign. It was a curious mix of information being relayed and her team knew it was leading somewhere, and would have some significance to the plan she was going to detail.

Before outlining the tasks she was setting, Melanie divided her team into working pairs, allocating one person with some traditional skills into each duo, hoping the traditional skills being rejuvenated would compliment current practices. To each couple she handed a précis of the rapist's attacks and corresponding statements along with investigations and outcomes to date. Then, reporting the success of the DNA campaign, and now reduced numbers, she instructed her team to go off to study the reports and reconvene after lunch with their thoughts on the information and any ideas of progressing it further. Melanie knew they'd already seen this data, and had her own ideas as to what should happen next, but wanted the team to look at its entirety and sound out their thoughts on the progression of the investigation. As the meeting broke up Melanie was pleased to see the duos go off together and hoped their lunches would bring about fruitful thinking. She wasn't to be disappointed.

Reassembling after lunch, Melanie was relieved to see her earlier announcement hadn't daunted the team, but sparked a new level of energy. It appeared they'd not only been working in pairs but had formed into three defined groups to thrash ideas out over the break, exactly what Melanie had hoped for. The ideas the teams came back with all hinged on reducing the number of unregistered DNAers, and the potential number of cases which could realistically be solved as a consequence, just as Melanie had predicted they would.

The next piece of information she imparted was what they'd been hoping to hear, but hadn't been expecting. Again, through Melanie's insistence, the Crimedical Department had agreed to the usual Case Solved Rewards under the existing scale of remuneration. The team twittered excitedly, double checking Melanie's statement, and were told if all went according to plan they could expect to double their salaries that year, to which Melanie then added anyone found not pulling their weight would be relegated to another team. This immediately sobered up her audience, even though Melanie had only issued it as an official statement, as the officers in this room were the elite of the elite and she'd no reason whatsoever to doubt their dedication to the task in hand. The team, knowing this was now serious business indeed, in terms of recompense and the credence of the Crimedical Sector in the UK and beyond, immediately set about putting their ideas forward, which were all recorded for reviewing later.

By late afternoon the teams, which had formed naturally over the break, had been allocated their agreed tasks and issued instructions for reporting back any information to keep the entire team updated. Each team's workload was as onerous and tedious as the others, but with the incentive of doubling salaries there was no lack of energy evident.

Melanie had named the three teams: Motor, DNA and Forces, which titled the tasks allocated. With the provision of the new motoring policies, put in place and updated over the past thirty years, each and every car travelling on UK roads was monitored and its position could be tracked and verified at any given time, past and present. The Motoring team were tasked with collating every vehicle in a fifty mile radius from where each rape had taken place. It was a humungous undertaking, but one which would be calculated primarily by the UK Roads Network System. From the information held they'd be able to cross-reference and identify all cars whose owners weren't DNA registered. Those unregistered would be passed onto the DNA team who'd then set about procuring samples from the car owners and cross-reference results with the Outstanding Crimes Register. It was from this register the bulk of perpetrators, for unsolved crimes, would be identified and arrests made. The task, Melanie believed, should have been instigated nationally several years ago with strict penalties imposed on those flouting the rules. She'd make sure car dealers, as well as car owners, faced the consequences and if her team were going to get the accolade and financial recompense for the prosecutions then who were they to moan?

Her third team, the Investigations Team, was assigned to collate all official and unofficial information relating to each of the force's investigations, and interview any parties involved to date. Of the six rapes committed there were five forces involved, including themselves, yet to date no one had actually collated the entire case load and carried out multi-purpose cross-referencing. Why, Melanie had no idea, as this was something that should automatically have been done previously.

*No wonder there's a lack of public confidence in what should have been infallible procedures. It'll be interesting to see what comes out of these co-ordinated investigations,* Melanie thought contemptuously.

When everyone had departed Melanie and Froud sat discussing the case and their team's reactions. Despite them being given arduous, and seemingly basic tasks, they'd not moaned, in fact since the announcement of the recompense scheme they'd not even complained about having to revert to traditional policing methods, instead of relying exclusively on the currently used push-button ones. Maybe they all saw some credence in the old methods, which weren't addressed by present procedures.

Meanwhile, in the adjoining office, Alan was reflecting on the meeting and the way Melanie had handled it. Alan had been allocated the task of looking into car movements in the Manchester area. A huge task and although possibly one of the smallest areas geographically, after London, it showed the greatest volume of traffic. As he and his partner, Jim, discussed how they were going to tackle it, Alan's thoughts drifted to Melanie.

*Her skills are superb and her track record second to none,* he thought. *Even the way she'd handled the negative responses to traditional methods had been overcome by announcing the recompense scheme she'd secured for them. No wonder everyone wanted to get on this team,* he thought appraisingly. *With leadership like Froud and Melanie no one could want for better.* Only half listening to his partner, as he pondered on Melanie, Alan made a sudden decision to put himself forward as Melanie's right-hand man. Heartened by the decision he set about his task with relish, outlining the systems he was going to implement and how he'd get the information in the most usable format and quickest route by calling in a favour from a past colleague. Alan was a keen advocate on keeping in touch with associates, as you never knew when you'd need to call in or ask a favour, he was constantly telling everyone. This was one such time and he thanked his lucky stars for practising what he preached. Making the call, which would save hours of trawling manually through data, he was promised the information would be at his desk first thing. Knowing the promise would be honoured he set about creating a records base to merge the information into. The system he was working on was one that had become virtually obsolete since the push button methods, but Alan still used it knowing how to manipulate the information with more dexterity than the modern systems allowed. Secretly he hoped to be able to gain his information and formulate it far quicker than anyone else in order to impress Melanie. If things went according to plan he was going to be spending much more time with Melanie in the future, than he had in the past.

It was later, after everyone had left, that he got his opportunity to speak to Melanie alone. She came out of her office almost staggering under a load of boxes and other paraphernalia.

'Hold up Melanie and I'll do the doors for you,' Alan offered. 'In fact why don't you let me help with some of those boxes,' he added quickly, deftly relieving her of several. Melanie instantly accepted his offer and together they made their way to the car park.

'I really admired the way you handled the meeting today, Melanie,' Alan told her. 'It's a smart move reverting back to old policing practices for this case. I cut my teeth on the old systems and, if there's ever anything I can do or you need a sounding board I'll help wherever I can,' he told her matter of factly, not ingratiating himself at all. As they walked Alan started outlining the system he was setting up and by the time the boxes were safely stored in Melanie's car they were deep in discussion. Never one to miss an opportunity Alan asked if Melanie had eaten yet, knowing she hadn't, and suggested they go for something to eat to bounce a few ideas around.

With Melanie's agreement they set off for one of the quieter eateries, often frequented by the Crimedical team, where several of the team were already eating. Disappointed they wouldn't be alone, but valiantly hiding it, Alan led Melanie over to the others greeting them cheerfully. Joining them, the talk automatically turned to the case and several ideas were bandied about. Alan's enthusiasm and competitiveness was clearly evident, much to the amusement of the others.

Drink had been flowing freely and the evening was becoming rumbustious. Being off-duty and pleased, Melanie was with them and obviously happy to be there, the atmosphere became more relaxed. They were all laughing, regaling tales and telling jokes when a question was directed at Melanie. Unusually though she wasn't addressed as Melanie but as Mel, her Achilles heel. The address came from one of the newer team members but the others, aware of how sensitive Melanie was about the hated nickname, and believing there was a hidden agenda behind it, instantly froze anxiously waiting to see what would happen.

'So you've worked on murders and all sorts of crimes, Mel, but this one really seems to have grabbed your attention. I mean don't get me wrong, you're dedicated to all the cases you work on, but this one seems to have more of your attention than usual. So what do you reckon to the twat who's doing them then?' Judy asked, obviously the worse for wear.

Melanie sat and groaned good naturedly before saying, 'Aw, I hate being called Mel, you can call me anything else – tosspot or whatever,' she joked lightly, 'but please… not Mel!' For a moment she sat in thought, idly playing with a fork in front of her. The rest of the group waiting silently, as if they were expecting some sort of revelation to be announced. Whenever anyone called her Mel it always set them wondering why she was so set against the name, but they never questioned it, liking her too much to upset her. As for the question about the rapist they'd all felt the tension change when it'd been asked, and been aware Melanie had used her pet dislike to give herself thinking time.

'I just think anyone abusing another person in that manner should be taken off the streets, castrated in the most painful manner and banished from this country to teach others a lesson. whilst giving him a punishment he'll live with for the rest of his life,' she said in a low cold voice, her face almost devoid of colour.

The group, aware Melanie had consumed quite a bit of alcohol, knew her statement probably held more depth than the words and sat spellbound. Maybe this was going to be the revelation of Melanie's focus on crime and her long term passion, or was it obsession? she'd spoken about over the years. They waited with bated breath to see what would be revealed next. Suddenly the tension was broken by Alan knocking over his pint, which went pooling across the table and all over Melanie.

'Oh god! Oh Melanie I am so sorry,' Alan apologised profusely, clumsily mopping at her clothes. 'Let me go and find something to clean up with,' he offered, searching the nearby table for something to use.

'No, no,' protested Mel. 'I'm so drenched I'll have to go home.'

'At least let me give you a lift,' Alan offered. 'After all it was my clumsiness in the first place. It's the least I can do and as I didn't get to finish my drink I'm not over the limit,' he added hastily, by way of explanation. Agreeing without hesitation, and telling the team to put the bill on her account so it could be claimed as expenses, Melanie and Alan left the restaurant leaving the others to speculate quietly.

'She's got something to hide,' Judy said thoughtfully, to the rest of the crowd. 'And mark my words Alan's got a soft spot for her too. Did you see how he knocked his drink over her to save her from having to answer?' she asked the table in general.

'You're about as subtle as a sledge hammer,' Tony chided her. 'If you'd been a bit more gentle we'd have probably found a bit more out and as for Alan... well he's had a thing about Melanie for ages. I for one, hope they get it together. They'd be good for each other and it would ease some of the pressure on us, if Melanie had something other than work to think about.' Put in her place, Judy moodily muttered some incomprehensible and defensive answer and within minutes the party began to break up.

As the half-hearted argument was breaking out at the table, Melanie was being driven home by Alan. She knew Alan had deliberately spilt the drink in an attempt to save her and thanked him for it, grateful he didn't try to deny it.

'You did it to save me from Judy's prying mind, didn't you?' she asked.

'She's not exactly Miss Subtlety is she? Anyway I saw the expression on your face, so thought I'd do the gallant knight-in-shining armour bit and rescue you from the prying dragon,' he told her laughing.

'Did it ever occur to you I might have liked to answer it and get a few things out in the open?' Melanie challenged him.

'Did you?' he responded, to which Melanie shrugged her shoulders silently.

'So what did you want to say?' Alan asked gently, as he drew up outside her flat.

'Fancy a coffee?' Melanie's asked. 'And I'll tell you about it.'

Normally a very private person Melanie sat with a steaming hot cup of coffee and for some obscure reason started to tell Alan the tale which made this case so important to her.

'This case is making us a laughing stock and putting the UK under constant watch from WPPL. We've allowed this rapist to stay free far longer than is acceptable, and he's taking us for mugs,' she told him passionately. 'He knows the country's being monitored and doesn't give a toss. In fact,' she continued, 'it's probably making him take more risks. If we didn't have the media in our pockets, well, things would be much worse,' she finished.

After a few moments silence Alan said thoughtfully, 'I hear all you have to say, Melanie, but it doesn't explain where you're coming from in all this. And please don't fob me off with what you've just told me, because you know that's not what I mean. What I want to know is where you are in all this? What does it mean to *you*? Come on Melanie, it's me here, Alan. Friend not foe. You can trust me you know and no one will ever know what you've said, unless you want them to,' he added gently.

He watched in silence as the normally emotionless Melanie struggled to keep her face expressionless, failing miserably. Alan watched as anger, bitterness, sadness and pain swept over her plain but appealing face. With dismay he saw her eyes fill with tears and spill over. It was obvious there were battles raging within, and she didn't know whether to tell her tale or not. Not moving an inch, and barely daring to breathe, Alan sat and waited for her to respond.

Finally Alan got slowly to his feet and went over to sit next to Melanie. Putting his arm round her in a fatherly fashion, he pulled her into the warmth of his embrace. He half expected her to pull away, but she didn't.

'Come on Melanie. A problem shared is a problem halved. Don't torture yourself like this. It's obviously something that's touched you deeply,' he told her, wondering if she'd been a rape victim herself. After a while Melanie started to speak in a quiet, tremulous voice.

'Everything I said I believe with a passion. But... but something happened a long time ago that's been a driving force for me since I was in my teens. It was my mother,' she told him in a shaky voice. 'When she was pregnant with me, about seven months on, well she... she was... she was raped,' she said in a barely audible voice. 'She was so badly raped and beaten the rapist left her... left her for dead. Oh, she was found fairly soon afterwards and taken to hospital for treatment but... but she didn't make it, and as soon as she was pronounced dead

150

they delivered me. I was in a pretty poor state too and only just survived. I always knew my mum had died in childbirth and dad hadn't got there in time to say goodbye, but…' Melanie paused, getting control of herself, taking comfort from Alan's arm draped round her shoulders. 'When I was in my teens my dad became ill, which was when he told me about my mum being raped. I don't think he'd ever got over her death and having to bring me up by himself, and it took its toll on us and we were never close. I'd always thought him calling me Melanie, instead of Mel, was a cold thing but just before he died he told me Mum had always said she'd never shorten my name to Mel. That's why I never answer to Mel now.' Alan was listening intently knowing instinctively there was more to come.

'Anyway when he knew his illness was terminal, he told me the full story. He showed me all the press clippings, the statements and the court hearing of a man who'd been arrested and tried, but proven to be innocent by his DNA. So if the murdering bastard is still alive today well… he's never been caught. The bastard who raped and murdered my mother is still out there somewhere. Even though they've got his DNA and everything else he's never, ever been caught. I've got all the DNA details and every time a murder or rape case comes in, or we get new records or reports of a death, I cross-reference the details. I know I shouldn't,' she added quickly, knowing she was admitting to was a dismissible offence and aware she'd already said too much.

'Shh,' soothed Alan. 'What you've told me is between us only and I'll never repeat it to another living soul. That I promise you,' he said, taking Melanie's face and turning it towards him so she could look at his eyes and see the sincerity he was saying it with. 'Is that why you became a detective?'

'Sort of,' Melanie admitted. 'At first I thought if I had a medical degree and knew how to treat a victim's injuries I could make up for my mum's death. But I'd always been interested in detective novels and started reading them in my early teens. It was after my dad told me the truth about my mum I started building my database. It made me feel as if I was doing something positive after I was told about my mum.'

'Agh. The infamous database,' Alan said quietly. 'I knew the supposed legend behind it of course and I've used it a few times too. So that's why it came into being then?'

'It's not just built on factual books, but mainly from crime novels written by retired detectives. Every time I've read one I've logged the techniques and strategies down so I can use it for reference or inspiration. Then when they created the Crimedical Sector it seemed the perfect route for me to follow,' Melanie told him.

'So you never met your mum then,' asked Alan quietly, 'and were never close to your dad either?' Melanie shook her head sadly. 'And I suppose you think because you lived and your mum died, somehow it was your fault and you were to blame?'

'No, not really, well not after my dad told me the full story,' Melanie agreed. 'That's when the sorrow I felt turned into anger. After all I'd lost my mum and never been close to my dad all because of some vicious rapist who ruined our family,' she said with venom in her voice.

'You do know the likelihood of ever finding him after all these years is pretty remote don't you?' Alan advised her. 'The most likely thing to have happened is he went abroad.' Melanie nodded her agreement. 'Have you ever talked to anyone about this?' Alan asked. 'Professionally I mean,' he added quickly.

'When I was going through the interview process it was part and parcel of the process,' Melanie told him. 'If I hadn't agreed to the counselling and re-programming then I wouldn't have had a chance at this job.'

'And did it help?' Alan asked.

'In some ways yes, but in others… no, not really. I've learnt that my reactions to everything were pretty normal and there's a grieving process to go through, not just for my mother but for my lost childhood and the lack of love in it too. My father's attitude towards me didn't help and his hatred for my mum's murderer continued to fester after her death. I could always feel it and can remember the frustration I used to feel with not understanding, until he told me and then everything fell into place.'

After a few moments silence she jumped up with more energy than seemed natural.

'There, now you know. Another coffee?' she asked, and Alan could almost see her detaching herself from the feelings and erecting emotional barriers again.

'Melanie, don't run away from this. Face it whilst you're with me, when you're not alone. It'll be easier with someone to listen you know.'

Melanie stopped in her tracks and, turning, cocked her head to one side and asked sceptically, 'Is it, Alan? Is it really easier with someone else to listen?' Alan nodded, his eyes looking directly into Melanie's, trying to convey his understanding across the short void between them.

'Maybe my pain isn't the same as yours Melanie but I do know what it's like to lose someone you love. It's not easy to cope with but it's easier if there's someone to help you through it.'

'Your wife?' Melanie asked, receiving a sad little nod in reply. 'How long is it now?'

'Six years, nearly seven,' Alan said sadly, although he could have told Melanie to the hour just how long it really was. Melanie stepped closer to him and, laying her hand gently on his shoulder, said, 'Maybe if we work through it together… it'll become easier.'

Alan got up and walking over to Melanie said, 'I think we could both do with a hug. Don't you?' Melanie stood rigidly, her arms straight down by her sides, not stepping into the outstretched arms or avoiding them either. Finally Alan moved to her and wrapped his arms round her, rhythmically rubbing her back comfortingly. After a few minutes, Melanie began to relax and finally, putting her arms round his back, gave way to the tears she'd held back for so many years. Alan didn't take advantage of her vulnerability, but just held her warmly, the strength of his arms providing the comfort she'd never had before.

~ ~ ~ ~ ~

It was a month since Daryl had returned from his course and several things had changed. He'd arrived home to his mother's moans, groans and disparaging remarks, but was no longer prepared to put up with her evil tongue. Whether it was because he'd the support of friendship or something else he didn't know, but his Mam's merciless treatment was over, as far as he was concerned.

When he'd stood up to his Mam, he didn't know who was more surprised, him or her. Her mouth had dropped open and she'd stood blustering, gathering herself together to launch into a vitriolic attack and had physically lashed out, which was a mistake. As she'd swung her arm Daryl had caught hold of it wrenching it upwards, making her almost lose her balance. She'd glared at him with hatred but had been doubly shocked when Daryl had wrenched her arm again, gripping her wrist so tightly she'd winced with pain, shaken by the hard, ugly look on Daryl's face.

'That's the last time you'll ever take a swing at me Mam and you'll learn to hold that evil tongue of yours too. What's more, there's going to be some changes round here, if you want me to pay more than the bills.' He'd then launched into a long list of things she was going to do and not do, to which she listened pale-faced with her mouth hanging open, she was so flabbergasted.

'Now go and make me a cup of tea and sandwich,' he demanded, anger still in his voice. Massaging the angry red welt circling her wrist, his mam was in two minds whether to give him another mouthful or burst into noisy dramatic tears. She had the ability to do both and used whichever suited her best, but she'd hesitated just a fraction too long and was mortified when Daryl burst out laughing, sneering scathingly.

'What's the matter Mam? Can't decide whether to give me a gobful or the waterworks? Well don't bother with either 'cos yer going to make me something to eat and drink. Now!' he demanded fiercely, and was surprised when she meekly did as bade.

Daryl went into the front room and sat on his Mam's chair switching over to a programme he was interested in. Coming back, with the demanded snack, this had been the final straw, and, not prepared to give up her cherished chair and role of matriarch without a fight she stood, hands on hips and screamed, 'Yer fucking little half wit. Get the fuck out my chair. How dare you come in here and tell me what to do you little shi...' but before she'd finished Daryl had leapt up and grabbing her arms had propelled her backwards unceremoniously dumping her in an ordinary chair and with his face just inches away had growled.

'Don't you dare speak to me like that again old woman.' His spittle sprayed her face as he enunciated each word carefully. 'And in future you give me the respect I deserve if you want any money I earn. Understand?' he demanded dogmatically, pushing her further back in the chair.

'I said did you understand?' he yelled at his Mam who, shocked and frightened by this new and assertive Daryl, had shed real tears and an inability to speak. Satisfied his message had got through, Daryl went back to sit in his Mam's chair, picked up his sandwich and ate it as if nothing had happened.

Although life at home had changed, his time at work was much the same. He was still rubbished and although he was involved in the maintenance of the new system, spending less time on the shop floor, the workers still took a pop at him whenever they had the chance, but he ignored the barbs as if they were water off a duck's back.

There were only two things really marring his life now. Firstly he still didn't know if his behaviour had been reported anywhere, and he lived in dread that his closely kept secret, of being beaten by a woman, would get out. His other problem was his health. He was still suffering problems from his blood poisoning and the sabotaged cut was only just beginning to heal again. Both these issues prevented him playing pool and he'd only had a few games since the tournament, dreading the fact someone may have heard about him losing to Sonia. The last thing Daryl wanted, or needed, was to be even more of a laughing stock than usual.

Missing his game and just getting back in practise now his hand was healing, he was considering getting in touch with Sonia to take up the offer of a rematch, which Patrick had offered to referee. Still not confident with the opposite sex, especially those who beat him at pool, he kept putting it off. Finally the decision was made for him when he received a message from Patrick, who needed help with sorting out a problem on his own system. Daryl was delighted. Not only had Patrick, a bloke he liked and respected, contacted him but he'd got in touch asking for help. Daryl felt ten foot tall as they worked through the problem together sorting out an easy glitch Daryl had already had to NapPals' equipment. The problem sorted, Patrick asked if he'd recently spoken to Sonia who was, apparently, waiting to hear from Daryl about their rematch. The unease Daryl felt at this news was put more in proportion, when Patrick also told him Sonia reckoned she could learn a thing or two about pool from Daryl. This admission gave Daryl enough courage to admit he too could learn some tricks from Sonia and muttered something to Patrick about contacting Sonia soon.

It was another week before he finally got in touch with Sonia; after he'd played a few games and made sure his hand was holding out. Waiting nervously for Sonia to answer her phone, he was more than pleasantly surprised to hear her sounding genuinely pleased to hear from him. After a few minutes chatting, about their respective systems at work, it was Sonia who broached the subject of a rematch.

'How's your hand healing Daryl? Is it ready for our rematch; that is if you still want one?' she asked. Daryl grunted his response then found himself having to repeat it more clearly when Sonia hadn't been able to interpret what he'd said. Quickly turning his grunt into throat clearing he apologised to Sonia for the 'frog in his throat'. Sonia had laughed good-naturedly agreeing the changing season's cooler moistness made her voice gravelly too. Daryl, amazed at how easy the conversation was going, quickly accepted her invitation to a rematch setting a date for two weeks' hence and agreeing to finalise arrangements nearer the time. Terminating the call Daryl felt more elated and happier than he'd felt in a long time, if ever. Things were better at home, had definitely improved at work and now he had a date. How life was changing.

His new-found status at home, meant he was no longer obliged to go away weekends and at last his Mam was cooking for him, she wasn't a bad cook either. Every so often, he'd verbally throw his weight about reminding her his threats still stood, and when she'd tried on one occasion to better him, he'd quickly raised his hand to scratch his head, deliberately making her think he was about to hit her. The only downside to home cooking was his consumption of traditional foods was making him put on weight and his clothes were getting tight, especially round his expanding middle. He also found himself suffering from indigestion, but it was a small price to pay after all the misery his Mam had put him through over the years.

It was his expanding waistline which finally persuaded him to go and buy new clothes for his meeting with Sonia. Instead of his usual attire he bought age-old traditional jeans and a couple of casual shirts and was surprised by how big the waists of his new trousers were, but at least they were comfortable and he could fasten them, and he vowed to watch what he ate before his weight escalated out of control.

As he made his way to meet Sonia, he reflected on the past few months, marvelling how much his life had altered and how easy it had been in the end to change things. Feeling excited at the pending meeting his stomach was turning somersaults ten to the dozen. He found himself more pent up, with meeting Sonia, than before any of his other liaisons. He'd never had butterflies like this before, and wondered if he was falling in love. The fact Daryl didn't harbour any remorse or guilt, and didn't really see his sexual encounters as rapes, spoke volumes about him as a character. As far as he was concerned they'd only got what they'd wanted and had led him on, so they must have wanted what he gave them. Without thought for any of them he carried on driving, proud of his newly-acquired car and whistling loudly as he drove.

He was looking forward to seeing Sonia and Patrick again and going off to meet friends, which he'd never done before, it made him feel good about himself and life. He looked across at the large bunch of flowers he'd bought Sonia and the assortment of sweets for Patrick's two children. *Presents! What pleasure he'd had buying them*, he hugged the warmth the small act had created in him.

*Maybe there could be romance in the air for me and Sonia. But do I want that?* he mused.

The meeting with Patrick and Sonia had gone surprisingly well and they'd appreciated the gifts Daryl had brought along, although they'd protested it hadn't been necessary. Daryl confided in them they'd made such a difference to his life, by befriending him, it had given him pleasure to go out and buy the small items. This declaration reinforced Sonia and Patrick's belief Daryl's life had been pretty much void of human kindness and affection. However, it didn't make them feel any more comfortable about him, and their feeling of unease persisted.

Their game of pool, umpired by Patrick, had thankfully been a draw, and to avoid any unpleasantness, it had been decided to leave it as that. In terms of talent, Sonia and Daryl were well matched, although both employed different techniques and styles. Oddly enough, instead of wanting to outdo the other, they were more interested in learning each other's techniques, surprisingly learning quite a lot from each other.

Before leaving Patrick had asked Sonia if she was happy being left alone with Daryl, or if she was going at the same time. Sonia assured him she'd only be staying a while longer, as she was going to a concert, and would play pool and get to know him better until it was time to leave. With Patrick gone they continued to play but used the table to set up awkward shots and learn each other's techniques, rather than playing actual games. It was after six when Sonia looked at her timepiece and was surprised to see how late it was, suddenly becoming flustered. Feeling awfully guilty, at having to run out on Daryl at such short notice, she was just about to dash out the door when, seeing Daryl's crestfallen face, she'd turned to him and laying a hand on one cheek kissed the other, suggesting they meet up again. Daryl's face had lit up and agreeing with enthusiasm had promised to ring her mid-week.

Despite being disappointed at Sonia leaving so quickly a big smile played on his face during the journey home. He kept laying his hand on his cheek, where she'd kissed him, smiling with warmth at the memory. No one had ever kissed him with kindness before, with the exception of his grandma when he was a tiny pre-school boy, and he wasn't going to forget Sonia's kiss in a hurry.

~ ~ ~ ~ ~

Within a month of losing their baby, Jack and Chloe, had been away for a two-week break for their intensive re-programming, which enabled them to come to terms with the loss of their babies. The programming didn't eradicate the memories of their two babies, who'd survived long enough for Jack and Chloe to think of them as their children, and whose development they'd watched in the Brooder's and then in Chloe's womb. Their photographs would be treasured along with the memory of cradling their tiny bodies in their arms. Memories never to be forgotten but remembered without the pain, which gave them the freedom to talk openly without the heart wrenching emotions they'd otherwise have experienced. This was what re-programming was about, managing feelings and putting them into sufficient perspective to continue life as an undamaged person, but not obliterating memories.

Knowing they'd never be parents: how could they if Chloe had no womb; the future would have looked incredibly bleak without the re-programming. They were forbidden by the laws of marriage to adopt or have full surrogacy babies, which was the privilege of other couples who'd not achieved the life-long marital status and weren't able to have babies. The system seemed so unfair, especially as they were deemed to be of the elite, in terms of the government selecting parents for future generations.

Before going away Jack and Chloe had felt bitterness at the unfairness of this which, coupled with their raw grief and disappointment, was emotionally eating them up. They berated themselves, and silently each other, for their short-sightedness and for opting for the life-long marriage, which precluded them from having a baby not of Chloe's womb. Chloe blamed herself for being so pig-headed and Jack for not standing up for what he really wanted, and believed should be his. The volume and intensity of their emotions were phenomenal, and coping with the other's feeling was just as hard. Inwardly Chloe blamed Jack for being weak, but deep down knew he'd bowed down to her demands purely out of his love for her.

It didn't help either that Jack, no longer able to cope, had gone out before their baby was even buried and had sex with another woman, even if she was a Gobi. That, in Chloe's mind, had been the ultimate insult and betrayal, and his infidelity had caused as much grief as her ultimate state of barrenness.

*So much for the government's 'wisdom' of providing Gobis. They've obviously never thought through the reasons men might turn to them, and the resultant damage it could inflict,* Chloe thought.

It was therefore surprising when they learnt Jack's reaction, to seek solace in the arms of another woman, was not uncommon and not so much a betrayal of the heart as a detachment from emotions a bereaved man underwent. Also the fact that sex would no longer mean an act of procreation but would be one of love and fun, which had been redressed for Jack in the arms of another woman who'd recognised many of those issues. It was for this reason Gobis existed when the government, with foresight or was it insight, created a special status for barren woman in their Fornipubs and Forniclubs. After all, the last thing anyone wanted was for a bereaved father to make another woman pregnant if he sought solace. What could be more insulting after a last chance of procreation had been lost? Learning this hadn't made Jack's infidelity any less distasteful but, as the programming became more intense, their grief began to lose its bitter rawness.

Along with their cruel loss, they were reminded of their love for each other; what had attracted them and kept them together over the years. Once again they began to discover the warm intimacy of love-making, which had been missing over their long years of trying to have a baby. In each other's arms they again found the sweet tenderness of intimacy, which now served not just as pleasure but as support in their need to grieve together. Without this re-programming they may never have found that closeness again; certainly not after all the trauma they'd encountered.

The couple had been due to move when the baby was a year old but, with no baby, they made the decision to move anyway. There was already a house allocated to them, in their childless state, where they would become involved as ancillary parents on a young children's estate, a concept dreamt up by the government in the mid-twenties. They may only be moving a short distance away but were relieved to be moving on so quickly.

Their new housing was in an area with other young couples, who'd been successful in becoming parents, along with two other couples who, like them, had not succeeded in having children. The couples on the estate were all in their mid-twenties to early thirties and were at various stages of parenthood, some with one child and expecting another, others having achieved their full breeding potential, of two pregnancies, and others just expecting their first.

By moving onto the estate, Jack and Chloe wouldn't be totally excluded from living without parenthood. Through the 'extended family' structures they'd still have day-to-day contact with children and become major players in the extended family concept the Government were nurturing. Despite this, when Jack and Chloe finally moved into their new home, it was with some trepidation. They wondered how they'd cope being with young families when they couldn't have a child of their own. It needn't have concerned them though as they received a warm and understanding reception from their new neighbours and immediately found themselves integrating into life on the estate.

Whilst Jack had returned to work almost immediately, Chloe would not be returning for some time, her body needing time to heal after all the treatments and great number of pregnancies it had endured. The extra time off would allow her space to readjust to the new situation and 'nest' them into their new accommodation, something found to help with readjustment following failed pregnancies.

Both she and Jack liked the new house and area along with all the neighbours, without exception. It was wonderful to be involved with the local children, even if it wasn't the same as having their own child and never would be. The intensive re-programming they'd undergone now meant the distance between them had almost disappeared, and once again the love they'd had when they'd met and married, seemed to be re-emerging. Jack knew, as he'd always known, the deep seated passionate love he felt for Chloe had only been misplaced in recent years, and was relieved to see it reappearing with extra strength. He didn't regret his time with Zoe, who as a Gobi, had given him a new perspective on life and love. Zoe had reminded and shown him there was fun, laughter and tenderness in love-making, which had until recently been lost with Chloe. For that he was profoundly grateful and, although he knew his visit to Zoe had hurt Chloe deeply, with what she saw as the ultimate betrayal, she now understood his needs at a time when only another woman's arms would have sufficed.

Chloe stayed at home but it was a relief for Jack to be back in his work routine. It gave them both the space they needed, Chloe had time to settle in and organise their home, whilst at the same time work provided a distraction for Jack, although these days he found himself feeling constantly tired and drained. In the six weeks since they'd lost Jenny, physical activities were becoming an effort and it was nothing for him to doze off during the day. They'd both been warned to expect periods like this, as nature's way of helping the mind and body cope, and been advised not to be concerned by it. As it was still early days, and there weren't any other physical symptoms to concern him, it didn't send Jack scurrying off to the doctors, although it was beginning to become an embarrassment. He was just grateful those at work understood his situation.

Time would slowly allow them to adjust to their status as a childless couple and they could re-sculpt their lives together. After all there was nothing now to detract from their future life together and life could not throw any other tests for them to endure, or that's what they believed. If only that were the case.

~ ~ ~ ~ ~

Liam and Crawford got along famously and began meeting on a regular basis. As they were both based in the same building, although Liam travelled the country most of the time, they met for lunch as often as possible. Crawford even managed to seduce Liam into a passion for working-out, and together they'd spend many hours working-out in the gym. It wasn't long before their friendship evolved into spending passionate nights and weekends together, by themselves and together with Tanya, where a deep and intimate relationship began to flourish between them. One that was based on a firm foundation of friendship, but with a unique bond of support and passion too.

Liam was all too pleased to spend this time with Crawford and to fall under his expert guidance. Although Liam was only young, as a leader of the social groups he ran he found it a refreshing change to have someone take responsibility for him, even if it were only in the gym for a short time. He'd never liked the regime of exercise, but it was made far easier having someone to do it with, who cared what he looked like and gave him a true enjoyment of working-out, with the view of looking better than he already did.

The other thing Liam found surprising was that the intensity of his feelings for Tanya, although as strong, had become less urgent. To counteract this Tanya's feelings for him seemed to be strengthening, not just for him but for Crawford too. Liam, still with strong feelings for Tanya, also found himself beginning to have similar feelings for Crawford. It didn't create a puzzling conflict at all, but became a source of comfort and completeness for them all. It was as if Crawford was the balancing pin connecting them, and as a consequence there was a very definable ménage a trios developing between them. None of them noticed it happening and it was only one night when they were at a Forniclub Tanya happened to point out none of them seemed to have as many partners as they had done previously.

'In fact whilst we've got each other we don't really need anyone else. So why don't we do something about it?' Tanya had suggested.

'How do you mean 'do something about it?" Liam asked.

'Well Crawford here is coming to the end of his probationary period and you're coming to the end of your apprenticeship,' Tanya explained laying a delicate hand on each of the men's arms. 'So you'll be eligible for a government pad and Liam here will be eligible for an upgrade,' she explained, sweetly to them.

'So what does that mean in Tanya terms?' Crawford asked, in a teasing voice.

'Well why don't you combine your upgrades and get a place together. Let's face it, Liam's only here once or twice during the week and just comes home to an empty place. You two have developed a nice little bond between you so why not live together? You wouldn't have to commit yourselves and could still go out and have some fun by yourselves but wouldn't have the solitude either,' she continued to explain.

'And what about you?' Crawford asked, trying to hide a big grin. 'Where do you fit in to all this?'

'Well I've already got my place but...' She paused, looking coquettishly from under her long thick eyelashes. 'If I'm going to start up my business I could really do with reducing my costs and having you guys help.'

Liam and Crawford, who were now so much in tune with one another, looked at each other and grinned simultaneously.

'Does that mean we'd have all your stuff cluttering up our place? Liam asked, with a tragic look on his face.

'No, no not at all,' Tanya protested, totally unaware she was rising to the bait of their teasing.

'God can you imagine it Liam?' Crawford groaned with mock horror. 'All those uniforms and accessories. Some packed, some unpacked and more than likely some only half packed and we'd have to do the packing ourselves just to get them out of the way.'

'Yeah! And when she gets something new one or both of us is going to have to try it on and make sure it's to madam's satisfaction,' Liam chipped in.

'God!' said Crawford, clapping his hand to his forehead dramatically. 'We'd never get any sleep.'

'Do you want to sleep?' purred Tanya, caressing their naked thighs.

'Well occasionally would be nice,' Crawford told her with an exceptionally stern look on his face.

'Pity,' Tanya responded. 'I thought I could have kept the two of you entertained.

'Well as long as you let us sleep occasionally,' Liam joined in. 'Otherwise...' he gave a huge wink to Crawford, 'we'd never be able to service you.'

'What? What do you mean?' Tanya challenged, then all of a sudden realised they were winding her up. 'Oh you...' she said, slapping them both at the same time, realising she'd fallen hook line and sinker into their little game. 'Anyway what do you reckon? Should the three of us get a place together?'

'So it's the three of us now and not just Liam and me?' Crawford challenged, once again pretending to be stern.

'Yeah, well none of us want to settle down and anyway if we all had our own rooms we could just sleep with each other when we wanted.' Tanya told them.

'But what about all your stuff Tanya?' Crawford asked seriously now. 'I personally couldn't bear to be cluttered up all the time. What would you do with it?'

'Well if I moved in with you guys, then I can afford a small unit and work from there. I needn't have any of it in the flat, which would mean I could get away from work as well as you guys.'

'But could you afford to do that?' Liam interjected. 'After all this is a new business you're talking of setting up and we all know it'll take a while to get going.'

'I've got a better chance of it working if I move in with you guys,' Tanya told them, completely innocent to the fact she might be taking advantage of them. 'And it's been agreed I can work part-time until it gets going so I've got enough income to cover my costs, at the unit as well as the pad.'

'You've got it all worked out,' Crawford acknowledged, not sure how he felt about it. 'It could work but I'd want to think about it first and then talk about it properly before I did anything about it. What do you reckon Liam?'

'Out of the blue for me,' Liam told him. 'Like you said it's something to think about but worth considering,' he agreed. Then turning to Tanya he asked her quite bluntly. 'Whenever did you think all this up?'

'I didn't,' Tanya replied, very much on her mettle. 'It came into my head just now but if you think I cooked it up to get a cheap ride then forget it,' she told them both, embarrassed she'd even mentioned it.

'No, no,' Liam and Crawford both intoned together, reaching out to touch her reassuringly. 'It's worth thinking about,' Crawford told her.

'Yeah. Not a bad idea,' Liam conceded approvingly.

'Really?' Tanya asked hopefully, and together they sat and talked about the type of place they'd look for. It was the start of something far bigger than any of them had ever dreamt about.

~ ~ ~ ~ ~

By the middle of July, Jed's room had been stripped of his childhood and recreated to illustrate Jed as he saw himself today. The ceiling had a projected sky, which Jed could predetermine as cloudy or clear by programming in the weather conditions. He often watched the stormy sky whilst lying on his newly-acquired slumber-pit, as the miniaturised clouds rolled about in the room, as if they were miles above him in the sky. His parents had really splashed out investing in doing the entire room with Image Receptive Gel and buying a really good machine to run the images. Jed loved some of the settings, especially the beach and club scenes.

When Jed told Ben his parents were doing his room with Image Receptive Gel, Ben warned him his parents would block some of the best scenes, as they might not be regarded as suitable. He also suggested Jed should ask Fiona to create a block breaker for it and get her to programme it into a door contact. This would mean the image would automatically turn off his chosen images and revert to default, when the door was opened from the outside. Jed's default happened to be a beach scene, which he could add people to and decide what state of clothing they'd be in, which was something his parents weren't aware of. The door contact made their images disappear, reverting the room to a state of innocence. However, Jed often lay on his slumber-pit with naked women strolling round his room, every so often one stopping to wave. It really did Jed's ego a lot of good, even though he knew they weren't real flesh and blood.

Ben also managed to get hold of a load of other imagery too, which turned out to be a mixture of erotic, pornographic, gruesome or just downright evil images. Most of them Jed enjoyed but one, of street warfare where Jed was the target being hunted down, frightened him so much he had difficulty sleeping for the next few nights, it had haunted him so much. Ben finding this highly amusing, had called him a 'mummy's boy'. The smile was on the other side of his face though when Jed challenged him to spend just an hour in his room with it on. Ben didn't last the hour out before he was banging on the door demanding Jed to turn off the imagery. It really was incredibly realistic and not something to be taken lightly at all.

Fiona, without being asked, had also created a wristlet blocker for Jed's room. She warned him if he used it, when he didn't need to, it would increase the chances of alerting his parents to the fact a blocker existed. If he only used it when his parents were out, or for short periods when he wanted total privacy, then it should be ok. She also rigged it so that more than one person could have their wristlets blocked at the same time. An enormous risk for Jed, running it, and for Fiona who'd provided it, but what the heck… it was a hoot!

With a new room, Jed was no longer embarrassed to invite people over. With the constantly changing and programmable ambience, plus the existence of his own blocker, he was in his element. The first time he invited Ben round he almost swelled with pride at his new surroundings. Ben was awestruck and so impressed Jed actually confessed why he'd not invited him round for so many years. Ben, as Jed knew he would, laughed long and hard, imagining his friend's infantile room, but was quickly shut up when Jed pointed out how advanced his room was now, compared to Ben's.

Jed's bedroom being decorated had been quite a big event for the foursome, giving them all a new collective focus as a group, in addition to their skate boarding. Whilst Fiona had programmed the blockers and Ben produced additional software Jade, who was a very talented artist, had actually created a couple of sculptures and other items which now adorned Jed's room. The cleverest thing was Jade using some of the Image Receptive Gel to finish them with, which meant they took on the same imagery as the room's theme. Jed had been enthralled by these more than anything else. In fact, he reflected, both girls seemed to be incredibly talented and creative compared to him and Ben.

Jed felt quite a dullard when he listened to the girls talk about their creations, but when he'd finished his parent's garden, as promised, all that changed for him. He'd created quite a masterpiece and finished it off by persuading Jade to create a couple of small statues to put by the entrance to the gate. His parents, impressed and delighted with it, were astonished at Jed's dedication and the talent and foresight he'd used to create it. It was then Jed realised he too had talent, and was even more thrilled when his friends saw it for the first time and had openly admired it. In fact Jade and Fiona had gushed over it so much he'd been embarrassed, but was interested to hear they thought he should pursue garden design when he went off to camp. Jade, Jed knew, was going to be following creativity, Ben was plumping for sciences and Fiona was obviously going into the computing sector. Until that time though Jed had no idea what he could find to develop, but his newly-found gardening interest gave him an avenue to explore. He'd never considered it before and decided to discuss it with his father.

Jed and his dad were getting on better these days. Jed suspected it was because he was no longer a child, knowing his father didn't particularly like children. Whilst they weren't big pals there was a quiet acceptance between them now, which enabled them to talk about things without shouting. His dad spent more time with Jed at the skateboarding park too, coaching Jed and his friends. They'd actually managed to persuade him to get back on a skateboard one weekend and, despite his stiffened knee, he had shown he was still pretty good. Jed's mum had thought it hilarious, questioning what had happened to make her husband mellow so much in so short a time. The relationship between her two men seemed to have created a new peace at home, with Jed seeming to have mellowed and calmed down. It was only on rare occasions he came across as surly or mardy and although he still got involved with minor scams his ambitions of doing more risky ones seemed to have abated, not that his parents knew any of this. In general both he and his dad were happier people and far more approachable.

Jed and Fiona often went out on a foursome with Jade and Ben, mostly to the skate park. Both girls were now members of the Traditional Section club and Jade was proving to be a naturally talented skateboarder with great courage. Her expertise on the board was quickly becoming a match for Ben's speed and dexterity, although she still hadn't mastered the number of tricks he had, and she was becoming one of the club's star members, being primed with plenty of coaching for the display team. When this was initially announced there were great ructions between her and Ben, as it was a position Ben had coveted for a long time. However Jade, ever the diplomat, had pointed out that had she been a male she wouldn't have had a look in, as male members far outnumbered the female ones. Female team numbers still remained low, despite Jade's recent recruitment, and she reminded Ben she'd never even have tried the sport without his introduction and continual coaching and he should take the credit for her achievements. This, to a small extent, seemed to appease him.

Fiona still struggled with the sport but really enjoyed it and the people involved. She also loved the meal they enjoyed, guilt free, afterwards having expended an enormous amount of energy boarding. Jed, forever at her side, made an exemplary coach, always calm and supportive when she wasn't able to accomplish the task at hand, or if she fell off her board – which was frequent. She invariably left the park with bumps and bruises but the treatment, provided by the medics, certainly helped to keep damage to the minimum.

Fiona found the physical activity a real respite from the rest of things she was occupied with during those summer months. She spent considerable time with her uncle and his family going though the developmental needs for the Colorbs and how she'd present herself and invention to the NHS. Despite his earlier reluctance for Fiona to pursue a role as a government protégé, instead of university, he was certainly standing by her helping to prepare for the interviews ahead.

Fiona had gone to stay at her uncle's for a couple of weeks during the summer vacation and was delighted when the others joined her on the Norfolk farm for a long weekend. As poor as she was at skateboarding Fiona was a confident rider and it amused her highly to see her friends struggle with horsemanship, as she had with boarding. She'd laughed delightedly when Jed couldn't make his mount move, and although initially alarmed when Jade fell off found it highly amusing when Jade discovered she'd landed in a cow pat. Ben on the other hand was totally cack-handed, as inept on horseback as she'd originally been on a board. When their first session had ended the others, stiff and not as confident as before the ride, had readily agreed it wasn't necessarily a bad thing not being the best, as long as they were enjoying themselves. Ben even admitted he had a grudging admiration for Fiona's sticking ability, and then told her he wouldn't be mounting a horse again in a hurry, which he reiterated the following morning when he woke up stiff and bruised from the previous day. The horse riding experience had certainly changed the balance of the group and their respect for Fiona's doggedness enhanced.

It had been obvious to Fiona's aunt and uncle that Jed was smitten with her, but they couldn't understand why Fiona didn't feel the same. They were fascinated to hear she saw young men as a form of entertainment and company but her ambitions for the Colorbs and her own future still remained her first priority. It had led onto discussions of what it must have been like for previous generations, who'd been constantly blighted with the fear of getting pregnant and how it must have stifled their freedom. Fiona hadn't realised how lucky she was, having the freedom of sexual expression, which was openly accepted now pregnancy was no longer an issue with contraception being initiated at birth and removed as and when the time was right. The eradication of sexual diseases also gave a freedom they'd not had in her aunt's teens and with Fornipubs and Forniclubs now being run by the government sex was now recognised as a respectable form of recreation. Fiona reflecting on this, thought how much better it was these days, and then turned her thoughts to the new substance Ben had been offered.

It was the talk with her aunt which helped her decide she'd like to try it out and be ready to enjoy the experience she hoped it would give her. Once back home Fiona broached the subject of her relationship with Jed and, although he tried to hide it, Jed was mortified Fiona didn't feel the same way as he did. He'd admitted to his father, in one of their man-to-man talks, how much he thought of Fiona. His father had dismissed this, laughing and telling him not to get involved but play the field whilst he was young. Biting his tongue Jed had managed to refrain from telling his dad he'd been doing exactly that for the past couple of years, but knew his dad wouldn't have appreciated the information. Now he needed to find out exactly where he stood with Fiona.

To Jed's surprise Fiona wasn't committing herself to outlining exactly where they stood. Even more surprising she broached the subject of the sex-enhancing drug telling him she wanted to try it out.

'Why do you want to try it, Fiona? What difference do you think it'll make?' Jed challenged her. Fiona outlined the conversations she'd had with her aunt.

'I trust you, Ben and Jade to try this out with,' she replied. 'Who knows where I'll be in a year's time, five year's time or whenever? I might never be in a group of friends I trust like you three and if I am it'll probably be too late and I'll be married. We're young and there's no stigma attached to this anymore. I just want to try it out. Is that a crime?'

'You know this drug isn't legal and not certificated don't you? It's a risk Fi, physically and criminally. You know the consequences if we're caught don't you? So why get involved if you're likely to get caught?' Jed demanded, getting highly irritated.

'That's rich coming from you, but for a start I'd be taking responsibility for my actions and because I'd really like to find out what sex without inhibitions is like, Jed,' she told him sincerely. 'I'm sixteen and didn't lose my virginity until a short while ago, most of my friends lost theirs years ago, but it didn't happen like that with me. I was too busy working on the Colorbs,' she continued. 'And now? Well now I want to make up for lost time. What's wrong with that?' she asked in a voice that dared him to challenge her.

'Fiona,' he faltered. 'I thought you knew how I felt about you. I want it to be just me and you.'

Fiona shrugged his arm from her shoulder and jumped off the bed angrily, planting her feet firmly on the floor, she stuck her hands on her hips and told him, 'That's not what I want, Jed, especially when you're like this. You're a nice guy, fun to be with and I like the fact you're not totally straight and have lots of different interests. But that's it Jed, nothing more. I want fun in the next two years and when I go off to camp I want more fun. With lots of different people,' she added. 'And if that's not what you want to hear, or what you want, then I'm sorry but I don't want any more. Yes, sex with you is great, but it will be different with other lads too, and I want to have sex with a girl, and probably in a group which is why I want to take the drug and see how it makes me feel and I want to be with people I trust so I know they won't do anything I wouldn't want to. That's why I want us to be together but I'm not interested in getting serious. Just go and find another girlfriend Jed and have some fun – like you used to,' she finished angrily.

There then ensued an argument, so heated, it almost split them up. It was only through Jed virtually grovelling, and agreeing to talk to Ben, that stopped Fiona walking out.

A week in the life of a young man can see a lot of changes, so sometimes a month can seem like a lifetime. Since their row Fiona had stepped back from their relationship, seeing it as being far more casual than Jed was comfortable with, and she was now openly seeing other lads too. When he'd talked to Jade about it she'd told him how much Fiona felt she'd missed out on, with being an only child, and wanted to make up for lost time. As an only child himself Jed couldn't really understand this and his confusion was further confounded by Jade telling him how much he'd changed recently.

'How do you mean I've changed?' Jed asked guardedly. 'In what way?' He'd listened, partly mortified as Jade told him how serious he was these days and how conscientious he'd become about doing things at home.

'Is that such a bad thing?' Jed had challenged defensively.

'Not at all Jed, but where's the old you gone? You know, the one Fiona fell for? It's not long since you were a 'Jack the lad' and up to all sorts of things. Now you're so serious and seem to spend more time with your dad than with us. Especially with Ben, you always used to be together,' she added. 'If you want to keep Fiona interested just lighten up a bit, give her some of the fun she wants, instead of trying to restrict her. It's like you want to pin her down, but she's had enough restriction. What she wants is fun and if you can't provide it she'll go and find it elsewhere,' Jade warned.

Jed knew some of this applied to him but it took all his inner strength not to retaliate and explain how much spending time with his dad meant to him. He knew he'd changed, but he didn't see it as all bad. The atmosphere at home was so much better now, making life much more pleasant. And sure, he was more serious, but he'd done the chasing round and casual sex thing. He wanted more now and had thought that's what Fiona had wanted too. He realised he was totally wrong there.

'Personally, Jed,' Jade told him shyly, 'I for one like the new you. I know it's important to spend more time with your dad and I think it's great he's getting more involved, but don't change just to hang on to Fiona because I know it won't work,' she told him.

'It must be hard not having brothers and sisters,' she said, thinking out loud. 'But then my situation's so different. I know that I'm so much luckier than most 'cos I've always had my mum at home and it's made a difference to us all as a family.' Sensing Jed's mood, and without thinking, she put an arm round his shoulders and gave him a chaste kiss.

*It must be as hard for Jed as it is for Fiona,* she thought, *which is probably why Jed tries to be such a wide boy.*

Jed turned to look at her and was surprised to see her face suffused with a deep red blush. She quickly moved away from him and was now sitting on her hands swinging her feet, but momentarily catching his gaze her blush deepened. Jumping up energetically she suggested, a bit too brightly, 'Hey how about we go for a few circuits round the skate park?'

Recognising an awkward moment handled brilliantly, Jed jumped up enthusiastically and challenged Jade to a 'race you there' and like a couple of kids they sprinted off towards the park laughing as they went. Jade, being the sportier of the two, easily reached the park before Jed.

171

'Well there's a turn up for the books,' Jed joked a couple of hours later, Jade having coached him. 'A few months ago you'd never been on a board and now here you are showing the old hands how to do things.' Jade accepted the compliment graciously and suggested they ended with a double circuit race, which she allowed Jed to win.

Their conversation had set Jed thinking and walking home by himself Jed found his thoughts even more confused.

*Jade is just so easy and uncomplicated to be with,* Jed decided, *but does she fancy me or is she just trying to make me feel better about me and Fiona?* For the rest of the short journey home he pondered on those thoughts. He really liked Jade and could see why she and Fiona got on so well. Neither of them were at all boastful of their talents, which were refreshing compared to the competitive edge that existed between him and Ben and, for that matter, most of the lads he knew.

Later in the evening, Ben came round to talk to Jed about the Sexulent Grains they'd been offered a few months before.

'He finally got the clearance on them but has promised I can have some from the last batch before the licence kicks in. I know Jade and Fiona are up for it so are you mate?' he asked Jed lewdly. "Cos I reckon we can get the girls to be pretty sweet with each other. What says you?' Typical of lads their age they spent the next hour or so speculating on what they could get the girls to do together. Their imaginative minds were further inflamed by Ben selecting a 'free for all' orgy onto the Imager. As the figures round the walls cavorted with abandon, so did the boys' imaginations.

Then out of the blue Ben told Jed nonchalantly, 'Reckon Jade's got a spot of the hots for you mate,' and gave Jed an almighty dig in the ribs, making him yell out loud.

'Would it bother you if she did?' asked Jed, partly flattered but also a little concerned as to how Ben might really feel.

'If she wants to screw you, mate,' Ben replied crudely, 'it just leaves the way free for me. I quite fancy having a crack at Fiona if you've no objections. I reckon with those grains she could be a right little goer, and I know she'd be up for it. Then you could have a crack at Jade and give her a bloody good fucking. We could swap, what do you reckon?'

Jed cringed at the crude and callous manner in which Ben spoke about the two girls, but at the same time wasn't adverse to giving it some thought or even a go. All the same it wasn't easy for him to think of Ben and Fiona together, but he needed to show Fiona he was happy for this to happen. Maybe it was his chance to win her round a bit.

'September mate, that's when we can get the grains so all we've got to do now is work out where we can go to block our wristlets for a few hours.'

*September,* Jed thought. *I think I know just the person to sort this out and the place. It'll also show Fiona I'm as happy for her to be as free as she wants.*

From then on Jed was on a campaign to make it a night to remember, unaware it was to be a night he'd never forget.

~ ~ ~ ~ ~

Daryl and Sonia met up again a few weeks later. The jeans Daryl had bought previously were now beginning to feel uncomfortably tight and when he fidgeted with them Sonia had jokingly patted his stomach declaring his mother must be feeding him too well. Daryl looked down at his belly with dismay, thinking Sonia's remark was a criticism, and, in defence, added he kept getting indigestion and if he didn't know better would've suspected she was trying to poison him. As soon as he'd muttered the words he regretted them immediately, seeing Sonia's face, and quickly laughed to show he was joking. Thankfully Sonia had laughed with him and the momentary awkwardness had quickly passed, with Sonia reassuring him the extra weight suited him, and commented on how nice it must be to have proper food again instead of food pearls.

Daryl nodded agreement to this then followed it up with, 'Me Mam's a lot better now. She's not watching soaps all the time and she's actually talking to me. She's still got an evil tongue but if she goes off on one, all I have to do is give her a look and she purses her lips and says nowt more. I reckon you were right about her being lonely and still missing me dad. She won't tell me the full story of how he died but I know she knows more than she's letting on 'cos I've heard the rumours.'

'What sort of rumours?' Sonia asked, and Daryl reiterated all he'd heard about the gang bang and how the eight, who'd reputedly been involved, were now all dead. Sonia shuddered at the story, a chill running through her blood at the thought of such a horrendous act being committed on another human being. Although she wanted to ask Daryl if he thought his dad had done it she didn't, for fear of what his answer might be.

'Do you have time to stay so I can treat you to supper or do you have to get off?' Daryl asked tentatively. He'd had to pluck up a lot of courage to ask for fear of being turned down. Much to his delight Sonia had agreed and together they walked out to their cars to store their pool cues. Sonia had admired Daryl's car, a veteran Subaru from the nineties, which was his current pride and joy. Walking to the restaurant, which boasted the best roasts in town, Daryl regaled her with all the attributes of his wonderful automobile and the love of his ever changing old cars.

The evening progressed surprisingly well and Sonia, for the first time, talked of herself and the sadness of when her husband and daughter had been killed in a car accident. Although it had happened many years before the pain was clearly evident in her eyes and Daryl hugged her, somewhat clumsily. He'd seen another person's pain, and realised the hug he'd given in sympathy made him feel good too. He was on cloud nine and whilst Sonia wasn't the prettiest woman on earth, she wanted to be with him, as he wanted to be with her. Sitting in the pub later Daryl even plucked up courage to put his arm round Sonia, relieved she didn't shrug him off.

*Maybe if we take things slowly we could become a couple*, Daryl fantasised, and with his arm protectively round Sonia's shoulders he felt as though they were taking solace from each other.

Daryl was reluctant to say goodnight at the end of the evening, although another part of him was relieved he wouldn't have to go to the next stage of the relationship just yet. Sonia, sensing his reluctance, suggested they meet again and spend more time together. Daryl eagerly nodded his agreement, afraid to ask exactly what she meant, and once again found himself driving home on a high, trying to imagine just what was in store for him with Sonia.

During the week, Daryl had rung Sonia and they'd agreed to book into the hotel, in separate rooms. Getting up on the Saturday Daryl had scrubbed and washed himself scrupulously, the ablutions giving him comfort. Living a hundred and fifty miles apart had great disadvantages in the courting stakes, Daryl could see, but at least this way they could see how their time together panned out and neither would feel obliged to sleep with the other. The thought of sleeping or having sex with Sonia quite bothered Daryl. At thirty-four he'd never slept with a woman. In fact, apart from the nightclub disaster, he'd never kissed a woman romantically.

*How will I know what to do or how to behave? What if I make a fool of meself?* he worried and wondered just what Sonia would expect of him and when.

Having arrived early and booked into the hotel, Daryl waited for Sonia. He was so nervous his stomach was turning somersaults at record speed. Added to this he kept getting a griping pain round his middle, even though he'd not eaten yet. His recent stomach problems concerned him and he worried they may be something serious. Yet despite his concerns he knew he couldn't go and see a doctor as his DNA would be passed on to the authorities, which couldn't be allowed to happen. As his stomach continued to churn the realisation hit him that he'd never be able to see a doctor again, and prayed he'd never need to.

*Mam's tried to kill me with blood poisoning once,* he thought. *She better not be trying the same with her food 'cos it's since she's been cooking for me me stomachs been playing up,* he calculated. *I'll just have to be careful with what I eat,* he told himself, *and keep her under control. I know she ain't happy with the way things are, now I'm in charge, but I'm damned if I'll let things go back to how they were and let her take me for the ride, like she's done since I started work.*

Sonia arrived just before midday and having found a stylish bar they shared a leisurely lunch. Then, after Daryl had suggested he could do with some new clothes, they'd wandered companionably round town until they were laden with parcels, which included everything from shoes to underwear. Daryl had never spent as much on himself before and had even insisted on buying a bag he'd seen Sonia admiring, for all her hard work. Making their way back to the hotel Daryl had never been happier in his life, evident from his glowing face and not just from the autumnal air. Daryl was one very happy man.

It was later when things started to go wrong. They'd played a few games of pool, Daryl managing to keep everything in perspective, and they shared a pleasant evening meal. Even the time they spent in the bar, dissecting their pool shots, had been ok. It was afterwards, when it was time to part ways for the night, things began to get sticky.

When they'd arrived back upstairs, Daryl had pulled Sonia clumsily into his arms. Although Sonia hadn't resisted she'd been so reluctant, even Daryl couldn't ignore it. He smarted against what he saw, as her rejection.

'Don't rush me,' she pleaded, with beseeching eyes. 'Let's just take our time shall we?' Daryl, not knowing how to respond had two options as far as he could see. He could either go off in a huff or take her in his arms and try and kiss her. He chose the former and muttered something about supper and shopping and stomped off to his room leaving Sonia, at a loss, wondering what to do.

For some inexplicable reason, Sonia was drawn to Daryl, despite logic and an inner voice telling her she was being a fool. She couldn't bear the thought of Daryl going off feeling bad about her, or even himself, so after a few minutes indecision followed him along the hallway and stood outside his door, steeling herself to knock.

*I've been here before*, she told herself, and at the same time wondered why she was here at all.

Answering his door with a sullen look, Daryl stood back to let Sonia in. It was awkward, neither of them knowing how to approach the other.

It was after an hour of reasoning, pleading, explanations and a whole load of other emotions having been examined, explained and put away, that they'd ended up in bed together. Who was most surprised neither knew, but they lay side-by-side as if in a double coffin. Daryl had been mortified, having to get undressed in front of Sonia, he was so ashamed of his body he'd insisted on turning out the light, leaving only the glow of the rooms ethereal blue lighting. Now, undressed, he lay unyielding next to a plump, semi clad Sonia. He'd no idea what to do or how to make the next move. For the umpteenth time, both he and Sonia silently regretted being there, not knowing how to go about remedying the situation without causing massive insult and untold damage to the other.

Feeling confused, about Daryl's modesty, Sonia assumed Daryl had either never had a relationship before or there was some physical impairment he was reluctant for her to see. She even wondered if he was still a virgin and if so, and they didn't actually consummate the relationship, she hoped they'd still be able to spend the night together.

Daryl was in a quandary about how to progress with Sonia and even if he wanted anything to happen. He still wasn't sure if he found her attractive or not but he did feel safe with her and enjoyed her company. He didn't even mind now when she beat him at pool, so he must find her attractive, he surmised. He lay straight and regimentally rigid, his arms tight by his side, as if a sentry on duty. He'd no idea what to do and daren't move, praying he'd get an erection and wouldn't let himself down.

*What will I do if I don't?* he panicked and broke into a light sweat. *What if I can't do it and make a fool of himself?* Mentally and physically he shuddered, prompting Sonia to invite him into her arms for a cuddle. He moved over into her embrace and lay stiff and awkward, not knowing what to do with his hands and arms and wondering what she looked like naked. He'd seen pictures of naked women, wantonly showing off all they had to offer, but never seen a woman in the flesh naked before. He turned his head to see, but it was too dark, so his mind began to wonder what she'd feel like, but before touching her he touched himself, relieved to feel himself growing hard.

In amongst all these jumbled thoughts, one jumped out ahead of everything else. *Sonia's a lonely person just like me*, he thought. *She's sure to jump at the chance of living with a successful man and a good income like me.* The thoughts of being with Sonia and moving out of his uncaring house flitted through his mind giving him confidence. Finally he reached over and touched her hair.

'You can put your arm round me Daryl and kiss me if you want,' Sonia offered quietly. Daryl tentatively put his arm beneath her shoulders, still not relaxing. Sonia snuggled into him and laid her arm across his chest letting her fingers caress his arm. Daryl found it quite pleasant, but still didn't know how to respond or how to go about kissing her. Thankfully Sonia removed this worry by leaning over and kissing him gently. He responded greedily, and none too gently, making Sonia draw away telling him there was no need to rush and neither of them needed to do anything they weren't comfortable with.

'Can I touch you Sonia?' Daryl asked bluntly, turning towards her and clumsily grabbing her breast and squeezing tightly.

'Ouch, Daryl be careful,' Sonia protested, mildly taking hold of his hand to draw it away from her slightly. 'It's much nicer if you caress me, rather than pummel me,' she told him gently, relaxing her grip on his hand. Daryl tentatively kneaded her breast, as if testing a piece of dough. He liked its soft pliant feel and shifting round took his other hand from beneath her and none too graciously clasped hold of the other breast in his enormous hand. He kneaded away, lost in the sensation of the warm flesh and without thought pushed his face into Sonia's and pressed his straight lined lips hard against hers.

Sonia, shocked at the force of the kiss, pulled her head down into the pillow trying to turn her head to breathe. Surprised that she didn't seem to be enjoying his kiss, Daryl felt himself becoming annoyed and without thinking accused her of leading him on and not wanting to kiss him. Sonia, trying to make light of a situation, laughed softly and told him she'd rather kiss him like this. Taking hold of his head she held his face slightly away from her and kissed his lips gently, teasing this mouth with the tip of her tongue and telling him to relax. Daryl tried to relax, but could feel himself harden and a desperate need to thrust himself into her. The thoughts were overtaking his logical thinking and he began pawing relentlessly at her breasts, tugging hard at the flimsy fabric so he could feel her naked flesh.

'Daryl, Daryl wait. Slow down,' Sonia instructed him, concerned with the way things were going. Sitting up she took off her bra hoping the action would slow him down, but demonstrate to Daryl she was willing. Her heavy pale breasts hung low without any support and now, accustomed to the dark, Daryl wasn't sure whether he liked what he saw. He reached out and lifted the heavy breast, letting its weight rest in his hand. Pushing it upwards he caught hold of the nipple and without thinking pinched it hard, making Sonia cry out.

He looked at her and apologised then said, 'I've never seen a naked woman before. Well not in the flesh,' he explained hesitantly, kicking himself for having said anything at all. 'I don't want to hurt you but can I touch you?' he asked with an expression on his face that Sonia couldn't quite work out.

Sonia lay back submitting to his scrutiny, hoping he wouldn't continue to be as ham-fisted as before, and ready to stop him if he was. Daryl sat looking at her for what seemed like an eternity, a range of expressions passing over his face as he looked at the naked orbs then lowered the sheets to stare at the dark thatch of hair at the top of her plump thighs.

*It don't matter if she's no centrefold*, he told himself, *this is a real woman in the flesh and all his*. Daryl looked down at his own belly, now so fat it hid his semi erect penis from his view. He was unaware of what Sonia was doing and was shocked when she reached out and touched him. He was so stunned his partial erection immediately disappeared and he knocked her hand roughly from him.

'Don't touch me,' he snapped, and from that moment on Sonia knew with certainty the night wasn't going to be a success.

Daryl had been mortified when Sonia had touched him and he'd become flaccid. No matter what he did or how he touched himself, he could not raise his poor excuse of manhood to perform. All his worries and nightmares of being with a woman had come to the fore and yet Sonia lay there shushing him and reassuring him everything would be alright. Which he knew it wasn't and his reaction, which had seemed so unnatural to Sonia, rang warning bells again in her mind. Daryl didn't have to ask twice when he asked her to leave. Sonia did so, willingly and shaken.

Sonia was not behaving rationally, as her mind was in conflict. The logical part of her thought processes told her to walk away, whilst the irrational part was telling her to stay and she'd make a difference. Since losing her family there was a big part of Sonia not being addressed, a huge void with a cache of untapped love and the need to be needed. She thought of her loss, knowing nothing could ever replace her loved and lost ones, but knowing she needed someone in her life who'd make a difference. Daryl seemed so sad and she thought long and hard of how she'd describe him, and the only word she could come up with was 'damaged', but she was reluctant to even think the word out loud, let alone say it. She knew all about his mother, but had her treatment of him been enough to undermine his confidence to this level? She'd no idea but felt as if there was a menace of violence not far beneath the surface, which sometimes made her feel exposed and vulnerable. This was what her rational brain was telling her to avoid, whilst the illogical side was telling her she could heal it and make a difference to his life. Whatever, she'd have to be careful, as she didn't want to be the catalyst to unleash whatever might lay beneath the surface.

Daryl was incensed, how he'd kept his cool he'd no idea.

*She's totally humiliated me, the bitch. How could she have done that to me? I should've known not to trust the bitch, the cheating cow,* he thought viciously. *Having to lie there pretending to be calm when I was bloody seething. Having to hide how I feel so's she wouldn't know how much she'd degraded me. I can't believe I was stupid enough to trust her, and yet she was good company and was kind to me,* he mused irrationally. *Well kind enough to set me up for a fall and make a fool of me, the bitch.*

As the thoughts ran through his mind, the more they raged, the more confused and angry he became. His stomach was also doing somersaults and he desperately wanted something to eat, which would hopefully settle his churning belly. Finally he could stand lying there no longer and got out of bed to get his sardines and jam. Seeking solace within its glistening sticky mass he stuffed the odd combination into his mouth as quickly as he could. Within minutes he was regretting it, his indigestion, which seemed to plague him constantly these days, was taking hold with a vengeance. He prowled up and down the room burping loudly and doing his utmost to appease his stomach, which was turning somersaults ten to the dozen.

As he paced his anger became virulent and his confusion more extreme. He'd no more idea what to do now than he had last night, but he did know he didn't want to lose the friendship and having a girlfriend quite appealed too. He was sure too he'd lose Patrick's friendship if he and Sonia fell out, and yet, no matter how much he thought, solutions continued to evade him.

By five in the morning, his humiliation and stomach had settled enough to allow him some sleep. The only decision he'd made was to go down to have breakfast with Sonia as arranged and take it from there. With those final thoughts in mind he fell into an unsettled and uncomfortable sleep, his stomach still playing up.

~ ~ ~ ~ ~

# Third Trimester

## September – November 2032

Dogmatically Melanie and her team continued to work. Each day more information was gleaned and used to solve a variety of outstanding crimes, but not the one they were looking to crack most of all. The Investigations team were carefully trawling through the casework and from their investigations several similarities were identified, not noted before, and slowly they were beginning to build a picture of their perpetrator. What they really needed was for him to make a mistake, which they knew wasn't likely, as each attack became more vicious than the last. They needed to apprehend him, fast.

For the Motor Team it was a slightly different matter. They'd downloaded the registration numbers of over one million cars from the six areas, but none of the cars listed had been in all of the areas, which indicated the rapist had probably changed his car since he'd started his campaign of attacks. It was a long laborious task and if they'd been looking to do a 'quickie' on the case, Melanie would have suggested tracing only the rapist's fingerprints matching any vehicle purchase. However, due to the adverse attention the Crimedical Sector was receiving, and the chance he could have an older car, Melanie was on a crusade and insisted each car, whose owner wasn't DNA registered, should be fully investigated enabling them to bring the Government DNA Database up-to-date and solve a substantial number of crimes, be they minor ones.

The team started working their way through the different car schemes. Where non-DNAers were found the details were passed onto the DNA team who instigated arrests and DNA sampling. These were then cross-referenced with the National Crime Register solving several crimes, the number of prosecutions soaring and unsolved crime figures dropping rapidly, even if many of them were only minor misdemeanours.

The first tranche of vehicles they investigated were those manufactured since 2023, where all cars were iris and fingerprint activated and the transaction could only be sanctioned if the purchaser's details were on the Government DNA Database. Although the scheme was reputedly impossible to cheat, they'd still checked the records and found a number of anomalies. Consequently they'd apprehended both the dealers and purchaser in each case, unearthed several serious criminals, but unfortunately not found their rapist.

Scrutinising cars registered between 2010-2023, was a far more arduous task, as car buyers didn't need to produce finger and iris imprints to act as 'keys' for their cars, so the details weren't automatically registered with their vehicles. There were three times as many cars in this section, than in the post 2023 category, and a staggering number of owners who didn't have their DNA registered. It was going to take much longer and far more people to investigate these numbers than Melanie wanted. This tranche of cars had been manufactured with hidden 'detection chips', which meant each time it passed a Vehicle Detection Post, its details were registered on the Vehicle Location programme and held on file for a minimum of five years. The chips also imposed speed limits on the car, by activating a high-pitched alarm, which was only de-activated by slowing down to the prescribed limit. The scheme had caused an enormous uproar when first launched but had reduced speed related accidents drastically.

It wasn't long before the team realised their attacker's car had been produced before 2010. This in itself wasn't a problem but meant an incredible amount of manual cross-referencing. This batch of vehicles had been manufactured pre-hidden chip days, and the Vehicle Detection Posts recorded the numbers as images, rather than data. This huge workload wasn't helped by the fact they were convinced their attacker had changed his car at least once since starting his wave of crime. Whilst a setback like this would normally have depleted morale, especially if they didn't identify their attacker, the escalation of their salaries, as they solved a number of other crimes, kept morale and determination at a premium.

Whilst this was going on, the DNA team were launching a major coup in organising arrests for non-DNAers. With it being a criminal offence, not to have DNA registered, any car owner identified as not being registered was arrested and kept in custody until their samples were analysed and run against outstanding crimes. It was almost like sweeping the country to ensure they found their rapist, but in reality was identifying far more criminals than they'd ever imagined possible and updating the Government DNA Database at the same time.

With the investigation workload being so extreme, due to the additional elements Melanie had incorporated, the energy levels of the team were at risk of becoming depleted. A lot of the workload incorporated extensive admin, and other elements demanded traditional policing methods, so Melanie quickly brought in a number of other personnel to help with the task at hand. Within weeks there was a new back-up team of cadets and retired officers brought in to assist with the routine work. In addition she recruited Jerome Hardy, a fellow officer who'd just returned to work after a horrendous climbing accident, to oversee the additional officers. None of her own officers were interested in the role, and besides, were too valuable for Melanie to release just to supervise extra staff. Within days Jerome had them all licked into shape and began the rotation of their roles, to keep the work interesting and maximise on talents as and when they were revealed. It made a huge difference to the morale of everyone involved, including Melanie.

~ ~ ~ ~ ~

Although Sonia and Daryl were still in touch a month after their visit to the hotel, there was a distance between them neither seemed able to breach. The distance, irrationally, seemed to make Daryl's negative emotions fester to such an extent he couldn't contain them.

*The only way I can even things out,* he thought, *is to teach some-begging-for it bitch a lesson.* Finally one night, no longer able to cope with his rage, he threw a few items into the boot of his car and set off to find his next floozy.

He drove some seventy odd miles to where he'd already done a recce, and selected a well-used thoroughfare, about half a mile from where he planned to park, the route taking him through a series of different terrains. His chances of avoiding detection were easier with a variety of different footways, making it harder for the Path Tracker to follow his route, especially if there was water to walk through. Unusually there'd been quite a bit of rain in the past few days and the area had plenty of deep puddles and would hamper the Path Tracker nicely.

Having parked in a busy street and changed into dark clothes, putting his jacket on lighter side out, Daryl set off towards the parkland. The air had a cold, damp snap to it and he noticed the trees were beginning to shed their leaves in the cooling month of October. Whilst leaves could hamper his progress, they were also an ally and he'd make sure to kick plenty about on his way back, to confuse the Path Tracker further.

En route to his lair he noted different things he could use to break his step on the way home. Besides the leaves and puddles he'd also brought new plastic slipovers, planning to stand in a puddle and put them on over his shoes after his tryst. Their bulk and shape would make it almost impossible for them to follow his path once they were on. It was these devious methods and precautions which had helped him stay a free man to date.

Arriving at his destination Daryl sauntered across the park and exited into the street passing a middle-aged man out walking his dog, who'd see him leaving the park rather than entering. As was customary Daryl returned the man's greeting and walked away from the park and into an adjoining street, which doubled back to a wooded area in the park. Before re-entering the park he took his jacket off, turned it inside out and put it on black side out. Apart from his keys, handkerchief and balaclava he carried nothing in his pockets, for fear of leaving a vital clue to his identity. As he changed his jacket round he felt a gripping pain shoot round his stomach, and cursed not having had anything to eat. Not eating always seemed to make the churning and cramping pains worse, but fortunately, this one wasn't bad enough to double him over. Waiting for it to pass he pulled out his handkerchief, mopped his brow and blew his nose as quietly as possible, before stuffing the snotty article back in his pocket.

With balaclava in hand, he made his way silently through the trees, watching the man and dog circuit the park. Any description he gave would depict Daryl as wearing a light-coloured jacket, and wouldn't be connected with the man in black, as the girl she was about to entertain would describe him. Silently watching for suitable prey who used this route, knowing several barmaids did, he waited silently as four women, two walking together and two singly, crossed his path, none spotting his lair. When he'd staked this spot out, there'd been eleven women who'd walked across the park an hour after the pubs closed, which had been the deciding factor for choosing this spot. Taking a calculated risk, he'd decided to target the eleventh tonight, hoping there would be eleven but not a twelfth. Getting impatient he considered attacking the ninth, but could hear the footsteps of the tenth before she'd even entered the park.

As the tenth woman made her way across the park, Daryl made his way to a small clearing, where he planned to make the grab. He had clear vision to both ends of the park and in addition an excellent escape route should anyone come before he'd finished. He rubbed his groin in anticipation mentally licking his lips, relieved to find himself growing hard. Moving along the track he found his balance compromised and cursed his Mam and her cooking for his weight gain. Finally in position, he heard his chosen woman's footsteps, and pulled his thickly padded balaclava well into place.

The woman walked nonchalantly along the path, not at all concerned about being out alone in the dark, since crime had become almost non-existent. Her high-heels rang out a jaunty rhythm as she made her way home, happy after her shift in the Fornipub. Without sound or warning she was suddenly grabbed from behind, the arm round her throat dragging her backwards into the bushes. Something was forced into her mouth, stifling the scream automatically rising from her throat. As she was dragged her feet valiantly tried to match the momentum in a vain bid to keep her balance. Suddenly her fear and confusion were abruptly ended, by an almighty blow to her head. After that, and for the next few minutes, there was nothing. No light, no sound, no feeling, no fear – and no chance of fighting off the attacker in her unconscious state.

Daryl dragged the woman into the darkness away from the path. She'd not had a chance to make a sound and no one else had entered the park. All the black feelings, which had festered throughout his adult years, seemed to come to the fore. He was going to pour the lot of them into this slut in front of him. He sneered now he had another slapper laid at his feet. Well he'd teach her what a real man was about, and show her good and proper.

The woman remained unconscious, although Daryl saw it as submissiveness, the slut. Making sure his snot soaked handkerchief was shoved well into her mouth, he ripped open her coat, the buttons flying off to land soundlessly in the surrounding grass. He ripped apart her flimsy blouse, which tore like tissue paper, and grabbing hold of her bra his long fingernails gouged the pale delicate skin, the strength of the movement momentarily lifting her upper body from the ground. He grabbed roughly at the small pale breasts, squeezing hard and pinching the nipples viciously, letting one of his fingernails slice into the fragile skin.

The moon was high and full enough to give sufficient light to his lair, enabling him to see what he was doing as he denuded the woman. Taking hold of her feet, and wrapping her legs round his waist, he dragged the unconscious body away from the path, inwardly laughing at how easy she was going to be to service. In a more sheltered place he unceremoniously dumped her on the ground and reaching down, tore the thin nylon tights and pants, exposing the woman. He chuckled aloud at how easy this tart was, quickly unfastened his trousers and released his manhood. Expecting it to be rampantly hard and up for it he momentarily froze when he found his penis only semi-erect. Quickly pumping his hand up and down it, he was dismayed to find it wasn't stiffening, but decided to ram it into the woman anyway. Just at that moment she began to stir and angered he hit out at her again, hoping the action would stir him into hardness. The strike was so violent the woman's head snapped back, and once again she lay motionless on the ground. Kneeling between her semi-naked thighs, he thrust himself into her groin ramming hard against her, but was unable to penetrate her with his flaccid member. He thrust again, and all that happened was his dick folded softly to his own body. He took hold of it again pumping it frantically, roughly pummelling the woman's breast, his fingers digging into the flesh and drawing blood. Nothing stirred, neither the woman or his manhood.

For a split second the world seemed to stand still. Then in a nanosecond he saw red, and all the resentment and humiliations he'd endured over the years came to the fore. Raising him arm high he drove his fist down into the woman's groin. Again and again he punched and thumped the woman until blood ran freely between her legs. He tried to thrust himself into the woman again, but without success. He hammered his fists onto the woman's stomach, banging forcefully, as he'd thumped his desk in temper as a frustrated child. Finally he rammed his fist between the woman's thighs, forcing it into her body. Pummelling his forearm like a piston he drove it deep into the now horrendously damaged depths of the woman's body. By now he was heaving noisy sobs of rage, and it suddenly came to him he was exposing himself to being heard and found. Mentally he pulled himself together staggering to his feet and fastening his trousers. Quickly checking the area, to make sure no one was about, he was just about to leave when he stopped short, and looked at the woman lying unconscious on the ground, the tart.

'You fucking bitch,' he raged silently, kicking her full in the face. 'You fucking whoring bitch. You shitty excuse of a woman.' With each insult he aimed vicious kicks at her body and head. If he'd been wearing his normal shoes the woman would not have survived this onslaught. As it was she hung on to life by a mere thread, her substance for life ebbing away, as the blood oozed from her body.

Finally satisfied she'd learnt her lesson, Daryl turned his back on the scene and stormed out of the empty park. The night was silent, with the exception of a resident owl, which helped restore Daryl's rational thinking. Realising he needed to be extra careful to avoid being caught, he looked about to make sure no one else was around. As he willed his breathing to slow he then looked down at himself, and to his horror saw the dirty bitch had left him covered in blood. It was on his hands and shoes as well as his jacket. Stooping to rinse his hands in a nearby puddle he carefully took his jacket off and turned it inside out, managing to do it without staining it with more blood. One problem solved. He shoved the balaclava into his pocket and thrust his hands in too, before setting off to leave the park at what he believed was a leisurely pace. Stopping a short way past the park gates, he stood in a deep puddle and pulled on his overshoes. Then checking to see no one was about, he climbed onto the drystone wall and made his way precariously along its length, cursing his mother silently for his cumbersome body.

*Just a few more feet and I'll be in fallen leaves and can walk on those and kick them about. That'll confuse 'em,* he told himself. Then, as he made his way back to the car, calling on every reserve he had to keep calm, he created as many footfall diversions as possible, and was relieved not to meet or hear another soul until he turned onto the busy road where his car was parked.

Reaching the main road and walking past a shop window, he was relieved to catch a glimpse of his reflection and see he looked quite normal. Passing a couple of people he nodded and grunted good evening trying to make his voice sound as normal as possible, despite his heart beating wildly and his stomach churning frantically. It seemed an eternity before he was back at his car and if it hadn't been parked in such a public area, he'd have taken his trousers off to avoid getting blood on the seats. As it was he had no choice but to get in. promising himself he'd replace the seat covers when he got back, just in case his car was ever checked.

Two hours later, arriving back in Armley, he put his car in the garage, removed the covers and wiped over any areas he could have left bloodstains on. Locking the garage after him, he walked the short distance back home and, entering a false alibi into the door security, provided himself with the additional two hours he'd calculated he needed for cover. Checking his Mam was ensconced in her soaps, which thankfully she was, he made his way upstairs stripped off his clothes and put them in a laundry processor. As he made his way to the cleansing room, he was horrified to see he was covered in the bitch's blood.

*The dirty fucking bitch of a slut,* he raged inwardly, scrubbing at his skin angrily. *The tart,* he screamed silently, and burst into noisy tears. *She made me look like a fucking idiot and it was all the fault of that evil cow downstairs,* he thought, feeling mightily sorry for himself. Those irrational thoughts stayed with him whilst he dried himself and, helping himself to his late night snack, the thoughts continued to bombard him, as he reassured himself over and over again it was the woman's fault and not his. *She'd looked at him, the bitch. She'd asked for it,* he told himself, and finally fell into a sleep steeped in nightmares.

~ ~ ~ ~ ~

Life once again began to settle into a comfortable routine for Jack and Chloe, who were now both back at work. With continued counselling and reinforced programming, past traumas continued to recede and their existence as a couple seemed to be regaining its original shape. Together they redecorated the house, spending several happy hours shopping for bits and pieces to make the house seem more like theirs. They weren't exempt from spirited arguments, but unlike past years once again enjoyed the making-up afterwards, which helped strengthen their rediscovered feelings for one another.

They'd been truly welcomed onto the estate, with a party which everyone attended, giving them an opportunity to meet all their new neighbours, young and old. Most of the children, or those who were old enough, had drawn pictures or made cards for them, which had been the start of an ever-changing children's gallery in Jack and Chloe's house. As a consequence, it caused further amusement when it progressed from being a children's playroom and gallery to one for the adults, when Jack added 'toys' for the big boys. It wasn't long before their house became a focal meeting point, and the already busy social life on the estate became more prolific. The highlight of the week was Friday when on alternate weeks, either the men or women met at Jack and Chloe's whilst their other halves had their social in someone else's house. Neither Jack nor Chloe could have dreamt they'd find this sort of peace and happiness in their lives again, especially as they were childless.

As the weeks passed by they began to look at their own lives and to revisit old loves and passions they'd not addressed in the past few years. They spent long hours at the weekends walking the countryside or visiting museums in the area and began planning weekends away, to explore further afield. They even considered getting a puppy and, after numerous and long discussions, decided to research the different breeds, finally deciding on a bearded collie. With only a handful of breeders, they began to plan their mission to find the right pup for them.

When they announced their news, the neighbouring children were delighted to be getting a new pet on the estate, as there were very few. The estate's two eldest children, at just five and six years old, plagued Jack and Chloe until they agreed they could go and look at the litters with them. Their parents, happy for the lads to go along, got Jack to explain to the boys they could help with the new puppy but weren't to expect one of their own. Jack reiterated this to the boys regularly, who quickly became frequent visitors to their home even before the pup arrived.

Finally one Saturday Jack, Chloe and the two lads, Harry and Thomas, set off with a huge picnic to go and see the two nearest litters. It was to be a full day expedition, and the first time Jack and Chloe had taken any of the estate children out of the area. Relaxed and happy with the couple the boys babbled excitedly in the back of the car, it being the first time they'd see a litter of puppies and also the first time they'd gone out for a full day without someone from their family.

Jack found the two boys' enthusiasm exhausting, but it also gave him a new lease of energy he'd not experienced in weeks. Chloe, sitting in the front seat doing her best to answer the boys excited questions, also felt an exhilaration she'd not felt in a long time. She knew this wasn't anything like having a baby of her own, but having a small and vulnerably puppy held more appeal than anything else she and Jack had considered for ages. The couple, contented if not happy, were looking forward to their day out with the boys and to finding their pup.

The boys were barely able to contain their excitement but, on arriving to see the first litter, showed what appeared to be a very impressive display of self-control as they quietly went into the room where the pups were. Hearing the sounds of human beings the puppies were instantly awake and, coming to life quickly, rushed over to where everyone was gathered. The boys squealed in delight as the pups clambered over their shoes and bending down to fuss the pups got their faces licked for reward.

Harry loved it but Thomas, less confident than Harry, wasn't too sure and quietly moved over to Chloe's side after one of the pups had taken a small nip at his chubby finger. Taking Chloe's hand he stuck his thumb into his mouth and nestled alongside Chloe's legs. Chloe, a doubting Thomas at her side and five lively pups at her feet, felt touched and looking across at Jack experienced a real mix of emotions.

*It's good Jack and I are back on such good terms and so much in love again*, she thought, *but sad these two young lads are the nearest we'll ever get to having children around us*. As a lump of emotion begin to well in her throat she felt Thomas tugging at her hand, and looking down saw his appealing eyes looking up, silently asking for reassurance and guidance.

Recognising Thomas' need for encouragement, Chloe sat on the floor beside him scooping a pup in her arms for Thomas to stroke. Within minutes, Thomas' momentary fear of the pups overcome, found him rolling about the floor with pups jumping and climbing all over him and Harry. The joint sound of giggling, and the pup's attempts to bark, made both Jack and Chloe laugh delightedly. Looking up they caught each other's eyes, a look of pure love and understanding passing between them. Stepping over squirming giggling bodies on the floor Jack took Chloe's hand in his and squeezed it gently. Then dropping down onto one knee he picked up a lone pup, its tail wagging and eyes beseeching.

'You see this little one?' Jack said. 'Well he's the same appealing look in his eyes you have. So how about we have this little chap?'

Chloe, gently taking the pup from him and nuzzling it to her replied quietly, 'Only one problem with that buddy,' a huge grin on her face as she turned the pup over to expose its belly. ''Cos this little chap just happens to be a girl.'

Shaking his head and laughing Jack told the two boys it would soon be time to leave for their picnic.

'Which one are we taking?' Thomas asked excitedly.

'Yeah!' chorused Harry, 'and can we get one of the others this afternoon?'

'Whoa, whoa,' laughed Jack. 'We can't take any of these little chaps home because they're too young to leave their mummies yet and like I said,' he told them squatting down on his hunkers. 'We have some more to look at after our picnic and we're not taking any home with us today. Five more minutes and then we must go,' he told them, ruffling their hair affectionately.

Ten minutes later they detached the boys from the milling, excited pups and went to talk to the owners telling them they'd make their decision later in the day and let them know. Then taking the two bouncing boys by the hand they bid their farewells and made their way back to the car, the two lads waving energetically to the unresponsive pups.

After they'd picnicked and run off some of the boys' energy, they settled the boys to play quietly on the swings to eat their promised ice creams. Sitting at the edge of the play area, Chloe diligently watching the boys, Jack sat with his body slumped and head cradled in his hands. Chloe, turning to look at him, was suddenly concerned by Jack's stance and the paleness of his face. Looking more closely she noticed beads of sweat glistening on his forehead.

'Jack?' she queried 'Jack? What's the matter? Are you alright?' gently she laid her hand on his arm as if to give comfort.

Slowly Jack lifted his head. His face was drained of colour and a distant look seemed to haunt his eyes. Shaking his head he said in a low slow voice, 'Yeah, yeah I'm ok. Just felt dog tired. Just need a minute to myself so will you keep an eye on the boys?' he asked. Chloe did as she was bade and went off to play with the boys, leaving Jack some time to pull himself together before they set off to see the second litter.

They chose their pup, a bitch, almost immediately which, despite its minute size, appeared to have a huge personality. All of them had been drawn to the same one when it had systematically sniffed them all and then, much to everyone's amusement, had squatted down and peed over Chloe's feet, the wee running between her toes exposed in her open sandals. The boys and Jack thought it hilarious and even Chloe, wet though she was, couldn't help but laugh. Picking up everyone's mood the pup began to run round in circles chasing its tail, making them laugh all the harder and making their decision of choice so much easier.

'That pup is going to be a right little clown and it'll certainly keep you on your toes,' Jack finished laughing. Chloe, glad to see him looking brighter and more relaxed took hold of his hand and looking down at the boys said, 'Well boys I think this is the one. What do you think?' Jumping up and down, the two lads demanded to have another hold of the puppy and began suggesting different names for it.

Having officially secured the puppy they set off home, the journey's entertainment being a discussion of the pup's name. Both boys kept laughing about it weeing on Chloe's foot and how fast it could race, so the name Wiz was finally decided on. Once the boys had argued and agreed the colour of the collar, lead and bed, it wasn't long before they fell silent. Looking round to check on them, Chloe saw they'd fallen asleep, their tousled heads resting together. Seeing this lovely peaceful picture Chloe's heart lurched, as she momentarily remembered her two lost children who'd never be able to have the same enjoyment these two youngsters had enjoyed today.

Looking across at Jack, she was concerned to see his face pinched and pale, drawn with concentration as he drove. Leaning across to him Chloe lay her hand on his leg and squeezing it affectionately told him, 'Jack, you need to get checked out at the doctors. Promise me you'll sort it out first thing next week?' she cajoled, thinking the last thing she could bear was to lose this wonderful man who was still a major part of her life, despite what had happened. *Losing the children was one thing but to lose Jack as well,* she told herself, *is something I know I couldn't bear.* And as if hearing her unspoken words Jack reassured her he'd get checked out with the doctor but whatever was ailing him he was sure it wouldn't be life changing. How wrong could he have been?

The next two weeks seemed to go by in a haze for Jack, who felt constantly tired and often light-headed. His medical had shown up nothing more than raised blood pressure and slight anaemia, his ailments being put down to the toll of the past few years. Reassured it was nothing to worry about, Jack and Chloe left the surgery with a suggested diet in hand to address Jack's ailments.

The doctor had also suggested Jack went off for four days intensive re-programming and relaxation, to re-address past years' events by himself, without the focus being diluted by him being re-programmed as part of a couple. Jack, knowing this was something he needed to address, readily agreed and the week before the pup was due to arrive set off to a centre in the Cotswolds.

Jack enjoyed his break alone, revelling in the time he'd been given for himself. With the intensive therapies and beautiful surroundings Jack found himself looking at his life as if from a distance. His love for Chloe still ran deep and their recent problems he knew were mainly due to the disappointment of lost parenthood. It wasn't long before he found himself beginning to re-evaluate everything with a new clarity, and able to look at the future with a new perspective.

His time on retreat also gave him time to walk in the beautiful countryside, and when he wasn't out walking he took advantage of the extensive old-fashioned library where he was staying. Taking a first cursory glance along the shelves, he came across a whole selection of books on pets, several relating to dog training, and set about studying the different methods. Although he'd had a dog as a pet, when he was a boy, he'd never actually been involved in training a puppy before, so the books available to him were a godsend.

Returning home from his retreat, rested and successfully re-programmed, he was also well read on puppy training and looking forward to the distraction the pup would provide for him and Chloe. He had more energy than previously, but was still encountering light-headedness and dizzy spells. Hopefully, with plenty of the right foods, that would soon abate, but in the meantime he felt more relaxed and confident about his future than he had done for a long time.

Whilst he'd been away, Chloe had taken the two boys to the market to buy the pup's bed, collar and lead. Jack hadn't been home long before Harry had come rushing round demanding to show off the puppy's new items. Chloe, who'd missed Jack terribly, watched Jack lovingly as he gave his full attention to the child, wondering how long it would be before she had her much missed man all to herself. To her relief it wasn't long before Harry's Wristlet activated telling him it was time to go home.

'I like living here,' Chloe said, as they watched Harry depart home. 'And it's so good to have you back home again and all to myself,' she said, with an inviting smile.

'I'm very happy to be home with you too,' he said, nuzzling her neck. Then, in a mock serious tone, added, 'But I'm worried about your forgetfulness. Especially when it smells as if my supper's burning.' Chloe quickly pulled away throwing him a playful punch as she dashed into the kitchen to rescue their meal from incineration. The ploy had distracted Chloe, as Jack had known it would, and prevent her from seeing him almost swoon, as he began to feel an almost overwhelming intensity of light-headedness wash over him.

Two days later they went to collect the pup, without the boys, stopping off for a leisurely lunch on the way. Enjoying each others company, they waxed lyrical about the new addition to their family. Everything was prepared ready for the pup's homecoming, just as they'd planned and organised everything for bringing a baby home. Both were aware of the simile and when Jack mentioned it during lunch it was a poignant moment, but sharing it made it easier to bear. A pup may not be the same as a baby, but it would be a distraction for them and entertainment for the children on the estate.

Arriving home, late afternoon, it wasn't long before a reception committee had gathered, headed, of course, by Thomas and Harry. It was like a scene from the Pied Piper of Hamlin, all the little people trickling out of the houses with parents in tow to see the puppy. By the time the last child had said hello the bewildered and very tired Wiz, had a wide variety of presents and treats. Having a pup was going to be an interesting experience, Jack and Chloe decided, not just as a pet but as another focal point for the estate's residents.

Having introduced Wiz to her new home, Jack settled her onto an old woolly jumper, the breeders had provided them with, and collapsed drained onto the sofa with a cup of tea. Exhausted, Jack reflected on the day's events and the different reactions of the children. Deep in thought, he was brought out of his reverie by Chloe standing in the doorway.

'A penny for them?' she asked, a note of anxiety in her voice.

'My thoughts are worth more than that,' Jack replied, bringing his thoughts and sight back into focus. 'My thoughts are worth a golden guinea,' he told her, grinning. 'And I'll tell you about them after I've had a quick nap. Are you going to curl up on the settee with me for an hour?' he asked quietly. Chloe, needing no further invitation, joined Jack on the settee, where they entwined in each other's arms and fell into a companionable sleep, the pup curled in a tight ball at their feet.

Woken a short while later, by the whimpering of the pup, Chloe opened her eyes wondering what the noise was and jumped with shock when a cold wet nose pushed against her bare toes. Realising it was the pup she reached down to see the tiny creature standing in front of her, its tail wagging frantically. Scooping it up into her arms the pup frantically trying to lick her face, Jack was woken to the wonderful sound of Chloe's tinkling laughter and watched as Wiz squirmed excitedly in her arms.

'Looks like someone's got the measure of you,' he chuckled, swinging his legs round to sit up. Stretching and shaking his head to rid himself of sleep he offered, 'You fancy another cup of tea? Might be an idea if we take her out to do her business too, if it's not too late,' he suggested with a grin. Standing to stretch, he suddenly cried out, groping blindly to sit down again. Looking up quickly Chloe saw Jack's face was drained of all colour and glistening with sweat.

'Jack, Jack? What's the matter Jack?' Chloe asked in a concerned voice.

'Urgh, urgh,' groaned Jack. 'Just got up too quickly and went all dizzy,' he explained. 'Must have woken up too quickly,' he said feebly, having slumped back down, his head pounding in his hands.

'Put your head between your legs Jack and let the blood back to your brain, if it can find one,' she added, trying to make a joke of the incident, but actually feeling quite alarmed. The moment passed and Jack, troubled by Chloe's concern, made light of the matter. Not fooled by Jack's bravado for a minute Chloe suggested he play with the pup whilst she prepared supper, and set about cooking a meal with as much natural iron content as possible. The meal prepared, she then took out one of the jellies Jack seemed to be exceptionally fond of at the moment, wondering what on earth their appeal was to him.

Despite the new occupant in the house, Jack and Chloe decided to turn in early, something not uncommon for Jack of late. It wasn't to be a night of rest though, as downstairs the pup whimpered continually with Jack insistent they didn't go down and pander to it, adamant the pup's domain would not include upstairs. Smiling to herself at the impossibility of this, and wincing as the youngster downstairs whimpered, Chloe snuggled down beside Jack to spend a night which seemed to be almost devoid of sleep.

Jack, so exhausted, had slept well, but knowing what a light sleeper Chloe was, had left her to sleep-in when he'd woken in the early morning. Going downstairs he found carnage in the kitchen, where Wiz had done her business in various places and chewed a number of items. Feeling nauseous anyway, the sight didn't make Jack feel any better, but he also knew it would ruin the start of Chloe's day. Putting Wiz's lead on he took her outside, restraining himself from picking her up to cuddle until she'd performed, and then had lavished praise on her. Sensing the change of atmosphere Wiz started to gamble round and round, as if showing off. It took Jack ten minutes playing with the pup before he felt able to brace himself and go back inside to clear up the wreckage. Thirty minutes later, with the kitchen pretty much back to normal, Jack's sickness was still threatening to get the better of him. Determined not to give into it, Jack made drinks to take back to bed and, spotting a jelly, picked it up and devoured it quickly, not giving a second thought to how odd it was to eat one so early in the day.

It was later on when Jack had another funny turn. They'd been sitting on the settee with their mugs of tea discussing the pup's training, continually bending over to fuss the dog which was trying to gain a place on the settee and access to their affections. As Jack noticed the pup starting to behave differently and recognising its need to go out, he'd jumped up energetically to let it out. As he leapt to his feet it was like a heavyweight blackness had struck him down, and the next thing he knew he found himself lying in a crumpled heap on the floor, Chloe almost in tears as she tried to rouse him.

Finally back on the settee, Jack sat with his head between his knees feeling sick and dizzy. He'd never passed out before and the experience had been so sudden and unexpected it had frightened him. He felt crap and wasn't comfortable with this situation, and knew Chloe was as terrified by what was happening as he was. A while later Chloe presented him with more tea and a slice of toast, which Jack looked at dubiously but then accepted gratefully. Looking at the toast he noticed it had honey on. Looking questioningly at Chloe he said, 'Chloe why have you put honey on my toast? You know I don't like it.'

'Yes, but you hate sweet tea even more, and you need something sweet to eat, Jack. Just humour me and eat it without a fuss will you? I need to take the dog out before it makes another mess. Then I quite fancy a boiled egg. Do you fancy one?' she called, as she made her way back into the kitchen to deal with the pup. Jack recognised her over-bright efficiency as her typical 'this is how I'll cope with it', mechanism, and obediently ate the snack.

'Chloe?' he called. 'I'm going back to see the doctor,' he told her, beating her to the topic he knew would be foremost in her mind. 'I'll make an appointment for as early as I can next week,' he finished as a worried Chloe stood in the doorway looking relieved.

'Thanks Jack. I hoped I wouldn't have to nag you into it. Do you want me to come with you?' Jack declined this offer, wanting to air his concerns without Chloe being present, knowing how worried she was. Momentarily he thought about going back to see Zoe, the Gobi he'd seen before. She'd been so easy to talk to and he knew he could talk about his concerns, without her becoming over-protective or fussing as Chloe did. He let his mind wander back to his experience with Zoe and, although in some ways he regretted his wandering, he'd still have liked to go back. She was very much a font of wisdom, and he'd enjoyed the coupling between them which had been exhilarating yet devoid of emotion, unlike sex with Chloe. Dismissing the idea of a revisit he drained his tea, ate the last mouthful of toast and steeled himself to get up, afraid he'd feel dizzy or keel over again. Gingerly he stood up, Chloe hovering at his side, and relieved to find he was ok, the concern at doing something so simple reinforced his resolve to go back to the doctors. He also vowed to take the rest of the weekend easy, new puppy and constant young visitors notwithstanding.

~ ~ ~ ~ ~

The camaraderie between Liam, Crawford and Tanya was almost tangible. There was such a comfortable liaison between them it automatically rubbished the old saying of 'two's company, three's a crowd'. The three of them just naturally gravitated together and within a short space of time none of them could imagine ever being part of a couple. It didn't matter whether it was Liam and Tanya meeting up, Crawford and Tanya, Crawford and Liam or all three of them together, there was no jealousy and no pecking order, just extended communications and a genuine warmth of being in each other's company.

It was mid-September when the three of them moved into one of the government's spacious penthouse suites overlooking the Thames. Liam and Crawford, pooling together their privileges, were able to secure one of the larger and more luxurious top floor apartments in a nineteenth century converted warehouse. The property sported huge banks of windows and, being the loft apartment, benefited from cathedral-like skylights in the living area ceiling which added to the illusion of spaciousness.

There were three large bedrooms and a smaller room, which was still large enough to use as an office and house Crawford's gym equipment. The rest of the apartment was open plan, with a spacious area they chose to allocate for sitting and dining in. The entire communal section overlooked one of the Thames bends, where they could watch the passage of water and numerous activities that took place on the river. To Liam's delight there was a beautiful, ingeniously designed and enviable kitchen area, which he planned to make full use of.

Tanya had managed to find a small, reasonably priced unit within walking distance, which meant she'd save on travel and by working part-time, with reduced living costs, she was optimistic her business had a fair chance of survival. With their pad being a government property for employees, Liam and Crawford had very little rent to pay, and between them they'd agreed to split the costs three ways and share their reductions with Tanya so she was still able to hold her head up financially.

On the day they moved in Liam insisted on showing off his culinary skills and produced a superb meal, the first of many to come. Serving it at their newly-acquired ancient dining suite, he'd warned them that, although he loved to cook and found it relaxing, they weren't to expect him to cook all the time. However it wasn't too long before the kitchen became recognised as Liam's domain. Although Crawford and Tanya had promised to do their bit they warned Liam their talents might lay elsewhere. Liam, raising an eyebrow at this had hurriedly cleared the dishes and the three of them promptly set about christening every room and piece of furniture they could with their sexual antics.

Finally exhausted, and ready for sleep, Crawford was the last to climb into the huge slumber-pit, where Tanya was already fast asleep and Liam just dozing off. They both lay in the bed, barely touching each other in the enormous slumber-pit, and carefully Crawford crawled in between them, quickly dropping into a deep and dreamless sleep as the three of them curled round each other.

When they all woke the next morning, luxuriating in their entwined yet sexually dormant bodies, Liam complained, for the first time, how tired he'd been feeling lately and if he was to keep up with the other two he'd have to do something about it. Laughing good naturedly, Tanya patted his plump belly affectionately and told him they'd soon help him lose his belly and get him in shape with plenty of activity between the sheets.

Wanting to reassure, Crawford couldn't resist the temptation to bend over them and kiss them both. Turning over he kissed Liam, the kiss long and their tongues snaking into each others mouths. Tanya watched in fascination as both men immediately started to become aroused. Their growing hardness would never cease to fascinate her, or how quickly it happened. She loved watching it and knew Crawford was aware the sight excited her. He smiled inwardly as he watched her take Liam's hardness in her hand and began to stroke the silken shaft. He knew exactly how Liam would react and sure enough within minutes Crawford's huge black erection was in his hand. Crawford responded by gently stroking Tanya intimately. Within minutes the three of them were in the deep throes of passion, satisfying each other's urgent needs. It was the way they would invariably start their days in their new flat, when all three of them were home, and a wonderful way to start the first day in their new abode.

A couple of weeks after moving in, Crawford had a gym unit installed in the spacious office area. What Crawford didn't reveal straight away was, he'd selected the equipment to use in their sexual antics as well as for keeping fit, knowing they'd get enormous pleasure using it in a more imaginative manner. It wasn't long before their office took on a new meaning, and provided an ingenuous focal point in their luxurious accommodation.

Using the equipment conventionally, on a regular basis, it wasn't long before Liam began to look much better, his puppy-type fat gradually being replaced by slowly toning muscle. It was only his stomach the exercises didn't seem to be making an impact on, but with his skin glowing, hair shinier than ever before, he looked and felt better than in previous months. Living together with Tanya and Crawford was, for Liam, idyllic. Life was good and his feelings for them deep and whether together or apart their ménàge à trios gave him a feeling of deep seated security in his new life. His family, when they came to visit, were impressed with the set-up and how the three were settling in together. His mother in particular was happy, to see Liam settling down in what was obviously a beneficial relationship. She saw in her son a new inner confidence and peace, which pleased her immensely. As for Liam's new shape, well if she was honest, she couldn't see any difference, but what did that matter as long as her son was happy?

Work wise things were panning out better than any of them had been expected. Tanya's business was surviving, just, but still necessitated her working part-time at her old job. She was a meticulous planner, something neither Liam nor Crawford had been aware of before, and were quietly impressed by her business acumen. They'd both wondered if they were doing the right thing letting Tanya give up her own flat and move in with them, expecting to have the business overtake their flat, but nothing could have been further from the truth. She worked diligently for long hours, but knew when to stop and take stock of a situation. She'd just secured the full support of the Forniclubs in London, who were going to use her as a source of reference and supply for individuals wanting to buy or hire specialist outfits. Hiring was one thing Tanya hadn't considered previously, but soon found herself earning more money from this than through purchases. All in all things were going well, but what pleased Liam and Crawford most of all was she didn't bring her business home.

Liam's career continued to flourish and now he was a fully fledged member of the team he was tasked to plan, set up and pilot a new project to run alongside some of his current work. It was a brilliant opportunity and showed his employers had faith in his abilities. His scheme was to be aimed at individuals who showed promise but lacked the confidence to make the most of their talents. When the project had first been outlined, Liam had worked an entire weekend identifying individuals from his groups who fitted the criteria. By the end of the weekend he'd identified a full compliment of candidates and compiled a list of research to do before deciding how he was going to implement his scheme. He was determined the pilot would work, as it would then be rolled out across the UK and really pave his road to success, if it proved successful.

Liam was an ideas man, unlike Tanya who was a meticulous planner, which was why they worked so well together. Before he set about developing ideas, for his pilot scheme, he, Tanya and Crawford put their heads together to thrash out ideas, Crawford playing a major advisory role due to his senior position and greater understanding of the nation's needs. It was a true team effort and after a lively brainstorming session, involving a number of heated debates, Liam had enough information to set about preparing his portfolio which, completed and well rehearsed, was due to be presented to the managers and team midweek.

However, the presentation of his plan was not accepted with the success he'd hoped for. It was deemed unmanageable and impractical in terms of delivery and support, although they'd liked his basic concept. With several constructive suggestions, and far clearer guidelines, Liam left undaunted to tackle the task again. Although he'd been initially disappointed with the outcome, Liam had thought long and hard about the comments and suggestions, and decided to once again follow in Tanya's style and put it back into the 'pad thinking pot', as they now called their brainstorming sessions. Tanya and Crawford agreed to help, but only if he cooked them one of his wonderful meals. Primarily miffed, but then secretly flattered, Liam agreed to the terms and a few nights later, served up a Mexican feast. Dining done, they set to the task of re-evaluating the information and the suggestions and criticisms it had been met with.

Surprisingly, it was Tanya who came up with the most appealing and workable suggestion and Liam and Crawford, looking at her admiringly, were once again struck by how innovative yet practical her ideas were. With the concept taken on board enthusiastically by Liam, and sanctioned by Crawford, the three of them set about putting together the presentation. After a couple of hours hard work and imaginative thinking, Liam felt as though he had a presentation plan fit to impress a king – if royalty had still existed!

It was the following week when Liam next presented his plan, and this time the ideas were accepted with relish and enthusiasm. With one or two minor adjustments, it was agreed Liam would be able to launch the idea as a pilot in the spring of 2033 and if successful would be rolled out across the UK the following year. With three months left before the year end, Liam would have the chance to contact and secure the cooperation of the individuals he'd identified, do an extensive amount of research and set up the programme format ready for the following spring. This was the first project Liam could truly call his own, and he tackled it with fervour and enormous energy, determined to make it a success.

Despite the fact that Liam now worked out diligently with Crawford, almost to the point of obsession, his weight stayed static and although it was evident his limbs were more toned, his waistline continued to expand. Liam, struggling now to fasten his trousers, was convinced he was doing the stomach exercises incorrectly, which were expanding the size of his belly. Crawford, having checked his technique diligently, begged to differ. But Liam, having been warned about his weight, at the last two obesity checks, came slamming home one night after attending his monthly check and, much to Tanya and Crawford's surprise, had almost wept with frustration as he'd relayed the outcome of that day's weigh-in. According to the Company Medics his blood pressure was up, his weight not reduced and they'd detected swelling in his ankles. The results had astonished him, but not as much as his outburst had surprised his two flatmates.

Liam's anger was not easily calmed, as he and Crawford had worked long and hard to tone Liam up, and reduce his weight. Although the tests had identified greater muscle and less fat, the differences weren't enough for him to avoid the government weight programme. The only thing to still Liam's anger was Crawford's promise to get him registered on to his own programme, and to examine Liam's diet again in minute detail.

Liam's appetite in the past few weeks had noticeably changed. He'd lost the taste for synthetically sweetened foods and recently started eating summer fruits in copious amounts. His one weakness though, was bananas and raspberry ripple ice cream sprinkled with sugar. That, Crawford had told him, was the first thing he'd have to knock on the head. But no matter how determined Liam was, he had such dreadful cravings for the sweets he couldn't totally resist them altogether and only managed to cut down on the quantities he ate. Sweet things didn't really bother Tanya, but the extra fresh fruit Crawford began stocking the bowls with certainly enticed her. Like Liam her hair and skin looked more radiant, and Crawford put this down to more natural foods and less food pearls. He'd even noticed he had a healthier glow, and surmised it wasn't just the food but the camaraderie and depth of feelings that obviously suited them all.

Somehow this ménage à trois, which had sprung up from nothing, seemed to have afforded them all a peace and serenity in life not many found. With no apparent jealousy between them, and the fact they all had their own rooms, and didn't need to live in each other's laps, they found themselves seeing and having sex with fewer people than they had done previously. It was Liam who decided to point it out to the others.

'Do you realise,' he started, 'that in the past few weeks we've only had sex with one another when we've gone out? And I've not slept with anyone else for weeks now, even when I've been away. I don't need anyone else when I've got you two and I'm happy with the way things are, even if we do decide to invite someone else along every now and then. Does it bother you I like the way things have become?' he asked, his eyes glistening with emotion. 'What about you Crawford?'

'You've got me thinking,' Crawford replied, stirring his coffee as he contemplated the situation. 'There's something pretty good between us but I for one wouldn't want to stifle either of you from going elsewhere, 'cos it would probably spoil things,' he added. 'Let's just take it one day at a time shall we and see how things pan out. What do you reckon Tan?' he asked moving the focus to her.

Unconsciously mirroring Crawford's motions, she too was stirring her own drink. The conversation had quite thrown her as she herself hadn't had as many partners recently and had to admit she didn't want to either. She'd deliberately avoided any commitment with Liam in the past but now Crawford was in the relationship as well, she felt as though she had everything she needed. They still went to the Fornipubs and clubs, and indulged in their various fantasies, and both of her men really encouraged her when it came to the business, and suddenly she realised she was part of something she'd never dreamt of being part of before.

'Yeah well things have changed haven't they?' and she gently reached out to touch both men simultaneously. 'Crawford and I seem to spend far more time together than we do with you because you're away so much. Somehow the house doesn't seem the same without you but when you come breezing through the door after a spell away, the whole atmosphere changes. It's like greeting an old friend returning from a long distant journey, rather than a flatmate who's just been away for a few days.'

Crawford nodded his agreement to this. He knew the feelings between Tanya and Liam had become more deeply seated since they'd all lived together, and he himself, felt a love for both Tanya and Liam he'd not felt for anyone before. He also knew that the perfect situation was when the three of them were together.

'I for one know I feel more for you two than I ever have for anyone else. But I know as well that if one of us was to leave this trine it would be the end for all of us. Do you know what I mean?' Crawford asked.

'Yeah, exactly,' Liam agreed. 'I've thought the world of Tanya since we first met, but I knew there was something missing. Now it's the three of us, for me it's complete. It would never have worked for Tanya and me without you, but then it wouldn't have worked for you and me if it was just the two of us. But the three of us – well that's a different matter altogether.' Tanya and Crawford listened, understanding exactly what he meant but, finding no need to respond, just nodded their agreement.

'Here's to the three of us,' Crawford toasted, raising his glass. 'And long may we all be together.'

~ ~ ~ ~ ~

The night arrived when, as planned, Jed, Jade and Ben all turned up at Fiona's to experiment with the sex drug. Fiona had worked hard at setting up a blocker, which would give them a few hours privacy from their parents without raising any alarms. Having tried it out a few times before they'd all arrived, they were all excited yet somewhat nervous about the experience they were about to undergo, praying none of their parents would want them for anything. They'd agreed it would be an alcohol free night, as they were told they wouldn't need it with the drug. All of them were edgy, especially the girls, and to cover up their nervousness they acted with more bravado than they felt.

Once in Fiona's study, the blockers were set, wristlets checked and with everything set they popped the grains, with lots of nervous laughing, wondering what was going to happen to them. They'd been told it would be half an hour or so before the grains took effect; so whilst they waited Fiona turned on the music, tuned in the Colorbs and together they cavorted about, the Colorbs emulating their dancing.

Initially there was an awkwardness between them but the fascination of their personal Colorbs capering above them soon had them laughing and becoming crazier by the minute. As their actions grew wilder so did the Colorbs, egging them on to be more outrageous, until finally all four of them collapsed in a heap, their limbs entwined, as were those of the Colorbs. If it hadn't been for the blockers their parents would have been onto them in an instant, so high were their spirits and boundless their energy.

Finding themselves in a tangle on the floor Fiona, inhibitions gone, kissed Jed passionately, pouring into it a torrent of steamy romantic emotions. Jed, having been aroused for sometime, didn't hold back and, kissing and caressing Fiona, manoeuvred her over to the settee, where he eagerly undressed her, Fiona not protesting despite the presence of Jade and Ben. Jed's thoughts of Ben and Jade ceased to exist as he slowly seduced Fiona, caressing her with his hands and mouth. As far as they were concerned there was nothing and no one in their world except them; inhibitions ceased to exist as the passion burned between them. Fiona, her lack of experience a thing of the past, responded just as eagerly as Jed, and together they climbed to peaks neither had experienced before, until they collapsed panting and spent. Above them the merged colours of the Colorbs imitated their resting, the tiny stars spangling the shapes above them gradually disappearing.

It seemed only a short while before Jade and Ben were beside them, and they seemed to have swapped partners, although later, none

205

of them could consciously remember when it had happened. Jed kissed Jade just as hungrily as he'd kissed Fiona and, to his surprise, found he had no objection to Ben and Fiona becoming sexually entangled. Half keeping an eye on Fiona, which he found incredibly erotic as she and Ben touched each other, he and Jade explored one another eagerly. Whether it was their pleasure at this new coupling or the sight of the other two neither knew but Jed found Jade to be an extremely agile and eager lover, completely different to Fiona or any other girl he'd had sex with before. There was more spontaneity between them than there was between him and Fiona, and he found Jade's receptiveness a heady aphrodisiac. Frantically and athletically they fornicated and Jed was delighted to see Jade arch her back and cry out her pleasure, as she hadn't done with Ben.

Just as Jade voiced her pleasure, and Jed experienced his own powerful climax, Fiona came over to join them, and Jed found himself instantly becoming aroused again, on seeing the two girls kiss. He sat back to watch, his semi-erect penis still inside Jade. Gently rocking backwards and forwards he touched Jade, the pleasure of being inside her and watching the two girls an experience he'd only ever dreamt of before. Beside them Ben looked on, his eyes ablaze with sheer delight, and Jed wondered how long it would be before he muscled in on the act.

'Fucking hell, Jed. These tabs are something else. I always knew those two fancied each other,' and he reached out and began caressing the girls together.

The four of them cavorted together on the floor kissing and caressing each other, girl-to-girl, boy-to-girl and, without realising boy-to-boy. Their touching of each other wasn't rough or intrusive, but was done with an intimacy that was beyond their years and experience. Above them the Colorbs emulated the frantic antics of the young people beneath and the normally vacant space near the ceiling was awash with a myriad of colours, like the northern lights of a wintry sky.

Finally, as the drugs began to wear off, rationale returned and Ben and Jed, finding themselves kissing and touching each other silently separated, but not until they'd momentarily enjoyed the other's hands upon them. As the music continued to play, the security devices holding out despite the heightened emotions, they once again found themselves an entangled mass of limbs, spent and exhilarated by the experience.

The music, by vocal command, changed to more gentle rhythms and as they slowly caught their breath, talking animatedly about the past hour, they slowly returned to their normal selves and shyly got up to dress.

Despite things going back to normal, the mood between them stayed euphoric, their friendships now laced with an odd affection and admiration. If only the mood had continued to exist, and been drawn upon nearer to Christmas, then they'd all have coped differently with a scenario none of them, especially their parents, could ever have dreamt of. The only word to sum up their evening was 'Wow!' but if they'd known the consequences of their cavorting, they'd have used a far stronger expletive, and it would have been spoken in fear.

The closeness they'd shared was incredible; the consequences they were to face even more so.

~ ~ ~ ~ ~

The first real breakthrough, in the investigation, finally came at the latter end of November, the morning after the barmaid had been attacked. When the woman was discovered, as head of the serial rapist case, Melanie was immediately called to the scene. By the time she arrived, less than an hour later, the Forensics Detector which all detectives were issued with, had confirmed this was another of their rapist's attacks. It was actually less than two hours from the attack taking place when Melanie entered the cordoned off area, where detectives were grid walking and evidencing the location. The victim, barely alive, had already been flown to the nearest Crimedical Centre.

Whilst Melanie took a brief reconnaissance of the area she issued a number of orders, and fed various elements into her own Forensics Detector setting the analysis programme in process before even departing from the site. Leaving a string of orders, of areas she wanted looking at thoroughly, she stepped into the gyrocopter to follow the victim to the Crimedical Centre.

On arrival, however, there was no point in her being present whilst the medics examined and worked on the woman, whose life hung in the balance. Although Melanie had as much medical expertise as any of the medics in the room, there were other factors needing her attention first. All she'd needed to check on, that the woman had been linked into the

Subliminal Voyeur, which would monitor her subconscious memory as well as keep tally of her vital signs and injuries.

As Melanie carried about her work, checking occasionally to see how the woman was faring, she found herself sickened by the extent of the woman's injuries. As the results filtered through, Melanie knew they had to apprehend the rapist and soon, otherwise they'd soon have a murder on their hands as well.

*This isn't someone out to belittle women through intimidation and rape,* she ascertained. *This is the act of savage revenge and whoever this bloke is he's no consideration for his own consequences, let alone his victim,* Melanie thought as she reviewed the charts and scans.

Going through to the annexe, where the woman lay deathly pale against the contrast of bruises and contusions she'd suffered, Melanie had a momentary flash of it having been the same for her mother, although this woman wasn't pregnant. Instantly banishing the thoughts from her mind, Melanie steeled herself to her usual cool professional manner and set about checking the Subliminal Voyeur to see what, if anything had been revealed by the piece of equipment. As she studied the readings she was barely aware of the ventilator breathing for the woman and the bed undulating gently. Subconsciously Melanie wondered if this equipment would have saved her mother had it been available thirty years ago.

Knowing the woman would remain like this for sometime, through injury and the cocktail of drugs she was receiving, Melanie was just about to leave the room when an urgent message came through from the ground team. Leaving the annexe she hurried back to the room allocated to her team to find out what had just been discovered.

'Is this… don't tell me,' Melanie asked, taking a bagged item from the technician, who was nodding his confirmation with great pride.

'Yes it is. It's the handkerchief, found not far from the scene. Untested so far.'

Before the words were out of his mouth, Melanie had reached for her phone to contact her team back in Leeds. In a voice, full of energy yet devoid of excitement, she quickly instructed them to get their forensic specialists over pronto, to start testing on a handkerchief now in their possession found near to the last victim. The officer at the other end of the phone knew exactly what was required and, conveying the information to the rest of the team, set about assembling their forensics team to get over to Melanie. From that moment on it was all actions go, and not even a blade of grass would miss their scrutiny.

Whilst initial results began to come back before the day was out it was two days before they'd got something extra to work with. The handkerchief had shown five lots of DNA, besides the rapist's. As the traces were so minimal, and obviously diluted many times by laundering, they weren't the easiest to analyse, and clarify as indisputable information. Trace samples also showed several processing elements, which had been linked into the manufacturing sector. Unfortunately the substances identified were used extensively across the industry, but looking at them collectively would enable them to narrow the field considerably.

Of the six DNA samples isolated, one was from the rapist; another the current victim, two from previous victims and the other two as yet unidentified. It was these two unknowns that would hopefully provide the vital link they were looking for, and would be their number one priority in the investigation.

As one team worked on the site and its findings, another group were tracing the chemicals identified on the handkerchief. Another team was looking into the banned adhesive, they'd detected, and all round it was a hub of activity but worked in such a methodical and understated way an outsider wouldn't have realised they were working against the odds and the clock. Melanie had called in their profiler, who was now looking at the victim's pattern of injuries and studying the Subliminal Voyeur readouts, Melanie working at his side formulating the machine's readings to correlate with the different aspects of the attack.

Rob, the profiler, confirmed what Melanie suspected and feared most of all. The rapist was becoming increasingly dangerous and out of control. Something had happened and he'd been rendered unable to penetrate the woman, proven by the lack of semen. It appeared he'd been unable to achieve an erection and taken it out on the woman by using his fist and arm so forcefully, the woman had been damaged almost irreparably. So what had happened to make him flip like this? It was going to take some time to unravel the mystery but unravel it they would – no matter how long it took.

It was soon established that the bulk of traces found on the handkerchief were used in the packaging industry for the bottling trade. There were other elements too which, strictly speaking, didn't fit with the industry but were chemicals normally associated with the manufacture of computers. It was one sample in particular which held interest for them, which was the presence of an adhesive substance banned more than five years before. This had been used in the computer industry but, having been linked to a severe skin condition, had quickly been removed from the market and prohibited in the UK and several other countries. For some inexplicable reason there were relatively fresh traces of the substance, so was there a company still using it illegally, or had someone got hold of a supply illicitly? The discovery of the substance could either assist or hinder the investigation enormously. It was unlikely there was a company still using the substance, but had a quantity of it been stolen at some point in time? What were the chances of someone getting hold of a quantity? And what was the presence of silver paint? Did it indicate a hobby of some sort and if so did it include both paints and electronics? It was possible, but then millions could use the same quality of paint, but how many could get hold of the banned substance? Everything they'd found so far would mean extensive research, tracing and following up. Nothing they'd got would give them instant answers, but at least they were making headway.

To date, everything Melanie and her team had been following up, had been sheer hard slog with little reward, in terms of getting nearer to finding their rapist. Although the salary increments had kept spirits high nothing could have lifted them as much as finding the handkerchief had. All of a sudden it seemed as though the team, one and all working in situ and at different locations, had been given a renewed zest for life. It was finding the other DNA samples which had excited everyone most. These could lead to a partner, or someone else living with or in close proximity to their rapist and could help locate him.

Everyone was working incredibly hard but Alan, who was working closely with Melanie, was becoming increasingly concerned by the way Melanie was driving herself. It was as if she'd become obsessed with the case, and getting unduly anxious about her reputation in the world of crime detection. There was no reason for concern there, Alan knew, as her reputation went before her with the number of cases she'd solved and systems she'd put in place over the years. But Alan knew this almost obsessive drive went deeper than that. Since he'd 'rescued' her that evening, and driven her back home, they'd become quite close. In her private, personal world Melanie was a much softer, less dismissive person than portrayed at work. It wasn't easy getting close to her but their relationship was slowly progressing and Alan hoped she'd soon have enough confidence to allow the relationship to become one of intimacy. Only time, support and nurturing would allow it to go that way and, after so many years of being widowed, Alan had all the time in the world and didn't need to rush or spoil things. After all he knew Melanie was worth waiting for.

What concerned Alan most though, was what drove Melanie. When she'd told him about her mother's rape and her own premature birth as a result, she'd also admitted to programming the murderer's DNA onto UK Forensic Detectors. When he'd started to remonstrate she'd stopped him mid sentence, and been a little too quick to point out all wanted serious criminals' DNA was on the devices. Alan knew it would be pointless to remind her it was normally only criminals who'd committed crimes in the last twenty-five years, but knew this wasn't something Melanie would want reminding of.

The DNA registration figures were looking good, along with the increased solved crime rate, but when Melanie checked them daily he knew she wasn't just looking for the rapist's identification, she was looking for her mother's murderer too, who'd obligingly left DNA samples to trace him by. Alan however, wanting to protect her, didn't feel this was a healthy situation for Melanie to be in.

~ ~ ~ ~ ~

Daryl's life continued to be difficult, and, in addition, his health was becoming a problem. To make matters worse the factory girls had started mocking his expanding waistline by mimicking his waddling walk. Not only was his belly getting bigger, it felt as if it were forever churning, whether he ate or not. He also kept getting griping pains and his indigestion was getting increasingly worse and, if he was honest, his debilitation was beginning to frighten him, along with the fact he couldn't get medical advice. He was just grateful he wasn't in the factory all the time now, as being in the office gave him the chance to sit down, which he needed to do frequently.

Another problem which was on the increase; was the trouble he was having with his breathing. He often became short of breath with the minimum of exertions, with simple things like bending over the pool table, which caused a great deal of discomfort and left him breathless, then straightening up he'd find himself light-headed. He was always battling fatigue too, and by the end of the day it took all his energy to climb the stairs to his room, where he invariably fell asleep on his slumber-pit, whether he'd had his tea or not.

There was no one he could talk to and anyhow they'd only advise him to go to the doctors, which he couldn't if he wanted to keep his freedom. Gradually Daryl became more and more despondent and desperate for a solution. The only saving graces were Sonia and Patrick, who still kept in touch despite the disastrous weekend he and Sonia had spent together. He and Sonia still met for the occasional game of pool and their potential relationship had finally settled into a tentative friendship, much to Daryl's relief. Whether Sonia had ever told Patrick the events of the weekend he neither knew nor cared, he was just grateful they continued to be his friends.

When he met Sonia, a few weeks later, it was obvious how much weight he'd put on. Sonia couldn't help herself but to finally comment on his increasing weight.

'Daryl you're finding it really difficult to lean over the table today without getting breathless. I've noticed its worse than the last time we played. Have you seen a doctor about it?' she asked, praying he wouldn't take offence.

'Yeah, a couple of times,' Daryl lied easily. 'He reckons it's all to do with me Mam's cooking and too much beer. An old-fashioned beer belly,' he laughed, patting his stomach, which was doing its usual somersaults as if it had a life of its own.

'But what about your breathlessness?' Sonia probed.

'Same thing. Just less room for my lungs to expand,' he fabricated, trying to be as glib as possible.

'So what are you doing about it? You can't let a bit of food spoil your health. What about going back to food pearls for a while?' she suggested.

'Yeah, 'spose I could but then I'd miss out on me Mam's cooking,' Daryl explained. 'She's not a bad cook yer know,' he added as if this would excuse all.

'Is it really worth struggling like this just for a bit of extra food? If you keep putting weight on you'll be hauled up on the government's weight programme if you don't lose some before your next check-up.'

'What?' Daryl asked looking totally lost at what she'd said. Then as if working out how to respond, he quickly added, 'Oh that, yeah, right. The doctors already told me that's my next step if I don't do something about it,' he lied, not even having the grace to blush at such an outrageous untruth. 'Still it won't hurt if I leave it a while, will it?'

It seemed that later during the night Daryl was paying for his lies, his stomach being more active and painful than usual. He'd the most horrendous indigestion, with griping pains which were so extreme he could see his belly moving as the trapped wind rolled about inside. Watching it anxiously he saw what seemed to be a lump appear, then just as quickly disappear. It frightened him, the fact it was so bad he could actually see the movement. Even the indigestion tablets he continually sucked didn't seem to help now. Feeling sorry for himself, his arms wrapped round his undulating stomach, he finally fell into a disturbed sleep, unable to get comfortable no matter how he lay.

The next morning when he got out of bed, showered and dressed, Daryl could have sworn his beer belly had dropped during the night. Even so his trousers were so tight he still couldn't fasten them, no matter how much he breathed in. He just prayed his trousers wouldn't fall down before he managed to get out and buy some bigger ones.

*Maybe food pearls wouldn't be such a bad idea for a while*, he told himself miserably.

~ ~ ~ ~ ~

A week and visit to the doctors later, Jack was still no nearer to knowing what was the matter with him, despite having had several more tests. The nearest the doctor could tell him was his blood pressure was raised, his anaemia no better and he seemed to have a mild form of oedema. Giving Jack a prescription and telling him he wasn't unduly concerned, that it wasn't a life shattering condition, he sent Jack on his way. How wrong could his prognosis have been?

Wiz was a godsend, acting as visitor magnet and distraction device. She was a source of constant amusement and drew anecdotes and questions from the local children like nothing they'd known before.

Feeling decidedly under par the entertainment, provided by the small ones on the estate, constantly amused Jack, Chloe and their neighbours. Jack also realised how careful he'd have to phrase things because of the literal minds of the children. This was really brought to light when he spoke of potential burglars being licked to death. It wasn't his comment about being licked to death but his reference to burglars.

'But will there be burglars then?' Harry had asked, and Jack patiently explained how years ago there'd been lots of burglars, but there weren't many left now, as they knew if they stole from peoples' houses they'd be badly punished and anyway, he'd told Harry, burglars were nearly extinct now just like the Bengal tigers were years ago. Harry, who'd been doing a project on animals at school, contemplated for a moment and then told Jack worriedly.

'But Jack there's lots of Bengal tigers now.' Realising he'd not used the best example Jack had ruffled his hair and told the youngster, 'Yes but we wanted more Bengal tigers so spent lots of money so there would be. But the government's spent even more money making sure there won't be more burglars so it's ok, Harry. Ok?' Much to his relief Jack saw this was accepted happily, and Harry got back to the serious business of playing with Wiz, leaving Jack chuckling quietly as to how literal the child's logic was.

His next problem presented itself later the same day, when he was recounting the tale to Chloe in bed. They'd just finished making love and in the aftermath of their passion Jack was telling her Harry's tale, sniffing as if to punctuate the story. After he'd finished he still continued to sniff, which Chloe couldn't bear and quickly got irritated.

'For goodness sake Jack, can't you blow your nose and stop sniffing,' she complained, their moment of passion forgotten. Jack, ever the one to keep the peace, turned on his light and got out of bed to sort the problem. Chloe, now wide awake and feeling irritable was just about to say something scathing but instead, catching sight of Jack, gave a loud gasp.

'Jack? Jack what's the matter?' she chided, hurriedly getting out of bed to go to him.

'What?' asked Jack as he walked across the room.

'Jack look at you. You're covered in blood,' she told him.

'What?' asked Jack again, not understanding what she meant.

'Your face Jack, it's covered in blood. It's all over you,' she told him in a high-pitched voice of worry. Jack you're having a nose bleed, look it's dripping. Jack what on earth is going on? What's wrong with you? Do you feel all right?' she fussed.

By this time Jack had reached the bathroom mirror, and was stunned by his appearance. His entire face and upper torso was either smeared with blood or had splashes of blood from his nose, which was bleeding profusely.

'Oh god,' he muttered, pinching his nose hard. 'What the hell's made this happen?' he asked Chloe, as she ushered him over to sit on the toilet whilst she wrung out a cloth in cold water to clean him up. It was some time later before the nose bleed was stopped and Jack cleaned up. Both of them were shaken by the event, and even though they'd been reassured by the doctor's report this just caused them further concern.

'This isn't right Jack, despite what the doctor says. I know you've got anaemia and we've both been through a tough time lately, but you're usually so fit and healthy. Jack I'm really frightened there's something seriously wrong with you. I'm really scared, Jack,' she finished, her eyes bright with unshed tears, and then burst into noisy sobs.

Jack took her into his arms, cradling her against his chest making crooning noises, which rumbled through his chest and gave Chloe comfort.

'It's alright, sweetheart,' he told her 'I'm back at the doctor's again on Tuesday and I'll tell him this latest episode. Maybe it's just psychosomatic but there's no need to get upset over it, so stop worrying,' he told her unconvincingly.

'Come on, sweetheart, let's get back to bed. We both need the sleep,' he said, taking her by the hand and leading her back to the now clean bed. Getting into bed and snuggled down the house was once again silent, even the pup seemed to have settled down. Trying their hardest not to fidget and keep the other awake they finally fell into a light, but troubled, sleep. Neither would admit to the other how worried they were, but both of them knew something was amiss, but had no idea the cause would affect them so much – and threaten their relationship.

~ ~ ~ ~ ~

In general Liam's life seemed to be getting better and better. His career was ticking along nicely and his home life even better. The individuals he was talking to, for his pilot scheme, were mostly in agreement to becoming one of his guinea pigs, mainly due to the way Liam approached them and because he was so popular. People had confidence in him and being in his company, socially or otherwise, created the 'feel good' factor in them, especially for those who lacked confidence.

It wasn't just the task of getting someone to take part in the scheme though. Once someone had agreed, there was a whole tranche of research for Liam to do. This was something he insisted on doing himself first time round, just to find out exactly what information he needed and where to find it, even though it was increasing his workload. In the future he could pass it on, when he'd formulated a workable plan, but as it was the extra work was putting a real toll on him even though it was giving him a buzz. He was becoming so tired these days, despite feeling well and full of energy the majority of the time, he'd got into the habit of power-napping whenever he could. He'd started off by taking forty winks in his lunch break, and eating food pearls instead of traditional food, but it wasn't long before he began napping whenever he could.

Part of Liam's job was to socialise with his groups so when he started to disappear during the lunch break, it wasn't long before they began to complain. It was fair comment and Liam tried to counteract their moans by pointing out he still socialised with them at night. For most of them this was enough and only a handful continued to carp about it, for which Liam was grateful, as he didn't want anything to jeopardise the pilot scheme or question his ability to stay the pace.

If Liam was working away his first port of call, at the end of a stint, was a twenty minute nap back at his hotel. If he was home it was a little more difficult, but he always tried to get some sleep before Tanya or Crawford got home. He didn't know why but he felt embarrassed by this need, and didn't want the others to see him as being weak. His energy levels were beginning to cause him some concerns too. Whereas he seemed to have ample energy during the day if he didn't manage a cat nap at lunchtime, or first thing after work, he felt dreadful. It was now getting to the stage where he wanted to stay at home and unwind by cooking, rather than going out. Tanya and Crawford still went out at least twice a week to a Forniclub, or somewhere similar, and when Liam had first refused their invitations they'd been openly insulted. Liam sometimes wondered if it would be better to summon-up the energy, just to go and keep the peace, but the thought of a long sleep was becoming a greater attraction than a night of fornicating.

Tanya and Crawford couldn't believe how much Liam was changing, or why he was so tired all the time. He was also getting very tetchy and emotional and on several occasions had cried, or been on the verge of tears, for what seemed like no apparent reason. They knew he had a heavy workload, with his pilot scheme, but it was draining his energy for socialising. Between them they decided to keep a more watchful eye on him and make sure he didn't start to really run himself into the ground, which was the last thing they wanted.

The length of time he was spending in the shower these days was also beginning to cause some concern. Neither Tanya nor Crawford felt it fair to take him to task about it, but both agreed it was something they should keep a tally on. It didn't seem rational behaviour for Liam to spend over an hour in the cleansing room and locking the door to keep them out. The only consolation was that afterwards he seemed to have more energy, and was more likely to agree to play out with them, so they refrained from challenging him about it.

Their other concern was Liam's weight. He was still working-out most days, and put loads of energy into his workouts, but no matter how much he exercised and how little he ate his girth continued to expand, but the rest of his body didn't. It was a real mystery and Crawford, ever vigilant, kept a close tab on how Liam did his exercises but couldn't fault his techniques. Whilst Tanya and Crawford didn't find his protruding stomach repulsive, neither did they find it appealing either, so why, when he seemed to be doing everything properly, was he getting fatter, they asked themselves?

~ ~ ~ ~ ~

Always on the lookout for some sort of distraction, Ben and Jed had set up a distillery some months ago from equipment they'd unearthed at Ben's grandparents, and finally produced a batch of fiery, barely drinkable moonshine. Neither of them liked it, yet Jed was determined it wouldn't go to waste. The liquid was vicious and seemed to burn a tract through Jed whenever he drank it.

Since he'd started drinking it he'd not been feeling particularly well, mainly in the mornings when he got up feeling sick, although he'd not actually succumbed to being sick yet. Getting up, showered and ready for school had not been an easy task of late. It seemed to take an enormous amount of energy, when he was feeling so sick, and it wasn't until he'd actually had a hot drink and some cereal he began to feel better. His parents, never about in the mornings, were not aware of Jed's malaise, and Jed was not overly aware of it himself. After the first week or so he began to put it down to the fact he'd been overindulging in the 'moonshine'. However, like many a man before him, and undoubtedly many in the future, the aftermath of being drunk did not balance sufficiently to forego a night's drinking.

Jed made the conscious decision to halve the quantity he drank, even though it seemed to be a miniscule amount, but he was not prepared to give it up altogether so kept the bottle well hidden in his room. After all, it made him have the most amazingly bizarre dreams, especially if he set his Imager for some of the more extreme scenarios, and it was the dreams, rather than the drink he couldn't or wouldn't sacrifice. Whatever scenario he set up on the Imager, whether it be sex, adventure or violence, he could guarantee he dreamt about it that night. It was so easy to control the subject of his dreams, and they were so vivid, he knew they were good enough to enter into dream competitions as long as he could get hold of a Dream Machine. His problem though was how to get one, as his parents would not entertain having one in the house and none of his friends had one he could borrow. Until he got hold of a Dream Machine there was no way he'd give up the moonshine.

Ben found it highly irritating Jed was so extremely affected by the drink and told him, in no uncertain terms, he'd be better off not drinking it if he 'wasn't man enough to handle it'. This didn't amuse Jed and he dismissed Ben's caution telling him he wasn't being funny.

'Drinking shit stuff like this was what led to alcoholism years ago so stop pissing about with it,' he'd told Jed angrily. This cautious side of Ben was not one Jed had encountered before, it being out of character for his friend, and the warning went way over his head.

'No, Ben, you're not listening,' Jed protested, frantically trying to make Ben understand why he drank it. 'I can control my dreams when I drink some and set up the Imager. The dreams are bizarre and would win dream competitions – easy they're so vivid, so we could be into a breakthrough here 'cos there's big money to be won.'

'Look mate, if you're that bothered then get your parents to get you a Dream Machine and tell them why,' Ben said in exasperation. 'None of us have a portable Dream Machine and I don't know anyone who has either,' he added impatiently. So get it sorted yourself and stop mythering about it because I am fed up of you harping on about it all the time.'

'Hey, mate, I'm telling you, these dreams are weird. It's not like you're watching them from a distance, it's like you're there as a main player and it's happening around you. They're mega. Last night...?' he started before Ben cut him short, 'Jed, fucking shut up about it. I'm sick of hearing about it. You bang on enough about how many credits you've earned and you're still getting work at weekends so you must have enough to buy one yourself,' he told Jed. Jed shuffled his feet about, kicking at the small stones that lay at their feet in the garden area they were sitting in.

'Yeah well it's not that easy is it?'

'What do you mean it's not easy? What's so difficult about spending your hard earned dosh on a Dream Machine? Either you've got your credits or you haven't. Which is it?' Ben asked impatiently.

'I've got the credits, no problem,' Jed started, 'but I've not got access to it unless I get Mum's or Dad's consent.'

'So what's stopping you? You earned it so you can spend it surely? Just ask them for fuck sake, Jed, and be done with it. At least then you'll be off my back,' he snapped in exasperation.

'Mum and Dad don't approve of Dream Machines and reckon if I buy one, then I've more money than sense. When I told them about these weird dreams and I wanted to enter them for Dream Makers competitions Dad hit the roof and went off on one. Bloody hell, Ben, he's not gone off on one for ages and he really let rip. If I go and buy one neither he nor Mum will give their consent for the transaction, so I'm stuffed. That's why you've got to help me mate, we could enter all the different categories and clean up on those competitions. And if you help me sort out a Dream Machine I'll split everything fifty-fifty with you,' he gabbled on excitedly. 'Come on Ben, old mate. It's too good an opportunity to miss,' he finished pleadingly.

They sat silently for a while, deep in thought. The problem with credit systems was parents had too much control over what could be spent. Even if you set up a secondary account, and tried to use a different identity and age, it didn't work once you went past spending the smallest amount. It automatically recognised the iris and fingerprints and, until reaching eighteen, put it through parental control. It was all well and good iris readers detecting illness early on, but trying to overcome them as a minor, or illegally, was impossible, even with iris and fingerprint distorters; with the two readers combined there wasn't a chance of spending money if your parents didn't approve the purchase.

Even though the two lads couldn't think of a way round the problem it didn't stop Jed taking his nightly nip and setting up his Imager so that he could escape into his Technicolor wonderland. If he drank more than one small measure of moonshine his dreams became violent and unpredictable, and on more than one occasion he'd woken in a cold sweat, terrified his dream was reality, and the intense atmosphere and feeling of realism seemed to hang in the air long after he'd woken.

The others, knowing Jed always woke up feeling sick, were losing patience with him and told him what a fool he was. No matter how much Jed tried to explain things to them, and in whatever tone, he couldn't explain the extremities of his dreams and his desperation to get hold of a Dream Machine.

'What are you going to do when these dreams stop?' Fiona asked one day.

'Stop?' asked Jed stunned, the thought never having crossed his mind before. 'Why should they stop?' he asked in a worried tone.

'Well how much moonshine is left?' she asked.

'Not much,' Jed responded, working out in his mind how long it would last him. ''Spose I better get some more made for when this runs out,' he said out loud.

'Well if you do you're a fool and don't be surprised if your friends aren't around. Don't think we're going to stop around to see you destroy yourself,' Fiona warned.

'I don't intend to destroy myself,' blustered Jed. 'How could I?'

'Well you are by drinking that shit and then to even think of making some more… you are such an idiot. Do your parents know about it?' she asked, rhetorically, 'because I think they should.'

'Oh come on Fi, surely you're not going to tell them are you?' Jed pleaded. 'Just let me get some of these dreams recorded then I promise I won't have any more and won't make any either. But please don't tell them Fi. Promise? Just let me record the dreams first,' he added, his eyes glistening with tears, which took Fiona aback.

Fiona exasperated and with a look of disbelief on her face, got up to go.

'I've got to go Jed,' she told him and then, so there would be no argument 'I'm meeting my mum,' and without giving Jed a chance to protest left quickly.

Jed stayed where he was and sat worrying about his dreams stopping and where he could get a Dream Machine from. His sickness was the least of his concerns. It was only a matter of minutes before he realised he was crying. He really didn't know what had got into him lately but this wasn't the first time he'd been in tears lately. Maybe the moonshine was doing some sort of damage to him after all. He'd just have to find a Dream Machine then he could stop drinking it.

It was a week later when Ben came round, claiming he had a solution to Jed's problem. Arriving at Jed's and once inside his room they closed the door and set the blocker. Ben, who treated the room as his own, programmed the Imager to a beach scene. Within seconds slim attractive women strolled naked about the walls, their pert breasts firm and full and their long slender legs tanned to a honey-gold.

'Reckon I've sorted your problem, mate,' said Ben, distracted by a particular blonde whom he began to interact with.

'What problem?' Jed asked distractedly, annoyed by Ben's behaviour. 'You know they're not real women don't you?' he snapped.

'Yeah!' Ben drooled rubbing his crotch, 'but couldn't you just give her one?' he leered.

'What problem do you reckon you've sorted?' asked Jed, pulling his T-shirt off over his head.

'Your Dream Machine of course,' Ben told him, looking at Jed with a puzzled expression on his face. 'Went to see my chemical contact this afternoon and he's expanding his lab at home. You should have seen him trying to put up some shelves, he hadn't a clue so there's no chance he can fit a bench. It was obvious he hadn't a clue where to start.'

'Anyway,' he continued, waving cheerily to a brunette who stood before him looking invitingly at him from the beach. 'Since his dad died he's got no one to do the practical things and his mum's got no more idea than he has, so he's talking about paying someone to do the work for him. So I suggested you, mate,' he finished in a triumphant voice.

'Suggested me for what? Doing the work?' asked Jed taking off his trousers and standing there in front of Ben, in just his skin-hugging underpants. 'Lot of good that's going to do me when I can't spend it,' he said in exasperation.

'No, no that's where we'll get the Dream Machine sorted,' Ben interjected quickly. 'If you do the work, instead of paying you credits, he'll go and buy the machine. If it costs more than the work you've done, all you need to do is buy him some shoes or something and your parents'll never know. Neat eh?' he crowed triumphantly.

'Really?' asked Jed in delight, one leg in the trousers he was putting on. 'That's brilliant. I could get one of those portables and you guys could borrow it too,' he mused in an excited voice, but stopped as he saw an odd look on Ben's face. Ben was looking at him in an odd way, but Jed had no idea why.

'Ben? What's the matter? Why're you looking at me like that?' Jed asked struggling to fasten his trousers quickly.

'Nothing mate. Just that,' Ben hesitated, not sure whether to say what he was thinking. 'Well, you've started to put on a bit of weight. You had quite a six pack awhile back. I noticed it when we were, we were… well I just noticed it all right?' he added in embarrassment. 'And now… well… you're getting a gut and can hardly do your trousers up,' he finished quickly.

'Yeah! I'd noticed that too,' Jed said, looking down at his stomach. 'In fact most of my trousers are too tight yet I'm not eating more or doing less exercise. Maybe I'm just filling out as I'm getting to the end of my teens.'

'Yeah, maybe,' agreed Ben not convinced. 'But maybe it's more to do with the moonshine,' he added then, dismissing Jed, turned to a group of women on the beach in the corner of the room.

Jed quickly dressed, uncomfortable with Ben making personal comments about his body, and winced at the memory of him and Ben kissing and touching when they'd had their foursome. He hoped to god Ben didn't fancy him 'cos he just wasn't interested. Wondering how to diffuse the situation, Jed pointed to a woman on the beach, who was getting undressed.

'Now that's an eyeful,' he pointed out, to illustrate he was interested in women and not Ben. As if to diffuse the sudden awkwardness between them Ben stood up and walking over to where the woman was poised said, 'You could almost reach out and touch her couldn't you? What a body! Just imagine what fun you could have with her,' he told Jed, grinning. 'Who'd ever want a bloke with dolls like that around?' he finished, and saw a look of relief cross Jed's face.

'Christ, man. I thought for one awful moment you were coming onto me just then,' Jed said with relief. 'So when does this bloke want the work doing? We could look at the Dream Machines at school tomorrow. I might as well get a decent one 'cos I tell you my dreams will win us megabucks,' he finished. 'Is he the guy who got us the grains 'cos I wouldn't mind trying some more? Anyway what's his name?'

'His name's Guy and no, no tabs at the moment. He can't risk losing any more tabs for the next few weeks now he's got the licence, but once he's got his lab expanded he'll be making bigger batches and it'll be easier for him to lose some along the way,' he explained as they made their way out to meet the girls, Jed's head full of the sort of Dream Machine he was going to plump for.

All of a sudden Jed felt completely overcome by emotion and, almost in tears, grabbed hold of Ben's arm and in a tearful voice told him, 'Look mate, I really appreciate you helping me like this. It's brilliant and I owe you one.' To Ben's horror tears were trickling down Jed's cheeks and wiping them away with embarrassment Jed started to stroll quickly ahead, embarrassed he'd ended up crying in front of Ben and for no reason at all. Ben ran to catch up, grabbing his jacket and pulling Jed round.

'For fuck sake, Jed, what's going on? What are you snivelling for? Look mate you can rage at me, shout or even fucking thump me but just don't cry in front of me. Ok?' he demanded, really embarrassed but not prepared to let it go unchallenged.

'I don't know what the fucks up with you these days. One minute you're in a temper and the next crying like a fucking baby. You better promise me you'll stop drinking that stuff as soon as you've recorded the dreams otherwise I won't be around to be embarrassed by you anymore,' he finished, striding away with long angry strides, totally unaware of how to cope with Jed when he was like this.

They arrived at Fiona's shortly afterwards, the atmosphere between them thick enough to be cut by a knife. When they arrived, Fiona and Jade were sitting at a desk, their heads close together.

While they waited for the girls to finish what they were doing Ben said lewdly, 'If you ever hear these two are getting it together, then give me a shout and we'll film it for your Imager. Don't know how we'll keep the camera steady though, 'specially when I muscle in on it,' he told Jed giving him an almighty dig in the ribs, their earlier spat forgotten.

'Do you reckon they're at it then? They're so bloody secretive they won't say anything one way or another,' Jed said intrigued, and the two lads sat happily, quietly fantasising about the girls, whilst they carried on with whatever they were doing.

'I'm surprised you and Jade are still together, mate,' Jed told Ben. 'You're not usually in for steady relationships and you've been seeing her quite a while now. She's certainly keeping you on yer toes about Fi. I reckon you're hooked, mate.'

'Yeah, well,' Ben began to boast. 'She's not the only one you know. I've a couple more on the side although I have to say they're not a patch on Jade. She's all right is Jade and'll help me bide time 'til we're off to camp, I reckon.'

'If that's what you want then go for it, but don't be surprised if she decides to dump you. There's a lot would take her out. Even after she's been out with you,' he joked, getting ready to dodge a playful punch.

Finally Jade left the computer screen and came over to sit on the sofa with Ben, whilst Fiona shut down the system and made her way over to sit with Jed, who immediately began to grumble about her not spending enough time with him. His whiney comments quickly started off an argument and both Jade and Ben, sitting on the sidelines feeling uncomfortable, agreed they'd try to slope off unnoticed. It was Fiona who noticed them going and, grabbing her bag, told them she was coming too, preferably without Jed.

'That's right, bugger off without me,' Jed complained. 'There's nothing new there is there?' and promptly burst into tears.

Ben, Jade and Fiona stood in horrified silence, appalled and embarrassed by Jed's outburst of emotion.

'Why do you always have to go off without me? What's wrong with spending time with me?' Jed wept.

Before he could say anything else Fiona was spurred into action and retorted angrily, 'No one ever knows where they stand with you these days, Jed. One minute you're all happy and laughing, the next you're as grouchy as hell and if that's not bad enough then you're in floods of tears. It's bloody pathetic, Jed, and you've been like this ever since you've been drinking. Well as far as I'm concerned until you've got yourself sorted, I want nothing more to do with you so I suggest that when we leave you leave too, and don't come back.'

Ben and Jade were stunned at this forceful Fiona, they'd not seen before, and embarrassed by Jed crying openly in front of them. They weren't going to wait around to see what was going to happen next so scurried out the door, hoping to leave without being spotted. Just as they were leaving they cringed to hear Fiona say, 'We've all had enough of you, Jed, and it's time your mum and dad knew about the drinking so they can do something to stop you before you kill yourself.' Neither Ben nor Jade heard the response to this but disappeared as quickly as they could. They weren't going to hang round to find out what would happen next, they'd find out soon enough.

~ ~ ~ ~ ~

Over the next few days Daryl found breathing easier, but he was having more trouble bending over and he seemed to be constantly going to the toilet too, and once he'd been it didn't seem five minutes before he needed to go again. The worst thing of all though was the constant dull nag of pain in his lower back. No matter what he did he couldn't get comfortable. He wasn't just thinking it was new trousers he needed but a new bed as well, if things went on as they were.

As a distraction he decided to think about Sonia and what she'd say about his secret life. He knew she'd be shocked and disappointed if ever she found out who he really was, and shuddered at the thought of her finding out and cringed at how close she'd come to getting the same treatment from him. Twice he'd nearly been beaten by his urges, firstly after she'd won the match and then when they'd slept together. He felt saddened by it all and his misery was compounded even more when he realised how little chance there was of them ever having a proper relationship. Deep down he knew he wasn't really her type and wondered if he ever could be.

*Some chance*, he thought bitterly, *and now I'm ill I can't even go to the doctor's or talk to Sonia about it. If only I'd told her I was too scared to go then maybe she'd have helped me out. But then,* he'd thought, *how could she have helped me?*

As Daryl pondered on all these thoughts he realised he spent too much time brooding about things he couldn't change.

*He couldn't undo the rapes and anyway,* he told himself, *they'd all been up for it and gagging for him. Now it looked as if the silly cow from the Fornipub could still die.* In the last couple of weeks he'd not given much thought to the last woman he'd attacked, even though it was constantly on the media about her life still hanging in the balance.

*Even if she does die it won't make much difference,* he told himself miserably. *If she lives or dies the punishment'll be the same and I'll be imprisoned, castrated and deported so why should I give a shit about what happens to her? Anyway she'd been begging for it, the stupid cow.*

Needing something to distract him from his self-pity, Daryl looked round the room and decided to give it a really good clean, not that it needed one. Within a couple of hours anything and everything in Daryl's room had been picked up, cleaned and moved to a different place. The work surfaces shone, the cleansing room was scrubbed, the slumber-pit covers changed and everything else thoroughly cleaned. He'd emptied and cleaned the drawers and cupboards and finally, in his manic phase, not just vacuumed but shampooed the carpet, even the windows sparkled in the early afternoon sunshine. Daryl, one hand on his aching back, his belly hanging low, looked round with satisfaction, pleased with his afternoon's work.

*'If only life was this easy to sort and my back and belly would stop hurting,* he thought to himself as he made his way for a pee, for what seemed like the hundredth time that day. Absolutely exhausted he found his slumber-pit pulling him towards its warmth and comfort and decided he deserved a short rest after all his hard work. Getting undressed and settling himself between the comforting cleanness of fresh sheets he fell asleep almost instantly, but only for a short while. Within half an hour he was awake, his stomach in a spasm of cramp. Reluctant to leave the

comfort of his bed he stayed where he was, sweat pouring down his face. As suddenly as the pain had started it ended, but his back still ached dreadfully and he felt really nauseous.

As the pain subsided, he got up to go to the toilet and get a drink and, picking up a magazine, climbed back into his pit. Leafing through the magazine he realised he'd also got a headache so, tossing aside the magazine, once again lay down unable to get comfortable as his stomach was cramping again, his back ached and his head was thumping. In a vain attempt to ease his discomfort he got up and began to prowl round the room, his hands in the small of his back massaging it in a vain attempt to relax his muscles.

Unable to get comfortable, no matter what he did, Daryl went to bed early, but was kept awake by his intense backache and the griping cramps he kept getting periodically. No matter what he did or how he moved he couldn't find relief from the pain and, although tempted to take time off work, reasoned that work would at least be a distraction and being busy may take his mind off his problems.

~ ~ ~ ~ ~

Dragging himself to work the next day, Daryl felt dreadful; his lower back was agony, his head aching and even though he'd not eaten breakfast his indigestion was so bad his stomach still kept cramping. To add to everything else he was informed, when he arrived at work, the new system was playing up and would need his attention immediately otherwise production would be interrupted. Daryl was just thankful he could analysis the problem from his desk, as he really didn't feel like crawling about in the factory, with tools and diagnostic equipment, at the mercy of all the women.

The day was tough and gruelling, in terms of work and Daryl struggled to keep going. By close of play, was seriously considering not working the next day if he felt as bad. Feeling dreadful he was just about to leave when Patrick called, asking him for help with sorting out a problem first thing in the morning, if Daryl wasn't too busy. Feeling on cloud nine, at being asked to help again, Daryl vowed no matter how he felt he'd be there the next day to take Patrick's call. It was easy saying that then, but his backache and stomach cramps worsened, with waves of intense pain gripping him throughout the night. By morning, as much as he'd have liked to have stayed in bed and die, he dragged himself out of his pit and, determined to impress Patrick, walked out of the house and to work, for what was to be his last time.

~ ~ ~ ~ ~

Despite another inconclusive visit to the medics, the past month for Jack had been quite uneventful. His health hadn't changed, and although there were still problems he didn't feel particularly unwell. In fact, with the exception of his dizzy spells and nose bleeds, he felt really good. Now using an oral spray, for his blood pressure and anaemia, he'd begun to feel better within days. Apart from these minor signs his doctor assured him he had a clean bill of health and even agreed the symptoms he was experiencing could be an aftermath of Jack's recent trauma, and his body's way of getting him to slow down. He advised Jack to submit to the forty winks he fought against, which amused Chloe, and advised Jack to go home, relax and enjoy the company of his wife and puppy.

Finally reassured nothing untoward was wrong Chloe teased him mercilessly about becoming an old man. She even pointed out gleefully he was getting what used to be known as a beer belly, an old man's gut and he wasn't even forty yet! Jack put it down to all the rich foods he'd been eating, in a bid to overcome his anaemia, and his constant consumption of jelly and custard of all things.

When Chloe had quizzed him about the constant array of jellies she was forever finding in the fridge he'd blamed it on the children from the estate, who thought it was brilliant when they were always offered a bowlful when they went to see Wiz. Yet no matter how much Jack bought it never seemed to appease his yearning, and the puzzle was that with all the extra dog walking he was doing he shouldn't be gaining any weight, but he was. He only had to look down at his belly to know this, and fastening his trousers was becoming increasingly difficult.

Jack really looked forward to the evening walks, when they'd venture further afield than in the mornings, hand-in-hand and often with Thomas and Harry in tow. No matter how tired he felt he was determined to keep doing these walks, especially as his girth continued to grow. If he and Chloe walked alone they set a brisk pace, but when the boys joined them they'd sauntered along, Jack invariably entertaining them with stories, making them up as they went along, and encouraging the boys to join in. They were happy times and Jack and Chloe, having found requited love, relished their time wandering under the trees' spreading branches, the weak evening sunlight gently filtering through.

Invariably when they got home Jack would make a pot of tea and they'd sit together, the pup exhausted and asleep at their feet, and halfway through his second cup Chloe could guarantee Jack would be asleep too. Waking an hour or so later, to the aromas of cooking, Jack invariably felt guilty leaving Chloe to do the cooking but she loved it, was a superb cook and used only raw ingredients. Her only stipulation was Jack sorted the dishes and kitchen after supper. It was preferable to his attempts at cooking, Chloe told him, which was usually out of packets and invariably resulted in disasters.

It was late November, just a couple of weeks before Jack's annual check, when he woke from his nap to the aroma of stew and dumplings, his favourite meal.

'Mmm, that smells good, Chloe,' he said, yawning. On hearing her master's voice, Wiz came trotting through to see him, pouncing playfully on his feet.

'Is there any chance of a sponge pudding for afters?' Jack asked hopefully, bending to stroke the pup. As he leaned over he felt an odd lurching sensation in his stomach, which was barely discernable, so he dismissed it without a second thought.

'Jack!' Chloe said in mock astonishment. 'Would I really be doing you any favours if I made you a sponge pudding with your belly growing by the day and your annual check-up next week? I don't think so,' she told him, a smile in her voice.

'I'm really hungry tonight, my stomach's graunching with it,' he told her, rubbing his belly. Why aren't you doing a sponge pudding?'

'Because we're having something different,' Chloe told him, coming over to sit next to him. 'Which isn't as detrimental to your waistline,' she told him, patting his stomach affectionately.

'Pudding Jack, if you insist on it, will be fresh fruit but not,' she emphasised, 'jelly and custard. You're forever eating it and you're not to buy any more 'cos they're not doing you any good. Just look how much weight you've put on lately,' she instructed in a now serious tone. 'If you stopped eating it, the extra walking would soon put it back to rights so

I'm making this a jelly and custard free zone. Otherwise you'll start wobbling around as if you are one,' she finished with a laugh.

Appearing to agree with Chloe, on the no-jelly front, he consoled himself with the fact he'd still be able to get some from the eaterie at work, and if that wasn't enough he could always sneak some in when Chloe wasn't around.

'You're a very hard woman, Mrs Baird,' he told his wife in a low intimate voice. 'But I love you – despite your cruelty,' he finished, quickly dodging out of her way to avoid the swat he knew she'd try and aim at him.

'Get away with you, Mr Baird, and park your butt over there. You've been so idle tonight that I've even had to set the table myself,' she admonished mockingly. Throughout the meal they continued their bantering and when it came to pudding Chloe produced, not fresh fruit as threatened but, a homemade soufflé she knew Jack loved but wasn't as calorie laden as a stodgy sponge pudding.

'You're forgiven, Mrs Baird,' Jack told her grinning as he tucked into the rich but light dessert. 'Exceedingly forgiven you wanton woman,' he told with a wink.

'Thank you kindly sir,' Chloe responded, using the same tone as he had 'But I really think you need to do some extra exercise tonight,' she told him winking back.

'Oh? And what did her ladyship have in mind?' Jack asked, a twinkle in his eye.

'Well I thought a few acrobatics in the pit might just work off a bit of that stomach.'

'Huh,' Jack responded with mock offence. 'You'll be lucky, lady, with the insults you've been throwing about today. Do you want a cuppa?' he asked, as he cleared the plates from the table.

'No thanks. You want help with the dishes?' she asked.

'No, you're Ok. Sit down and put your feet up. After all you're older than me,' he teased.

'Oh yeah!' Chloe called. 'All of three weeks so you better start taking better care of me as I'm an old lady,' she shouted in an old lady voice.

'Well, old lady,' Jack retorted. 'If you're a smelly old lady you better get a tub run for us, and put some nice smells in it to cover up your pong.'

'Cheek!' retorted Chloe making her way up to the bathroom, where Jack joined her a while later. The house boasted a superb bath, programmable for scrubbing, massaging and cleansing, but not drying. Chloe was already in the bath, the lights turned off with candles lit, when Jack climbed in behind her.

Chloe lay between Jack's legs leaning back against him, as he whispered sweet nothings in her ear, kissing her neck and caressing her breasts. Chloe arched her back with pleasure at the silkiness of the bubbled caresses and reaching behind her searched for his penis. She settled its semi-erect length in her hand, knowing exactly how to pleasure Jack, who moaned with desire.

Jack dipped his hand between Chloe's legs, feeling the silky smoothness of her arousal.

Jack, lets go to bed,' she gasped with breathtaking pleasure. 'I want you. I want now,' she moaned and unsteadily got to her feet and pulled Jack to his. Wrapping self-heating towels round them both she led Jack through to the bedroom where Jack knelt beside her, his hand gently caressing her until she orgasmed. Chloe moaned with pleasure, their love-making these past few weeks had been exquisite and erotic and their coupling out of this world; sweet, poignant and very evident of their feelings for each other.

She continued to enjoy Jack's feather-light, sexual touches and reached over to take his manhood in her mouth, savouring Jack's unique taste. As she started to draw his length into her mouth Jack stopped her, hauling her up level with his head and kissed her hard.

'Not tonight baby,' he whispered softly. 'Tonight is all about your pleasure, my love for you,' he told her, kissing her hard on her lips, tasting his own saltiness as he did so. Once again his hand slipped between her thighs and with his other hand he caressed her breasts.

'I love you Chloe. I love you so much,' he whispered, as he continued to caress her.

'I love you too Jack. I just want you so much,' Chloe replied throatily, and again reached for his throbbing manhood, except it wasn't throbbing and it wasn't rampant. It was only semi-erect, so Chloe, taking it into her hand to arouse Jack to full erection, again began to caress him but Jack stopped her, instinctively knowing he wouldn't be able to respond tonight. Hoping she wouldn't recognise his lack of prowess he took hold of both of her hands and pinned them to the warm towels beneath them. Straddling her lower body, Jack ran his tongue across her neck. Chloe groaned in pleasure. Tantalisingly he trailed his tongue across her shoulders and breasts and with each sweep of his tongue, travelled a little lower down her body. Chloe moaned with the sheer pleasure and tried to release her hands from Jack's hold, but Jack was having none of it. His tongue continued to travel down her body, stopping to linger at the sweet centre of her body, where he knew he could drive her past oblivion.

'Jack,' she called out hoarsely. 'Jack I want you now. Please Jack. I want you. I want you so much!' she begged. But knowing he'd not be able to pleasure her that way tonight, Jack continued to caress her bringing her to yet another heart stopping orgasm. As Chloe came down from the height of sensitivity Jack continued to caress her gently, her slender body shuddering occasionally, like the shockwaves following an earthquake.

Her mind, totally overtaken by the sensations of her body was on a different plane and drowsy in the sweet aftermath of their love-making. Jack lying beside her on the towels stroked her hair gently, willing her to go to sleep so she'd not realise the lack of his penetration. If she questioned it tomorrow then he'd have thought of some plausible reason as to why he hadn't – and maybe by then he'd have worked out why he couldn't. But that was another story.

~ ~ ~ ~ ~

Liam, Crawford and Tanya had only been living together for a matter of months when cracks started to appear, which was surprising considering how good everything had been previously. The niggles usually seemed to be aimed at Liam, who was aware of it to the point of feeling uncomfortable. It wasn't something he was used to, nor did he want to be, so one evening in his usual manner decided to do something about it. He suggested to the others he'd cook one of his specialities if he knew they were both going to be around to enjoy it. With experience of Liam's gastronomic skills both readily agreed.

Being owed quite a bit of time off work, Liam took an afternoon off to prepare the meal. The first thing he did on arriving home, after dumping the shopping, was to have a long and much needed sleep in the silence of the flat. It was bliss, and he woke up feeling energised and took a leisurely wake-up shower before finally starting on the meal preparations.

Not only did Liam enjoy preparing and cooking the food, he also loved dressing up the table to give it the right ambience for the type of meal he was cooking. Knowing Tanya's tastes, better than Crawford's, he'd decided on a traditional Greek meal, emulating one they'd shared several times abroad since they'd known one another. It turned out to be a culinary masterpiece, as he knew it would.

Crawford arrived home first and on seeing the set up of the table, and smelling the stiffado cooking, he immediately knew there was big business afoot. Although they'd only lived together a short while it hadn't taken Crawford long to pick up on the hidden messages that passed between his two partners. He grinned from ear to ear and almost burst out laughing as he saw Liam's face drop, when he realised Crawford was on to his motives. Crawford responded by walking over to him and folding him into his big black arms, stroking his back soothingly. He'd have done just the same if it'd been Tanya needing comfort and reassurance, because that was the type of guy Crawford was. As Crawford held Liam, and felt his tension ease, the embrace quickly progressed from one of comfort to passion. It wasn't long before they both found themselves greatly aroused, and were very soon making urgent love against the kitchen surfaces, quickly satisfying each others burning needs of the moment.

They'd barely finished their love-making, when Tanya arrived home and, without realising her two men were busy, sauntered in making appreciative sounds to the aromas drifting out of the kitchen area. She stopped midway, when she saw them still sweaty from their sexual exertions, and muttered a disappointed 'oh' followed by some reference to them starting without her. Liam, seeing her disappointed expression went over and taking her by the hand, led her over to Crawford and without premeditation or spoken word, folded Tanya into the comfort of their embrace, holding her warmly against them.

Liam was the first to walk away, to check his cooking was still bubbling and not burning. Quietly he left the kitchen and went into the cleansing room where he turned on the shower knowing Tanya and Crawford would be joining him in moments, seeing as he'd left the door open. He wasn't to be disappointed and within minutes they were soon busy soaping and massaging each other's bodies satisfying yet more sexual urges in their playfulness.

Their Greek meal eaten, with great relish, it was Crawford who took the lead by opening up the conversation for Tanya and Liam to air their grievances. Tanya's problem was that she'd moved in with the two men on the terms it be a threesome, and although, she'd realised Liam was away a lot she hadn't realised how much it would change the dynamics. As much as she loved her time alone with Crawford, she didn't have the same time with Liam, and she didn't like the fact she found herself missing his presence and the atmosphere the three of them created together. Not only that, but Liam never went out with them anymore. It was as if he was excluding himself from the threesome, and she didn't want to be closer to one than the other.

Liam took this all on board carefully trying to work out his feelings as Tanya talked.

'You're always so tired Liam, and when you're tired you're just no fun. You don't want to play out, you don't want to screw and you don't want to spend time with us. It's like you don't like our company.' Liam let out a great lungful of air in sheer exasperation before setting off on his own tirade.

'Tanya I work damned hard.'

'As if Crawford and I don't,' Tanya snapped back.

'That's not what I meant and you know it. I've got this new project to work on and it's my big chance to make a name for myself. You've just got to understand I want to give it my best shot ever. It's important to me and I've already admitted I'm doing too much and I've promised to slow down. We supported you Tanya when you set up the new business and still do,' he said, halting Tanya by putting up his hand to still her a while. 'So is it unreasonable for me to ask for the same support?'

'No it's not. But I don't come home dead beat and miserable do I?'

'No you don't come home 'dead beat' as you put it Tanya, but I don't come home miserable. Just tired. If you guys hadn't made such a big thing about me taking naps I wouldn't find it necessary to go into the shower and sleep there would I?' he snapped, his voice louder than before.

'You do what?' asked Crawford in shock. 'You sleep in the shower?'

Liam hung his head and then immediately pulled it up again and glaring told them, 'Yes I go for a sleep in the shower. Some nights I'm so dog tired all I want to do is get twenty minutes' sleep. Twenty minutes,' he guffawed, 'and I feel so damn guilty, knowing how uptight you two will get about it, I sleep in the shower because it's the easiest way to keep the peace. Pathetic isn't it?' he said getting up from the table and making his way into the kitchen area.

'Oh!' he said stopping mid-way and spinning round on his heel. 'And as for this,' he said, indicating his protruding belly, 'I know it upsets you Tanya but I've done my utmost to do something about it. I've worked out, I've cut down on traditional food and it's not shifting. I know you don't like it to the point of despising it, but I don't like it either. And I can't get rid of it,' he said, and to the shock of the others started to cry, quickly damping away his tears by dragging his hand across his eyes. Acting as if he wasn't upset he carried on into the kitchen and noisily set about getting mugs out to make the coffee, trying to pretend he wasn't upset or crying.

It was a few minutes before the stunned silence was broken, Tanya and Crawford so shocked they'd not said a word since Liam had left the table. Silently Tanya had followed him into the kitchen and crept up behind him to twine her arms round his waist, surprised they barely encircled him.

'Tubs, aw come on Tubs,' she coaxed softly, leaning against his back and kissing his neck.

'Don't... don't call me Tubs,' Liam said, in a pleading voice trying his hardest not to cry.

'But you're my Tubs, always have been and always will be,' Tanya told him soothingly. 'It's just that... oh hell Liam, I'm just worried about you, that's all. It's so unlike you to be tired all the time and I know you've always verged on being tubby but you've never worked out so hard before either. I'm concerned Liam, that's all. Come here,' she told him turning him round and reaching up to put her arms round his neck and was surprised when Liam started to sob onto her shoulder..

Kissing him chastely she told him, 'I love you Liam, but I worry about you too.' Just at that moment another voice chipped in with, 'Room for a little one here who's worried too?' and turning towards Crawford they opened their embrace to welcome him into their arms, cuddling each other and giving comfort.

235

'If I didn't know better, Liam, I'd have said you were pregnant with your tiredness and pop belly. But I'm glad you're not.' Tanya joked trying to make light of the situation, unaware of just how accurate her throw-away line would prove.

Liam was due to go to the Company Medic for his annual check-up the following week and before the night was over, they'd agreed Liam should have a full medical check to see if there was any underlying reason for his tiredness. Liam agreed willingly, relieved when Crawford, his personal health overseer at work, told Liam he'd set everything up for him. Having cleared away the dishes and flopped down comfortably in the sitting area, instead of engaging in their usual sexual activities, Liam actually admitted he was getting concerned himself. It was comforting to hear the others reassure him he'd be alright and they were there as friends and partners to support him whatever the outcome. None of them though, at that precise moment in time, could ever have imagined what the outcome would be!

~ ~ ~ ~ ~

Within a week Jed had installed the new shelves and benches for Ben's friend and in return got his Dream Machine, one of the better portable models. He'd researched the competition criteria carefully and, having decided which categories to enter, he'd set up the Dream Machine and drunk the moonshine and, over several nights, recorded a number of dreams deleting everything except the best. He was surprised at how vivid and sharp the recordings were and knew he'd got some winners recorded. He wasn't just doing it for the competitions though, now he was doing it to show the others just how bizarre the dreams were, which would explain their importance to him too. He'd got some really good entries, some funny, others erotic and one or two that were downright chilling. The others had been avoiding him since he'd made such a spectacle of himself and he wondered how best to approach them with the view of showing them his dreams. Having pondered on it for some time, he finally came up with a solution. All he needed to do was make sure he could get them all together first and issue his invitation.

Although Fiona hadn't actually spoken to Jed's parents, as she'd threatened, they were becoming disturbed with his uncharacteristic behaviour. Over the past week Jed had been going to bed early and when they were around to see him in the mornings, which wasn't often, then were concerned with how pale and pallid he looked. His mum, who'd been taking some time off work, had challenged Jed about it on a couple of occasions and been openly surprised when Jed had either cried openly or been near to tears. What they didn't know was, Jed woke each morning feeling dreadfully sick and was quite often sick; which so far he'd managed to keep from them. He knew it would pass once he stopped drinking the moonshine.

His supply of moonshine was dwindling fast and, wanting one last bizarre and violent dream, Jed decided to increase the measure and set up his Dream Machine to record a really intense dream for the nightmare section. Once he'd got one for that category he'd be finished, he decided. It was the Friday when he took his double dose, set up the Imager for the scene he and Ben had been so frightened by, and gone to bed to dream. He had a horrendous night.

Getting up the next morning Jed felt worse than he'd ever felt before. Going downstairs to the kitchen he was surprised to be greeted by both his parents; he'd forgotten it was a weekend. They took one look at him and his mum was immediately alarmed.

'Jed, whatever is the matter? Are you feeling alright?' she asked going over to him. 'You look dreadful. Your eyes are all shadowed and purple. Here come and sit down,' she invited, leading him over to the table. 'And I'll get you some breakfast. That'll make you feel better. Do you want bacon and eggs? I'm just doing your dad some.'

The thought of bacon and eggs and the rising smell of them cooking was too much and Jed rushed out of the kitchen, his hand clamped tightly over his mouth, and into the toilet where he was violently sick as he'd never been before.

His mum stood outside the door as Jed retched up the few contents of his stomach. He put his hand on his belly, as if to steady it, and fleetingly was surprised at how much weight he'd put on, but the thought was quickly forgotten as he began vomiting again.

Finally he stumbled out, as weak as a kitten, and made his way to his bedroom, his mum supporting him as he staggered up the stairs. As he gratefully sank onto his slumber-pit he told his mum weakly, 'There's a stomach bug going about at school. I must have picked it up. I'm going to try and get some sleep now ok?' he dismissed her, hoping and praying she'd leave him in peace and not start to ask questions.

'Poor baby,' his mum crooned, stroking his forehead as she'd done when he was a tiny child. 'You get undressed and go to sleep and I'll bring you a drink. The last thing you need when you've a stomach upset is to get dehydrated. Ok babe? I'll go and get some now.'

Jed, probably because of the non-intrusive sympathy, felt ridiculously pampered and, as his mum left, he got undressed and under the covers. Just as he was about to burrow down he suddenly sat bolt upright, quickly looking round the room to see if anything had been left out which would reveal the life he'd been hiding from his parents. Relieved to see nothing was likely to be spotted he snuggled in under the covers, listening for his mum coming back.

Within minutes she was back with water and the controller for his slumber-pit. She came in and fiddled with a few switches and he felt the bed begin to gently undulating to rock him to sleep. He'd forgotten the bed had this facility, but as he drifted off vowed to himself he'd set up the slumber-pit to see if it would alter his dreams.

*Funny I've never thought of using the slumber-pit for my dreams,* he thought to himself as he drifted off into a wonderfully deep and dreamless sleep, unaware that not only had his stomach's peace been broken by his sickness, but that a tiny life was stirring.

On the Tuesday, having spent ages persuading the others to meet up with him, Jed set off to school armed with a bag filled with items he hoped would interest and appease his friends. Arriving at their usual rendezvous he felt as though he was going to a clandestine meeting, and felt tense with anticipation. It felt as though there were a hundred butterflies fluttering around in his belly.

Only Jade was waiting for him when he arrived, but she convinced him Fiona and Ben were coming. Whilst they waited they chatted idly about skateboarding, Jade telling him about the plans for the girls' team. It seemed like an eternity, but was less than ten minutes later, before Fiona and Ben arrived. Jed couldn't help but notice Ben and Jade kissed on seeing each other but Fiona had chosen to sit as far away from him as possible, which hurt.

When everyone was sitting down and Jed had their attention, he reached into his bag and pulling out a bottle, half filled with a milky looking liquid, passed it to Fiona telling her, 'This is for you. Just open the bottle and pour the contents on the ground,' he instructed.

Fiona looked at the bottle quizzically and, taking the lid off it, sniffed at the contents, sitting back hastily as the acrid aroma hit her. Pulling a face of distaste she held the bottle at arm's length looking at it with disgust.

'Is this what I think it is?' she asked with a look of disdain. 'The moonshine you've been drinking?'

Jed nodded.

'So why have you given it to me?' she asked with an edge of hardness to her voice.

'Because I've finished with it and thought you might like to pour it away, seeing's you're so concerned about it,' he told her.

'How do we know you haven't got any more?' Ben butted in. 'I know what a devious bastard you can be. Anyway what about the dreams if you've not any more moonshine?'

Jed, digging his hand into the bag, pulled out a small disc which he displayed on his outstretched hand.

'I've finished recording my dreams and this is just a couple of them. I'd really like you to come and watch them and see for yourselves how bizarre and vivid they are. Then maybe you'll see why I was so adamant about the Dream Machine and moonshine,' he told them. He looked round at their faces, trying to gauge their thoughts. After what seemed like an eternity of silence he turned to Fiona and said, 'Well Fiona what about it?'

Fiona sat silently and then in an offhand, almost dismissive tone asked, 'What difference is us watching your dreams going to make to the way you've been behaving in the past few weeks?' and then, scrutinising Jed's face, 'or how haggard you've been looking?'

'So you don't want to watch them then?' challenged Jed and before another argument could erupt, Jade, ever the peacemaker, jumped in with, 'Well I don't see anything wrong in watching them so you can count me in. Ben, you?'

'Yeah, count me in. I want to see what all the fuss's been about,' he agreed eagerly and turned to Fiona.

'Come on Fi, after everything we've done together you've got to come to this freak show.' Begrudgingly Fiona shrugged and promptly raised the bottle, pouring its contents to splash on the ground, openly watching Jed's face to see how he'd react, relieved he wasn't making any objections.

'Well here's to the old Jed,' she announced, as if making a toast. Let's hope we'll have him back after all this rubbish.'

At three-thirty the following day they walked to Jed's and, helping themselves to refreshments, made their way up to Jed's room and activated the blocker. When they entered, the Imager was set to its default and once settled, Jed activated the Dream Machine, which he'd taken out of its hiding place and quickly hooked up. When they'd sat and watched four of the dreams they openly admitted to having been mesmerised, realising Jed had actually been right about them being something special.

'Fucking hell, mate they was brilliant,' said Ben admiringly, in his usual bad manner speak.

'And you reckon that's all down to the moonshine?' asked Fiona.

'No, not just the moonshine, but setting up the mood on the Imager, so I could take the setting into my dreams and, I suppose, choose what I was going to dream about,' Jed explained. 'But they're not the best. You've just got to see this one; it's awesome, but I warn you it's not for the faint-hearted.'

The four of them settled to watch the next three minute dream and when it was finished sat there, ashen faced.

'God, Jed that was awful. I can't believe anyone could have such an evil, violent dream. It was horrendous,' said Jade in a small voice.

'Awesome,' Ben said, in what sounded like a shocked voice. 'Those gangsters,' he muttered. 'And when they caught up and slit him across his belly and ripped that thing out, ugh!' he shuddered. It had been obvious to them all it had been a hideously deformed child with the face of an evil-looking old man. The gangsters, who'd torn it out, had flung it away and a long and piercing screech of 'Nooooo,' of the discarded monster, seemed to echo on until the end of the dream, then seemed to bounce around in their skulls, so haunting was the scream.

Before anyone said anything more, Jade burst into tears and cried inconsolably. She wasn't sure whether she was crying for the baby, Jed, or the images of his tortured dream. Even Ben sat at a loss for words. It was Fiona who seemed to stir their stumps and spat out crossly, 'Well it just serves you right, Jed, for drinking all that lethal moonshine. I just hope you were telling the truth when you said you didn't have any more left. That last dream was absolutely despicable and I just hope you weren't thinking of sending that one away. It would be tossed in the garbage straight away. And if it wasn't,' she continued 'then it damn well should be.'

'I didn't choose to have that dream, Fiona,' Jed retaliated.

'Oh yes you did, Jed, by drinking then setting up your room with nightmare scenes. Although, why god in heaven, you ended up dreaming about male pregnancy and such a hideously deformed and ugly specimen I have no idea.'

Jed squirmed, aware Fiona's accusations were nearer to the truth than he was comfortable with. He had set everything up and taken a double dose of moonshine in the hope of having a really horrendous nightmare. As for the baby? Well he had no idea why he'd dreamt that.

'What did you think to the other dreams I had, though?' he asked the others, trying to break the strained atmosphere.

Gathering his wits about him, Ben answered, 'The one about fast cars and stunts and everything was brilliant. Not too sure about the space one though, it was a bit naff even if it is topical again. I reckon the other two would be ok to send off, though. What do you two think?' he asked the girls.

'Yeah go for it,' Jade agreed, now much calmer. 'But Jed please don't send the nightmare one. Just get rid of it, destroy it or something. It's evil and I'm sure I'm going to dream about it tonight,' she finished with a worried expression on her face.

'Well I think the whole thing's a total waste of time. How much did you pay for the Dream Machine Jed? 'Cos whatever it was it was too much?' Fiona added disparagingly.

'Well if any of you want to borrow it and see if you can dream better dreams than mine, be my guest,' Jed offered. 'But you won't get the same 'in your face dreams' I had because there's no moonshine left.'

'Can I borrow the Dream Machine please Jed? Not to compete with your dreams but just to see if anyone can interpret a dream I keep having. It would actually help me if you could.' Jade pleaded.

'You're having recurring dreams?' asked Fiona shocked. 'You've never said anything about them before. Why not?'

'Just didn't want to,' Jade answered, shrugging her shoulders and looking a little embarrassed.

'Course you can borrow it,' Jed offered generously. 'It's dead easy to set up and I can show you how it works within minutes it's so simple. I'll bring it to school tomorrow,' he told her, glad the subject had been changed and the heat taken off him.

It was about an hour later before they left and, signalling for Ben to hang back, Jed discreetly gave Ben a small disc.

'Couldn't really show the girls this one mate so enjoy it on me,' he said, punching Ben on the arm as a form of saying goodbye. Ben looked at the small disk and, as it dawned on him what it probably contained, a huge grin spread across his face. Winking, but without saying a word, he left hurrying after the girls.

What Ben, Jade and Fiona didn't realise, as they made their way home, was that within days they'd all be in total awe of Jed, when they believed he'd just revealed to them today what they'd see in the future as a rare and hidden talent. Within a week their perception of Jed was going to change radically.

~ ~ ~ ~ ~

# The Birth
## Tuesday, 7th December 2032
### December Second Trimester

# June – August 2032

It was Tuesday 7th December at 09:15 precisely when Patrick rang; Daryl had already been in work for almost two hours. Together they worked through Patrick's systems synchronising it with Daryl's until they finally resolved the problem. Throughout the call Daryl found himself encountering more and more spasms of pain and a couple of times couldn't help but gasp in agony. Picking up on this Patrick asked if Daryl was ok, to which Daryl told him he'd had a dose of food poisoning over the weekend, the first excuse he could come up with. After several more groans Patrick suggested he should think about calling it a day and go home to rest. By quarter past ten, just as they were finishing their call, Daryl had resolved to do just that, and asked Patrick to ring his mobile later on to let him know if they'd completely resolved the problem.

The call terminated, Daryl, now in acute agony with both his back and stomach, decided a hot drink might help before he called it a day and set off home. Taking a detour via the toilets, where he finally achieved what seemed like a slow and never ending pee, Daryl wondered if this was another health problem developing. Finally finished, Daryl pulled his trousers together, unable to completely fasten them, and made his way, in excruciating pain and on the point of collapse, to the drinks machine.

With dismay he saw Lucy and a couple of the other girls in the restroom and, despite the fact he felt like shit, Daryl grinned at the memory of the lesson he'd taught her. Lumbering over to the drinks machine, and keying in his drinks request, he was suddenly gripped with such an intense cramping pain he doubled over, unable to prevent himself from crying out. It seemed to be forever before the pain eased and he was soaked with sweat and his face so screwed up with agony the girls couldn't help but ask, 'You alright Daryl?'

Daryl's response was to immediately double up again crying out in pain as another wave of agony gripped him. This pain was so intense the only thing which prevented him from falling was his holding onto a rail, which he was gripping with all his might. Just as he managed to stand straight he felt a warm wet sensation run down his legs.

'Yer dirty bastard,' Lucy shouted. 'Yer fucking dirty bastard you've pissed yerself.' Daryl didn't even get the chance to look up before he was bent double again, this time screaming in agony.

Totally overcome by the intensity of the pain Daryl had no idea what was going on around him but suddenly felt strong arms grab him and help him to a seat.

'Daryl? Daryl? You alright mate?' a concerned male voice asked. Daryl could do nothing but scream in pain. 'Ok mate, ok. We'll get yer sorted,' the voice said, then barked, 'Lucy, you girls, one of you do something! There's something seriously wrong here,' he told them as Daryl continued to scream. 'For fuck's sake Lucy, ring a fucking ambulance,' the voice finally commanded, 'and tell the bastards to be quick.' Then the voice told Daryl, 'It's alright Daryl. Help'll be here soon. It's on its way.'

Suddenly it dawned on Daryl what was happening – if they called an ambulance, and he was taken for medical treatment, they'd have his DNA and if they did he'd be a dead man – or as good as.

'No...' he started finding momentary respite from his pain. 'No, I'm alright now...' but before he could finish his sentence yet another pain gripped him, stronger and more intense than the last one and with it Daryl screamed, as if the devil himself was trying to rip his heart out.

By this stage quite a group had gathered to see who was making all the noise and whoever was sitting with Daryl told them all to, 'Clear off and get on with your work. If you want drinks,' the voice told them, 'then go to the other area. If it's just a show you want, then you can all fuck off.'

'Lucy, pass me a drink of water and help me here.' Lucy quickly passed him a cup of water but she'd done her bit, she'd rung the ambulance and given them instructions and as far as Daryl went she wasn't going to do any more.

'Dirty bastard pissed his pants,' she told the gathering crowd. 'I'd get out of the way if I were you he'll probably shit them next,' and with that she walked off. Daryl, having caught every word, was mortified anyone had seen him piss himself, but it would have to be her of all people. Barely had the thought passed through his mind before he found himself crippled with pain again, this time the pain so intense it felt as if his balls were on fire.

*Fucking hell,* he thought. *If I'm going to die let it be quick.*

In the ten minutes it took for the ambulance to arrive, Daryl was in almost constant pain. The pains were coming in intense waves, but at shorter intervals and with more power than the last couple of days. By the time the ambulance arrived Daryl was in total turmoil, desperately wanting help, but terrified of losing his freedom, if they treated him. Despite protesting vehemently he was ok his statement was interspersed with screams of agony, which echoed throughout the factory premises.

Unable to treat him, let alone examine him because of the struggle he was putting up, the medics gave him a spray of sedation and pain relief and started to get him ready to transport to the hospital. With no opportunity to examine him, and despite their patient experiencing chronic pain, they had no idea what was the matter with him, but it was clearly evident he needed medical attention.

Unfortunately for Daryl, the hastily administered drugs were not addressing his pain and the medics, reluctant to administer any more, had their worst journey in memory. In between Daryl's ear-piercing screams he cried noisily and when they'd wheeled him through the factory everyone had stopped working, so piercingly eerie was the noise. They'd all gathered about, waiting to find out what was causing such a furore and so nervous and disturbed were the onlookers that once Daryl was driven away a pall of silence hung in the air for a few seconds, before everyone started speculating. Rumours were rife, the favourites being someone had tried to murder him or he'd lost his hand in a piece of machinery. But no one really believed these, nor could they fathom out what had been the cause of such loud, ear-splitting screams.

The short five-mile journey to hospital was fraught and the two ambulance crew, with thirty-seven years service between them, had never known anything like it. No idea what was wrong with their patient, having had no chance to examine him, their nerves were frazzled by the time they arrived at hospital. Daryl was being totally uncooperative, threatening violence should they touch him, as he repeated over and over again there was nothing the matter. He wouldn't even give them his doctor's name.

The story was much the same when they arrived at hospital. As Daryl continued to scream, the gaps between them becoming shorter, he'd not allow anyone to examine him and fought frantically when they tried to take a blood sample. He wouldn't even allow them to undress or scan him and in-between screams, when the pain had obviously subsided, made determined efforts to get off the trolley to leave, but never made it before the next pain ripped through him.

Daryl was terrified to the point of being petrified. He didn't know which was worse – the escalating pain or samples being taken, which would identify him as the serial rapist. All of a sudden the decision was taken out of his hands as a searing pain ripped into his balls, making him feel as if they were on fire and about to split open. He gave the longest and highest pitched scream yet, grabbing hold of his balls, the tears streamed down his cheeks mingling with the beads of sweat pouring down his face.

'My balls, my balls,' he sobbed. 'They're splitting open. Help me,' he pleaded desperately.

'Ok Daryl, calm down and let me take a look. You must let us examine you if we're going to help you,' a disembodied voice told him.

'No!' Daryl protested, roughly pushing away the hands. 'Noooooo,' he screamed, as another pain ripped through his body. Then all of a sudden he screamed.

'My cock. My fucking cock. It's got a huge lump in it…' and again he screamed an unbelievably high pitched scream.

The doctors by this time had virtually given up hope of being able to examine him without injury to themselves and unless he stopped struggling no one was prepared to get too close. Having outlined this ultimatum the doctor was just about to walk away when Daryl's demeanour changed and he begged the doctor to come back to stop his prick from dropping off.

The doctor gave Daryl a long searching look, as if trying to establish whether Daryl meant what he was saying and if he was going to calm down. Realising Daryl was genuine about co-operating he beckoned a male nurse forward to remove Daryl's clothes. As Daryl's underpants were finally removed the doctor almost reeled back in shock. He could see the entire length of, what had been Daryl's penis, had swelled to the proportions of a rugby ball, and was not dissimilar in shape. Without being able to stop himself the doctor took a sharp intake of breath, causing the nurse to look in the direction of his gaze. They looked at each other, a ripple of revulsion running through their bodies.

*What the hell was causing such an enormous swelling?* the doctor asked himself with a look of disbelief on his face. He'd seen some things in his time but never anything like this!

Daryl, letting out another blood curdling scream was immediately pushed back down on the trolley as the doctor laid his hands on Daryl's abdomen. He felt a hard mass and tracing it down found the same solidity in the groin too.

'Christ!' he said. 'This Guy has one hell of a tumour by the feels of it. How the hell's he been able to walk with this thing? Did you say he was picked up from work? With this thing hanging between his legs?' he asked with utter incredulity. As he said this, the doctor was amazed as he detected a slight movement beneath the skin, and placing his hand on the stomach felt the strength of a contraction, not that he immediately recognised it as this.

'Ok,' the doctor said consolingly. 'We'll soon get this sorted out,' he told Daryl, following the statement through with instructions for the trolley's scanning devices to be set up, as Daryl still thrashed about in screams of agony. Just as he issued the order a security officer arrived informing them there were instructions for them to leave the cubicled area and move the patient to an adjoining room. Issuing instructions for the scanner to be set up in the allocated room the doctor, along with his entourage of medics, readied Daryl to be wheeled from the cubicle. By the time they'd made the few yards journey, and the scanner had been set up the doctor was astonished to see the enormous lump seemed to have moved nearer to the end of Daryl's penis, and Daryl appeared to be pushing.

'It looks like he's trying to discharge this thing. Quick! Get that scanner up and running so we can find out what's happening,' he instructed the nurse urgently. It was merely seconds before the scanner was up and running and as the images appeared on-screen the doctor could not believe what he was seeing. Taking a closer look he uttered, 'Jeeeeeez. I don't believe this.'

The nurse immediately looked at the screen, his first impression making him think he was hallucinating.

'What...' he started before another ear piercing scream split the air.

'Get it out of me,' Daryl screamed. 'Get it the fuck oooooout,' he screamed.

Quickly gathering his wits about him, despite his disbelief, the doctor turned to Daryl, who was grunting and pushing as if he'd been constipated the best part of his life, and announced, to no one in particular, 'Bloody hell I don't believe this. This man's having a baby!'

'Daryl, Daryl,' he told him. 'You're about to deliver a baby so we're going to have to work together on this one.' Daryl's only response was to put more exertion into his efforts to get rid of it, but to no avail.

Examining Daryl more closely the doctor could see Daryl's scrotum beginning to tear with the strain, and the length of his penis looked about to split too. The doctor, shuddering with empathy and momentarily clenching his own legs together, asked rhetorically, 'What the hell am I supposed to do here?' Suddenly springing into action he demanded, 'Quickly pass me a scalpel. If this is actually a baby about to arrive in the world it needs help. Come on! There's no time to waste,' he commanded, just as a uniformed officer was ushered into the cubicle.

By this time several staff from the area, along with one or two patients, were crowding round the cubicle listening in disbelief, wondering if what they were hearing was genuine. Inside, the doctor, who'd quickly donned gloves, had taken a scalpel and raising Daryl's engorged penis, as much as he was able, started to cut from the tip of it right down the length and into the scrotum. Nothing was visible apart from blood and quickly swabbing it away the doctor examined the area carefully, watching as the walls of the penis strained as Daryl pushed.

Quickly instructing two of the staff to raise Daryl's legs up in the air and draw them apart, he pulled the light closer and carefully began to cut the remaining flesh, making small deft cuts as he tried to find where the baby was likely to exit. Several of those present were looking askance, one or two of the male members holding hands over their mouths looking ready to be sick or pass out. All of the sudden there was an almighty crash and turning briefly the doctor saw the police officer lying prone on the floor.

Having located the area, where the doctor thought the baby could be located, he urgently instructed Daryl not to push, and started deepening the incision, which exposed the baby's head, and then cut a second identical incision. Despite this, nothing else seemed to be happening, so mentally changing gear, and putting on his female delivery head, the doctor instructed, 'When you feel the next pain Daryl I want you to push as hard as you can.'

Within seconds, Daryl started to groan and push, the baby moving only fractionally as the doctor urged Daryl to keep pushing. The baby appeared to be moving along, what the doctor supposed was the male equivalent of a birth canal, and it being 'external' meant it was much easier to gain access to the baby. However, the baby was obviously not far enough along for the doctor to be able to intervene, without causing it or its 'mother' more trauma.

'Come on Daryl you need to push again at the next pain,' the doctor instructed.

'I can't... fucking push,' roared Daryl, and the last word turned into a scream as another spasm gripped him.

'Push. Come on Daryl, push,' the doctor encouraged, but again the baby made insufficient movement for the birth to progress. Whilst he didn't need forceps to get hold of the baby, the doctor needed to do something to help its progress. By now a midwife had arrived and admonished Daryl with, 'For goodness sake Daryl there's no need for all this screaming. Women don't scream like this you know.'

'Fuck women.' Daryl screamed. 'Anyway how do you know what it's like?'

'Because I've delivered hundreds,' the nurse responded, 'and had two of my own, so don't try to tell me it's any harder for you. It's just different.'

'That was rather harsh,' the male nurse criticised in defence of Daryl's predicament. 'After all this is different.'

'Only because he's a male,' the nurse responded scornfully, cringing as Daryl screamed again.

'Come on Daryl, one more push should do it otherwise I am going to have to manipulate the baby's shoulders.'

'What... what... what does that mean,' Daryl asked, totally horrified and stunned by what was happening. Before the doctor could respond, another vicious contraction gripped Daryl.

There'd been five people attending Daryl, but once it was established they were coping with a delivery the doctor instructed the two attending Daryl's legs, to hook him into stirrups, then released them for other duties, not that they'd left, as they wanted to be present at what looked like being the first ever male birthing.

The doctor was becoming increasingly concerned about the baby becoming traumatised, with Daryl having been in the final stages of labour for nearly half an hour. As he worked on Daryl, trying to manoeuvre the baby to a better position, a sudden shout was heard.

'The media are here.'

'That's all we need,' the doctor muttered. 'Can we get security in to give us some room and privacy?' he demanded curtly. Just as he instructed this, a female officer and colleague came in, informing the doctor who they were and reassuring him everything was in hand. The doctor grunted acknowledgement just as the officer, who'd just arrived, spotted what was happening and fainted, with yet another noisy clatter onto the floor. Obviously cringing herself, but at the same time annoyed with her officers, the female officer rudely roused her colleagues and hauled them both out of the now overcrowded, cubicle.

Finally there was a muttered, 'Almost there Daryl,' from the doctor and then a triumphant, 'its ok Daryl it's all over now,' as the baby finally emerged safely into the doctor's strong hands.

'It's a...' but the doctor, unsure exactly what sex the baby was, said no more. He looked more closely and then in an uncertain voice said, 'a boy – I think,' in very quiet tones so only those directly round the table would hear.

'Take this child away, check it out, and keep it away from everyone else,' he instructed laying the baby gently in the midwife's outstretched arms and into the sterile wrap she held out.

Turning his attention back to Daryl, he wondered what sort of afterbirth would be delivered. Looking down at Daryl's penis, which lay open like a discarded banana skin, the doctor calculated it would need extensive stapling, stitching and gluing, but quickly instructed the team to reset the scan to see if there was anything else about to surprise them, apart from the placenta. After all, this was anything but a normal delivery.

Within minutes the scanner had again been activated and the sophistication of the ultra sonic technology clearly showed the passage the baby had just taken during delivery. With the advanced 3D imagery it gave crystal clear images of the obscure elements within Daryl's body. Almost ignoring Daryl himself, so engrossed was the doctor in this phenomenon; he set the machine to record mode, regretting he'd not done it earlier.

*If it was possible for one man to have a baby, surely it was possible for other men too*, the doctor hypothesised with himself, *and the more detail and information I get the better.*

Dr Emsam, who'd attended the birth, was in his early thirties and an ambitious, dedicated doctor. To date, his career had been pretty standard, with nothing unusual having happened previously to make his name on.

*If I handle this correctly,* he told himself, *and record as much as possible, it could be the turning point of my career.* With that he decided to get as much data and as many samples as possible, and keep the gathering mob at bay. Just as he was about to check his patient the female officer informed him they would need three samples from the patient, for DNA purposes, and any recording of the proceedings. Before the doctor had a chance to respond, urgent beeps began to sound from the machines Daryl was connected to and his attention was diverted, before he could even ask what the samples were required for. Once again it was action stations and, determined not to let another doctor muscle in on the glory, the doctor diligently set about attending his patient.

Within the last couple of minutes Daryl had deteriorated rapidly, his blood pressure dropping drastically and his skin becoming cold and clammy. His breathing was also become rapid and shallow.

'Daryl?' the doctor asked calmly, to see how responsive Daryl was. Getting minimal reaction he ordered a cocktail of drugs, at the same time checking the scanner and monitors. Making ready to stitch Daryl's penis, he decided to wait a while until, he'd established what was happening with the placenta, its image clearly showing on the monitor. He'd presumed they'd be a placenta, which had been confirmed by the images on the scanner. Daryl, for some time now, had been losing blood steadily and although they were addressing this, the infusions didn't seem to be tackling the problem.

'Damn! I've no idea what to do here. If he's got no womb then where do I remove the placenta from,' he muttered to himself. 'This is so alien I can't make head or tail of. Hold on. Hold on there's some movement here,' he said, relieved to see something moving on the screen. Tracing his finger on the screen he imagined the exit route it might make.

*The problem was,* he surmised, the *first scan showed the baby in advanced presentation and the delivery was too far advanced to see where it had developed.*

Adjusting various dials on the midwifery machine he placed the equipment arms over Daryl's abdomen and initiated a programme to massage Daryl's abdomen, which would hopefully hasten the delivery of the placenta. It worked on women but whether it would work on a man he'd no idea. Daryl was now unconscious and readings showed his condition to be deteriorating and approaching critical. He was obviously in shock, which wasn't surprising in the circumstances, but there was something else not right too. As the doctor pondered on his next action he heard the strident voice of the hospital director challenging what was going on and demanding if it was true a man had just given birth. Dr Emsam chose not to answer, with his patient's needs being more urgent than massaging the ego of his superior. He tried to switch off from the barking demands, which were audible right across the department, scoffing inwardly at the lack of answers being given. He was grateful the police were in control of things, as the last thing he wanted was anyone giving statements to the media and taking his thunder, a privilege he wanted for himself.

Finally the monitors showed a large mass was moving downwards, which the doctor hoped was the placenta. Once it was eventually delivered he could set about the onerous task of gluing, stapling and stitching Daryl up, and pondered whether he should insert two skzips as an alternative, just in case they needed to run tests in the future.

*It would be interesting to know why this man hadn't sought medical attention, as he must have had some pretty severe symptoms over the past few months.* Wondering if the lack of medical attention was somehow connected to the police presence, and their request for DNA samples, he promised himself he'd find out later. Directing his full attention back to the patient he finally set about delivering the placenta, making a mental note to take additional samples for his own research.

*After all he was probably the only doctor in the world ever to have delivered a man of a baby and even if other men gave birth he'd still have been the first doctor to ever have encountered it.* As the enormity of this realisation hit him he realised his eminence was now set for life. *This incredible event will give me the opportunity to become the leading authority on the topic and help launch a high profile career for myself,* he thought as his head buzzed with the events of the last hour. *Who'd have thought any of this was going to happen when I got up this morning,* he pondered, thinking how bizarrely events had unfolded.

Despite the medical care, Daryl had now slipped into a coma and his condition was not good. Determined to keep his patient alive, Dr Emsam decided to move him to the high-dependency unit once he'd finished repairing the incisions. Finally, having finished and stabilised his patient, he gave Daryl drugs to take him into a restorative level of unconsciousness. Alerting the police he was ready to be moved, a route was cleared to transfer Daryl to another area of the hospital. There he'd be guaranteed privacy and isolation, and the police would have easier security controls. There were a variety of escorts for Daryl's transfer, headed by Dr Emsam and protected and flanked by a variety of police and Crimedical staff.

*Anyone would think they were escorting some serial killer or famous celebrity*, Dr Emsam thought as they made their way through the corridors. Which, in effect, their extraordinary patient was, or was to become – but not in the way any of them would like.

~ ~ ~ ~ ~

The morning the real breakthrough in the investigation happened, was a day Melanie and her team would never forget. Of the two unidentified DNA samples, one had finally been identified through the Government DNA Database and a name and address passed on to Melanie's team. Sonia Williams. Who or what she was to the rapist no one had any idea of, but as soon as the information was passed to them, Melanie called air transport to take her directly to the woman's address. At the same time, with it being a working day, she instructed the team to find her work address and pass it onto her, mid-flight. It was more likely she'd be at work, rather than home, and she'd have officers posted at both addresses until they'd talked to her.

Within three quarters of an hour, Melanie had completed the hundred odd mile journey and was met at the woman's home address by the local Crimedical specialist and two constables from the local police force. As they hammered on the door Melanie found herself holding her breath. There was no one in, which wasn't a surprise, so Melanie left the local constables to keep a watch on the property and quickly made her way to the works address she'd received on alighting from the gyrocopter.

Arriving at the works address only minutes later, she was met by another Crimedical officer, who'd discreetly checked the register of personnel on site and ensured the building was electronically sealed against anyone leaving. They'd no idea what connection this woman had with the rapist, what her relationship was with him or even if she was another victim, who'd not reported an attack. It was going to have to be handled sensitively, which wasn't easy when they were going in mob-handed to take the woman to the nearby Crimedical Centre.

Arriving in Sonia's department their purpose was quickly outlined and Melanie, accompanied by the manager, made her way to Sonia's desk. Quietly informing the woman her presence was required at the Crimedical Centre, they waited whilst she retrieved her coat then escorted her, in a mixed state of trembling fear and curiosity, to the awaiting police vehicle outside. They'd given her no indication of what they wanted her for and had not given her the chance to contact anyone either, but quickly swept her away with several dozen colleagues watching her departure from the windows.

Despite being reassured, during the high-speed short journey, she wasn't in any sort of trouble and had nothing to worry about. Sonia was too stunned, confused and frightened to comprehend or demand to know what was going on. All would be explained to her when they arrived at the centre, she was told, although somehow this didn't reassure her. Sonia wasn't used to being picked up by the authorities, the Crimedical bods at that, and she wasn't at all happy, despite reassurances.

Arriving at the centre Sonia was shown into an interview suite, which had all the facilities she'd need during her stay and would give her no reason to leave the area for any reason whatsoever. Still not thinking straight, Sonia sat bewildered as microscopic tabs were adhered to her, connecting her remotely to the Subliminal Voyeur. One of the methods used in the Crimedical Department was not to inform anyone why they were being questioned until they were linked to the Subliminal Voyeur, this way they could monitor reactions, subconscious thoughts and record the spoken word all at the same time, using all the information to correlate responses throughout the interview process. The equipment was even more effective at analysing responses than body language was at portraying feelings, but it recorded those too, adding to their arsenal of information.

Once Sonia was connected to the device, Melanie and her co-officer, Chris, linked themselves onto the Observations Link, which allowed them to communicate silently with their thoughts appearing in written format on their monitors. Once all the monitors were seen to be working efficiently they ran a series of standard questions to establish base levels. From these recordings the equipment would identify any deviations from the norm as different questions were posed and allow them to see when a subconscious thought needed assistance to become consciously recognised.

Melanie began the interview, carefully watching the monitors for Sonia's responses. She started by relating to Sonia how they were seeking a serial rapist, and a link between him and Sonia had been identified, which they were looking to explore. Not only did Sonia's face register non-comprehension and complete shock, but was reinforced by the Subliminal Voyeur's recordings.

The fact that somehow Sonia was associated with a rapist and her DNA had been discovered linking them together appalled Sonia. Her eyes opened wide with revulsion, as she listened to and tried to take in this horrendous piece of information.

*Had she been stalked or in touch with someone who could do something as heinous as rape?* she asked herself. Searching wildly about in her mind the thought she could be connected with a criminal, a rapist at that, made her feel physically sick. All this information was detected and logged onto the machines quietly working away in the background.

She was further shocked when Melanie asked if she'd ever been attacked or raped or believed herself to have been followed, and not reported it. With a look of total horror and confusion on her face, Sonia ran a series of scenarios through her mind before answering. She knew she hadn't been attacked, but wondered if maybe there was some menace she'd not picked up from someone? Finally she shook her head emphatically, dismissing any suggestion of an attack.

Melanie, linked in jointly to a personal Subliminal Voyeur with Chris, pressed a tiny tab on her wrist and deliberately thought, *She's not a rape victim*, which Chris clearly picked up on the monitor in front of him.

'Can you tell me Sonia,' Melanie continued, 'has there ever been a time when you've felt threatened or uneasy with an individual in the past year or so?'

Again Sonia ran through past memories then shook her head confirming again she hadn't. However, as she'd been running through her memories there'd been two signals sent out silently, indicating there was something which had pricked her conscious but she'd not acknowledged it. Both Melanie and Chris had immediately picked this up from their screens.

'Sonia, I want you to think more carefully about any incident you felt threatened by or uncomfortable with. Can you think back again more carefully and see if you can remember any incidents?' Melanie persisted gently, knowing there was something this woman hadn't recognised or was subconsciously blocking. Again Melanie sat and thought, carefully scanning her memories. At one point, Melanie saw a puzzled look on Sonia's face, which correlated with the monitor indicating she was reviewing an incident which could fit the question.

One of the more advanced techniques of the Subliminal Voyeur, was its ability to prompt or screen a subconscious memory. However at this stage, Melanie hadn't linked into this element, as she wanted to hear what Sonia could tell them first. After what seemed like an eternity, which Melanie and Chris patiently sat throughout, Sonia finally opened her eyes and said hesitantly, 'No... I... I don't think so,' but the worried, puzzled look was more intense now.

Melanie once again spoke and this time, with more forthright persuasion, telling Sonia, 'Sonia, there's a memory which you've partially remembered which showed up on the monitor the first time as something you just thought of and then discounted. The second time you came across it though, the monitor showed you remembered it, were concerned about it but decided to dismiss it. Can you recount that memory to us please?'

Sonia sat with a look of total shock on her face. 'You mean... you mean the monitor can show you all those details? Does it show you the events too?' she asked.

'Only if we choose to change the setting,' Melanie told her, 'or you seem unable or unwilling to remember it.'

'What if I wasn't able to remember it?' Sonia asked reasonably.

'If you weren't able or willing to think about it,' Melanie explained, 'or were obstructing it for any reason, whether it be deliberately or subconsciously, we could use the machine to help identify and replay your thoughts. We won't need to do that with you though, Sonia, as you've nothing to hide. Thankfully you're not a victim of this rapist and I don't believe you're shielding him in any way, but I think there's something you've just stumbled across which caused you some alarm at the time of the event and the memory's just tried to resurface. It doesn't look like a one-off situation either, so can you think more carefully and try and recall the situation? Do you think you could do it or would you like me to stop you when I know you're thinking about the incident?' Melanie asked encouragingly.

Sonia, deeply shocked and frightened by some of the things Melanie had just told her, found herself close to tears.

'Do you mean,' she stumbled with her words, 'what I mean is... when you brought me... when I came here with you... you thought I could have been one of the rape victims?' she asked, mortified by the thought and wondering if she'd been a potential victim at some stage.

Melanie, seeing Sonia's distress, explained that when they'd collected her from work they'd no idea what her connection was, but there had been a possibility they could've been dealing with another victim. When Sonia heard this big, fat tears trickled from her eyes and, reaching across, Melanie passed her a box of tissues. She could see Sonia was visibly shaken and confused, but was prepared to do whatever she could to help solve the mystery. Whatever that was.

Collecting her thoughts Sonia shook her head and said, 'No! You asked me if I knew what I was thinking and I can tell you, but I don't think it'll be anything to do with your investigation.' As she spoke she slowly shook her head, as if trying to convince herself the memory was insignificant. The horror of the situation suddenly found her with a terribly dry mouth, and just as she was about to ask for a drink, Melanie reached over and poured her one, her plight having been highlighted by the Subliminal Voyeur. Taking the proffered glass of water, Sonia started to recount the memory.

'I was thinking about an incident a few months back. I was away on a company training course and whilst I was there, the hotel we were staying in was hosting a pool tournament. A colleague and I entered the tournament and, by default, I won the game. The other player from our group had injured his hand and the referee stopped him playing the last game,' she explained then continued. 'He didn't take kindly to that at all, and the following day at breakfast he was really nasty about it and made quite a public spectacle of himself. I'm afraid it didn't end there,' she continued, as Melanie and Chris sat listening to her story. They knew this was the thought she'd dismissed earlier, the monitor having confirmed it, and sat silently communicating their thoughts to each other as they listened to the tale.

'When he came down to the course later,' Sonia told them. 'The tutor forbade him to join us without an apology to me and to the rest of the group. I don't know all the ins and outs of it, but he finally apologised and, well that's it really.'

'So what happened after he'd apologised?' Melanie asked, having noticed a change in the monitor's display as Sonia had quickly ended her explanation.

'Nothing really,' Sonia told her, not really giving it the credence it warranted.

'So the group just accepted the apology and forgot all about it?' asked Melanie sceptically.

'Well…' said Sonia thoughtfully. 'Well, no not really. Daryl came and apologised, he was really upset and contrite and then all of a sudden, he started telling us about his upbringing. Apparently his dad had died when Daryl was young and his mother was a tyrant. He became quite emotional and then all of a sudden he called me 'Mam' and when he realised what he'd said he got really upset and… well it looked like he panicked and ran from the room,' she finished lamely, with thoughts of confusion clouding her normally lucid thinking.

'So what happened then?' Melanie encouraged gently.

'Well Patrick and I, Patrick was one of the others on the course,' she explained, 'we went up to see if he was ok. Anyway we agreed it would be better if I talked to him alone, as the argument had originally been against me and it was me he'd called 'Mam', but before I went in Patrick insisted I set up my mobile with an urgent help signal.'

'And did you?' Melanie asked, to which Sonia nodded her confirmation. 'Any idea why Patrick suggested you do that?' she prodded carefully.

Sonia sat thinking, looking puzzled, then shrugged her shoulders and added, 'No, not really, except he'd seemed so aggressive at breakfast. I suppose that's why.'

'In what way aggressive? What sort of things did he do or say?' Melanie probed gently and Sonia explained his reaction and some of the names and accusations he'd used in the heat of the moment.

'So tell me about what happened when you went into the room to talk to him,' Melanie asked gently. Once again Sonia started to reiterate what had gone on and how Daryl had behaved. Both Melanie and Chris listened intensely, whilst at the same time watching the monitor to see what sort of effect the story was having on Sonia as it unfolded.

When she'd finished Melanie asked, 'So did you have to activate your signal to Patrick?' Sonia shook her head. 'So what happened next?' Melanie asked, and Sonia explained how she'd gone down to meet Patrick, told him what had happened and how Daryl's life had seemed. Then just before going back into the course, Daryl had joined them and they'd all gone back in together as if nothing unusual had happened, two days later going off their own separate ways.

'And did you keep in touch with Daryl?' Melanie asked, and pressing the tab again, asked Chris if this was the link, but telling him she didn't want to push it too hard just yet. Chris confirmed he thought they were onto something too. The monitor certainly seemed to indicate it.

'Both Patrick and I kept in touch with him and started meeting up once a month.'

'What right from the time you left the course?' Melanie asked innocently.

'No,' Sonia responded shaking her head. 'It was Patrick who got in touch first because he was having problems with his system. I think he got in touch with me and someone else first, but our companies produce different products to Patrick's. Finally he got hold of Daryl and I think they sorted the problem out pretty quickly. It wasn't long afterwards we all met up, and you could tell Daryl was over the moon about solving the problem,' she recounted. 'It was quite sweet really because it was as if he'd done something really clever for the first time in his life and been acknowledged for it. He was like a dog with two tails he was so proud of himself. But not in an officious manner,' she added quickly.

'So when did you finally meet up with Daryl then?' Melanie asked, checking the monitor where Chris was prompting her to ask when and why they'd finally met up.

'About six weeks later,' Melanie answered in response to the question.

'Which would have been when?' Melanie asked, and Sonia, racking her brains trying to remember when it was, suddenly remembered it was the day she'd been going to the theatre and gave Melanie the details.

'What sort of products does Daryl's company manufacture?' Melanie asked.

'Nappies and baby bottles I think. He works for NapPals in Leeds,' she told them. 'It's pretty miserable for him there by the sounds of it. He told us no one likes him where he lives, and he hasn't any friends. His colleagues at work weren't the nicest to him either and his Mam couldn't bear him, so at weekends and when he was on holiday from work he had to go away, because his mother couldn't stand having him in the house,' she waffled. Whilst she was imparting this information Melanie could feel the excitement in her rising.

*This was their man,* she communicated to Chris via the Observations Link. *It's got to be because it fits in with everything and if he keeps going away his attacks may well fit into the pattern of his excursions.* Chris, who'd sat up straight as the realisation of what Sonia was telling them, quickly agreed with Melanie.

'So you met up, the three of you, and then what happened?'

'Well we all met up for lunch and then played the rematch of the pool game we'd talked of playing once Daryl's hand was ok. We'd both agreed Patrick should referee, which he did,' Sonia told them.

'You mentioned, 'when Daryl's hand was better', so what was the matter with it?' Melanie asked, and Sonia explained how a healing cut had reopened whilst they were playing, which was why the match had been stopped in case it soiled the table.

'So hadn't he had medical treatment for it?' Melanie asked sending another silent message to Chris that this could be it.

'Well apparently he'd had blood poisoning and the doctor had been looking after it,' Sonia told her with a shudder, 'but it was an awful mess, all red and inflamed and the sides looked really jagged.' Again Melanie sent a silent message to Chris saying this looked like an indication of medical attention avoidance from the description of the wound.

'So you had the game of pool and everything was ok, was it? I mean who won?' Melanie asked, disinterested in the game's outcome but wanting to know how things had progressed and how this fitted in with the picture she was forming about Daryl's character.

'Well I won the game, but only just,' she added hastily. 'We were quite evenly matched skill wise, but I suppose I got lucky. Daryl took it quite well this time, but then we'd both learnt quite a bit from each other.'

'Then?' Melanie asked having to restrain herself from asking Daryl's full name for a few moments.

'Well Patrick went home and I stayed on a while longer,' Sonia explained casually.

'And you say you met on a monthly basis, so how did things progress from there?' Melanie asked. To which Sonia outlined their meetings.

'Did you and Daryl ever have a relationship?' Melanie asked in a bland tone.

'Well… sort of,' Sonia replied shuffling uncomfortably in her chair.

'Go on,' encouraged Melanie feeling a stir of excitement start as her instinct kicked in telling her they were definitely on the right track.

Sonia explained how they'd booked into a hotel together, in separate rooms, but ended up sharing a bed for part of the night. Neither of them had planned to sleep together but Daryl, who'd behaved quite oddly over the topic of sex, had turned the night into a disaster and things had become quite ugly.

'How do you mean it was a disaster?'

'Well I'm not sure if Daryl had ever had sex before,' Sonia started to explain.

'What made you think that?' Melanie asked, just as Chris sent a sarcastic but pertinent message through saying it was probably the 'first time he'd attempted to have consenting sex,' and Melanie had responded silently by agreeing with him.

Sonia shrugged her shoulders, indicating her puzzlement over the situation and then said, 'Well… well it was like he didn't know what to do or was… well… I don't know… somehow frightened. He'd no idea how to touch me and was really rough,' she said shivering with the memory.

'Did he hurt you?' Melanie asked. Sonia's head shot up as if to protest and then she stopped herself midway and seemed to change track. Her face furrowed, in a frown of memory, and after a few moments silence said, 'Well, yes, I suppose he did. He grabbed my breasts really roughly. Roughly enough to bruise me,' she added as the memory came flooding back. 'But then...' Sonia's colour rose as she looked worriedly at Melanie then at Chris.

'Go on,' Melanie encouraged gently. 'What happened next?'

'Well... well I could see that he wasn't... wasn't... fully aroused,' Sonia said as quickly as she could in embarrassment. 'And then... so I... well I reached out to touch him and as I did he... well he just lost it altogether, his erection I mean and then... and then he started shouting at me and calling me names and... and...' It was at that moment the realisation Daryl could potentially be the rapist hit her, and the enormity of this morning's events and her liaisons with Daryl started to crash in on her.

'You don't think... you don't mean... please tell me... please don't tell me Daryl's the rapist?' she asked Melanie desperately, the full horror dawning on her of what the events that night could have entailed.

Melanie, by this time, was pretty convinced that if Daryl wasn't the rapist, then he was hiding something else. Chris was thinking along the same lines and their collective and individual thoughts flitted from screen to screen, filling up scrolls of the monitor to be looked at and studied later, when the interview was analysed.

Now was the time to ask for a name, Melanie decided, and just as she was about to ask a message came over on the monitor, which was linked in to an observation room outside, that she was urgently required.

'Sonia, what's Daryl's full name and do you have an address for him?' she asked urgently, desperate to get the details and be able to leave the suite as soon as possible.

'Well all I know is that his name's Daryl Payne and he lives in Armley, just outside Leeds. I haven't got an address but he works at NapPals so they'll have his details,' Sonia finished and before she could put a full stop at the end of her sentence, Melanie was excusing herself to take an urgent message.

As Melanie left the room, still linked into the Observations Link, she sent a silent message to Chris to keep Sonia talking but not to give too much information away.

*Looks like this could be our man*, Melanie conveyed to him on screen. *And with him working in the baby bottle industry it links with the trace elements we found. I'll keep the link open so I can be kept informed of how the interview's progressing. In the meantime I'll send Judy in to act as female officer.* Chris responded to all this adding a 'fingers crossed' and set about ordering refreshments to while away time until Judy joined them, and they could recommence.

When Melanie shut the door behind her one of her officers came hurrying over to her and told her urgently, 'We've got a positive identification on the other DNA sample. It belongs to a Sharon Payne at Oldham Road, Armley. She's sixty-two years old, so could be the mother.'

'And Daryl could live with her and if he does, he's been on our doorstep all the time,' she added with annoyance, gathering her thoughts ready to issue orders to her staff who were waiting in expectation.

'Right,' Melanie responded, strolling determinedly into the control room with the police constable hot on her heels. 'It looks like we have a name, address and place of work for our rapist. Whether he is or not I want all action now with utmost discretion. I want Sharon Payne, who could well be our rapist's mother, to be brought in for questioning and for a watch to be put on all entries and exits to the house if this Daryl isn't there.' As she did this she pointed at different officers, whom she wanted to carry out her instructions.

In the meantime I want you, you and you,' she said, indicating her three best officers 'to come with me in the scrambler. We're going to NapPals in Armley, where Daryl Payne works. Inform the local police and get them to go in now and seal the premises, but to do it discreetly without police vehicles being evident in case he's not in the factory. Now go,' she instructed in her no-nonsense tones.

Within minutes the officers were all on their way out, to their various tasks, and Melanie was leaving instructions for the rest of the team as to what they were to carry on doing. Her final instruction was for Judy to attach herself to the Observations Link and go into the interview room and to relay everything to Chris via the monitor, and to find out what they could about Daryl and the relationship between him and Sonia.

'Lets just hope this is our man,' she told the remainder of those left in the control room, holding her right hand up with the index and second finger crossed in a childish gesture. 'But every instinct in my body tells me this is it,' she finished as she rushed from the room and out to the Scrambler, ready to take yet another long journey in an amazingly short space of time.

Arriving at the factory Melanie was pleased to see police strategically but discreetly placed by the numerous entrances to the factory and there'd been an area cleared for the small aircraft to land. Scrambling out of the craft, and back onto terra firma, Melanie made her way quickly to the entrance of the building. As she approached the main door the local Crimedical guy stepped out of the entrance and waylaid Melanie in an authoritative manner.

'Morning Melanie. Looks like there's been some sort of incident here this morning and the staff are pretty fazed.'

'What sort of incident?' Melanie asked, immediately concerned.

'It appears the bloke we're after collapsed with stomach pains. He was taken to hospital a short while ago but not without a load of fuss first.'

'What sort of fuss?' Melanie asked.

'Refused to let the medics touch him. Wouldn't let them examine him or touch him and they ended up having to sedate him he was in such a state.'

'What – in a state through pain or something else?' Melanie queried.

'Sounds to me like a bit of both. According to the staff here, he didn't want anyone near him and he got quite aggressive. Said it was weird when he was in such pain,' Jock told her.

'So where is he now?' Melanie demanded. 'We need to find somewhere we can catch up on everything and find out what the situation is here.' She started to move away and just as she was turning to walk away she stopped in her tracks as if a thought had just struck her.

'Isn't this where Lucy Johnson works? You know the last victim he raped? I'm sure this is where she works.'

'Don't know Melanie. If you hold on a minute I'll just check the security records,' she was told.

'Right, you do that, I'm going to get someone posted at the hospital,' Melanie instructed him.

Within minutes she was connected to the hospital and put through to the department where Daryl had been admitted. Immediately the Ward Manager came online and Melanie formally introduced herself, outlining her rank and authority within the Crimedical Department. Checking they'd had a patient by the name of Daryl Payne admitted, and confirmed, Melanie outlined the situation and the need for security to be posted nearby until her officers arrived.

'When my officers arrive I'll need one of them posted inside the treatment area and two others posted outside.' Melanie explained. 'Is it a securable area or a curtained cubicle he's in?' she enquired.

The manager explained he was actually in a curtained cubicle but was being moved into a diagnostic room shortly for scans and other detecting tests and there were two doors in the room.

'Would that make any difference?' she'd asked.

'Is it possible to have both of the doors manned by your security or one of the doors locked?' Melanie asked, and explained how vitally important it was their patient be kept under close surveillance with a strong police presence at all times.

'What's he under surveillance for?' the sister asked innocently.

'I'm afraid that's something I can't disclose at the moment, but I can advise you he's a tendency towards violence and shouldn't be antagonised,' Melanie told her.

'I don't really think that'll make much difference at the moment,' the sister told her. 'The pain he's in he'll be as weak as a kitten before long, although we'd already noticed his violent tendencies.'

'Has he harmed or threatened anyone?' Melanie asked solicitously, 'Because if he has we'll need reports.'

The ward sister assured Melanie there'd been verbal threats and his trying to physically restrain anyone from touching him. She then went on to explain the situation had since changed, and Daryl was now in so much pain he'd been drugged and wouldn't be going anywhere.

'What I need is for you to move him to the diagnostic room now and have the area secured. Can you get your security guards stationed in the area until my men arrive, but until they do, it's imperative your patient is not aware we'll be arriving and he must not, under any circumstances, be allowed to leave,' Melanie instructed her.

At this statement the ward manager laughed heartily and told Melanie cheerfully. 'You really don't need to worry about our patient going anywhere. He's in extreme pain and letting everyone know about it. In fact you can probably hear him in the background now,' she told Melanie with a scoffing laugh.

'Good god!' Melanie exclaimed on hearing a high pitched scream in the background. 'Is that him? For god's sake what's the matter with him?' she asked.

'That's something only time will tell. We've not diagnosed him yet, which is why we're moving him for scans,' the manager laughed. 'But he's been like this ever since he arrived. Wouldn't let anyone touch him and was really aggressive to start with. We've sedated him now, and administered pain relief, but he's still letting everyone know about his pain. Anyone would think he was having a baby with this carry on. Not that,' she added, 'I've ever heard a woman making half as much noise as this. It'll probably be a tiny kidney stone or something. I just hope they get him sorted soon, as his racket's driving everyone mad and frightening the other patients,' she told Melanie in exasperation. 'Right oh, we'll get our security sorted and wait for your men to arrive. I presume you'll be coming over yourself?'

'Yes I'll be there shortly and check in with you when I arrive.'

'Sounds good to me. I'll start a fresh brew of coffee shall I?'

'Don't worry about the coffee, although one wouldn't go amiss,' Melanie added as an afterthought. 'I'll see you shortly.' Just as they were about to terminate the call, the ward manager quickly interrupted with.

'Oh, just a minute. Looks like your officer's just arrived. Can you just hold on whilst I check?' Without waiting for Melanie to reply she left the phone and walked over to the officer. Melanie could hear the conversation in the distance and knew her men had arrived and would deal with the situation as was required.

Having sorted out security at the hospital, Melanie went back into the factory to find Jock had arrived, and was surprised to see Lucy standing talking animatedly to him. She had a big grin on her face and a glint of malice showed clearly in her eyes. Melanie couldn't help but smile back in response, this was a totally different woman to the one she'd originally seen who'd been brought in battered, bruised and raped with little confidence and an enormous font of fear hanging over her before they'd started the re-programming.

Lucy and Melanie went off into one of the small offices and Lucy told Melanie everything that had happened that morning.

'Can't believe the dirty fucking bastard pissed hisself though,' she finished, sniggering at his misfortune. 'Anyway he's a creepy bastard and gives me the shivers. He's forever creeping round the place on his

Silent-Sole shoes, and making me jump. Spooky it is so I hope the bastard continues to be bad for a while. It'll teach him a lesson,' she told Melanie. Then, as if it had suddenly dawned on her that she didn't know why Melanie was there she asked innocently, 'Anyway what you here for? You come to tell me you've caught the bastard wot raped me?'

'Lucy?' Melanie asked, her head cocked questioning to one side. 'Has Daryl always crept up on you?

'Nah. Don't fink so,' she drawled after a minute. 'But he's been doing it ever since I came back to work, yer know after I was attacked.'

'Are you sure about that?' Melanie asked. 'I mean are you sure he didn't do it before, but you weren't aware of it, until you became more jumpy?' Melanie watched as Lucy thought carefully about it. Finally she responded with, 'No. Definitely not and I tell you why. When he started doing it and I complained to the rest of the girls they pointed out he'd new shoes. You know some of those silent footstep ones or whatever they're called. He's always given us the creeps but those shoes made him ten times worse 'cos we couldn't hear him. Even after he got fat he managed to creep up on me and make me jump. Hey did I tell you about that time in the club?' she asked out of the blue and went on to tell Melanie about the time he'd gone to the club and when he'd kissed one of the girls had come and left a big wet stain on his trousers.

'Anyway we reckon he's still a virgin,' Lucy sniggered unkindly.

The more Melanie heard about this character the more he fitted in with their profile of the perpetrator.

'Lucy,' Melanie asked again, but in a quieter voice than before. 'Does Daryl ever use a handkerchief? You know a cloth one?'

'What his granddad snotter?' Lucy asked with a scathing laugh. 'That's what we call it 'cos no one's used those since last century and...' And then slowly it began to dawn on her why Melanie had come to the factory. The colour drained from her face as she asked in a frightened but astonished voice, 'Do you... do you mean that... that he's ... he's the bastard wot raped me?' she asked, a look of horror on her face. Melanie did not answer but watched Lucy steadily go through all the emotions of what that moment meant to her.

Unfortunately at that moment Melanie's mobile rang, and she quickly excused herself whilst she answered the phone. Through her trauma of emotions Lucy half heard the conversation, but her mind was in such turmoil she hadn't really taken on board the shocked and intrigued expressions on Melanie's face as she'd listened to her caller.

Finally Melanie terminated the call and turned her attention back to Lucy, who looked to be in a state of angry shock. Checking she was alright, Melanie told her she was just going to have a word outside, and before Lucy could respond went out closing the door carefully behind her.

Catching Jock's attention, Melanie beckoned him over.

'Jock!' Melanie said urgently 'Jock I've just had the most astonishing call but it's in total confidence until it's confirmed, including your workmates,' she warned.

Jock nodded his tired assent, having heard it many times before. Everything was confidential as far as he was concerned, but he certainly wasn't prepared for what Melanie told him next.

'Daryl Payne. I've just had a call from the hospital. Apparently our man's in labour and about to give birth to a baby.'

'Oh yeah Melanie, very droll. I thought you'd better taste than to joke at a time like this,' he said, jerking his head to the door, behind which Lucy sat, possibly one of the bastard's victims.

'Jock, I'm not joking,' Melanie told him, her hand on his arm and looking directly into his eyes. 'I have just been informed our bloke's in hospital and about to give birth to a baby.'

Still Jock didn't believe her and guffawed at Melanie's wit, even if it wasn't appropriate. Then as he watched her steadfast expression he began to realise she wasn't joking.

'Nah,' he said dismissively. 'Someone's winding you up.' Melanie said nothing, but carried on looking directly into his eyes until Jock, taking on board what she'd just told him and the reality of it all was finally sinking in, his eyes opened wide, his eyebrows rose dramatically and his mouth dropped open.

'I want you to go back in there Jock and sit with Lucy. We're going to have to take her to the Crimedical Centre to interview her again and if what I have been told is actually happening it's going to hit the media big time and she's going to be completely stunned. Especially,' she added running ahead of herself, 'if he's become pregnant through carnal means with one of his rape victims.'

'You mean... you mean she could be the... the mother?' he asked with shock and incredulity.

'Don't run ahead with your imagination, Jock, and for Christ sake don't let anyone else know what's going on. If he's having a baby there might be a second parent otherwise he could be self-producing. Who knows? After all who's ever heard of a man having a baby before?' she asked, going back to the room to speak to Lucy. Just before opening the door, she stopped and turning to Jock told him, 'I'm trusting you on this one, Jock. If you let anything out about this to Lucy, or she hears it from anywhere else, I personally will see you're severely disciplined. You know the state she was in when they found her, so just imagine what this could do to her, which is why she mustn't know until we've got her to the Crimedical Centre and know exactly what the story is. Do you understand, Jock?' she asked once again looking at him directly to assert her authority and the severity of the situation to him.

Jock, totally bowled over by the news, but an element of him still sceptical, nodded mutely and then, as if mentally pulling himself up with invisible marionette strings, straightened up, brushed his jacket down as if there was big business afoot, and responded with, 'Melanie, you can trust me implicitly. I'll protect Lucy from coming into contact with anyone between here and the centre. Think we should get her moved straightaway?' to which Melanie agreed. Entering the room with Jock they found Lucy pacing angrily.

'If it was that fucking bastard,' she spat as they entered the room 'And the dirty fucking bastard pissed himself. He had that dirty fucking thing inside me,' she said the tears flowing swiftly down the highly coloured cheeks. 'He fucking raped me the dirty fucking bastard,' she wailed, her voice rising dramatically. Melanie went over to the distraught woman and putting her arms around the thin shoulders led her over to a chair to sit down.

'Lucy. Lucy, listen to me,' Melanie instructed her gently. 'You remember Jock don't you? He was at the Crimedical Centre after you were attacked. Remember?' she waited for Lucy to acknowledge this. 'Well I'm going to have to leave but I want you to stay with Jock. We're going to order transport and I want you to go back to the Crimedical Centre so we can interview you again and record your subconscious memories. All right?' Lucy nodded dully at this. 'Then we'll look at different ways in which we can help you get through this, but just remember we're not totally sure it was him. We've still got to establish that for sure. Ok?'

Lucy looked at Melanie with a tear stained face. 'It is him. I know it's him. It all makes sense see?' she told Melanie bleakly and promptly started crying again.

Patting Lucy comfortingly on her arm Melanie turned to Jock, one of the best men she'd ever worked with, and told him unnecessarily, 'Look after her Jock, and don't let anyone get to her. If what we've heard is true it'll be with the media before the hour's out and on every outlet imaginable. Get her to the centre and start recording every thought and memory possible. Ok?' Telling Lucy she was leaving and would see her later, Melanie left to make her way to the hospital.

When Melanie arrived she could see chaos was about to break out. There seemed to be an extraordinary amount of media vehicles with more approaching, she noted as their Scrambler hovered overhead. Melanie quickly linked into her colleagues on the ground, and for what seemed like the umpteenth time that day, barked out a string of orders to take control of the situation before it got out of hand. She assumed the press were there because they'd heard about the impending male birth and wondered how the hell the news had got out so speedily.

Quickly alighting from the aircraft and making her way into the hospital, she knew immediately their rapist was still in the building, by a shrill high pitched scream echoing through the corridors.

*Typical,* she thought, *everyone's always joked about the world's population being brought under control if men were to have babies. If this is anything to go by,* she winced as another scream, ear piercingly close rent through the air, *then they were right. Couldn't he make more noise about it,* she laughed inwardly comparing a woman's bravery next to this man's cowardice at just a little pain. Especially after all the pain and suffering he'd inflicted on others.

Melanie followed the noise down the corridors and through the crowds which were gathering as if at a messiah's arrival.

*They'll be bowing at his door and proclaiming miracles at this rate,* Melanie muttered to herself in disgust. *If only they knew what I know it'd be a different story.*

Melanie finally arrived at a door guarded by a local policeman who had, until a few minutes before, been stationed inside the room as instructed. His face was ashen but it didn't stop Melanie demanding to know why he wasn't inside the room.

270

'With that going on?' the policeman said shakily. 'He'll not be going anywhere. Anyway they've locked the other door,' he told her.

'I don't care if they've bricked up the other door and all the windows,' Melanie said tartly. 'Your orders were to stand guard inside and you've totally disobeyed.'

'But... but–'

'There's no 'but'. Your orders were given to be followed so I suggest you get yourself in there forthwith. Otherwise you'll be facing a disciplinary hearing. Do you understand?' Melanie demanded and watched as the young officer reluctantly turned and made his way back into the room, just as Melanie spotted Sean walking down the corridor towards her.

'Is this for real?' he asked her as he approached. 'Our rapist's in there having a baby?'

Melanie nodded and immediately asked for an update on what was happening elsewhere with the case.

'The mother's been picked up,' Sean told her 'And Jock's on his way over to the Crimedical Centre with Lucy. Should be there any minute now,' he added looking at his timepiece. 'Have we managed to get any samples from this chap yet or is it too soon?'

'From all the noise and chaos in there it looks like there's no chance yet. Talking of chaos I've instructed extra police support for the security here. I did wonder how the news had got out so quickly but I got the answer when I came in and heard his squeals,' she told him, rolling her eyes upwards in mock exasperation.

'How's this baby being born?' Sean asked, and looking down Melanie was amused to see him almost crossing his legs as his imagination ran riot.

Before she had a chance to answer, they heard a loud bang followed by an even louder crash and both looked at each other, an ominous silence hanging in the air. In a split second, fearing the worst, both made a grab for the door handle and muscled their way into the room.

The first thing Melanie saw was their police constable lying prone on the floor. The next thing she heard was a 'Jesus fucking Christ. I don't believe this.' Looking across to where her colleague's gaze was focused she was astonished to see Daryl with his legs held up and apart in stirrups and a doctor positioned between his legs, carefully cutting down the length of Daryl's penis with a scalpel. Melanie felt a wave of shock wash over her and mentally shook herself. Just as she turned back to Sean she saw he was white-faced and starring transfixed at the sight before him. As the doctor started to insert his hand into, what looked like a glaring gash, Melanie saw Sean sink, in what appeared to be slow motion, into a faint on the floor, quickly followed by one of the male nurses. The men in the room were dropping like flies and, the only one who seemed unaffected by what was happening was the doctor, who was so intent on what he was doing he appeared to be totally unaware of what was happening to the others in the room.

Melanie herself was shaken out of her state of shock by the next ear piercing scream, which was so loud it necessitated Melanie putting her hands over her ears to block it out. When the long, soul wrenching scream finally ceased, and Melanie had taken her hands away from her ears and opened her eyes, she saw both her colleagues were coming round. In what seemed like a comical sequence they both sat up simultaneously, the young constable clamping his hand onto his head, which was bleeding from his fall, and all three of the men looked as white as ghosts. Amused by their faintheartedness, Melanie watched as each of them looked anxiously towards the couch where Daryl was being treated. Melanie went over to her two subordinates and said sarcastically, 'Thought you men were meant to be hardened?' she told them gruffly, not amused by her colleagues falling like flies at the first sight of blood. 'Women have been doing this for years,' she said to them, 'so I don't see why it should be any different for you men.'

As she finished speaking she turned to the table to see the blood smeared, crumpled head of a baby appear between the legs hanging in the stirrups. Melanie watched in fascination as the doctor carefully bent his head over the baby and tried gently to deliver its shoulders instructing Daryl all the while to either push or pant as the minutes ticked by. Finally, shaking his head, the doctor bent over the bloody mess of the baby and taking his scalpel once again began to elongate the incision down into the scrotum. Within seconds the baby lay in the doctor's outstretched hands, its umbilical cord attached between the baby and what Melanie decided had once been their rapist's weapon of destruction.

The young officer looked over at the couch again with a look of utter horror on his face, and quickly clamping his hand over his mouth, and making a hasty retreat, rushed out of the room as quickly as his wobbly legs would allow. Sean still sat on the floor, pasty faced, looking incredulously at the gory scene before him. Melanie on the other hand was intrigued by the birth, and the fact it was a male giving birth.

*This is one for the books, a bit of a turnabout,* Melanie thought to herself. *Definitely one for the grandchildren and after dinner speeches. Who'd ever believe what I've just seen,* she asked herself as she continued to watch in fascinated wonderment.

Daryl's screaming had now ceased and was replaced by an eerie silence, which created a hushed and tense atmosphere of disbelief and incredulity. The baby, now delivered and the umbilical cord dealt with, had been quickly checked over by the doctor and handed over to a nurse, who'd stood with her arms outstretched holding a white linen ready to accept the baby.

The doctor then started checking the monitors and screens surrounding the couch, activating scanners and other pieces of machinery. Melanie could hear him muttering to himself and making comments out loud and realised he was recording into a machine, and had been all the while she'd been present. Every so often he checked his dials, his patient, and then suddenly it was all action and something was obviously very wrong with the still, silent body laying inert atop the couch.

*Toxic shock,* Melanie thought, her medical knowledge battling against her criminal investigation discipline, as she willed herself not to muscle in and help with the treatment. Realising their rapist wasn't going to be running off, Melanie motioned for Sean to follow her out of the room, only to be met by a broadly grinning colleague from their Leeds division.

'Heard there was a bit of falling down going on in there,' he said mockingly to Sean. 'Me-lad-oh came rushing out as white as a sheet with his hand clamped over his mouth. Didn't stop to tell me what was going on but apparently he's gone to get his head checked out. Cracked it or summat I hear. Our man been throwing a few punches around then?' he said knowing full well it wasn't anything of the sort, and angling for information.

'You don't want to know,' Sean responded weakly, still looking green round the gills.

'Our rapist in there has just given birth to a baby,' Melanie told him. 'All a load of fuss about nothing.'

'What you on about Melanie? Our bloke in there is a... well he's a bloke,' Ian finished lamely.

'Precisely. Which is probably why he made such a fuss over nothing,' Melanie finished. 'Anyway if that's the result of one of his victims being raped, then he got his comeuppance didn't he? And I hope it hurt as much and more than he hurt them. Right what's the situation with his mother?' Melanie finished, as her colleagues looked at each other, shocked by Melanie's uncharacteristic attitude.

'You're something else you are,' was the disgusted response. 'If I didn't know better I'd call you a cold-hearted bitch.'

'Which is exactly what I am where vicious, callous rapists are concerned,' Melanie interrupted quickly. 'What's the situation with the mother? Has she been picked up or not?' Melanie demanded, leaving no further room for her feelings to be brooked.

'The mother's at the Crimedical Centre in York. Took her there rather than Leeds, seeing as Lucy's there. The house is sealed but we've not started a search yet, we're waiting for your instructions on that,' he responded, feeling suitably chastised by Melanie's previous response.

'And what's the situation with the media? The last thing we need is for the identity of our patient in there to get out and any whispers of his crimes to be broadcast until there isn't a shadow of doubt left. In the meantime I want you to stay here,' she told Rob. 'And you, Sean, can keep a check on the media activities out there.'

Then turning back to Rob she told him, 'I expect you to be in the room, and at the side of Daryl Payne all the time. You'll monitor each and every person entering or leaving and if any member of the media enters or any information leaves that room, by any of the personnel who attended him or by any other means, you can well and truly call your career over. The constable who left a few minutes ago can help Sean control the media along with hospital security and I'll send someone else along immediately to help control this room. As soon as samples are taken, I've already left instructions we'll need three lots, I'll be back to collect them and take them for analysis. Do you understand, or would you like me to repeat it for you?' she asked tartly, still smarting from his derogatory remarks earlier.

'We can't control rumours, and there's bound to be plenty,' she added regretfully. 'But we can control why this guy's under strict guard. If anyone asks, the official answer is because of the recent birth and unusual parentage. We can't expect to keep that under cover but the rest of the information will not leak out. Do you understand?' she demanded of them both. Having finished issuing orders Melanie was just about to re-enter the room when one of the male nurses came out with a metal receptacle.

'These are the samples you requested,' he told Melanie, handing them over and going straight back into the room.

'Right, I'm taking these samples over to Leeds for testing. On the way there, I'm going to get Alan to start on the house search. I know I can trust you to keep everything under control here and I'll keep you posted as to what's going on and where. And I expect regular updates please. I'll sort out some armed security that'll be able to release you from here as soon as possible. Ok?'

Much to Melanie's amusement Rob blushed beetroot red, shuffled his feet and with barely a grunt turned to enter the room, stopping momentarily as if having to steel himself to enter. Melanie couldn't help but let a broad grin spread across her face as she watched him. Once the door was securely closed she set off to speak to her other team members, to shore up security, before setting off to the Leeds Crimedical Centre to start testing the samples.

As soon as Melanie arrived at the centre, she made sure Lucy and Jock had arrived and how the interview was progressing, before quickly making her way to the laboratories. As soon as she entered the lab, Paul, their top DNA specialist, who'd arrived a short while before, immediately left the bench he was setting up and made his way across to Melanie.

'You've got the rapist's DNA samples then?' he asked Melanie without preamble.

'Well lets hope it's the rapist's,' Melanie responded, taking the samples out of the transporter she'd placed on the bench. Separating the collection into three identical lots she handed one batch to Rob, set her own samples in front of her and placed the third consignment in a lockable container. Placing a seal on it, which both she and Rob signed and added the date and time to, along with the source details, they then locked them away. Finally Melanie shrugged out of the coat, she seemed to have worn all day.

'You alright Melanie?' Paul asked. 'Only you look tired. You've done a fair few miles today, what with driving and flying. You want to take a break before starting these or shall I get one of the others over to test them?'

'No way,' Melanie responded positively. 'I may have travelled a few journeys but what a day! If someone had told me what was going to happen today when I got up I'd have told them to dream on. In fact it all seems like some sort of bizarre dream. Can you imagine it Rob? A man having a baby – and I saw it with my own eyes! If I hadn't, I wouldn't have believed it. It was a pretty incredible experience and I still can't believe I saw it,' her face shone with incredulity. 'I'm fine to do these samples. Let's get on with them shall we? The sooner we test, the quicker we'll have our results,' and then in an almost inaudible voice added, 'but I'm pretty sure it's him.'

Together, but separately, they started running the tests, double testing to ensure outcomes were indisputable. The third set of samples would be available to the rapist's legal representative if the crimes against his client were disputed. If it was Daryl Payne, the guy who'd just delivered a baby, then they must be totally sure and ensure nothing and no one could challenge the results. After all, if this was their rapist he stood to be incarcerated, castrated and deported, and they wouldn't want to make any mistakes with such an irreversible conclusion.

Thanks to the incredible advancements in science within a couple of hours, as the evening was drawing in, they looked at each other with relief and professional pride. They had their man. It was conclusive. The man, who'd just delivered the baby earlier in the day, was their wanted serial rapist. Bingo!

Quickly they gathered the entire team together, in their various locations via the numerous communication formats available to them, and once all 'assembled' Melanie made the announcement they'd all been waiting and hoping for.

'Our rapist has been apprehended; each and every sample has been doubly tested and there's no doubt the samples identify positively to the residual traces left on the victims. Therefore his identification tested positive, so we've got our man,' Melanie told them triumphantly congratulating them all for their contributions. Melanie waited a moment until all the sighs of relief, exclamation and cheers of jubilation had been expressed by her team.

'Now the next piece of news I have to divulge, whilst common knowledge, does not have the details I am about to divulge to you and under *no* circumstances must these be made known to any other party. That includes partners, spouses, other family members, friends or colleagues. This is privileged information about to be imparted over secure air waves and it stays that way. Does everyone understand this and understand that for this information to be repeated to any other person, until it's sanctioned, will result in instant dismissal without references and even if you're proven not guilty, your career within the Crimedical Department will be over. Does everyone understand this?' Again the same responses, although more subdued this time, were heard over the various connections.

'The rapist was apprehended this morning at the Leeds Royal Hospital. He's not yet been cautioned, as he's not conscious as we speak, but linked into a Subliminal Voyeur. He is however under armed guard and will remain so until he's moved to a secure location, which won't be for a few days yet. Our man, Daryl Payne, was taken into hospital this morning in the latter stages of labour.'

There were noises of non-understanding as they all took this in. Melanie waited until once again they'd quietened.

'Daryl Payne, our rapist, gave birth to a baby boy this afternoon. We have not yet obtained DNA from the baby but it is highly probable it could be the result of one of the rapes.'

Once again Melanie sat quietly, as they took on board the news and then waited for the deluge of questions to bombard her. She was not disappointed.

'You've no doubt heard this news already but what the media and hospital do not know, at this moment in time, is that the same man who gave birth today is the same man who's been sought as the UK Serial Rapist. His mother, along with one of his former victims, and a colleague of his who seems to have had a lucky escape, are all at Crimedical Centres and not aware of each other's presence. Nor do they know of the birth or identity of the parent. This information at the moment is being kept from them and, is to stay undisclosed until further notice. You all know what will happen if this leaks out so please take it as my one and only warning. Any more questions?'

The one question which was asked over and over again was, 'sure this isn't a wind up guv?' to which Melanie assured them it wasn't and she and Sean had actually been present at the birth, although, she added with a chuckle, Sean hadn't actually seen much. Obviously there were a number asking why, to which Melanie replied, 'Let's just say he decided to take a short nap shall we.' To which Sean, on view to everyone in the link, was seen to blush with embarrassment.

'The only thing left to tell you, is there'll be a full team briefing tomorrow at four sharp. In the meantime we'll hopefully have completed a thorough search of his property and have several other items of conclusive evidence to hand. In the meantime can I ask you all to continue with your allocated tasks and tomorrow I'll be reviewing your own findings and allocating tasks ready for Thursday? The more information we have by the team meet tomorrow the better. That's all ladies and gentlemen. Celebration on Friday, details to be announced at the end of the meeting tomorrow. In the meantime please remember the need of total confidentiality and the consequences should they be breached. Thank you and goodbye.'

With that Melanie terminated the connection, sat back in her chair and was immediately bombarded with questions from the team members who were in the same room as her. All wanted to know about the birth above anything else. After all, it was one thing catching a criminal but another thing for a man to give birth and even more astounding, some of their colleagues had unwittingly ended up in a front row position during it.

~ ~ ~ ~ ~

# After Birth

Liam, Tanya and Crawford weren't together when the news hit the world late on the Tuesday afternoon. Both men were away and Tanya wasn't expecting them back until the latter end of the week. Despite everyone round them buzzing excitedly, yet sceptically, about the news the trio only briefly touched on the topic when they spoke to each other from their remote locations. It fact, apart from checking they'd all heard the news, they'd been almost dismissive of the announcement, seeing it as inconsequential. Even on the Thursday evening, when they were all together again, the subject was barely mentioned. There were other activities of more interest to take up their time and energy.

It was because of their flippancy that the news, they were to receive the following day, would hit them like a bolt out of the blue and create such shock waves for them.

~ ~ ~ ~ ~

It was a week before Jack's annual check when the news of the male birthing broke out. Jack, still feeling somewhat out of sorts, was playing ball in the park with Wiz, when Chloe came charging across to him shouting at the top of her voice, 'Jack, Jack. Have you heard the news? Have you heard the news? I know what's wrong with you and why you're feeling ill. Jack come home,' she'd shouted even before reaching him, the pup bounding towards her yapping with excitement and running circles round her, threatening to trip her up as she neared Jack.

'Jack, Jack. You'll never believe what's just been on the news,' she told him breathlessly, panting madly.

'Jack they've just announced a man has given birth. Do you know what that means? It means you're pregnant. That's what's the matter with you Jack. Jack can you believe it?' she regaled, almost delirious with excitement.

'Chloe!' Jack calmed her, taking hold of her shoulders to make her stand still, as she was virtually dancing on the spot. 'Come on honey calm down. Tell me what's going on. Calmly,' he commanded knowing how upset she could get if overexcited, and then become disappointed and tearful.

'Jack it's just been on the news,' Chloe told him taking him by the hand and pulling him along in the direction of home. 'It's just been announced a man's given birth to a baby. There's no details yet, but can you believe it? And Jack! Jack all those symptoms you've been having are all the ones women have in pregnancy, so it means you've got to be pregnant,' she told him, as if what came out of her mouth was gospel.

Sceptical and annoyed with Chloe for taking everything at face value actually made Jack feel quite angry.

'Chloe, stop it. There's no guarantee any man's just had a baby. It could just be a hoax and whether it's a hoax or not, you shouldn't get excited about it like this. You can't cling on to any thread of hope just like that. We can't have children Chloe and one day, sooner or later, you're just going to have to accept it,' he told her none too gently.'

'But Jack all the symptoms…'

'Are just as likely to be something else. Look Chloe,' he told her, putting his hands on her shoulders and turning her to face him. 'I know you're disappointed at losing the baby but we've got to live in the real world. The chances a man has given birth are several million to one and for me to be pregnant will be several billion to one.'

'Yes but Jack…'

'No buts Chloe just stop this nonsense…'

'Nonsense is it Jack?' she snapped back. 'Well let me just tell you, you're pregnant. I know you are,' she almost spat at him. 'I know in my heart of hearts, my instinct, call it what you like but you're pregnant Jack, like it or not.'

'So if I'm pregnant Chloe,' reasoned Jack 'then how come you didn't know before?'

'Because men don't get pregnant un…'

'Precisely Chloe. Men don't get pregnant and that includes me. All you heard today was a hoax, and a cruel one at that. I'm not pregnant Chloe and sadly never will be. Neither of us will,' he added more gently, 'and tragically that's the way it will stay and something we'll have to accept and the sooner the better.'

By now Chloe was openly crying, disappointed Jack didn't believe what she'd heard, what she'd told him and how she felt. Bitterly disenchanted by Jack's lack of belief, and his inability to look beyond his nose end, Chloe pulled away from him and with a hardened look turned and faced him head on, stared directly and unblinkingly into his eyes and said, 'You can say what you like, Jack Baird, but I'm telling you it's a fact. A man has given birth to a baby and you yourself are pregnant. You can be as sceptical as you like Jack, but tomorrow I'm making you an appointment with the doctor and he'll show you just how pregnant you are.'

She spun on her heel to storm off but Jack caught hold of her arm and pulled her back. In just an angry a tone, as the one Chloe had used, he told her, 'You do that Chloe, and you'll just be making a monkey out of yourself and me. I have an appointment next week and I will not go to the doctors before then unless something bad happens. Do you understand me Chloe?' he said in a now cold voice.

'Oh I understand you Jack. All too well, and believe me, you will go to the doctor even if I have to knock you out and call an ambulance.' On that final angry note she stormed across the park leaving Jack, with an agitated pup pulling on the lead to follow Chloe. Jack, in his bewilderment at her news, and stunned by her agitation, turned in the opposite direction pulling the pup after him. He needed to calm down and think carefully about what she'd just told him.

Not able to face the tirade of emotions he knew Chloe would be giving into, Jack decided to walk awhile, to gather his thoughts and give Chloe time to calm down.

*What she said, in some ways, made sense,* he thought. *My symptoms are similar to those women have in pregnancy,* he reasoned, *but they're symptoms of a great many other ailments too. It's not fair to play into her world of hope and make believe, and I'm not going to go charging off to the doctor's either just because of one stupid hoax in the media. It's not my style and I don't want to have to face the thought, or even the hope, that men can get pregnant now we know Chloe can't. The thought of hanging onto such a frail thread of hope, and the damage it could do to us, isn't worth thinking about. It could be the final thing to push one or both of us over the edge, and I'm not about to let that happen,* he thought determinedly.

It was almost hour later when he finally arrived home and was surprised to find the house unlit and empty. At first he thought he'd find Chloe in their bedroom crying, but when he checked found she wasn't there. He checked the rest of the house but there was no sign of Chloe anywhere, she'd gone. He casually popped into a couple of the neighbours but, instead of finding Chloe, was greeted with the same news Chloe had told him only a short while ago – that a man had just given birth to a baby.

'It's a hoax,' Jack told them sharply. 'Just a cruel hoax and look at how it's upset Chloe. She never goes off without telling me first,' he'd told their neighbours worriedly.

Arriving back home, he walked into the kitchen where he saw the LED screen flashing, informing him there was a message waiting. He activated the panel and within seconds a message informed him:

*'I'm not coming home Jack until you've seen the doctor. I couldn't bear to sleep with you knowing you're pregnant when you won't acknowledge it. I love you Jack but I just can't do it. I'm at my mum's, but don't contact me until you're prepared to go for a check-up. Love you, Chloe.'*

Jack was both saddened and angered by the message and the hoax, which had caused all this trouble between them. Whichever station he tuned into there was nothing but the same news repeated over and over again with speculation as to why a man had given birth and how.

*Just check out your story and source first,* Jack pleaded silently to himself. *Don't you know how many people you're hurting?* He turned off every news delivering device in the house and without ringing Chloe, needing his space just as much as she did, went to bed with a heavy heart.

He'd lain awake most of the night tossing and turning, his thoughts drifting back over their years of trouble and strife and their disappointment at not being able to have children. Many times during the night he'd laid his hands over his belly wondering if there was life in there and if he could be pregnant.

*Dare I hope I'm pregnant? course not, it's only a dream and none of it is going to come true,* he told himself. *Dreams don't come true. If only… but then 'if' is the biggest word in the English language isn't it,* he told himself, *and dreams are for dreaming, not living. But then again you've got to have a dream 'cos is you don't have a dream how you gonna make a dream come true? Isn't that how the song goes?* he asked himself.

Wiz must have known something was amiss, as she didn't settle, but fretted to be with Jack. In the end, restless and not at all sleepy, Jack broke all the house rules and not only allowed Wiz upstairs, but onto the slumber-pit. Wiz, never having been there before, snuffled round detecting, but not finding, Chloe, whimpered then flopped down mournfully nuzzling close to Jack as if to take and give comfort. When

Jack finally fell into a fitful sleep he was still unsure what to believe or what to do about Chloe.

The grey miserable dawn of the next day didn't help matters either. Everywhere Jack went, everything he heard or saw from the media was about the male pregnancy, and Jack still didn't believe what was being reported. He knew the only thing likely to convince him was a report of the birth in the WiPPLe. Whatever was printed in there, or recorded on their site, was fact and included no fiction whatsoever. If it was in there he knew it would be true and would put his mind at rest, one way or another. With that one decisive thought in mind he entered his office and went straight to their site.

It didn't surprise Jack at all when he found 'male birthing' wasn't WiPPLe's headline news. He'd known it was a hoax all along, but decided to do a search anyway, just to see if there was any information at all. Scanning beyond the headlines he found what he was looking for, but it wasn't what he'd expected. In the stop press section was a small heading which stated:

'*Man Gives Birth to Baby*' and underneath was written, 'Topic to be investigated before full report made available.'

As he read those few words Jack's heart seemed to stop.

*So it was true,* he thought astounded. *So maybe, just maybe there is a chance I could be pregnant? Don't be so stupid,* he reprimanded himself quickly. *Dreams don't come true. Remember?* Even more confused than ever before his first instinct was to ring Chloe, but he couldn't. He just couldn't bear the thought of building up her hopes and seeing them dashed again.

*Maybe,* he thought, *I'll just go and see the doctor without telling her. That way I'll know for certain I'm not pregnant and telling her will put a stop to all this nonsense. Then again maybe I'll just wait until my appointment next week. This desperation to be a father is obviously unbalancing my rationale,* he thought with irony.

As these thoughts continued to conflict with his common sense, an icon popped up on his screen. It was a message from Chloe. Normally he'd have opened it immediately, but something was holding him back. He was frightened of raising or dashing her hopes, let alone his own. He just couldn't face any more trauma or disappointment at the moment and just wanted the world to go away and leave him alone. Not having had anything to eat before leaving home, he decided to go and get something from the eaterie. He'd think about accessing her message whilst he was away.

Getting back to his desk armed with coffee, a sandwich and tub of jelly, he was relieved to see there were no more messages. Taking it as an omen, that it was safe to read Chloe's message, he finally opened it and read:

*'If I know you, Jack Baird, you'll have gone on to the WiPPLe site as soon as you got into work. Now you know it's all true please will you go to the doctor and have your pregnancy confirmed?'*

Jack smiled as he read the first part of the message, once again reminded how well Chloe knew him. It was the second part of the message which made his body slump in despair.

*How could she be so gullible and have such a font of total belief without any basis?* Not wanting to hurt her, shoot her down in flames or fan her hopes, he had no idea how to reply. Choosing not to reply at all he made the decision to bury himself in his work, which he thought would be the best way to cope with the situation.

Jack worked diligently throughout the morning, not even stopping for refreshments mid-morning as he usually did. It was just after twelve when his phone rang, and with a sinking heart saw it was Cassie, Chloe's sister. Answering the phone, with dread, he'd not even finished his greeting before Cassie went off on a tirade about how upset Chloe was; how inconsiderate Jack was being and how could he treat her like this etc etc. Not stopping to draw breath Jack couldn't get a word in edgeways.

'Jack? Jack? Are you there? Did you hear what I said?'

'Yes,' Jack replied, 'but can I say something now?' he asked, pausing to make sure she was going to listen.

'I can't just build-up Chloe's hopes after everything she's gone through. Can you imagine how hard it would be if I went along to the doctor's and was told I wasn't pregnant? Just think what that'd do to her Cassie. Just saying I'd go would build-up her hopes just to have them shattered again? I just can't do it,' he told her sadly.

'Oh! Jack do you think you could be pregnant?' Cassie asked in calmer tones.

'No I don't. This is just something Chloe's hanging onto. You've got to talk her out of the whole stupid idea Cassie. I've got an appointment next week, which is soon enough for her to hear I'm not.'

'Jack, you know what Chloe's like. If you leave it until then she'll have it all built up out of proportion and get into even more of a state. Couldn't you just go to the doctor's like she's asked so that she's not dangling all week?'

'I can't do that, you know I can't and it's not fair to ask me to.'

'Would you consider a compromise then Jack?' Cassie asked more gently.

'Depends what it is.'

'Would you consider going to the doctor anyway but just not telling her? Then at least we'll know one way or another and get the whole business out of the way now rather than later.'

'Oh yes Cassie of course I can,' Jack answered sarcastically. 'I go running off to the doctor's saying 'Doctor, Doctor I think I'm pregnant.' That'll give them all a laugh won't it? No I couldn't do that. Allow me some dignity will you?'

'It was only a suggestion, Jack. There's no need to be so sarcastic. I only suggested it as a compromise. You do know don't you Chloe won't come back until you've been to the doctor's? It's not a stubbornness Jack, it's the fact she doesn't want to put her arms round you not knowing whether or not you're pregnant. Please Jack. For both your sakes think about it and sort something out will you?'

Jack reluctantly told her he'd think about it and finishing the call made his way back to the eaterie. He was really hungry and the fluttery feelings he kept feeling seemed to be very pronounced today.

*It's no good my going without a midmorning snack*, he told himself hoping to calm his stomach with some food, which sometimes helped but not always. *And it's no good pretending I could be pregnant or even going down that road*, he reminded himself sharply. *It's bad enough Chloe hanging on to that hope. The worst thing I can do is follow her.*

~ ~ ~ ~ ~

The next day at the team meeting, Melanie's entire team, from across their various locations were in attendance. This was going to be one meeting not to be missed and wild horses wouldn't have kept them away, no matter what they'd had arranged previously.

They all sat with bated breath. Melanie had never had such a captive audience before and commenced the meeting with details of the rapist's admission to hospital and the consequent birth. As expected, this was followed with a barrage of questions and Melanie, wanting their full attention, insisted on a five minute break before commencing with the real business.

Finally resettled, Melanie asked for details of the house search to be relayed. She'd already had sight of the reports, but needed the entire team to be kept fully informed to give them the opportunity to pick up on something not considered so far, which might identify other information pertinent to the case.

This was exactly what happened when the subject of the robots, they'd found in Daryl's bedroom, was brought up. The prohibited adhesive they'd identified had been used during their creation, explaining the banned bonding agent on the handkerchief. When the description of the components was relayed to the team, one of the computer bods, happened to mention there were rumours the chips used in the robots were the ones they believed were being used, with modification, for altering entry and exit details, thus providing false alibi details on house security systems. Another piece of information which would be useful in the investigation and, would hopefully, break the validity of his house entry alibis and make that defence inadmissible. This information was greeted with yet more enthusiasm from the team as Melanie reiterated how impressed she was with the way the team worked together along with their vigilance and dedication.

The forensics team then went on to outline what had been found during the search. The one piece of information really puzzling them was, the fact they'd found a stack of tins of sardines and jars of jam neatly put away. In addition there were several empty tins and jars washed and discarded in the bin. 'What was that all about?' They'd asked innocently.

'Probably a craving from his pregnancy,' piped up a female voice from the back. 'I couldn't stay away from strawberries and ice cream when I was expecting.'

Everyone turned round to look at her, laughing as they remembered her constantly with a bowl of the proverbial strawberries and ice cream numerous times a day.

The forensic team, looking at each other as if the penny had finally dropped, quickly excused themselves explaining they hadn't been expecting their male suspect to be pregnant. This brought a ripple of laughter and ribald jokes from around the room.

On the subject of Daryl's mother, from comments Sonia had made during her interview, they'd not only been able to build up a more complete picture of their rapist, but also solved a crime that had lain unsolved for a good many years.

Following this through, they explained that when they'd questioned Sharon about the death of her husband the Subliminal Voyeur had identified her attempting to suppress a memory of him. When she'd refused to outline her thoughts, they'd re-programmed the Subliminal Voyeur to reveal the repressed memories. It had turned out her husband had been part of a gang which had gang-raped a woman some thirty years previously. When pressed she'd actually given the name of the victim and quickly followed it up by telling them the names of all the other men, reiterating over and over again her husband had never had anything to do with it.

Having checked the details in their archives, they'd indeed found details of the rape and the information of all the suspicious deaths matching the names of those mentioned by Sharon. They'd collected items from the house, still containing DNA from the dead husband, which had been tested. The DNA, left at the scene of crime and on the victim, had long been in storage and was just sitting waiting to have the perpetrators matched to it. Sharon would soon know her beloved husband was as guilty as her son, but whether she'd accept the information was a different matter.

The team working with Lucy, and re-running her previous memories, had seen all sorts of other information come out during the process. It all made sense now they had their criminal, but at the time neither the team nor Lucy had been able to make anything of it.

*Obviously something that needs fine tuning on the equipment,* Melanie told herself. She'd watched the interview tapes and noted where Lucy's anger lay, as she had retold her experience to Jock. Melanie could see the fury lying beneath the surface when she'd realised Daryl had been her assailant. You could see her emotions bubble with resentment as she recounted the times he'd crept up on her, playing with her emotions and pretending to be so innocent and timid.

'The man was sick,' she'd told Jock. 'He must have a screw loose to rape me and not bat an eyelid when he spoke to different people about it.'

Melanie couldn't decide whether it was the humiliation of her plight or the audacity and coolness of someone she despised so much which was upsetting Lucy most. Whatever, he'd hoodwinked far more people than just Lucy. As Melanie had watched the footage, she wondered how Lucy would react when they told her Daryl had given birth to a baby. Would it dawn on her to ask who the other parent was and, more to the point would she even wonder if she could be the second parent? Melanie hoped, when she had her next session with Lucy the following day, the topic wouldn't be broached. There was going to be a lot of re-programming to do on Lucy and she was going to need an enormous amount of support when the news of the rapes and the birth of the baby continued to hit the news.

For a moment Melanie let her thoughts drift, wondering if Lucy was the other parent, which was likely if she looked at it in terms of a female pregnancy. It was doubtful Daryl had a partner. Unless another woman had been attacked, and not come forward, which wasn't likely, the odds were Lucy was the second parent, unless of course Daryl had been self-impregnated. But deep down, Melanie's instinct told her Lucy was the other parent, just as her hunch had told her Daryl was the rapist from the time Sonia had spoken about him.

Bringing her thoughts sharply back into focus, Melanie continued to listen to the various reports, questions and theories flitting round the table. Finishing the meeting, with new tasks allocated amongst the team, Melanie reiterated her congratulations and appreciation to the team telling them there was a celebratory function at the '*Scarlet Nells… No pimps*' Fornipub at eight on Friday night, which she hoped everyone would attend. As a final parting shot, Melanie then announced a piece of news which would be received with even more enthusiasm than the rapist's capture.

'I'm sure you'll all be delighted to hear one last piece of news, which is…' she paused for dramatic effect. 'With all the work undertaken to date cross-referencing vehicles and DNA, we have solved more than fifteen thousand outstanding crimes.' A chorus of 'oohs' and 'aahs' rippled round the room. 'This means once additional costs have been taken out of the proceedings, your bonuses for the work will more than double your salaries at the financial year end and we are now the number one force in the UK. It was a daunting task, not yet complete, but it's all been a very worthwhile and a financially rewarding operation. So thank you again for your hard work and dedication.'

An almighty whoop went up as they realised how much it would mean to them financially.

'We'll continue the exercise until it's complete and I'm recommending a number of changes regarding DNA registration and car sales, which should reduce the chances of this happening in the future, but, in the meantime let's congratulate ourselves on success and our just rewards. Well done.'

As Melanie gathered her things together she was surprised, embarrassed, and a little flattered, to hear the team, as one voice, followed it up with a 'Hear, hear', and 'Thanks Melanie', which Melanie took with high coloured grace.

~ ~ ~ ~ ~

When Jed went into school on Wednesday 8th December, he was greeted by the others as if he were some sort of messiah. Jed had no idea what their excitement was about and demanded gruffly to know what the hell was going on.

'Haven't you heard the news?' Fiona challenged.

'No. Why should I?'

'Didn't you hear about the bloke who's had a baby?' Jade asked excitedly.

'Bloke? Baby? Will someone tell me what is going on here or at least talk some sense,' he grumbled.

'It's been on the news,' Ben interjected. 'Some poor bastard's given birth to a baby. It's the headline on every news media imaginable.'

'Bloody hell,' responded Jed, wincing. 'Poor fucking bastard. How was it born?' he asked, cringing at the thought.

'No idea; they've not given out the details yet. No one knows who the bloke is either, what sex the baby is or even if it's all right. But you know what it does mean, don't you?' Jade told him.

'No?' Jed answered vaguely.

'Well you predicted it Jed, didn't you?' Jade said, as if exasperated by him being so thick.

'Predicted it? What are you on about? How did I predict it?'

'Well what was your dream if it wasn't a prediction?' Fiona reminded him.

'You what?'

'Your dream Jed or at least the nightmare. It was a man having a baby, a premonition. Yours!'

'Oh yeah!' said Jed, with realisation. 'A premonition! How spooky!'

'We reckon you've a sixth sense and saw it before it happened,' Fiona chipped in.

'You reckon?' Jed said, wondering if he had.

Whist this interchange was going on, Jade had detached herself from the group and was standing thoughtfully looking on. She'd just caught a glimpse of Jed's stomach and the sight had shocked her. For one horrible moment the most bizarre thought crossed her mind.

*What if Jed was pregnant? He certainly looks it* she thought 'as she visualized his stomach. *No! He couldn't be.* She tried to dismiss the idea as ridiculous and get back into the fray of things, but couldn't shake the image from her mind. Deep in thought she trailed behind the others until Fiona, waiting for her to catch up, tucked her arm into Jade's.

'You ok? You've gone quiet on us. Isn't it amazing news? A man having a baby. Who'd have thought? I bet it's something they've always predicted as never happening. I mean I know there's been films and books on it in the past, but for it to actually happen. Wow! It's unbelievable. I don't believe that,' she twittered on. 'Did you hear Ben then? Asking Jed to predict his future. Moronic or what? But don't you think its amazing. Jed predicted it? Do you reckon he could have a sixth sense and be clairvoyant or something? Jade you're being very quiet, what's up?'

Jade replied by drawing Fi away from the lads so she wouldn't be overheard then said, 'Fi what if…' *Shit,* she decided, *better not say anything yet. If Jed is pregnant then Fi will be the… who would she be?* As the thoughts bombarded her mind she frantically searched for something else to say so as not to rouse suspicion.

'Oh nothing Fi. I'm just thinking of the enormity of the situation and the consequences on the human race, physically and emotionally. I mean who are going to be the child bearers of the future? Men as well as women or is this just a one off?

Throughout the day it seemed to be the only topic of discussion, with everyone downloading endless articles on the subject, except Jade, who was getting information on female pregnancies to read later. She had a hunch Jed's behaviour in recent weeks was the same as that experienced by pregnant women and, as fanciful as it seemed, instinct told her Jed was pregnant.

By the end of the day rumours of the baby, its parent and delivery were rife. General consensus being the baby was a monster; the bloke had had to have his penis cut off to deliver it and as a result was now at death's door. The rumours were like Chinese Whispers, with everyone embellishing the story each time it was told. The problem was, until the true facts were reported, no one knew, and wouldn't until the story and details were stated in the WiPPLe, the only paper that reported facts alone.

Jade couldn't shake off the heinous image of Jed's nightmare, which stayed stubbornly at the forefront of her mind throughout the day. Listening to everyone's comments, dismissing the majority of them as fanciful, she needed to talk to someone about Jed, preferably Fiona, but would she want to hear her thoughts? Especially if Jed was pregnant and Fiona the other parent! She got the opportunity as they walked home after school.

'Fiona? Have you taken a good look at Jed lately? I mean a really good look and seen how much weight he's put on?' she asked tentatively.

'Yes, not Jed at all is it with his protruding belly? He's even getting boobs…' as she said those last few words she stopped in her tracks, looking suspiciously at Jade. 'Surely you can't be thinking Jed's pregnant,' she challenged. 'Good god, Jade, you're as bad as everyone else. Just because one man's had a baby doesn't mean to say someone we know is going to have one.'

'I never said anything about Jed being pregnant; it was you who suggested that,' Jade replied carefully. 'But let's face it, he has been acting oddly lately.'

'Hah! That's what you get for drinking moonshine like he's been doing,' Fiona snorted.

'I'm not convinced, Fi. Call it instinct or what I reckon there's more to Jed's behaviour than just the after effects of moonshine. Instinct tells me he's pregnant.'

'Tell you what Jade you call it instinct and I'll call it fanciful,' Fiona scoffed, but the seed of doubt was quickly beginning to germinate.

~ ~ ~ ~ ~

Lucy still had the look of bitter anger on her face she'd worn the day before when Melanie went to see her. To cap it all, as she sat down in a comfy chair, for the first time in days, it suddenly struck Melanie how tired she was and yet, knew she had to keep her wits about her for Lucy's sake, as well as her own.

Slowly Melanie told Lucy it had been confirmed Daryl was her rapist. Once Lucy had let go of a tirade of emotions and calmed down Melanie began to tell her about him giving birth. She watched as huge waves of emotion washed over Lucy's bronzed features, ranging from incredulity to disbelief and rage.

'He's had a baby?' Lucy finally gasped doubtfully after Melanie had finished. 'But how come…? That's ridiculous. Men don't have babies. This isn't some time to joke you know, Melanie. It's not funny,' she raged, getting to her feet and beginning to pace back and forth.

'Lucy, please come and sit down. You're not doing either of us any favours pacing about like that.'

Reluctantly Lucy did as Melanie bade and sat back down, crossing her legs. Within seconds her upper leg was swinging, a clear indication of how incensed and uneasy she was. Melanie waited a few moments until the angry motion had begun to settle. The Subliminal Voyeur, which Lucy was remotely linked into, was also showing a gradual calming of emotions but Melanie knew, from past experience, to get the best response from her interviewees she needed to wait until the levels were reduced even more, before continuing.

Finally Lucy's leg calmed and the monitor indicated the reduced level of anger. Once again Melanie started to relay bits of information to see how Lucy would react. She started explaining that when Daryl had, as Lucy put it, 'pissed himself' it had more than likely been his waters breaking. Lucy grinned at this and the machine indicated a change in emotional feelings for her.

''S'far as I'm concerned he pissed hisself. In fact I hope the birth was the most painful experience a human being could ever have,' she said venomously, but the monitor was actually indicating there was an element of sadness and confusion attached to this statement.

'How was it born anyway?'

Melanie cocked her head to one side trying to decide if Lucy really wanted to know, or if it was small talk to mark time, whilst she gathered her thoughts. Looking at the monitor Melanie saw there was a genuine curiosity but also other thoughts and feelings clouding Lucy's thinking. Melanie honoured this with the briefest and most clinical of descriptions of the event, carefully watching Lucy and the monitor's interpretations of her reactions. Although Lucy asked for elaboration Melanie was vague and wouldn't give all the gory details she'd witnessed, and knew Lucy wanted to hear, nor did she tell Lucy she'd actually been present when it had happened.

Under the surveillance of the Subliminal Voyeur, Lucy had reacted as they'd expected, wishing him a painful and mind altering experience she hoped he'd never forget or be re-programmed for. She'd not asked about the baby yet nor speculated on who the other parent was and, until they'd unravelled the baby's DNA they wouldn't know who it was either. So Melanie, reluctant to broach the subject and traumatise Lucy further, skilfully manoeuvred her way past the subject.

'How did he get pregnant?' Lucy eventually asked in a small voice. 'Do you reckon it was to a man or a woman?' she asked quietly tensing, as if afraid to hear the answer.

'We don't know yet Lucy. There are a great number of tests to be carried out before we can even start to answer that one.'

'Do you think DNA tests will show who the other parent is?' Lucy asked rhetorically, again in a quiet voice which, confirmed to Melanie that Lucy was going through a whole series of questions she didn't want answers to yet. Not answering, Melanie watched and waited for Lucy's next question or statement.

'Only it's just nine months ago since he raped me,' Lucy told Melanie, with an indefinable expression on her face. 'If it's the same as a woman's pregnancy could it be mine?' she asked, this time with a tremor in her voice. Melanie still didn't answer, aware Lucy's vocalisations were really her thoughts being spoken aloud instead of questions waiting for answers.

'I don't know what I'd do if it was my baby. I mean... would... would I be expected to take care of it because... because... I... I,' she said finally bursting into heart wrenching sobs. 'Because... I... I don't think I... I could bear to... to be near... near it... but... but I... the poor... poor little thing,' she gasped, between deep gasping sobs. 'Tell me... tell me I... I don't have to... have to see it...' she pleaded to Melanie.

In a quiet reassuring voice Melanie responded with, 'Lucy you don't have to do anything you don't want to. We don't even know if it's yours, so don't go upsetting yourself like this. You've been through enough and need to think about getting yourself through this without giving yourself more trauma. Ok?' she reaffirmed in a low supportive voice. Lucy looked up at her with appealing eyes.

'What... what would you... you do if you were... you were me, Melanie?'

Melanie smiled encouragingly at Lucy and said, in a quiet voice, knowing it was exactly how she wasn't thinking, 'I'd be looking into my own thoughts to see how I was feeling,' she told Lucy. 'I'd be trying to look at how I could deal with it all and handle it along with anything else, just to get through one day at a time.'

'What... what do you mean? How I would cope with everything else? What... what does that mean? What do you think will happen?' Lucy asked with a look of terror and confusion in her eyes now, as if she was expecting something even more heinous to happen. *After all wasn't this bad enough?* she asked herself.

'Lucy. There has never before been a man who's given birth. The media are like hounds baying for blood at the moment. What they don't know is Daryl's the rapist we've been searching for, and it'll stay like that – for a short while only. But in the next few days they're going to be looking into every aspect of Daryl's life and anyone who was involved in it. We can't stop them but we can stop the news he was the rapist leaking out for a while yet. Once it's out though, they're going to start speculating, and at the moment we don't know if a male pregnancy's a nine-month duration, longer or shorter. When it's declared he's the rapist the media will be looking into the lives of all his victims and asking the same questions as everyone else – who is the other parent? We've got you in here to help you cope with all this and to protect you when the next round of news breaks. Just as we will with all his other victims. But your case is a bit different, as we know he knew you and continued to torment you after the attack. We haven't established yet if he knew any of his other victims but we do know three of them didn't know him. It changes the picture for them in some ways but for you? Well, you'll need extra support and probably some more re-programming to cope with it all. Don't worry about who the second parent is though. It really is something you don't need to worry about.'

'But Melanie,' Lucy protested, as if Melanie was missing the point. 'If that baby's mine,' she shuddered at the thought. 'Then I've got to think of its future.' Melanie shook her head slowly from side to side.

'Do you think other rapists from the past have ever bothered about any child born as a result of their raping someone? No. And as far as you're concerned, Lucy you were the victim of this rape, not the perpetrator. It wasn't you who did the raping and you didn't have to think about getting rid of an unwanted pregnancy or giving it up for adoption when it was born. That's what would have happened years ago but at this moment in time just let the authorities worry about the child. It will be cared for and protected as much as we're able.'

'But how come Daryl didn't know he was pregnant?'

Melanie shrugged her shoulders and then said, 'How many men would have suspected they were pregnant? It's an unheard of phenomenon and when we checked Daryl's medical notes we found he'd not been to a doctor for over fifteen years, which is why we didn't have his DNA on the database. If he hadn't been to the doctors in all that time it's unlikely he'd have gone unless he was desperately ill.'

'Was that why he was so against going to hospital then?' Lucy asked, intrigued now rather than frightened, which was what Melanie had intended.

'Maybe or maybe he was just frightened by everything going on.'

Lucy grunted at this and then said out loud, 'He fucking deserved to be frightened, and I hope there's a lot more that'll frighten the bastard. It would be good for him to know what it's like to feel frightened all the time,' she told Melanie venomously.

'Is that how you've felt then?' Melanie asked quietly.

Lucy sat deep in thought for a short while before answering, 'I don't know. I just felt this menace hanging over me all the time. You know, as if I was being watched and... and laughed at, I suppose. Which in effect I was, wasn't I?' she challenged Melanie.

'Yes but there's no reason to feel afraid any more and knowing your instincts are so honed must give you some peace of mind. Did you never suspect him?' she asked keeping a close eye on the screen and on Lucy herself. She watched carefully as Lucy sat deep in thought, obviously replaying memories in her mind, the Subliminal Voyeur monitoring her thought patterns. Every so often, it was evident Lucy had come across a vague memory which could have triggered something. When she'd sat and thought for a while Melanie asked her if she'd like some help examining her thoughts, intending to set the machine up as she'd done for Sonia.

Lucy again sat thinking before finally agreeing to the help, knowing Melanie would set the machine up, and not sure if that's what she wanted. As soon as Melanie was certain she was in agreement and ready, she quickly readjusted the monitors and told Lucy to go through her thoughts again.

As she ran through her memories there were several occasions Lucy's thoughts were stopped and delved into, with the aid of the machine, and several questions both Lucy and Melanie asked which were answered or highlighted as needing to be looked into. It was a gruelling session and traumatic for Lucy, but with Melanie's professionalism, she was protected from being pulled into a melee of emotions.

~ ~ ~ ~ ~

On Thursday, the topic continued to be rife, but still nothing of significance had been reported in the WiPPLe. Fiona and Jade were discussing the topic when Jed and Ben caught them up and joined in their speculation. After a few minutes, much to Jade's astonishment, Fiona asked the boys the question she was burning to ask.

'So what would you do if you found out you were pregnant?' she asked.

'Don't be stupid, men don't have babies. That guy's a freak, it's a one-off, if it's happened at all,' Jed said, dismissively.

'Yes, but what would you do if you were?' she persisted.

'Get rid of it,' Jed told her without hesitation, to which Ben butted in with, 'Would you? I wouldn't. Just think what a money spinner it'd be,' he told them, a greedy expression on his face.

'So you wouldn't get rid of it then?' Jade asked, 'no matter how it was likely to be born?'

'What? A little gold mine like that? No way,' Ben laughed, with Jed nodding enthusiastically, having just twigged onto what Ben had said.

'Yeah, just think how rich that guy'll be,' Jed speculated. 'Every media source will want his story and they'll want to do all sorts of experiments on him. He'll be rolling in it. Wish it was me,' he laughed.

'Well you look pregnant anyway Jed,' Jade said, immediately wishing she'd bitten her tongue.

Ben, turning to Jed, laughingly, held his hands out theatrically and announced, 'And here folks we have the world's second male mother in the offing. Watch this space to follow his progress; how will it be born?' And Jed, picking up their old performing antics, gave deep body bows to the girls, which they laughed off.

'Hey, just think, Fiona, if Jed's pregnant you'll be the dad,' Ben taunted her.

'Not necessarily,' Fiona replied. 'After all, we had our cosy little foursome didn't we, so it could just as easily be Jade's.' Being more of a scientist, than an idealist, hadn't stopped Fiona wondering if Jed could be pregnant. Her conversation with Jade yesterday had set her thinking and she'd decided, whatever the outcome, nothing and no one was going to get in the way of her ambitions. Baby or not!

It was lunchtime before Fiona and Jade got the chance to talk alone, their topic of conversation based on female pregnancies, in relation to Jed's recent behaviour. They both agreed his symptoms could be from more than drinking moonshine.

'Fi, if he was pregnant and it was yours what would you do?' Jade asked Fiona carefully.

'Nothing. My future's mapped out and I'm not changing it for anything,' she told Jade with determination. Not surprised with the reply, Jade was still surprised by the cold tone, but as she contemplated the answer and tone Jed came in wearing a T-shirt, giving the girls their first chance to really get a look at him since the news had broken.

'He does look pregnant,' Jade said, 'and you're right, he's getting boobs.' But how would they be able to find out if he was pregnant?

~ ~ ~ ~ ~

True to her word, Chloe still wasn't home on the Thursday. Jack himself seemed to have hit a black spot too and couldn't bring himself

297

to speak to her. By Thursday lunchtime he'd decided to take Cassie's advice and take the middle road, by going to see a doctor without Chloe knowing. He'd managed to make an appointment for the following morning with his normal doctor, who'd diligently followed their unsuccessful attempts to have a baby ever since he and Chloe had first started trying.

When Jack walked into the surgery the following day, he was in a rare state of nervousness, unusual for him. Highly embarrassed, Jack told the doctor why he was there, explaining the situation which had developed between him and Chloe.

'Oh no Jack, please don't do this to yourself. You seriously can't be asking me this? Please say you're not?'

Jack, crestfallen and down in the mouth nodded and finally said miserably, 'I know it's crazy, Rich, but I'm not asking for me. If you just examine me and tell me I'm not pregnant then at least I can go back to Chloe and tell her once and for all I'm not. Then hopefully we can try and get on with our lives again. You've got all the equipment here and it won't take long. Please?' he finished with a pleading tone in his voice.

Reluctantly, Rich, their doctor of many years who'd been through their countless disappointments with them, instructed Jack to go and get up on the scanning couch. Adjusting the equipment, as Jack readied himself, he set the monitors and dials ready to confirm Jack's non-pregnancy.

Finally, the equipment ready, Rich set the scanner in motion and kept a close eye on the monitors to see what, if anything, would be revealed. He was uncomfortable doing this and Jack, he noticed, was deliberately not looking at the screen but seemed to have a dead look of acceptance in his eyes.

After what seemed like an eternity of the scanner moving over his body, Jack felt a change in the doctor's demeanour. The feeling was so strong it made him turn to look at Rich, who hovered at his side. His whole persona seemed to have stiffened, and Jack immediately thought the worst.

'Rich? What is it? You've not found something nasty have you?' Jack asked, suddenly afraid the scan had revealed a tumour, or something equally as sinister. The doctor shook his head, not replying but instead looked intently at the screen.

'I don't believe this,' he gasped in a whisper. 'This can't be real. Whatever…'

By this time Jack was becoming genuinely concerned and demanded in a higher pitched than normal voice, 'What… what is it? Is it bad news?'

'Bad news?' asked the doctor in a baffled tone. 'Well I don't know but it's certainly very interesting. Unusual.'

'Interesting? Unusual?' Jack parroted, struggling to sit up.

'Jack, lay still for just a minute will you please? Just let me get this checked,' he told Jack, deliberately not looking at him. Without saying a word he turned off the monitors, not wanting Jack to see what he was looking at, and left the room leaving Jack lying on the couch, tense and more miserable than when he'd arrived and feeling somewhat worried.

Within minutes, one of the other practice doctor's, an attractive small and trim blonde woman, entered the room with Rich. The doctor instructed Jack to lie back down and once again set the scanner running. In total silence, and with looks of intense concentration on their faces, the two doctors watched the screen intently. All of a sudden Jack heard a sharp intake of breath.

'Look!' she exclaimed pointing a finger excitedly at the screen. 'There! Right there! Well I never! Have you told your patient yet, Rich?'

'Told me what,' Jack demanded.

'Well Jack,' Rich started 'it appears that…' but before he could finish his sentence his colleague had jumped in with, 'You're pregnant! Expecting a baby!' she said, in a totally unprofessional and highly excited voice.

'I… I'm pregnant? I… I really am pregnant?' Jack asked in a voice full of awe. 'I… I… I'm going to be a dad?'

'Or a mum,' the doctor said, laughing and taking hold of Jack's hand shook it vigorously to congratulate him.

'I think we should get Chloe here, don't you think? As a matter of urgency,' he finished with a chuckle.

'Yes, but don't tell her why I'm here, will you?' Jack told him, the truth not having sunk in yet. 'Let her see for herself. Please?' and the doctor, nodding his agreement, ushered the woman doctor from his room warning her not to say a thing to anyone. He wanted to do that himself!

When the doctor had rung Chloe, refusing to discuss matters over the phone but insisting she come to the Medics Centre immediately, Chloe had been understandably concerned. Arriving at the surgery fifteen minutes later a receptionist ushered her straight into the doctor's office where Chloe found Jack lying prone on the couch, his eyes closed. As she looked at him lying there Chloe's heart froze with fear.

'Jack, Jack whatever's the matter?' she asked hurrying over to him. Jack lay there as if dazed. In actuality he was.

'I think you should see this Chloe,' the doctor told her in a solemn voice, and turning the monitor round switched it on so she could see the screen.

Chloe peered at the monitor, not knowing what she was supposed to be looking for. Then all of a sudden the penny dropped and she recognised what it was she could see on the screen.

'A baby,' she whispered. 'A baby,' she repeated in a slightly louder voice. 'Jack,' she said looking over at him. 'It's a baby. You're pregnant. A baby. I knew you were. Jack we're going to have a baby,' she almost shouted and getting up from the couch Jack and Chloe flung themselves into each other's arms and began jumping and dancing round shouting 'A baby. We're going to have a baby.' There were tears of sheer happiness pouring down the couple's faces and even the doctor's eyes were moist with happiness for them.

Finally persuaded to go and sit at the desk, they sat gazing at each other with love and wonder shining in their eyes, hanging on to each other as if they'd never let go. Then all of a sudden the mood between them changed and a look of horror crossed over Chloe's face.

'But what if Jack loses it? He might miscarry or something might be wrong with it. Oh I can't bear to go there again,' she told the two men and buried her face in her hands, as if to block out any negative thoughts.

'Chloe,' the doctor said in a stern voice. 'Don't go spoiling the moment by remembering past times. You both need to think positively. Now it looks as if Jack's between eighteen and twenty-two weeks pregnant, if we go by a female pregnancy, and if that's the case, he's passed the danger point you experienced in your own pregnancies. If a male pregnancy corresponds with a female one then I reckon your baby should be due sometime in April. You'll know better when you've been for testing.'

'What sort of testing?' Chloe asked. 'The same ones as I had?'

'Those and a lot more. We've already received directives from the government to forward details of any pregnant males, so no doubt they'll have a host of other tests to carry out, as well as the usual ones. So you can expect the very best of treatment and care', he told them matter of factly. Then in a more whimsical note he added, 'Who'd have thought this would have happened when you got your life-long marriage certificate eh?' he shook his head in wonderment, chuckling at the irony of the situation. Then on a more professional note told them, 'As you're probably one of the first to have a pregnancy confirmed, you'll more than likely be called up next week to go for testing. The one thing they're looking to discover is why, after generations of only women having babies, are men now starting to have babies too. Must be something in the water,' he laughed, and then suddenly stopped realising it could well be something to do with the water or anything else that mundane. Only time would unravel the mystery, he realised.

Still unable to believe their good luck and fortune, Jack and Chloe left the surgery with very different expressions on their faces compared to the ones they'd arrived with. As they walked home they couldn't stop grinning as they chattered excitedly about the forthcoming baby.

'We don't want to get too over-excited though,' Jack warned her. 'After all no one knows anything about men being pregnant and, who knows, what dangers there are during the time it's developing, or even if it's developing normally. And we don't know if the pregnancy's going to last for nine months either,' he speculated. 'Then there's the birth,' he said, a look and feeling of anxiety settling on him suddenly.

'Wonder how it will be born?' Chloe pondered aloud.

'I don't care how it's born, Chloe, even if they have to cut my todger off. All I want is for us to be a mum and dad.'

'A mum and dad, Jack. Do you think it'll really happen? Hey! How about we invite everyone round tonight and tell them the news? Everyone's been so worried about us after all we've been through, and our tiff this week hasn't helped either. What do you reckon? Don't you think it would be good to invite them round for some really good news for once?'

'I'm not sure Chloe. I mean I haven't really got used to the idea yet and… well I'm… Oh hang it all! Why the hell not. It'll make a nice change having something good to share for once.'

Arriving home together, they began ringing their respective families to invite them round that evening, being careful not to give any indication of what it was all about. By seven that evening, the majority of the family had arrived and been greeted by a bouncing Wiz and two sombre adults, the atmosphere quite strained. Finally, not knowing what to expect it was Chloe's mother who set the ball rolling by voicing everyone's fears, with the warning, that no matter how much they'd been through, divorce was still illegal.

Perturbed they'd taken it all too far, Jack and Chloe looked at each other, silently agreeing they should now liven the atmosphere and tell everyone their news. Chloe put her arms lovingly round Jack's waist, or where his waist used to be, and told everyone in an almost hushed tone, 'We found out today Jack's going to have a baby. He's pregnant.'

There was a stunned silence then round the room, as if in a game of Chinese Whispers, one voice after another could be heard to say 'Pregnant?'

'Jack's pregnant?'

'Jack's having a baby?'

Then suddenly someone said out loud, voicing what everyone wanted to know, 'What do you mean Jack's having a baby? How come?' and once again the whispering and twittering started with everyone voicing their uncertainty.

'Jack went to the doctor's today for a check-up and, whilst he was there, I got a call to say Jack was at the surgery and I was needed there immediately. When I got there they didn't tell me what was going on, but just showed me the screen,' she explained. 'And this,' she said proudly holding up a picture. 'Is a picture of our baby!'

'What?'

'Really?'

'How wonderful.'

'I can't believe it.'

'I'm going to be a grandma after all.' and for the next ten minutes or so, the room was filled with questions and exclamations interspersed with hugs and kisses for Chloe, Jack and each other. Everyone was ecstatic, but inwardly each and every one of them was praying this wasn't some cruel joke being played on the couple, after everything they'd been through.

As Jack and Chloe watched and listened, they hung onto each other, only breaking apart when yet another relation came up to hug and kiss them in delight at their news. Every so often, they heard a really excited voice saying, 'Chloe kept saying he was pregnant. She did! She did, she said she just knew.'

It was of course Cassie, who'd been their biggest source of support over the past few years.

~ ~ ~ ~ ~

On the Friday, Liam and Crawford had lunch together before Liam was due to go off for his medical. It came as something of a surprise, an hour after they'd parted, when Crawford received an internal call asking him, as a matter of urgency, to go to the Medics Room, as there was a problem with Liam. Crawford, immediately concerned, hurried off to the Medics annexe, anxiously scanning through their conversation in his mind trying to work out what could be wrong.

Arriving at the office he was greeted by the nurse and immediately shown through to the room where Liam sat, slumped and drained of all colour, in a chair. He was wearing his boxers and a robe, which hung open revealing his distended belly.

'Liam?' Crawford asked anxiously. 'You alright?' Not getting any response he drew a chair up beside Liam and put an arm protectively round Liam's shoulders giving him a reassuring hug.

'Liam? What's the matter?' Still getting no response he turned to the doctor.

'What's the matter with him? Is he ill or what?' Crawford asked, having totally forgotten, in the fraughtness of the moment, Liam was having his medical that afternoon.

'Liam?' the doctor said addressing the inert, unresponsive body slouched dejectedly on the chair. 'I'm going to tell Crawford what's going on, as you've given me permission to do so on your work records in the case of an emergency. Ok?'

Not getting a response he turned to Crawford and told him. 'This is what I term an emergency. Liam's been sitting in a non-responsive manner since I gave him his test results.' Crawford looking alarmed and then questioningly at the doctor and asked which tests and what they'd shown. It was then he noticed the flicker of excitement on the doctor's face and a restlessness in his manner which betrayed the exhilaration he was feeling.

'You booked Liam in for a full medical check-up the other day, remember? Well it's not often we're asked to do full checks and with your concerns over his weight, I decided to run a few additional checks after my initial examination. I ran a whole range of scans, a number of other tests and also an examination with our new Intrusional Scanner.'

Getting up from his desk, the doctor strutted round to the monitor above the examination couch, as if about to reveal something momentous. Crawford half expected him to produce a rabbit out of a hat, so flamboyant was his behaviour, and found an element of dislike for the doctor developing.

'It was during the scans I found this,' the doctor announced dramatically, unable to contain his excitement any longer. He switched on the monitor and turned it so Crawford would be able to see the picture he was about to reveal.

'This,' the doctor started proudly, pointing to an image on the screen, 'is a baby. Your friend here, Crawford, is pregnant,' he paused for dramatic affect as if expecting a round of applause. Crawford looked on nonplussed. The doctor, unsure whether to be annoyed or to take advantage of Crawford's lack of response quickly added, 'And it also explains his tiredness.' Still not getting a reaction from Crawford, who was still sitting next to Liam with his arm round him, looking as confused as Liam was shocked. The doctor, reluctant to have the air taken out of his sails, carried on with, 'And from my calculations, Liam is about five months pregnant, if the growth of a baby in the male body correlates with that of a woman.'

'What?' Crawford finally asked with a baffled look on his face, as though he'd understood nothing the doctor had just told him. 'Pregnant? How the hell can he be pregnant? That's ridiculous.' He looked at Liam with incredulity, instinctively wanting to move away as if the condition was contagious but, at the same time, wanting to hold and shield him. Deciding on the latter, he hugged Liam protectively to him.

'Well,' said the doctor, unable to contain his excitement any longer. 'Since the news hit the headlines on Tuesday, regarding a man giving birth, every doctor in the land has been hoping and praying a pregnant man would turn up on their couch. I can't believe it myself.

It's a miracle. It's just so exciting. Imagine? Me! With a pregnant man in my office. It's a dream come true,' he enthused losing all professional etiquette, as he waxed lyrically about 'his find'.

'Right you can stop right there,' Crawford snapped standing up angrily, every part of him wanting to poke this crass bastard in the eyes. 'This is not about 'you', this is about Liam here, and what needs to be done,' he said looking across at Liam, relieved to see he was finally beginning to stir.

'If Liam is pregnant he'll need looking after. If he's pregnant,' he stated emphasising the 'if'. 'Are your tests accurate? Conclusive? You've not brought up an incorrect screen have you?' he suggested clutching at straws.

'I assure you Crawford,' the doctor said carefully, feeling somewhat affronted, 'your friend here is pregnant and this,' he said, indicating the clearly defined image on the screen, 'is Liam's baby. Not another patient's, Liam's! I can run the scan again if you insist, just to doubly reassure you,' he added acidly, annoyed Crawford had dampened his euphoria at this extraordinary find.

'Do you want another scan Liam?' Crawford asked him.

'Well it could be a mistake,' Liam said in a tremulous voice.

'Right,' Crawford instructed. 'Let's clear the screen, reset the scanner and double check this shall we?'

The doctor reset the equipments and screens, under the close scrutiny of Crawford, and once again Liam climbed on to the couch for a second scan, the doctor at his side scowling, with having his professionalism questioned.

Within seconds of the machine being set in motion, a crystal clear image of a well formed foetus came into view. Clutching hands tightly, whether in fear or for comfort, Liam and Crawford gasped in unison and disbelief.

'Christ Liam, you're pregnant alright and that there,' he said, pointing to the screen in wonder, 'is our baby.'

'Our baby?' Liam repeated in a daze. 'But how can it be our baby? How can I be pregnant? I just don't believe this, Crawford. This is a nightmare but a miracle at the same time.'

Liam slowly sat up on the couch swinging his legs round so they dangled over the edge of the couch. He didn't cry, or laugh nor did he shout or whoop or punch the air. He didn't scream or shout, wail or even moan, he just sat motionless, lost in his thoughts, which were ones of complete and utter disbelief.

'The pregnancy explains the tiredness and increased weight,' the doctor explained, now having put his professional hat back on, metaphorically speaking. 'There's a lack of iron in the body and his calcium levels could be better, but they'll be easily remedied by a change in his dietary intake, and his workouts can continue but will need adjusting. Other than that, all I can suggest at the moment is you go home and talk about the situation.

'God! Whatever is Tanya going to say?' Crawford asked in wonder.

'Tanya? Who's Tanya?' asked the doctor quickly.

'Our partner,' Crawford explained. 'The three of us live together,' he added quickly, so the doctor could be left in no uncertainty. 'In every sense of the word. Come on Liam. Get dressed and we'll get straight back. I'll ring Tanya to tell her we're on our way and need her there. Ok?' he demanded brooking no nonsense.

With shaking fingers, Liam slowly dressed and put on his shoes. Picking up his electronic briefcase, which now contained an image of his baby, he followed Crawford out of the Medics room, having first stopped at the reception desk to make another appointment for Monday as instructed. The nurse, who'd been present at the first scan, didn't know whether to congratulate or commiserate, and it was obvious she was itching to tell the story, as soon as she possibly could, to all and sundry. Like the doctor, she couldn't believe her luck a pregnant man had turned up as one of their patients.

Crawford, sensing she was bursting to tell someone, hissed at her in a low tone that, 'if she didn't respect patient confidentiality and revealed Liam's condition or identity to another living soul he personally would make sure she'd be instantly dismissed and never be able to get a job again.' Well known in the department, and knowing his position in the hierarchy pecking order, the now chastised and subdued nurse took his warning very much to heart.

Arriving home, they found a very concerned and agitated Tanya waiting for them. Having received Crawford's extremely odd and worrying phone call, asking her to go straight home, she'd dropped everything and almost run home. She'd no idea what it was all about, except there was something wrong with Liam. Not knowing how long they were going to be, she was actually in the kitchen and, as soon as she heard the door open, literally dropped what she was doing, which was a stainless steel pan that made an almighty racket as she dropped it into the sink as she rushed out to meet her men.

'Liam,' she gasped going straight to him, appraising him as she crossed the room, trying to work out if he'd been injured or anything. 'Whatever's the matter? Crawford said the doctor had given you some shocking news. Come over here and sit down for goodness sake,' she said fussing round him, which was a new experience for Liam.

'What is it?' she asked having finally settled him down. 'Are you ill? Have you had an accident? Will one of you please tell me what's going on here?' she demanded, her voice rising in panic at their silence.

'Tanya. This may come as a bit of a shock to you. It did to us so maybe you'd be best sitting down,' Crawford told her in a deliberately expressionless voice. Unceremoniously Tanya sat down heavily on the settee expecting the worst.

'What is it?' she asked tears of worry threatening to spill over from her beautiful brown eyes.

'Tanya,' Crawford started, having taken full control of the situation. 'Liam went for his check-up this afternoon and during the tests they found…' but before he could finish Liam blurted out bluntly, 'I'm pregnant.'

Tanya looked from one man to the other totally confused, not sure if she'd heard Liam's statement correctly.

'What?' she asked innocently.

'Liam's pregnant.'

'I'm pregnant,' came from both men simultaneously, causing Tanya more confusion.

'What? Will just one of you tell me what's going on here? Liam what did you say?'

'I'm pregnant,' Liam told her bluntly.

'Pregnant?' Tanya repeated as if he'd been speaking in a foreign language. 'Am I missing something here or just going mad? What do you mean you're pregnant?'

Liam shrugged his shoulders but didn't speak so Crawford, still in a state of shock himself, suggested Liam show her the picture. Liam reached down to his briefcase, which he'd dumped unceremoniously on the floor, and took out the brightly-coloured picture of the baby and handed it across to Tanya. Tanya reached out her hand and touched it gently, almost as if she was touching the baby itself.

'A baby?' she said in wonder. 'But Liam, how wonderful. Oh!' she gasped clapping her hand in front of her mouth as if to contain unspoken words.

'I said… I said if I didn't know better then I'd think you were pregnant. Do you remember Liam?' she asked, as if having spoken those words only the week before had created this phenomenon.

'But whose is it?' she asked. 'And who are you? Are you the mother or the father? she asked, a question which would constantly visit Liam in the future. 'And… are one of us the other parent?' she asked Crawford. 'Oh god Liam, this is wonderful but so, so scary. Oh come here and let me give you a hug.' She threw her arms round his neck and hugged him tightly, then released him abruptly laying her hand wonderingly on his distended belly and whispered. 'A baby. Oh how wonderful! A baby.'

'Yes,' Liam responded, 'a baby but is this really happening to me? To us? What are we going to do when it's born, however it's born,' he said wincing.

'What are we going to do?' Tanya parroted. 'Well *we're* all going to love it to bits and bring it up together aren't we Crawford?'

Crawford looked across at Liam and Tanya and then crossing over to where they both sat, knelt in front of them, drawing them both into his arms and telling them reassuringly, 'Yes, we will bring it up together and love it very much, whatever it is and whoever's it is. Ok Liam? Ok Tanya?'

No words of response were spoken. They just nodded their heads before wrapping their arms round each other and hugging more tightly than before. The bond, which already existed, could easily have been broken by this earth shattering news. As it was it had just been made stronger – or had it?

~ ~ ~ ~ ~

It was the Friday before Daryl was allowed to come round properly. He'd been so traumatised by the experience they'd decided to keep him heavily sedated. At the same time the Crimedical team wanted to gain the maximum of information from him, via the Subliminal

Voyeur, so having squirreled Daryl away, giving them privacy from the hoards wanting to interview him, they'd set about conducting extensive interviews, receiving only the truth from Daryl's subconscious mind.

Daryl knew none of this when he was finally allowed to regain full consciousness. Coming to, he'd no idea where he was or why he was surrounded by a range of machinery with numerous stickers adhered to him. His living nightmare started when he realised he was in hospital, and only got worse when it was revealed he was hooked up to the Subliminal Voyeur, which had probably divulged the details of all the rapes and attacks he'd committed.

As the realisation of where he was finally dawned on him, an enormous surge of terror struck him. Trying to sit upright the sudden movement caused a bolt of pain to rip through his groin. The pain was so intense he'd screamed in agony, before falling back prone onto the bed. His mind was battling between fright, and the need for flight, clouded by the intensity of pain he'd just experienced. He laid his hands gingerly on his belly and to his disbelief found it considerably flatter than the last time he'd felt it and wondered why.

The monitors, and his shout of pain, had alerted staff and within minutes, a male medic had entered the room, accompanied by a uniformed guard bearing a stun gun. The guard stood on the opposite side of the bed to the medic, with the gun in full view. The medic, not looking at all comfortable with the situation, made Daryl feel really scared, convinced his worst nightmare was about to come true.

'Right Daryl,' the guard instructed. 'Let the medic carry out his duties without making any sudden movements. You're under arrest for the rape of six women and the attempted murder of Francis Mellor. If you struggle, become violent or attempt to escape I'll have no option but to use this stun gun to restrain you. In a short time DDI Roberts will be arriving to start your interview process and, as soon as you're deemed fit, you'll be moved to a secure unit until trial. Do you understand this, Daryl?' the guard finished gruffly.

Daryl nodded in response, too terrified to speak, as he tried to take on board the implication of what he'd just heard.

*What's been happening since I was brought here?* he wondered fuzzily. *Surely they can't have sent off my DNA and got results so quickly,* he thought, unaware he'd just woken after three days heavily sedated sleep.

The medic, checking, adjusting and monitoring various recordings on the machines said, in a quiet, nervous voice, 'Dr Emsam will be along shortly to explain the medical aspects of your being here. I'll order some food for you. Do you want traditional or food pearls?' he asked Daryl in a distinctly distant manner.

'Food pearls and a drink,' Daryl said, in what came out as a squeaky voice, so terrified was he. The medic nodded his understanding and having finished adjusting the machines left the room. The guard following behind him stopped at the door and turned back to Daryl, who lay looking pale and scared against his pillow, 'There'll be a guard right outside your door, which is electronically locked. There's no window and no escape from this room and any medical person entering will be accompanied by a guard for their protection. I advise you to co-operate fully and not try and make any false moves. By doing so, you'll be putting individuals at risk, and we'll not hesitate in stunning you. Do you understand?'

Daryl nodded his understanding and the guard left the room, a symbolic 'clunk' sounding as he closed the door.

Daryl was left alone in the silent room and, as the realisation of what was happening dawned on him, soundless tears slid from his eyes and pooled round his ears on the pillow.

It was another ten minutes or so before Dr Emsam arrived. His behaviour was confusing, as there was obviously an element of excitement about him, but also one of uncertainty. His demeanour added to Daryl's bewilderment, who'd no idea what had happened since he'd been admitted.

'It's been quite an eventful few days since you arrived here,' the doctor started. 'Were you aware when you came in you were pregnant? He asked.

'Pre... pregnant?' asked Daryl doubtfully. The doctor nodded with a show of excitement, which he immediately tried to hide.

'You had a baby. A baby boy.' he told Daryl.

'A... a baby?' Daryl asked even more confused. 'I... I had a baby but...' he asked stunned by what he'd just heard. 'Do you mean to say I had a baby? A baby boy?' he asked without any comprehension whatsoever.

The doctor nodded continuing with, 'Didn't you know or ever suspect you were pregnant Daryl? You never had any symptoms in the past few months that you didn't wonder about, or which caused you concern?'

Daryl looked in wonder at the doctor and nodded, dumb struck as he thought about all his ailments, but not relating them to what he was hearing.

All those symptoms, his weight gain and everything else – he'd been pregnant? he mused.

'But how...' he struggled to ask. 'How come I got pregnant? Men don't get pregnant. Is this some sick joke or something?' he asked, grasping at the chance he was party to some sort of sick joke or wind up. 'I don't have a girlfriend and I've not had sex with a man,' he said involuntarily shuddering at the thought. 'So how come...' he trailed off.

'Well that's just it Daryl. No one knows how, or why, you became pregnant. It's something we're still trying to work out.'

'But who... how...' he was at a total loss for words as he struggled to sort out all the questions swimming about in his head and the guard, at his bedside was having to bite his tongue to keep quiet.

'So... so if I had a... a baby then how... how was it b-born?' he asked wincing as he remembered the pain in his groin he'd experienced a short while ago.

'It was born via your penis. You were brought in during the final stages of labour and when we finally realised what was happening, we assisted the delivery. It was a shock to us all when we grasped what was happening, and the only way we could assist the delivery was by incising the length of your penis and scrotum.'

Daryl was half sitting up, with a look of incredulity on his face.

*They'd been shocked,* he thought, *what about me?*

'Then you went into toxic shock,' the doctor explained, 'and have been kept under heavy sedation for the past few days. I can't give you anything other than medical details, so you'll have to wait for DDI Roberts to inform you what else has been going on,' he finished, checking Daryl over and adjusting the machines surrounding him. He desperately wanted to ask Daryl a whole dialogue of questions, but had been advised he could face prosecution if he did so without express authority, which was unlikely to be given prior to Daryl being questioned whilst conscious. The doctor also knew his patient would have a host of questions too, but it was more than his job was worth to get into a discussion with this patient.

*It was a pity this man was the rapist,* he thought, having been informed of the DNA results. *I would have loved to find out more about him personally and his family background, to see if it would throw any light on him becoming pregnant.* Sadly this wasn't to be and the only privilege the Crimedics would allow him was to view the subconscious recordings, which was an honour in itself. Just as Dr Emsam was about to leave, the guard received a message telling him Melanie had arrived. Dr Emsam hastily left the room, with the hope of catching a few moments with Melanie before she went in. He wasn't to be disappointed.

Five minutes later, Melanie entered the room with a colleague, and the first thing she did was to recite Daryl's rights, and inform him of the charges he was facing; six rapes and one attempted murder. He lay in stunned silence as he took all this on board, his worst nightmare having come true, and knowing if he'd been here for three days his DNA would have been analysed. But worse was to come.

'Whilst you were unconscious you were linked into the Subliminal Voyeur and were questioned,' Melanie told him. 'Working back over the past two year's events it was you, yourself who highlighted the rapes and attacks. The DNA samples we obtained from you clarified each and every subconscious confession you made. In effect, you have given indisputable evidence against yourself,' Melanie intoned. She and her colleagues were ever thankful these methods no longer encroached on human rights, having been flouted by the individual committing a criminal act. Something unheard of at the beginning of the century.

'The Subliminal Voyeur is an extremely ingenious piece of equipment and, through programming, we were able to bring a number of interesting aspects into the forefront of your subconscious mind, including your health concerns. Incidentally the blood poisoning you believed you were suffering from, never existed, the symptoms were merely those of pregnancy.'

Daryl listened, frozen with fear as Melanie reiterated a number of other things they'd discovered whilst he was unconscious.

*There should be a law against anyone trespassing on someone's mind,* he thought. *There used to be so why isn't there any more? This intrusion is diabolical it's like... like... like rape,* he surmised ironically, unaware theft of his thoughts wasn't anywhere as near as bad to the rapes he'd committed.'

Daryl lay in frightened silence, wondering if he could use his illness to call everything to a halt. He wanted to die, he wanted to be out of this nightmare, he wanted his Mam, but all he could do was lay inert.

'We've also had it confirmed today, Lucy Johnson is the other parent of the baby?' Melanie informed him. This news finally caused an animated reaction in Daryl.

'Lucy Johnson? Lucy-fucking-Johnson? That dirty fucking bitch? Why did she do that to me, the mucky cow?' Daryl yelled, struggling to get up as his anger came to the fore.

'I wouldn't advise you to do anything stupid, Daryl,' warned the guard stepping forward. 'One false move and I'll use this stun gun. Just remember, Matie,' he continued with contempt, 'it was you who raped her.'

'She was up for it,' Daryl muttered in anger, and continued to mutter for sometime, as the surrounding equipment recorded his every muttering and imagining, which were displayed on monitor. Melanie wasn't surprised to hear Daryl accusing Lucy of inflicting this on him. He had the most bizarre grip on reality, and was very much the 'victim' of life in his own eyes.

'How dare she do that to me? How dare she even breathe when I'm in here? I'll bloody teach her a lesson,' he ranted. 'And as for you, you bitch…' he threatened Melanie, as he struggled to get out of bed. He hadn't even finished his sentence before an excruciating bolt of pain shot through him, at the same time as an intense pain tore through his groin. For a few moments he knew no more, but when consciousness returned the after-effects of the stun gun were clearly evident by the pounding of his head and the inability to move or speak.

The guard, who knew all about Daryl's misdemeanours and despised him for it, had been somewhat trigger happy which, on this occasion, Melanie was prepared to overlook. She had her rapist and he had his comeuppance and as soon as he was fit she'd have him moved to a high security prison where he'd be isolated, so as not to gain notoriety amongst his fellow prisoners.

~ ~ ~ ~ ~

Over the weekend, Liam's, Crawford's and Tanya's reactions ranged from shock to horror, excitement to concern; to one of hope and then onto something unfathomable and back again. All three were excited, yet stunned, and more than a little bewildered. Babies and children were not a thing they'd discussed to date, after all the relationship was still too newly-formed to have given the subject any credence. The issues were further clouded by it being Liam having the baby, had it been Tanya there wouldn't have been so many issues and mysteries. After all they'd automatically assumed any children, had they got to that stage by choice, would have been borne by Tanya.

Whilst all of them were perplexed, no one was more so than Liam. He'd automatically assumed Crawford was the second parent, and if so was he likely to be a child bearer himself? And if Crawford was the other parent, the father, then who did that make him? Was he the mother or the father? His identity seemingly lost, Liam became more and more confused by the whole situation, completely at a loss as to how he should set about working it all out in his mind.

Tanya and Crawford were surprisingly excited by the whole situation and, still not used to the idea, it had taken Liam some time to persuade them not to tell anyone before he'd got used to the idea.

'Let's keep it between ourselves for the moment,' he'd pleaded. 'After all the first people we should tell are my family,' to which they had reluctantly consented to. It didn't stop them setting up plans though, as to who was going to look after the baby after it was born. They even went so far as to go onto the internet to look at how they could incorporate a nursery into the flat and what furniture and equipment they'd need.

It was all too much for Liam, who sat very much on the fringe of the activities and wasn't enjoying all the fuss and attention being lavished on him. He just wanted things to go on as normal, like before, as if nothing different had happened, but neither Tanya or Crawford were going to let that happen, and the flat continued to buzz all weekend with excitement. As the centre of attention, Liam couldn't remember a time when he'd needed some isolation and space more, just to sort out his thoughts and feelings.

Unable to grasp Liam's problem, expecting him to be as excited and involved as they were, they finally became exasperated, and almost on the edge of a full scale row demanded to know what was up with him. As far as they were concerned Liam's pregnancy was the future ahead for the three of them, and they'd bring up the baby together.

After all it wasn't just Liam's baby and, how lucky was he his two partners wanted to take on the baby, they'd asked him. Somehow Liam couldn't get it through to them he didn't feel particularly lucky at the moment and more than anything he was feeling scared, with so much unknown and so many unasked and unanswered questions.

'Scared?' they'd challenged. 'What's to be scared about?'

'Well to start with I'm going to have a baby and men don't have babies,' he'd told them.

'Phew! It'll be a doddle, nothing to it,' Tanya said. 'Women have been doing it forever.'

'Yes but women's bodies are obviously meant to have babies,' Liam snapped back.

'And so's yours,' Tanya retorted quickly. 'Otherwise you wouldn't be pregnant would you?'

'Yes but how…?'

'Who knows and who cares? Lets just take it one day at a time and you just remember Crawford and I are here whatever happens,' and she hugged him tightly hoping it'd reinforce what she'd just said.

The final straw came when Liam went into the office to do a workout. Seeing him going in they'd automatically assumed he was going to visualise where the cot and everything would go, so decided to leave him to it. When Tanya walked in a short while later, laden with information she'd downloaded from the internet, she was horrified to find Liam working-out.

'Liam! Liam what the hell do you think you're doing?' she cried out urgently. 'You can't do that, you're pregnant,' she accused. 'Crawford,' she shouted at the top of her voice. 'Crawford come here and do something about this,' she demanded. Seconds later Crawford appeared in the doorway alarmed by Tanya's urgent shouts.

'What's wrong?' he gasped, his heart beating loudly, or so it seemed to him.

'This is what's wrong. This idiot's doing a bloody workout and doesn't know what he's doing,' she said, pointing an accusing finger at Liam.

'Oh for fuck's sake will you two get off my back,' Liam exploded. 'One minute you're telling me it's the most natural thing in the world being pregnant, and the next you're telling me to stop what I'm doing.

Will you make your bloody minds up and leave me alone,' he raged at Tanya. 'Get her off my back,' he demanded of Crawford.

'Whoa there, whoa,' Crawford cajoled calmingly. 'Tanya, stop charging round screaming like a banshee, and Liam, you need to be more careful.' Then turning to Tanya he told her, 'There's nothing wrong with Liam working-out but,' he said warningly, turning to Liam and pointing a finger at him, 'we need to look at your routine and adjust it a little, ok?'

'Tanya, go and make yourself busy for an hour or two because we're going to do a bit of male bonding here, and sort out a new workout for Liam. How's about you go and finish the packing you left yesterday when we called you out? Huh?' he finished as though he'd brook no argument.

Tanya, looking crestfallen, reluctantly agreed and going over to Liam gave him a warm, loving hug before going off to her tiny workshop. When she returned a couple of hours later, having left her two men to sort out a few things, peace once again seemed to reign and the atmosphere between them seemed far more normal, despite the bizarre situation they'd now found themselves in.

By the end of the weekend, their emotions had calmed considerably, and it was agreed they wouldn't plan or buy anything until they knew more of what was happening, and their excitement had calmed. They also agreed that, until Liam was more comfortable with the situation, and he'd told his family the news, no one else would be told of the pending baby.

It was during the afternoon at work, when it suddenly dawned on Liam that if he was about five months pregnant the baby would be due around early spring, March or April he reckoned. Just as the penny dropped it suddenly hit him, like a ton of bricks, his project would suffer for it. Despite constant reassurances from Crawford and Tanya, he couldn't just accept everything could be worked out and it'd be ok. In a panic he'd rushed over to Crawford's office, who promised to support him and speak to his team manager, suggesting it might be worthwhile seeing if Liam could train someone up to work the project in his absence. Liam shook his head emphatically, pointing out he'd lose control and credit for the project. As Liam saw it, the situation was impossible, and there was no persuading him otherwise.

'None of my life makes sense anymore,' Liam told him mournfully. 'This is the first project I've been given and it could potentially be a leading programme for the country, when out of the blue this happens,' he told him indicating his stomach, which seemed to have expanded over the weekend since he'd received his news.

'So now I've no idea where my career's going or even if it's going anywhere. I don't even know who I am any more. I mean am I the mother or the father? Go on tell me,' he challenged emotionally. 'Answer me because I sure as hell don't know.'

'Does it really matter who you are Liam? I mean whether you're the mother or the father? Let's face it, you've got a far better chance of getting through this and being a parent than most, since your parents were involved in the Parenting Skills Pilot. You've got months ahead of you to work things out before you need to make any decision and perhaps the best way forward would be to ask if the pilot can be postponed until after the baby's born and, then you could use the time off to really fine tune it, and maximise on research time. What do you think?' Crawford asked, hoping his suggestion would take some of the immediate pressure off Liam.

'You're well respected at work, Liam, just think about it. How many sixteen year olds were involved in the National Service project from before the start and got a personal recommendation for their work? You did. How many of your ideas were taken on board when you finished your National Service? Loads. So stop worrying and we'll explain your situation to the boss and put forward the proposal for a delayed launch. He's going to be surprised but I'm sure he'll agree and then you can go back refreshed and make a real success of the project,' he told Liam reassuringly. 'And don't forget Tanya and I are right behind you, we love you and we'll do everything we can to make it as easy and enjoyable as possible.'

Liam felt tears of gratitude well in his eyes. He'd heard of couples going through rough patches and weathering them, but he'd got two partners who thought the world of him, loved him and would stand by him whatever.

*We've got something special*, he told himself, *which few people find with one, let alone two. So I'll have to find a way round handling the project and work out who I'm going to be but with Tanya and Crawford beside me, and the support I'll get from my family, things will pan out ok.*

With that realisation, he suddenly found himself thinking differently about his pregnancy and the baby that lay within. He looked down at his proudly protruding belly and gently laid his hands protectively against it. Then he looked up at Crawford and nodded. It was at that moment Crawford knew, without a doubt; Liam had finally accepted his condition positively.

~ ~ ~ ~ ~

The following day, still reeling from the shock of everything that had happened, Daryl desperately wanted to see his Mam and Sonia. When he asked if he'd be allowed to see Sonia he was told curtly.

'She's not a relative and as it's not common knowledge you're the father of the baby and the serial rapist you'll be allowed to see no one,' the guard told him. 'You may have professed your innocence 'to the inspector yesterday, but the Subliminal Voyeur recording and the evidence of injuries and DNA from victims, tell a totally different and far more accurate story. Once the news hits the deadlines you won't want to be out in public, because they'll want to lynch you,' he told Daryl venomously. 'We'll contact your mother but there's nothing we can do if she chooses not to visit.'

'But, but… 'Daryl stuttered in defence. 'I didn't do anything. I'm the one who ended up pregnant. She's the one who should be under guard… that Lucy Johnson I mean, not me Mam,' but his words fell on deaf ears. As the medic had finished treating him and was leaving the room with the guard, Daryl was left feeling lost, alone and very blue.

*If only I could talk to Sonia,* he thought, *she'd understand and wouldn't believe these cock and bull stories. Surely she'd know I could never do what they're accusing me of. Those bitches were game and up for it. I never did anything they didn't want.* But deep down he knew that wasn't true.

~ ~ ~ ~ ~

Only days after the male birthing, a handful of men had had pregnancies confirmed with more coming forward all the time, not all pregnant but panicking they could be. Tests were being developed, emotions were running high and for every confirmed pregnancy Melanie was being called upon to coordinate the proceedings. Finally, with the rape case under wrap, Melanie was asked to set up the hastily formed Male Pregnancy Department.

It was something Melanie welcomed, as she felt ready for a fresh challenge, and somehow by solving the rape case she'd begun to lay her own personal ghosts to rest. She wanted to be involved in the proceedings, set up the new department and link her medical knowledge into investigating the reason for male pregnancies. She'd been present at the first birth; had the medical background and the means and power to tap into any necessary hierarchical structures to set up new governmental procedures. All these factors lead her to accepting the post and as it was to be attached to her existing team, in the early stages, it would give her the time to select the right staff for the job. She automatically selected Dr Emsam, who after delivering the rapist's baby was the logical choice, but Melanie had a high regard for him anyway, in the way he'd handled the case and not let the eminence tarnish his professionalism.

Going home on the Friday night only Froud, Melanie's boss, knew Monday would be a totally different ball game for Melanie, as her promotion had not yet been announced. She was in a heightened state of excitement waiting for Alan to come round, as he was going to be the first she'd share the news with. However, when she told him he took her news in a more subdued state than she'd expected and instinctively Melanie knew something else was afoot, and she didn't think it was anything to do with her pending career change.

All of a sudden it dawned on her Alan was not only quiet but had something of major importance to impart. She stopped stock still as it dawned on her she needed to quieten down and listen to whatever he had to tell her. What it was, and uncertain whether she'd want to hear it, she instantly froze, as rigid as a statue.

'Alan? What is it?' she asked timidly as if expecting bad news.

'Melanie. Melanie come and sit down here next to me,' he told her patting the empty seat beside him. Melanie, now feeling apprehensive did as she was told, which was unlike her, and sat nervously beside him. Alan put his arm round her and pulled her into him kissing her comfortingly on top of her head.

'I've been trying to find the right time to tell you this,' Alan told her, feeling her tense in his arms. He hugged her more tightly to him. 'But it's alright there's nothing to be afraid of,' he told her comfortingly.

319

'It's just that when I checked the Death Register I found this,' he told her dipping into his pocket to pull out a report.

Melanie sat away from him and looked at him searchingly. She'd a good idea what it was he was offering her, and almost felt as though her heart had stopped pumping. She felt cold and clammy as she reached out for the proffered piece of paper. With trembling hands she took it from Alan and felt him slip his arm round her shoulders more firmly.

Before she'd even opened the piece of paper Alan was telling her gently, 'It's your mum Melanie. Her killer died a few days ago. The same day as all this baby business started to roll. I've checked the DNA they took from him. Apparently he was on a flight back home from the USA, where he's been for the past thirty years. He was taken ill mid-flight and died before the plane landed. His DNA went through Deceased Testing and checking it against the records we've confirmed it was your Mum's killer. I'm sorry Melanie for everything you lost and for all the years you've been searching, but at least now it's over. You know he doesn't exist in this world anymore.'

Melanie was holding the opened paper and looking at it carefully.

*This was the information on the man who'd raped and ultimately killed her Mum whilst she was carrying Melanie. The bastard who'd rendered her motherless and blighted her life in the eyes of her dad. She knew the data off by heart, so many times had she checked them against the Death Registration, and there was no shadow of a doubt it was him.* As she stared unseeingly at the piece of paper in her hand she saw and heard, rather than felt, the fat wet tears land on the paper in her hands. Still she continued to stare blindly.

For his part Alan sat beside her, giving Melanie the feeling she'd a rock of strength beside her and suddenly knew it was so perfectly right for him to be there. She knew this was the end of one journey for her and the start of a new one for both of them together. They'd a long way to travel yet but now she could continue the journey having finally laid her ghosts to rest and quietened her aching heart. Alan, instinctively knowing things had just changed between them, continued to hold her comfortingly. He knew there would be time for kissing and getting intimate later, before the night was over.

~ ~ ~ ~ ~

When Sharon had been visited by the police, she'd known within hours about Daryl giving birth, and was inwardly making plans how much money she could make out of being the mother of the first man to give birth. Mentally cashing in on her son's fame, she'd been planning parties, holidays and spending sprees from the money he'd be given for his story, and planning how she'd squirrel away money from selling her own tale of what a wonderful mother she'd been. Mentally she'd been rubbing her hands with glee, and not once given any real thought to her son or grandson.

For some reason, much to her annoyance, something to do with confidentiality, they'd not allowed her to go home. She'd been obliged to stay at the Crimedical Centre overnight, in what was a lovely suite, not that she'd admit it. The following day it had come as something of a shock when her interviews had taken a turn for the worse, and they'd started to ask awkward questions, not just about Daryl but about her husband too.

*Why the hell were they asking about her husband and his death? They'd know what had happened if they bothered to look it up*, she thought angrily. He'd been in a hit and run accident, which was all on record, she'd told them.

It hadn't bothered her being linked into the Subliminal Voyeur, or hadn't until they'd started asking questions about the events leading up to his death. At first she'd been flummoxed by the questions then her feelings turned to discomfort as they delved further into her thoughts and set up the machine to reveal memories she was deliberately trying to suppress. Before it had got to this stage though, she'd demanded, belligerently, why she was being asked these questions when she was there to help unravel the mystery of her son giving birth.

It was then they'd dropped their bombshell, and told her Daryl was the UK serial rapist they'd been hunting for the past two years. It had momentarily stunned her, but again she protested it had nothing to do with the questions they were asking about her husband, who'd been dead and buried a number of years now. Which was when they dropped the second bombshell, far mightier than the first, and informed her it had just been confirmed by testing he'd been involved in a gang rape at the turn of the century? When she'd demanded to know how they'd reached that conclusion they informed her of the house search, which had revealed not only evidence from Daryl's crimes but from her husband's as well. At that point she'd gone white and started to have a

321

'funny turn' all the while protesting her husband's innocence and naming the names of those she knew had committed the crime. Sadly for her, the Subliminal Voyeur also confirmed she'd known about his involvement all along, and had been expecting his death before it had even happened. Even Sharon couldn't dispute this against the machine's superior abilities.

Very quickly her plans to cash in on her son's notoriety, turned from one of fame and fortune, to one of misfortune. To cap it all, she was told it would be an offence for her to profit from her son having a baby, it being crime related. She was already in enough trouble, they told her, by obscuring her husband's criminal activities and concealing the reason for his death over the years. No matter how much she protested his innocence they weren't going to accept it, but she remained determined they wouldn't tarnish her memories of him.

It didn't please her at all when she was told she'd have to stay at the Crimedical Centre until they were ready to release her son's identity and announce the crimes he'd committed. Although it was a treat for her to be looked after, and have her meals cooked, this didn't appease Sharon at all. She wanted to tell the world about being her being the Gran to the world's first male born child, and had been told she wouldn't be allowed to contact anyone, for fear of giving information they weren't ready to be released yet. It was obvious this was the reason she was so disgruntled, as she'd not once asked about her son or the baby, and the Subliminal Voyeur had confirmed her disappointment was connected to her own greed.

~ ~ ~ ~ ~

Things finally came to a head for Jed on the Friday evening, when they were all watching a film at Fiona's. The facts of a male birth had finally been confirmed in the WiPPLe, although the method of delivery and the man's identity still hadn't been divulged. Other men had been coming forward and having their pregnancies confirmed too, presenting the opportunity Fiona and Jade had been waiting for.

'So if you were pregnant, Ben what would you do?' Jade asked without preamble.

'Milk it for all it was worth,' Ben answered.

'Hah! Bet you would,' Jed retorted. 'When you've all the fame you want and it's time to give birth, give us a shout and I'll come and watch it make its way down your dick. Then we'll see if it was worth money and fame,' he laughed. 'Can you imagine a baby's head forcing its way down your dick and out that tiny little hole?' he taunted.

Ben couldn't help but shudder at the image.

'Ok, I see what you mean, but if it's born that way do you reckon your dick'd go back to the same shape and size?' he asked.

Getting up to help himself to a banana, Jed shrugged.

'Jed!' Fiona admonished without thinking. 'You're forever eating bananas, that's your third one today. You sure you're not pregnant 'cos food cravings are a classic symptom.'

Normally Jed would have laughed this off, but something seemed to click in his mind and he froze, the banana midway to his mouth.

'What do you mean they're like pregnancy symptoms?'

Unsure of how to proceed, Fiona started tentatively, 'Your dreams and the way you used to look in the mornings and...'

'That was the moonshine,' Jed interjected quickly.

'What and your mood swings, laughing one minute and crying the next,' Fiona challenged. 'Just look at you now, near to tears again, it's bloody ludicrous,' she added, realising she'd overstepped the mark.

'So... so what are you saying? You can't seriously think I'm pregnant?' Jed asked with a small voice, spreading his fingers wide over his distended abdomen.

'Do you mean... I mean do you reckon... are you saying?' he asked, obviously at a loss for words and then looked up with abject terror in his eyes. 'Fi, Jade, tell me you're joking,' he said, his voice rising in panic. Then he flipped. 'Nooooooo' he screamed. 'Nooooooo,' and started tearing at his clothes and clawing at the flesh of his belly.

The calm atmosphere of before changed instantly, and Jed's three friends stunned by his reaction, stood stock still, then everything started to happen at once. Fiona's dad, Barry, came rushing in, just as Jed's wristlet started buzzing urgently. Seconds later Ben and Jade's wristlets activated, probably set off by their raised pulse rates. Jed continued to scream, tearing at himself as if possessed.

'Fiona?' her dad demanded urgently, as he moved over to Jed. 'What the hell's going on here?' Just as he reached Jed there was a sudden silence then slowly, as if a statue gone limp, Jed's body crumpled into a heap on the floor. The pursuing silence was broken by, 'Jed? Jed? Are you ok son?' which was Jed's dad, his voice booming out of the wristlet.

Between them Barry and Ben got Jed onto the settee and Fiona's mum went off to call the medics. Then, grabbing Jed's hand, Gary started speaking to Jed's dad, via the Wristlet, telling him what had happened and advising him to get there pronto. Once that was done, he was just about to ask the others what had been going on, when Jed began to come round, looking ashen-faced and hollowed-eyed, haunted by what he thought was happening, he was speechless.

Within ten minutes the medic arrived, having given Barry enough time to find out from his daughter what had been going on. Ushering the medic into Fiona's den, everyone else was sent out, with Jade and Ben sent home by Fiona's mum, despite protesting they wanted to stay to make sure Jed was all right.

Having come in and assessed Jed's hysteria, and seeing the damage Jed was still trying to do to himself, accompanied by screams of *Get this fucking alien thing out of me, get it out before it eats me*, the medic quickly administered a spray sedative, which seemed to have an immediate calming effect. Once calmed, the medic began to check Jed over, noting his bodily readings weren't as a young lad's should be. Just as he'd finished doing a cursory examination, and dressed the gouges on Jed's stomach, Jed's parents arrived and came hurrying in. Telling them briefly what had happened the medic reassured them Jed was okay and it wasn't the first time they'd been called out to a male, thinking they were pregnant, as the panic of men being pregnant was spreading like the plague.

Arranging for Jed to attend the surgery late the next afternoon for tests, he gave Lauren, Jed's mum, a sedative spray and instructed her to take Jed home, put him to bed and let him sleep until he woke naturally, which he predicted wouldn't be until late the following day.

Despite Lauren demanding to know whether her son was pregnant or not, the medic couldn't tell her, due to Jed's muscles being rigid with fright. Leaving as quickly as was decent, he thanked his lucky stars for the intense training he'd received to keep an expressionless face, whatever the situation.

Lauren drove a much subdued Jed home to bed whilst Gary stayed behind to find out exactly what had been going on in Jed's life over the past few weeks, learning all about the moonshine and Dream Machine.

Jed slept right through until mid afternoon, despite Lauren checking on him several times. When he finally emerged she was shocked at how drained and haggard he looked but, having collected the Dream Machine and watched his dreams, could understand why they'd been so disturbing to him.

Lauren was sceptical about Jed being pregnant, and only the week before would've poured scorn on the idea. Sadly it had dawned on her how little she knew about her son, even whether he was a virgin, and her lack of knowledge and recent interest made her uncomfortable in her son's presence. By the time they set off to the surgery, Jed had barely uttered a dozen words from getting up.

Finally ushered into the examining suite, Lauren inwardly panicking and looking as if her mental dexterity was about to desert her, she was surprised at the medic's warm reception. After asking a number of probing questions, the doctor finally suggested Jed get undressed and onto the couch which, to Jed, appeared to be surrounded by a daunting array of medical equipment. Looking at the machinery in trepidation, afraid of what it might reveal, Jed finally undressed and lay down, rigid with fear. He kept his eyes tightly shut and barely dared to breathe as the machine set about its business. The room was silent, except for the low hum of the scanner and all Jed could feel was a faint tingling sensation as the beams swept just above his skin's surface, making the down on his body ripple in response to the rays. He could sense his mother standing nearby, fidgeting, and the whole setup felt surreal. All Jed wanted to do was escape from that moment in time.

The examination finished, Jed sat next to the doctor's desk dreading the results the medic might revel. Confirming his worst fears, that he was indeed pregnant, before it could even begin to sink in both Jed and the medic were shocked to hear Jed's mum demand, 'If that's the case, then get rid of it. I can't look after it so arrange an abortion.'

Jed was so stunned by her words it jolted him out of his reverie. He couldn't believe what his mum had said. The medic, amazed she'd not even questioned his diagnosis or this strange phenomenon either, knew that despite Jed only being fifteen, it was obvious he'd not even have a chance of the news sinking in with his mother there. Yet all the same he was surprised by her reaction, as it was so out of character from what he knew of this woman.

A short while later Lauren, persuaded to wait outside, left Jed and the medic to talk alone, leaving as if the world was on her shoulders, so shocked was she by the news. Once alone, man and boy sat and discussed the moonshine, Dream Machine and all the other recent oddities in Jed's life. As they talked it was obvious the news hadn't begun to sink in, and probably wouldn't for some time to come. To make matters worse, the medic had no idea what options would be available to Jed, whatever his mum wanted or demanded. He knew Jed was going to face adversity and uncertainty in the next few weeks, and just hoped his father would react differently to the mother. What the medic did know was the enjoyment he'd get from seeing his colleagues expression's when he told them about their pregnant patient, a male minor, and would dine out on the story for many years to come. The most surprising thing though, was Jed's last question before his mum came back in.

'Can she really make me have an abortion?' Jed asked, but the doctor didn't even know if male abortions were possible.

Whilst his mum's response had been a surprise it was nothing compared to how he'd expected his dad to react. Anticipating the worst Jed left the surgery making two conscious decisions; the first being to keep out of his dad's way and the second to let Fiona know the news as soon as he could.

Arriving home Jed promptly disappeared and made haste round to Fiona's, knowing it was best to avoid his dad for as long as possible. Fiona, fortunately by herself, greeted him with a look of anticipation on her face, eager to know what was going on. As Jed relayed his prognosis he watched an array of conflicting emotions pass over her features. She wasn't surprised, but was shocked it was happening to one of her friends.

'Jed, I... I don't know what to say. To say I'm shocked is an understatement but I'm not surprised. It makes sense – well it would have done if you were a woman. Have you told the others yet?' she babbled, playing for time and hoping Jed wouldn't ask any awkward questions. Jed replied by shaking his head.

'So what do you think Fi? Are you pleased about our baby or what?'

'Pleased?' she asked. 'Our baby? What are you on about?' she answered, almost snapping.

'Well if the roles were reversed I'd be telling you you're to be a dad...' Jed started, but stopped abruptly as he saw his fatal words register, with horror, on Fiona's face.

'You what? I'm not the 'father'! What makes you think it's mine? Even if it was it doesn't make any difference.'

'What do you mean it doesn't make a difference? 'Course it does, this is our baby Fi. Yours and mine,' he added, with less confidence than when he'd started.

'Why should it be mine?'

'Because you're the only one I've had sex with,' he told her lamely.

'No I'm not? Who's to say it wasn't one of your girlfriends from earlier?' she said, frantically searching through her mind to avoid this trap. 'Maybe its lain dormant for a while – and you slept with Jade,' she reminded him, snatching at straws.

'You can't take this in can you, Fi? Neither could I, and I'm the one that's pregnant,' Jed said, sounding more confident than he felt. 'Don't worry we'll get used to it,' he added, with more optimism than he felt.

'We? We? There's no 'we' in this. This is you. You! You! You!' she said prodding him in the chest with a forefinger. 'And it's time for you go,' she told him almost pushing him towards the front door.

'But Fi I've only just come. We need to talk about this.'

'No we don't. I don't want anything to do with it. My future's mapped out and you're not going to ruin it. Just go, will you?' Before he could protest any more she pushed him out of the door, shutting it behind him with a bang, leaning back against it as if to keep him out. She shook from head to foot, frightened by the implications if she was the other parent, and whilst she stood there shaking she knew Jed was outside feeling even worse than she was – and knew she couldn't do anything to help him.

The next day Jade turned up at Fiona's, having just left Jed and Ben together.

'How can you be so callous?' Jade spat in fury. 'Jed's distraught. His mum's reaction was bad enough but yours!' she scolded in scorn. 'So what are you going to do about it?'

'Nothing, because it's not mine. Let's face it Jade it could be anyone's, the number of girls he's slept with. Anyway what'll you do if it's yours?' she asked turning the tables. Jade was so taken aback by Fiona's denial and accusations she stood rooted to the spot, looking at Fiona as if she'd never met her before. Without saying a word she turned and left Fiona's study and house, closing the doors quietly behind her. She walked away from her best friend not knowing if she'd ever speak to her again, or even if she wanted to.

~ ~ ~ ~ ~

The meeting between mother and son was not as Daryl would have wished. He sat tentatively on the edge of his chair, terrified of moving in case his penis should split open or he'd experience a shooting stab of pain. The hospital was at liberty to refuse Daryl any treatment at all, with him being a criminal, but had decided to treat him but only provide the most basic of care and minimum of painkillers. Twenty years ago he'd have been treated with far more civility, and been able to demand the best of treatments as his right. He could even have sued his rape victim for making him pregnant, but even this loophole had been closed and Daryl had to be grateful for what little he received. WPPL had certainly closed ranks on the criminal element and all criminal rights had now changed beyond recognition. So, with the minimal pain relief, Daryl was being exceptionally careful of what he did or how he moved.

On arriving at the hospital, Sharon was halted at the door and told in no uncertain terms, a guard would be in attendance at all times armed with a stun gun. If she did anything to aid her son to escape or maim anyone, in any way whatsoever, she'd be shot with the stun gun and immediately put in custody. The consequences made no difference to Sharon, who had no intention of helping her selfish, hateful son, especially as he'd deprived her of so much fame and fortune. Even so, she felt nervous with the guard standing attention on them and inwardly prayed Daryl wouldn't do anything stupid.

As she entered the room she threw a look of contempt at her son.

'Hello Mam,' he said, in the whiny voice she'd hated for so many years. 'Thanks for coming to see me. I'm really pleased,' he whined with tears of gratitude glistening in his pathetic eyes.

'Shut yer fucking face yer little bastard and listen to what I have to say,' she ordered without preamble and launched into how, because of him, she was going to be destitute and would have to hide from the world. He'd always been a 'stupid, selfish bastard,' she told him, and brought his dad's good name into disrepute because of his antics. Daryl looked at her nonplussed, not understanding anything she was saying. 'You'll have to sign all yer money over to me otherwise I'll starve,' she finished dramatically.

'Yes Mam,' he agreed crestfallen, she really didn't give a toss about him. 'But if I'm going to do that I need you to do something for me,' he wheedled trying to put strength in his voice. 'I need you to get in touch with Sonia and tell her all this is a mistake,' he told her without batting an eyelid.

'Sonia? Who the fuck's Sonia?'

'Me girlfriend,' Daryl said in a small voice.

'Oh! I've heard it all now,' his Mam said pacing about. 'So you've got a girlfriend now have yer? Well don't think she's going to get any of yer money 'cos it's mine after everything I've done for yer. I can't believe yer'd be so stupid as to rape someone and get caught,' she spat out contemptuously.

'What like me dad, yer mean?' Daryl spat, suddenly sparked by anger. 'When he was in that gang bang with them blokes and they all ended up dead, yer mean?'

'Shh,' hissed his Mam, looking round nervously at the guard. 'Shut yer face yer dirty little liar. Yer dad did nothing of the sort and yer know it.'

'I know exactly what he did Mam,' Daryl told her, now so incensed he didn't care if the guard heard or not.

'How do yer know about it?' hissed his Mam. 'It'll only be lies yer know.'

''Cos I heard yer talk about it often enough,' Daryl snarled. 'Bragging to yer friends how much of a man he was and what a wimp I am. Well now yer know I'm just a chip off the old block don't yer?' he spat, standing up for himself. 'Anyway what have you ever done for me yer poisonous old witch? Nothing except make me life hell. If yer'd treated me a bit better I wouldn't be here now would I? Are yer going to get in touch with Sonia for me or not?' he asked in a vicious tone she'd never heard before.

'No I'll not. I've done enough for you and why should she muscle in and have all yer money? It should come to me. It'll not be any good to you here or where you'll end up, so just sign it over, as a good son should do.'

'You vicious bitch. If you'll not do anything to help me now and do this one small thing for me then you can forget about having me money, and there's quite a bit of it too,' he taunted. 'That's all yer ever wanted me for anyway. So just think on you ol' crow, when yer penniless and rotting in Armley, you'll not get another penny piece from me,' he finished, relieved he'd finally stood up to her. 'Now get the fuck out and go back to yer bloody soaps and fairytale stories of me dad,' he spat.

Sharon, stunned by the turn of events over the last few days, stood in silence, at a total loss as to what she should do or say. She couldn't leave without knowing she'd got his money, and knew she'd somehow have to get round her son before she left.

'What about the babby?' she asked. 'You'll not be able to look after it so I'll take it for yer shall I?' Daryl looked up at her with utter contempt on his face.

'Let you bring it up?' he asked cruelly. 'It's already a fucking freak and the only reason you'd want it is to cash in on it. You can go stew in yer own venom you old bitch. I'm not going to let you make the kid's life more of a hell than it already is,' he told her scathingly. 'It's got no chance now, so yer not going to make it worse just to line yer own pocket,' he said shifting in his chair and wincing with pain.

'Hah!' his Mam scoffed seeing his discomfort. 'Heard they'd split yer end to end,' she said indicating his groin. Pity they didn't cut the fucker off,' she mocked. 'It'd save them having to cut it off when yer inside,' she sneered, and turning on her heel without a backward glance demanded to be let out of the room, plotting as she went how she'd get his money anyway.

~ ~ ~ ~ ~

It had been a spate of surprises for Jed, and not all nice ones. First of all finding out he was pregnant; then his mum's reaction; followed by Fiona's and then his dad's. Jed reckoned his dad's was the most astounding. When he'd arrived back from Fiona's, and started to make

330

his way upstairs, he'd heard his mum and dad arguing so loudly they were almost shouting. His mum was insisting there was no question but for Jed to have an abortion and his dad... after the last twenty-four hours Jed couldn't believe it... was standing up for him and telling her to calm down and let them all get used to the news before she pushed Jed off for an abortion. Then when she'd challenged him, stating it was the only option, his dad had replied coldly, 'I'll not have you dictate what he does and doesn't do. This has come as a shock to us all, but not as much for us as it has to Jed. It's his body and he'll decide what happens, not you. And just so's you know,' he told her in a steely tone Jed had never heard before, 'I for one will be standing by the boy and making sure he's not pushed into anything he's not ready for.' If Jed had been shocked by this response his mother must have been too, as a long heavy silence followed.

Not wanting to be caught listening Jed hurried up to his room, before either of his parents came out and found him eavesdropping on the stairs.

Shutting his bedroom door and activating the soundproofing Jed threw himself down on his pit, instinctively placing his hands protectively over his belly.

*His dad was on his side,* Jed thought with wonder. *At least someone's going to stand by me,* he thought, immediately feeling happier. He looked down at his hands, realising for the first time where they rested.

*Could he feel anything?* he asked himself. *Did he feel any different?* He thought about it for a moment, deciding he didn't. Getting up off his bed he turned on his Mirror Imager, which would allow him to easily view himself from all angles at once.

He unfastened his trousers, which was a relief as they were getting tight, rolled down the waistband of his underpants and took off his T-shirt, leaving his body naked from the groin up. Standing in front of the Mirror Imager he pressed a button to view his reflections. Although he'd never actually developed a really defined six-pack there was undoubtedly a lack of muscle definition in the images he was looking at. Pressing buttons he viewed his body from different angles and could see his stomach, which whilst not distended was very slightly curved, and not flat as it had been during the summer. Laying his hands across his belly he thrust his hips forward, as if he were heavily pregnant, imagining himself as he would be in a few months time should he keep the baby. The idea both repelled and intrigued him, and he felt a momentary panic. He'd no idea what was in store for him, or what his parents or Fiona would expect him to do, but at least he knew his dad was on his side. Turning off the Imager he got back onto the pit marvelling at how quickly everything had changed, and in such a short time.

*I've one more demon to face,* he told himself, *before I can start getting my head round all this. School! How am I going to face everyone? How are they going to react? Will they think I'm a fucking freak? Shit how the fuck am I going to be able to go back to school. I can't do it. There's no way I can go in and have everyone laughing at me. I just can't do it. Somehow I'm going to have to get out of going to school but if I'm pregnant maybe I won't have to,* he told himself. *Shit! I need some sleep I'm bloody exhausted. Maybe it's 'cos I'm pregnant. Well I am aren't I?*

~ ~ ~ ~ ~

When Liam went back for his appointment with the Company Medic on Tuesday, he was greeted by the same nurse who informed him there were visitors waiting to see him. Ushering him into the room Liam was introduced to DDI Roberts and Dr Emsam who, he was told, were overseeing the male pregnancy project. Introductions over, Melanie, DDI Roberts, explained why they were there and what they were proposing to do. Liam, as one of the first confirmed male pregnancies they'd been notified of, would need to go through a whole series of tests and examinations, a host of questionnaires and he'd need to give them a list of all his sexual partners over the past six months, Liam baulked at the last part and was instantly relieved his number of sexual partners had decreased recently, otherwise just the one task would have taken forever.

'First of all though, we need to make sure your baby's developing normally and calculate how far advanced your pregnancy is. Ok?' she asked kindly. 'What we want to do first is take a scan and then run a few other tests whilst we're here. Then we'll set up an appointment for you to come into the Crimedical Centre with your partners and start doing further testing. Would it be possible for your parents to attend as well?' Melanie asked, much to Liam's surprise.

'My parents? What do you need to see them for?' Liam asked puzzled.

'Purely and simply to carry out some testing on them and to glean information as to the circumstances round about the time of your conception. Nothing for you to worry about Liam, we'll be doing this with all pregnant men to try and establish if there was any connection between when you were conceived that's pertinent to you becoming pregnant now.'

'Oh! ok,' Liam agreed reluctantly, 'but can you wait for a few days only I've not told them I'm pregnant yet. I've sorta been trying to get used to the idea myself,' he told her with embarrassment. Liam wasn't used to not taking things in his stride and this whole business of being pregnant had really thrown him.

'Of course, but it'll have to be fairly soon. If you can come in with your partners on Thursday, would you be able to talk to your family before then?' Melanie asked patiently.

'Well yes but I can't guarantee they'll be free then.'

'We've already checked and both, is it Tanya and Crawford;' she asked looking at her notes, 'are free. We've already spoken to them and they've confirmed they are free,' she informed him as though what she stated wasn't to be questioned.

'Then we can contact your parents and arrange a convenient time for them to come in too. It says here,' she said checking Liam's medical notes, 'you also have a brother, so we may need to see him at some stage too. Right! Let's get you up on this couch and run a few scans and tests. Ok?'

Liam went over to the couch and lay down for one of many scans and tests he'd be subjected to over the next few months. Within minutes the monitors were bleeping, taking measurements and processing a whole host of other data. Melanie, still intrigued by seeing a baby within a male body, invited Liam to take a look, even though he was already peering keenly at the screen, now unafraid of looking. Although the baby appeared to be perfectly formed it was turned away from the screen so he couldn't tell whether it was male or female. However, he could see the perfectly formed fingers and toes, and was relieved to see such perfection. Liam continued to stare at the screen not saying a word, just marvelling at what was happening to him. He felt, for the first time, an overwhelming feeling of maternal pride, or was it paternal? He didn't know and didn't care, but his baby was amazing.

The scan over, Melanie began to explain arrangements for prenatal care and outlining the lengthy process they'd need to go through scrutinizing his health records, sexual activities and use of social drugs. She informed him whatever he told her would be used in the strictest confidence and would not incur any comeback on him, unless it was revealed he'd committed a serious crime, she'd told him knowing they'd find nothing of the sort.

It was well past Liam's normal lunch time when they stopped for a break, and Liam dashed off to see to a few urgent tasks needing his attention, Melanie warning him as he left he was to get something to eat. Within an hour he was back with Melanie, where they began looking at his family background and extensive record of sexual activities.

It was over two hours before they'd completed the task and by then it was too late to make a start on the other aspects of his life, although they'd already started investigating his medical records. As Liam made his way back to his office, a renewed jaunt in his step and his mind full of enthusiasm and plans for his baby's future, it took all his self-control not to blurt out his extraordinary news to everyone, so happy was he.

The *sooner I tell mum and dad the better, then I can tell everyone else,* he told himself. How his news would be received by his parents and brother, let alone friends and colleagues, he had no idea.

It was later in the evening when he went to see his parents. Having told his mum and dad the news he was relived to see they were actually delighted, but concerned too. After the initial shock had worn off they'd sat and addressed a whole torrent of questions and concerns; why he was pregnant, how the baby would be delivered and what monitoring and support he'd receive during his pregnancy. Still involved with the Parenting Skills Department, Liam's mum saw this from a completely different angle to Liam, rather than just from an emotional point of view. She saw it as an extension of the work they'd been doing, and an opportunity to add additional services to the ones already existing, for pregnant men and their partners who would be coping with the shock and fears of male pregnancy.

'Thanks Mum,' Liam said sardonically. 'Nice to know you can profit from my misfortune as well as get a grandchild out of the deal.' He'd grinned broadly as he'd said this, and she'd immediately jumped to her defence with, 'That's not what I meant and you know it,' then seeing his huge grin and twinkling eyes, cuffed him playfully before hugging him tightly to her.

'I'm so pleased Tanya and Crawford have taken it so well,' she said, releasing him from the hug. 'You'll all have to come round for a celebratory meal soon. After all, they're family now aren't they? No matter who the second parent is,' she added hastily.

'Mum,' Liam said in a more subdued voice, 'there's one thing really bothering me.' His mum looked up concerned.

'What's that Liam?' she asked reverting back into her old protective role of mother hen.

'Well apart from the fact I'm pregnant, and men don't normally have babies, it's just that… well I'm not too sure of… well who I'm going to be? Am I the mother or the father? Am I both or am I neither? Somehow I just can't get my head round that bit. Do you know what I mean?'

'I'd not thought of it that way,' his mum responded, whilst his dad looked on with a furrowed brow. 'I suppose it's really confusing at the moment with loads of conflicting information bombarding your thoughts. Not only have you found yourself pregnant but your situation is sloughing away years of traditional procreation. Who'd have thought men would ever have babies? More to the point who'd have thought my son would be one of the first? It's a miracle Liam, but a shock I admit. Let's just take things one day at a time and I'm sure everything will come right. You're lucky because you've not just one but two partners who love you and think the world of you and taken the news really well. I know they'll support you, so thank your lucky stars and know your dad and I are here for you as well. We're not a million miles away and maybe this is an opportunity to look at ways in which the extended family structure can help those who'll be less fortunate in years to come. There's a reason for you being pregnant, Liam, and maybe that's it. As for being the mother or father that'll sort itself out,' she nodded knowingly.

Her speech finished, Liam realised how lucky he was to have parents like his. His mum was right, not everyone was going to be as lucky as him. He'd have several people there for him throughout his pregnancy, unlike many in the future who'd probably struggle and be spurned in the process.

'Yeah, Mum, as usual you're right. But anyway I've got to go now but will you tell Shane for me please? I'm on the end of the phone but if you're seeing him tomorrow, I'm sure it's better being told face to face instead of over the airwaves. Love you,' he told her giving her a big hug, then walking over to his father to let himself be folded into one of his enormous bear hugs.

'Take care son,' he told Liam, 'and just remember, whatever you need, get in touch with us. Day or night. ok?' he demanded, as Liam put his coat on to go.

'Will do Dad and hey! Thanks you two. Love you both.' With that Liam left his parents, who stood with their arms round each other's waists, and told himself how lucky he was to have parents like them.

~ ~ ~ ~ ~

Jed couldn't face school on the Monday. Over the weekend his mood had swung from self-pity to euphoria; from feeling a freak to being someone special. Jade and Ben had been to see him but, despite asking Fiona to come, he'd not seen anything of her since he'd told her their news, much to Jade's disgust. Not knowing what he was likely to face, going into school, and knowing everyone would know what was happening, Jade and Ben had offered to walk to school with him on the Wednesday, and give him give any support he needed. But, as imaginative as Jed was, he could never have imagined the reception waiting for him, even though he knew his pregnancy was now common knowledge.

There were at least a hundred or more milling about in the school grounds, obviously waiting for him. Jed stood stock still, feeling a momentary rush of panic with not knowing how everyone was going to react to him. The crowds' reactions were varied; some shouting greetings of encouragement, a handful jeering and many calling him a freak or other hurtful names. One group were openly laughing at him and several moved away hurriedly as he passed, as if he had a contagious disease. It was awful and for the first time ever he was pleased to see the security men making their way towards him.

Without preamble they escorted Jed to the school entrance, Jed feeling more like a criminal than a celebrity, and informed him there were visitors in the Medics Room waiting for him. As they left him outside the door, Jed cringed as he heard one of them mutter under his breath, 'fucking freak' which, Jed thought, said it all. Finally ushered into the room, that now felt like a welcoming sanctuary, he was introduced to two doctors, whose names he didn't catch because they informed him they'd come from the Crimedical Department.

'Crim... Crimedical Department?' asked Jed worriedly. 'Have... have I done something wrong then?'

Quickly reassuring him he wasn't in any trouble they told Jed they were waiting for his parents to arrive, because of his age, before they started talking to him. Jed, as with everything else currently, accepted this with silent misery, then deciding he didn't like the silence asked.

'How many pregnant men are there?'

'We're looking at over a hundred, at the moment, but you're the youngest we know about so far,' Melanie answered conversationally.

'So why are we getting pregnant then?' Jed asked with genuine interest, but the answer was interrupted by his parent's escorted arrival.

Greetings and introductions over it was explained they'd be a number of tests run on Jed and extensive questionnaires for each of them to complete, and with the urgency of the situation, they'd need to transfer to the local Crimedical Centre for everything to get underway. The journey, between school and the centre, was driven in an icy silence, Jed's parents still very much at loggerheads.

It was later, during the complex proceedings, when things turned tricky and Lauren upset the apple cart dictating, 'Jed doesn't want the baby. All we need is for you to terminate it.' as if showing a red flag to a bull within seconds Jed's parents were arguing heatedly about what Jed did and didn't want, both determined to be heard. It went on for several minutes before Melanie decided to intervene.

'I'm afraid it's not that simple, due to our lack of knowledge as to whereabouts the baby is developing. At this moment in time there's no guarantee we'll be able to offer Jed a termination or even a baby pouch. However, as he's only a matter of weeks pregnant then it may become a possibility before it's too late,' she informed them.

Melanie then upset the applecart further, by informing them that both Fiona, Jade and their parents would be required to come in for testing too.

'Fiona doesn't want anything to do with me,' Jed told her miserably.

'I'm sorry Jed but she'll have no choice in the matter, none of them will. This is a government directive to be adhered to.'

Jed accepted this silently, inwardly hoping it would at least make Fiona speak to him again. He liked Melanie and, when he'd talked with her earlier, she'd reassured him his parents wouldn't need to know anything about the other girls, unless it was proved Fiona or Jade weren't the other parent.

Before terminating the meeting, which had seemed very taxing, Jed and his parents were warned they could expect their lives to be turned upside-down, not just by the medical world but by the media too. None of them were happy with this news, and dismissed Melanie's offer to get them moved if things became too intrusive and difficult to manage. The media, she explained, would be very interested in Jed who was the youngest pregnant male identified so far, and no one could guarantee his privacy. In the meantime they'd do whatever possible to help them all through the next few months, whatever the outcome of the pregnancy.

Jed, Lauren and Gary listened and accepted all this with different attitudes and grey faces. None of them were sure how to react and all had a myriad of emotions and other thoughts running though their heads. Lauren, determined Jed would get rid of it, his father determined to protect him and Jed feeling more miserable than ever.

*Would Fiona completely forsake him or would she come round?* he asked himself, and thanked his lucky stars that Jade, and to an extent Ben, were still very much there for him. He wasn't looking forward to the Friday, when they were due at the Crimedical Centre for yet more testing, and was frightened by what could be revealed.

~ ~ ~ ~ ~

Friday, 17th December was a day Jed and his parents would never forget. The past few days had turned out to be difficult for everyone, with Jed's parents continually sniping. The atmosphere in the house, only a couple of weeks away from Christmas, was chilly to say the least. If it hadn't been for Jade, Jed didn't know how he'd have got through it. Along with his parents', Ben's attitude didn't help either. He'd childishly started tagging onto Jed's coat tails declaring their friendship and Jed's pregnancy almost as it was his own private achievement. As for Fiona, well at least she was speaking to him now, due mainly to her parents' insistence, but she continued to remain distant.

When Jed and his parents arrived at the Crimedical Centre mid-morning they found some relief, with being introduced to other pregnant men and their families. They were as much in the dark about their pregnancies as Jed and his parents were, but it was good to be able to talk to others in the same predicament. Jed went off in a group with some of the other men, who all began pooling their stories. Jed, young and naïve in comparison to the others; found it difficult to work out what was fact or fiction, as information and the rumours circulating made the conversation somewhat clouded. The one thing which was clear though was no stone was being left unturned by the government, in the bid to discover the cause of male pregnancies.

For Jed's parents, there were mixed blessings. Like Jed they found comfort talking to other parents, although none of the others had sons as young as Jed. The disconcerting thing was the news Melanie imparted to each parent individually, which they later shared.

It was during the interviews when it became apparent Lauren and Gary could be partially responsible for their son's pregnancy. Melanie had just enquired as to whether or not they'd had fertility treatment, or used any sex-enhancing drugs, round the time of Jed's conception. Much to Lauren's dismay Gary had replied, 'I don't know if it's of any consequence but,' he blushed deeply, 'we did use the recreational drug Viagiant about then. For a bit of fun,' he added lamely, trying desperately to avoid his wife's glare.

When Melanie pressed Lauren, to see if she'd taken it as well, Lauren very defensively replied curtly, 'Yes I took it as well, but I'm sure it's had nothing to do with the situation Jed's in now.'

'Probably not, but we need all the information we can get at the moment,' Melanie replied carefully. Although there were only a handful of men, who they'd tested so far, it was already becoming evident that the use of Viagiant was a common denominator round about the time the pregnant men themselves were conceived.

'Our tests show a peculiarity in Jed's DNA,' Melanie had told Lauren and Gary, as she did all the other parents. 'In fact in all pregnant men's DNA. We've been scrutinising this in conjunction with our tests and interviews and have been able to establish one common factor in all the cases. It appears all males, who've found themselves pregnant, were themselves conceived whilst one or both of their parents were under the influence of Viagiant. Apparent in ninety percent of cases so far.'

Lauren and Gary had looked aghast. *Did this mean Jed's pregnancy was their fault,* they wondered? The enormity of their casual use of Viagiant was impacting rapidly and in their incredulity and discomfort they turned to look at each other, as if trying to apportion the blame to the other and rid themselves of guilt. Melanie, watching the expressions on their faces change, stepped in with, 'There's nothing to be done about this now. You can't turn the clock back or alter Jed's DNA.' And then as if she'd been reading their minds. 'You're just going to have to accept this, and make every effort not to blame each other or feel guilty. What's done is done.' Her words, though, did not offer comfort, but only made them more aware of what they now saw as their failings.

How were they to face Jed, knowing it could be their fault his DNA had been altered because of their casual use of a designer drug? And a drug that looked as if it had resulted in their son becoming pregnant at that? At least they wouldn't have to tell him straight away, although the sooner they told him the less likely he'd be to find it out from some other source.

When they'd met with Jed later on, for their final meeting that day with Melanie, Lauren in particular found it difficult to face him. She saw Jed as a freak, with him being pregnant, and was now having to come to terms with the fact she could have been party to his plight. Despite the fact they knew Melanie wouldn't be telling him, about the part Viagiant may have played, they were dismayed by her next piece of news, which was made even worse by Jed's reaction.

'I'm afraid, Jed, we can't guarantee a termination or offer you a Babypouch yet. We may be able to offer them at a later date but at the moment they're not viable options. What you do need to consider is what's to happen to the baby when it's born, whether you'll keep it or give it up for adoption. You'll be fully supported whatever decision you make. However as it appears you're only thirteen weeks pregnant, time's still on our side. There are a number of men due to give birth in the next few weeks and through them, and the others, we'll be able to discover where the foetus is developing.'

Jed's face had paled and his mouth dropped open, as tears welled in his eyes.

'But… but… if I can't have a baby pouch and don't get rid of it then… how will it be born?' he asked using every ounce of control not to give way to his rising panic.

'There's no reason to assume we won't be able to do a caesarean by the time your baby's due, if it's not aborted. We'll have far more knowledge by then so don't worry about it Jed.'

'Oh Jed I'm sorry,' his mum suddenly burst out. 'It's our fault this has happened,' she finally confessed, giving way to noisy sobs.

'What… what do you mean it's your fault?' Jed asked, all of a sudden feeling a well of resentment, along with confusion, rise. 'How can it be your fault?'

'Er, what your mum means Jed, is when you were conceived we, er, we were using Viagiant and it seems it altered your DNA and made you susceptible to becoming pregnant.'

'Does that mean then,' Jed shouted, jumping to his feet, 'That I'm pregnant because you and mum used a sex drug, which wasn't even legal then, when I was conceived?' he shouted at them angrily.

'Jed! That's enough,' Melanie demanded. 'After all they're not the only ones who've messed with illicit drugs are they?' she said, and, much to her relief, Jed immediately shut up and sat down.

In shocked and guilty silence the trio stayed to listen to what else Melanie had to say, before booking their first session for the New Year and leaving to go home.

Jed, ashen, angry and tearful, walked to the car with his dad's arm protectively round him. This baby, or pregnancy, wasn't just changing their lives but the dynamics of their family too.

Bidding them farewell, with best wishes for the season, Melanie walked back into the Crimedical Centre whilst, unbeknown to her, Jed summed it all up in a nutshell as he settled in the car.

'So my choices mean that I might be able to have an abortion and if I can't, I can keep it, or give it away when it's born.'

'You're having an abortion Jed,' his mother said in a cold, no-nonsense unfeeling voice.

'No he's not,' his father snapped defying her tone. 'We'll all think long and hard about this and make a careful and informed decision about it when we've been given all the options. I'll not allow you to bully or browbeat him into making the wrong decision.'

In a tense, oppressive atmosphere they set off to drive home on what should have been a joyous occasion. Christmas and a new baby would normally be a happy event to celebrate. This situation was anything but. All it held for Jed and his family was uncertainty, fear and guilt. Sitting listening to his parents quarrel Jed was sick and tired of it all. Miserably he wondered what 2033 held in store for him and other pregnant men. As they drove out of the complex Jed looked back to the centre as if just remembering Melanie's final words.

'And a merry fucking Christmas and Happy New Year to you too,' he muttered miserably.

Ominously, the New Year stood threateningly before him. What atrocities, or surprises, it would hold for him only time would tell. But nobody would have been able to predict or even imagine just what was in store for Jed.

~ ~ ~ ~ ~

When Liam, Tanya and Crawford all turned up at the Crimedical Centre, where Melanie and her team were waiting to see them, they were introduced to three other men, who were in exactly the same boat as Liam. With hands shaken and names exchanged the small groups dispersed to go about the first of the many gruelling tests to come. When they met each other, at intervals throughout the day, Liam found each individual had a different story to tell. All of them were in completely different situations and had a host of questions to ask one another. The questions, Liam, Tanya and Crawford hadn't thought to ask yet, were raised by the others, which set off new parameters of thinking, concerns and probabilities polling through their minds.

With Liam and his two partners having been prodded, poked, scanned, monitored and tested, for this and that, they met up for their final meeting of the day in Melanie's office, to hear what the next stage of the game was and to find out what, if anything, had been discovered from the tests. Melanie watched the three of them, intrigued and impressed by the obvious ambience and closeness which existed in their relationship. It was obviously a balanced and loving ménàge à trois and, surprisingly, appeared more successful than a lot of couple relationships were. It was evident Liam was going to get all the support he'd need and, from what she'd heard about his family, would get extra support from his parents as well. Melanie was looking forward to meeting his mother in particular who'd been extremely instrumental in the inception and development of the Parenting Skills Project, which had been launched around about the time Liam was born.

She suspected, quite rightly, Liam had led a somewhat charmed life so far and nothing this devastating had ever happened to him before. Maybe it still was charmed and would really propel Liam forward in life; he seemed to be one of those characters who took a positive slant on life, always finding some good in the bad. His biggest problem at the moment, which was very obvious from the Subliminal Voyeur scan, was his inability and need to understand who he was, mother or father. However, counselling and re-programming would help sort it out for him, along with the support he'd get from his partners and family. She just hoped other men coming forward would examine their state of affairs with the same intelligent and caring way Liam was, although she doubted it.

When the trio left the centre, watched by a fascinated Melanie, Liam was unaware what the surprise Tanya and Crawford had lined up for him. They'd hinted in the morning there was a treat in store, but no matter how much Liam had tried to probe, they wouldn't tell him their secret.

Less than an hour after leaving the centre, they'd arrived at Harrods, still in existence after decades of serving the public. Together they walked up to the nursery section and wandered round the furniture displays. They ummed and aaghed about the style they should go for and how the nursery should be decorated, before finally making their way to the restaurant where a table, decorated with balloons and sporting a bottle of the finest champagne nestling in ice, was ready for them.

Having ordered starters, the waiter replenished their glasses with champagne under strict instructions, Liam's was only to be partially filled, and Crawford nodded to Tanya.

'Ready?' he asked her. Tanya nodded eagerly in response and fished in her bag, bringing out three small packages. Liam looking puzzled wondering what on earth they were up to.

'It's nearly Christmas,' Crawford started 'our first and only one together…' Liam looked up in alarm but Tanya just smiled, even more sweetly than usual.

'Because next year there'll be four of us and the patter of tiny feet,' she informed him, looking as though she was hugging herself in excitement.

Crawford grinned, seeing Liam's relief at her words.

'So, by way of celebration we got these.' Tanya handed out two of the boxes keeping one back for herself. None of them bore the name of the person who held them in their hands and again Liam looked at his partners with a look of puzzlement.

'Ready?' Crawford asked again. They both nodded simultaneously but Tanya with more enthusiasm.

'These are for the future,' Crawford told them. Liam looked again at his box, by now intrigued as to what lay within. 'Let's open the boxes.' he suggested, and they all opened them to reveal a gold band nestling inside. 'Tanya, you put your ring on my finger, then I'll put mine on Liam, and Liam you can put your ring on Tanya. Ok? Ready?' and he turned to Tanya who started the ritual. When Crawford put his ring onto Liam's finger it fitted perfectly and looking at it, and the one he held in his hand, he saw they were identical. Reaching over he put Tanya's ring onto her marriage finger and then, without a word, they all joined hands, placing their hands so Liam could see all three rings together.

'They're identical,' he said, in a soft, emotional voice.

'They're our rings of protection and perfection,' Tanya said. 'Here's to us, our baby and being together forever, whatever.'

'Here's to us,' Liam and Crawford chorused together, and in perfect unison they let go of each other's hands and picking up their champagne charged glasses raised them to clink the toast.

'But don't ever expect,' Liam told them with tears of gratitude and relief glistening in his eyes, 'that it'll be an easy ride because with surprises like this,' he said indicating his stomach, 'it never will be.'

A wry nod circulated the table and once again glasses were raised and the champagne sipped. Liam's words of warning were just the start of a real rollercoaster of a ride for the three of them. Would they be able to weather the peaks and troughs, the highs and lows? Whether they would or not, they'd be sorely tested in time to come. The first hurdle being who the second parent was, and once discovered and the novelty of their situation had worn off, would they still feel the same about each other? Would time be as kind to them in the future as it had been so

344

far? Would they all be able to accept the parentage to the child or would it shake them all? And would they stay together to support one another as they'd just promised? Only time and a torrent of emotions would dictate that.

~ ~ ~ ~ ~

It was the Friday when Jack and Chloe finally went to the Crimedical Centre in Cambridge to meet Melanie, who was investigating and overseeing the phenomena of pregnant men. Having been greeted and given refreshments they waited in a comfortable annexe with another couple who informed them rumour had it Melanie had been present at the first birth. As the two couples waited they chatted about their predicaments, discovering they had totally different views on the news of their pregnancies. As delighted as they were it had never struck Jack and Chloe before not everyone was going to be as happy as them with the same news. The other couple was obviously quite daunted by it, but Jack and Chloe quietly agreed they weren't going to let their disquiet spoil their happiness.

When they finally met up with Melanie Roberts, who it was said now had her career made because of this miracle, they were pleasantly surprised by her friendly but professional style. The combination was somehow reassuring, and just the right type of manner for Jack and Chloe to be dealt with, counterbalancing their excitement with addressing concerns. Both Jack and Chloe took to Melanie and her colleague Dr Emsam straight away; Melanie for her professionalism and Dr Emsam his warmth, they made a good combination.

Both had read Jack and Chloe's extensive medical records and knew the history of all their attempted pregnancies. As Melanie listened to the couple recounting their experiences of the tests, implants and medical interventions they'd undergone, she could see their pain clearly, and warmed to the couple immediately. Now, as they talked of the pending baby, she saw the sorrow, she'd seen only moments before, replaced with the elation they felt at this unexpected gift, but Melanie had also spotted the shadow of fear they were trying so valiantly to hide.

Finally they asked the question, which was on the lips of the world, 'How was the baby to be born,' but Melanie could not and would not tell anyone what had happened during the delivery of Daryl's baby, as the circumstances he'd found himself in were extreme to say the least. All she could tell them was they were still establishing the development and positioning of male pregnancy but they'd be working towards delivery by caesarean section and trying to establish how viable it was for a Babypouch to be fitted.

'But isn't that going to be risky with the pregnancy this far on?' Chloe asked anxiously.

'You can rest assured,' Melanie told her, 'we'll be taking no risks and if you thought you were getting five-star treatment before that's nothing compared with now,' she said smiling. 'But before we speculate on anything else, we do need to run tests and I'm afraid go through some very extensive questionnaires.

For the rest of the day Jack and Chloe, separately and together, answered question after question and underwent a number of tests and scans. It was exhausting but helped put the couple's minds at rest, reassuring them that although Jack did appear to be a freak at the moment, they were going to receive the best of care anyone could hope for.

Melanie, by the end of the day, had decided and told Jack and Chloe the pregnancy couldn't have happened to a more deserving couple. Inwardly she prayed silently everything would go according to plan but was aware of one aspect she wasn't at all comfortable with. Throughout the various tests it had been identified there were problems between the couple and how they felt towards each other, regarding the pregnancy. The Subliminal Voyeur, they'd been linked into, had identified both as being truly delighted with the pregnancy, but also recognised intense negative feelings too. Chloe felt a strong resentment to the fact it was Jack who was pregnant, whilst she was unable to fulfil the traditional maternal role. When she'd admitted this to Melanie's she'd glibly told her, 'but at least we're having a baby.' Melanie and the Subliminal Voyeur, not convinced with this response, knew Chloe would need careful counselling and re-programming to cope with these deep-seated feelings of failure and resentment, if they weren't to fester and take over her rational thinking processes.

Jack on the other hand, was a different matter altogether. His concerns were clearly identified as being based on guilt.

'Why,' he'd asked, 'was he able to get pregnant and carry a baby so easily and for this long after all the problems Chloe had endured in her pregnancies? It didn't make sense and he felt guilty at his ease of carrying the baby.' Added to that he'd also confided to Melanie there was a chance Chloe wasn't the other parent.

'Not that it'd make any difference to her accepting the baby,' he'd told Melanie, 'but how could it be hers when we've been together all this time and I've not got pregnant before? He also confided he was concerned it would just add to the feelings of resentment and inadequacy he knew she was already experiencing. When Melanie challenged him about Chloe already having cottoned on to the fact it might not be hers, Jack was more than ready to admit it could well have crossed her mind, even though she'd not mentioned it yet. Melanie decided in a split second how she'd approach that, and cringed at the crassness of her plan.

Finally back in the room together, to listen to the day's outcome and future obligations, Melanie reassured Jack and Chloe they'd get the best medical attention possible and their child, as one of the first male born babies, would be put onto a new programme being developed to check and monitor their health, development and other aspects of their lives. They weren't starting out with a blank slate, where parenthood and pregnancy was concerned, but they would need help to get them through the next few months intact as rational human beings and as a couple.

Explaining they'd be expected to attend extra appointments, throughout and after the pregnancy, she'd laughed when she'd added it was going to be far easier for them than others who'd not gone through the marriage application process. They'd have to answer all those questions too, she'd told them, and have all the Crimedical aspects researched and recorded too.

Then to Jack's embarrassment, and Chloe's annoyance, Melanie apologised when she told Jack he'd need to bring in contact details for the Gobi he'd slept with, and she too would have to be called in for testing. As Jack turned to look at Chloe, he knew in an instant she'd picked up the implications of Melanie's request, and dreaded how he would deal with it, knowing how upset Chloe would be.

As Jack and Chloe left the clinic, exhausted at the end of a long and demanding day, they were armed with the knowledge that times ahead were not always going to be easy. As they approached the railway station, Chloe finally broached the subject Jack had been dreading.

'Jack, the Gobi you had sex with in the summer she's the mother or 'other parent' isn't she?' Chloe asked bluntly.

'What? How do I know, or anyone know for that matter?' he responded defensively. 'It's far more likely you made me pregnant than she did. Anyway she's in the past. And for all you know I could have made myself pregnant,' he told her clutching at straws.

'So if you made yourself pregnant, or I made you pregnant, how come you didn't get pregnant before?' Chloe demanded petulantly.

'Chloe,' Jack protested 'is it really worth having this conversation when it's all just conjecture? Why torment yourself with these questions when no one knows the answers. Who's to say something's not been added to the water or I've taken something that's lain dormant over the years. There's just no knowing Chloe so why don't we just plan for the wonderful future we've got in front of us. We're going to be parents Chloe. Just think, it's what we've always wanted,' he told her trying to lighten the mood between them.

'Oh now we have the truth don't we? Mr Bloody Wonderful is making life all right again isn't he? Aren't you?' she spat at him. 'Well I hope you feel wonderful. You've stood by my side and watched me go to hell and back and then what did you do? You just buggered off and screwed someone else to make you feel better when you were feeling down. You just leave me, with our dead baby barely cold… whilst you – Mr-Fucking-Wonderful,' she swore, which was unheard of for Chloe, 'go off and get pregnant so you can still be a daddy,' she accused. 'Well where do you think that leaves me? How do you think it makes me feel? Well I'll tell you Mr-Fucking-Wonderful… I feel a complete and utter failure! A waste of space! Like a spare prick at a wedding! I couldn't get pregnant! I couldn't carry a baby and I couldn't make you pregnant! What is the point of being here? Tell me that?' she cried hysterically. 'What is the point of anything in my life?'

Out of control and beside herself with pain and misery she ran off, with Jack running hot foot behind her. People waiting on the platform, and just alighting from the train, stood and stared at such anti-social behaviour, and by a couple who should have known better. Jack, panic stricken himself, was terrified by what Chloe might do and continued to run after her shouting her name at the top of his voice. Within minutes he'd lost sight of her and, losing the last of any rational thought, began running round just shouting her name.

Suddenly he spotted her on the opposite platform, and catching her attention darted up the stairs, connecting the two platforms, shouting her name as he lunged up the steps, two at a time. He raced across the bridge and just as he started to tear down the descending steps his balance, out of sync with his burgeoning belly, faltered and he tumbled forward, hitting the steps and rolling over and over until he finally landed at the bottom of the steps in a crumpled heap. Instinctively he'd clutched his hands to his stomach protecting his unborn child, but a searing pain sliced through the middle of his body, tearing a long anguished cry from his throat.

Having seen Jack fall down the stairs, as if in slow motion, and hearing his scream, Chloe knew he was in trouble and immediately pushed her way through the crowds to get to where Jack lay. As she ran, thoughts of losing babies flooded her mind and she was instantly terrified this was going to happen to Jack and the baby now. She rushed over to Jack calling his name in concern.

'Jack! Oh Jack! Are you all right? What's happening? I'm sorry darling! Oh! I'm so sorry Jack. What's the matter? Oh please Jack, speak to me!' she cried desperately, holding his face between her hands, her tears splashing onto his face.

'Chloe! Chloe!' Jack gasped amidst his pain. 'Help me... I... I think it's the baby. Help me! Oh god, please help me! Don't let us lose this baby. We can't lose this baby. Our babeee...' he screamed as once again a pain ripped through him.

By this time quite a crowd had gathered and Chloe, beside herself with desperate fear, felt like screaming at them all to go away. She didn't want Jack to lose the baby and she didn't want these vultures here either. As she fought against the need to scream and shout at them all to bugger off, a firm but gentle hand was laid on her shoulder and a kindly, calming voice informed her an ambulance was on its way.

'He's... he's pregnant,' she told the faceless voice. 'He can't... he can't lose the b... b... baby... he mustn't lose... our baby,' she sobbed, her breath wracked between words.

Several people in the crowd had heard what she'd said and, with all the hype in the papers about men getting pregnant, and many still disbelieving it, the group surged forward twittering excitedly, jostling to get nearer to see this miracle lying at their feet.

Chloe, frightened by everyone crowding in on her, and doing further injury to Jack, screamed at them to go away.

*We can't lose this baby. It has to survive,* she intoned silently, frantically fumbling for her mobile. Both she and Jack had been made to programme Melanie's number into their phones and, shaking violently, Chloe sobbed as she activated the call, which should put her straight through to Melanie, or one of her team at least who would hopefully still be at the Crimedical Centre nearby.

Gasping and crying she sobbed into the phone, 'Melanie! Oh Melanie! It's Chloe here. Jack's wife. It's Jack... he's had a fall. Fallen down some steps,' she wailed. 'We're at... at the railway station. I think... I think... I think he's... he's losing the baby. Please come... Please help us... please won't somebody help us? Don't let us lose this baby,' she wept uncontrollably into the phone. Turning to look at Jack, her husband who'd always been there for her and who she loved so much, she saw he was now prostrate and unconscious.

'I love you Jack, hang on there love, hold onto our baby, don't leave me. Help'll be here in a minute,' she wept as she cradled his head. 'Please don't leave me Jack. Hang on. I love you Jack,' she kept chanting to him.

Would anyone get there in time to help them? Would anyone save their baby? Was Jack going to be all right and would Jack and Chloe ever be the mummy and a daddy they so desperately wanted to be?

~ ~ ~ ~ ~

Melanie sat thinking reflectively, in the quiet of the Crimedical Centre, now all her pregnant men and their partners had left for the day. December 2032 was a month Melanie would never forget, from having identified the rapist to going to apprehend him and finding him in the process of giving birth. Actually witnessing the birth had been mind-blowing and life changing, for her and many others. The papers had now identified Daryl Payne as the first 'father' and also the fact he was the UK serial rapist. It had caused a great outcry of protests from all sectors of the UK and the world, for numerous reasons.

It was finally confirmed Lucy was the second parent and somehow, sadly, the media had managed to get hold of the story almost instantly. Melanie and her team had only just started re-programming

Lucy, who'd not taken the news of her parentage at all well, especially as the media splashed her pictures all over the newspapers and were speculating as to whether or not she'd take the child in. Melanie and her colleagues had immediately got the media stories and speculation halted, with intervention from the government, but too late to prevent Lucy's pain.

The way the nation were handling the news of the bizarre mutation, which was causing male pregnancies, was spreading like wildfire. Despite the fact it was only days since Daryl had given birth the number of pregnant men continued to grow, and even more were coming forward suspecting they were pregnant but weren't. The biggest fear, which seemed to be spreading like an epidemic, was who was likely to become pregnant and how could it be prevented, without abstinence from sex. There was even a worldwide hunt for condom making machinery, which hadn't been required for the past two decades as condoms were no longer needed or produced, now sexual diseases and unwanted pregnancies were a thing of the past.

Melanie's new career, although attached to her original team, was incredibly busy and would need numerous new programmes developing and implementing in the New Year, along with a totally new department and research team setting up for male pregnancy.

As for Daryl their rapist? Well his future lay in the hands of the nation. It had been announced by the government his future was to be put to referendum for the nation to decide his fate, now he'd been proven as the rapist. Should he go through the normal punishment system of incarceration, castration and deportment? Or kept in the UK as a human guinea pig? It was for the nation to vote on, as Daryl himself would have no say in what happened to him. Nor would his mother, who was facing charges for a number of small misdemeanours.

The seven victims, who'd all suffered at the evil hands of Daryl, would be asked to start off the polls with their opinions. So would Melanie and one or two others seniors in the higher ranks of government, put their cases forward. No doubt there would be campaigns for and against each punishment proposed, and undoubtedly several support groups started up for the victims, Daryl, his mother and the new breed of male mothers. What the outcome of this mutation would be no one had any idea. It was all in the lap of the gods.

Melanie herself looked as if she might be further promoted and rumours were afoot she was going to be officially appointed to head up the new government department to look into male pregnancy and the provisions for new 'mothers'. She wasn't sure if she was going to take it, as she loved her detective work and the team she was attached to, but knowing her mother's killer was now dead was making her look at things differently. Maybe, she told herself, she could just look at police work as an interest, rather than a means to an end as she'd seen it up until now.

So many life changing events had taken place and were happening all too quickly. She'd no idea what would happen in the months to come. She thought back to the number of pregnant men she'd interviewed recently and in particular to Jed, the young lad who wasn't yet sixteen. Would he keep his baby, have it aborted, or, if he had it, put it up for adoption? The plight of him and his parents had been almost as eye opening as that of the rapist.

There were several other men who stood out from the dozens she had interviewed in the last couple of weeks. In particular Jack and Chloe, who'd just left her office and were delighted at their news after years of failing to have a baby. It was wonderful the news had been so happily accepted, but she'd already seen the battle of inner feelings raging within them and knew they'd need help to weather this unexpected pregnancy. Would they be able to cope with such extreme emotions and come to terms with them to enable their relationship to survive? It would be such a pity if the conflict of emotions spoilt such a magical event, and they must still have their fingers crossed that Jack wouldn't lose the baby, as Chloe had so many times before.

Then there was Liam, part of the ménàge à trois who'd come along with his boyfriend and girlfriend. They still hadn't worked out which of them was the second parent but time would tell. She suspected Liam wouldn't have too much to worry about there anyway, as he was so closely supported. His confusion, as to whether he was the mother or father, would finally unravel and he might even find a way of keeping his career progressing as it had been. If he did the government would have one very special person working for them, who Melanie believed could well become a prominent part of the new family structuring, as his mother had been years before.

What had surprised Melanie and the rest of the nation, more than anything else, was the fact men who were getting pregnant had been proven to have been conceived whilst their fathers were under the influence of Viagiant, the recreational sex drug from the turn of the century and beyond. Now that was a turn up for the books and had beggared belief when it hit the news. The announcement had caused wide spread panic across the UK and Melanie knew this Christmas the festive season wouldn't be celebrated in the traditional ways it had been honoured by couples for years, decades and centuries past – that was unless men were prepared to risk pregnancy!

What the New Year would bring who could tell? But certainly 2033 was going to be one to keep an eye on and one which would start a whole batch of news items and records rolling.

Melanie thought back to the night before, a smile lighting her face as she thought of Alan. Alan, who she knew loved her unconditionally and was as solid as a rock, and who she knew would wait patiently, without pressing, for her to answer his question. Last night they had enjoyed the first of many kisses, full of hopes and desires; a kiss that had been shared by millions before, but not by Melanie. Their kiss last night had identified a future Melanie had never dared look at before, or even considered. It had been a kiss for the future.

Who knew what 2033 and the years beyond might hold? For Melanie, for Daryl, Jed, Liam, Jack and all the others who'd found themselves pregnant; would become pregnant and were afraid of becoming pregnant. It was a future to be watched and not missed.

Suddenly Melanie's reflections were interrupted by the phone ringing. It was another story about to unfold.

~ ~ ~ ~ ~

# AFTERWORD

When it was announced a man had given birth to a baby, it had rocked the world. When it was revealed, several days later, that the birthing-male was the UK serial rapist, it created even more shockwaves.

Before he'd even left hospital, it was conclusively proven Daryl Payne was the serial rapist. As the story slowly emerged, of how he'd raped six women and left another for dead, the nation began to bay for his blood.

UK citizens were further astounded when it was announced his punishment was not going to follow set procedures, but was being left in the hands of the nation for them to decide, via the means of a referendum. It was an unheard of precedent and immediately stirred the population into action.

Was he to remain in the UK, under lock and key, as a human guinea pig for experimentation or castrated and deported as criminals normally were?

Seven days after Daryl had given birth he'd walked, in great pain, from the humanity of the hospital to the prison van. As he took his last steps of freedom, he openly cried noisy tears of self-pity. What had he done to deserve this? What would his future be? Would he be castrated and deported or would he become a human guinea pig? His uncertain future was made worse by knowing it lay in the hands of an unknown quantity. His future and punishment would, for the first time in history, hang totally in the hands of the nation. They would decide the outcome for him. They held his life in their hands and only time would reveal what it held for him. He wouldn't even be able to present his own case for clemency, not that he knew which punishment would be the worst.

# WHAT WILL THE
# FUTURE FOR DARYL BE?

Anyone over eighteen had a say in how Daryl would be punished. The choices they were given were as follows.

The nation could demand he go through the normal process for serious criminals; which would include incarceration, castration and permanent deportation from the UK and all other WPPL countries.

*ALTERNATIVELY*

They could vote for him to be detained, in isolation in the UK, to be used as a human guinea pig without rights. This would enable scientists to discover what had caused him to become pregnant, and enlighten them as to the mutations which had occurred and expand medical knowledge on male pregnancy.

---

How would you vote?

*Join the Fecundity forum and cast your vote:*

*Visit **www.fecundity.uk.net***

---

How do you visualise the UK in 2032?

If you would like to find out more, email the characters and get responses and help to shape the sequel *Anomalies,* then visit the *Fecundity!* website on

## www.fecundity.uk.net

*If you would like to contact any of the characters and find out how they are coping with their situation, please email them on*

**Daryl@fecundity.uk.net**

**Lucy@fecundity.uk.net**

**Jack&Chloe@fecundity.uk.net**

**Liam@fecundity.uk.net**

**Crawford&Tanya@fecundity.uk.net**

**Jed@fecundity.uk.net**

**Jeds-parents@fecundity.uk.net**

**Fiona-Jade-Ben@fecundity.uk.net**

**Melanie@fecundity.uk.net**

**Other-questions@fecundity.uk.net**

# Fecundity! - Glossary

**Babypouch:** A sterile and accessible pouch inserted into a woman's abdomen to allow human and medical intervention during pregnancy. Has a viewing panel, incorporating a magnifying lens, so the baby's development can be watched and monitored by parents and doctors alike.

**Brooder:** A woman employed by the government to incubate other women's eggs or foetus' in a partial surrogacy role.

**Colorobs:** Computer generated globes of colour that are suspended in mid air. When probes are passed over an individual the Colorbs takes on the individual's characteristics emulating movements and body changes, eg blushing and body temperature. Colorbs are interactive colour-wise and can also be programmed into music and other sounds. In early development stages for use in the medical sector for paediatrics.

**Communileash:** A small chip implanted in a baby's back at birth. Used for tracking, monitoring of behaviour and collating information about the individual. Activated when an individual goes missing and during National Service. The only other times Communileashes are triggered is when anti-social or criminal tendencies are evident and the device is used to monitor and control behaviour.

**Crime Register:** A register of all crimes solved and unsolved.

**Death Register:** The means of recording all deaths, evidencing that the person's DNA has been checked against registered DNA and the Crime Register.

**Gobi:** A female prostitute who is unable to have children and therefore safe for a life-long married man to have sex with.

**Government DNA Database:** where each UK Citizens' DNA is registered for cross-referencing with Crime and Death Register. Created as an aid to solving and reducing crime.

**Image Receptive Gel:** A decorating substance that allows programmed, interactive images to be displayed on the wall and ceiling surface.

**Justice and Social Behaviour System:** the system which governs, regulates, corrects and punishes unacceptable behaviour

**Mirror Imager:** A mirror that allows the individual to view their image from all angles at once.

**National Service:** Two years compulsory service to the community for all individuals aged between 18-22.

**Path Tracker:** A device which enables crime investigators to trace, single out and track an individual's footprints for several miles over a wide range or terrain.

**Skzip:** A re-sealable incision that avoids the necessity of incision and stitches for surgery, once a Skzip is inserted. The incision is electronically sealed by a machine and cannot be opened by anyone other than a medical person, who has specialist equipment and all patients' validity details. Skzips can be used in any area of the body where surgery has been performed. Skzips are almost invisible to the naked eye.

**Slumber-pit:** A multi purpose, programmable, vibrating bed for relaxation, sleep, medical purposes and fornication.

**Social Behaviour Unit:** The official body that looks at undesirable behaviour prior to the Justice System being involved.

**Subliminal Voyeur:** A sophisticated piece of electronic machinery used by the psychiatrists and the Crimedical Sector to explore the subconscious thoughts of an individual, in a conscious or comatose state. Used primarily during investigations to tap into a victim's subconscious state.

**Three Generation Ruling:** DNA, and other data of an individual, and their relatives of the past three generations kept on government file. Used for the purpose of marital and breeding applications, along with other situations where generation information is required. Property of the Government.

**Vibro Centre:** A chair used for relaxation that is programmed to provide an alternative treatment to medication for various conditions.

**WPPL:** World Peace & Prosperity Leaders. An organisation that replaced EEC in the 2020s of which the UK is a leading member.

**WiPPLe**: A newspaper produced by WPPL that reports only proven facts of news.

**Wristlet:** A device worn on the wrist by a child and their parents until the age of majority. Transmits images and communications between parent and child and activates warning signals to parents when pulse, blood pressure and stress levels reach abnormal levels. Enables parents to oversee and take responsibility for their child's behaviour at all times and gives constant and instant access between parent and child.

**Younage:** Complexes or villages where National Service schemes are based. Usually built on disused service bases, developed and maintained by National Service participants

Any UK resident is at liberty, and encouraged, to report the unsocial behaviour of others

*Under the jurisdiction of the WPPL rulings there are a set standard of behaviours that residents and visitors to the UK are expected to comply with. Those not complying will be referred to the Justice and Social Behaviour Unit for processing, correction and/or punishment*

*NO ANTI-SOCIAL OR CRIMINAL BEHAVIOUR WILL BE TOLERATED OR LEFT UNPUNISHED IN THE UK*

### MINORS & THE JUSTICE AND SOCIAL BEHAVIOUR SYSTEM

All infants born in the UK will be fitted with a Communileash at birth. Communileashes will be used to track and monitor an individual's behaviour as and when necessary. The behaviour of all minors, up until the age of 18, will be the responsibility of the parents and/or guardians. Parents and/or guardians, and the minor committing a misdemeanour, will be subject to processing through the Justice and Social Behaviour System.

From the age of 2 all minors, up until the age of 18, will be obliged to wear a Wristlet. Parents and/or guardians will be obliged to wear controlling Wristlets and are required to monitor and react to their charge's behaviour. Failure to respond will activate the Communileash Regulating System, necessitating the parents and/or guardians being answerable and complying to any jurisdiction imposed by the Justice and Social Behaviour Unit.

It is the parents and/or guardians responsibility to ensure no 'blocking' devices are used by their charge. Any minor or parent/guardian found to be using blocking devices will incur penalties as seen appropriate.

Minors found to be guilty of unsocial behaviour, criminal or violent acts will be referred to the social behaviour unit and subject to their Communileashes being activated. Behaviour will be monitored and corrected and individual rights reduced until such time as the social behaviour unit is satisfied the individual behaviour is meeting the required standard. Further anti-social behaviour and misdemeanours will be reported to the Higher Social Behaviour Unit for correction. Minors will be subject to residential re-training until such time as the higher social behaviour is satisfied set standards of behaviour are being met. Parents will also be subject to following and/or participating in the re-training process.

### NATIONAL SERVICE

All individuals aged 18-22 will be obliged to undertake 2 years National Service. This will involve 2 years residential training, in a Younage, addressing different aspects of serving the community and learning career and hobby skills. All participants will partake in a number of skill initiatives in a bid to identify and enhance talents and interests. Participants will receive remuneration during their service.

Communileashes will be activated and warrants for arrest issued for those trying to avoid National Service. Communileashes will automatically activate Awareness Alerts throughout the UK to assist absconders capture. Individuals will then be obliged to carry out their service, with reduced freedoms and payments, until such time as attitudes and compliance are of acceptable standards. Applications can be submitted as Conscientious Objectors, but it is anticipated the majority of those successfully achieving this status will be expelled from the UK.

#### ADULTS AND THE JUSTICE AND SOCIAL BEHAVIOUR SYSTEM

Any adult reported for anti-social behaviour will be subject to an interview with the Social Behaviour Unit. It will be the Social Behaviour Units decision whether further action or investigation is required and if the individual needs to undergo re-training. Where it is shown an individuals DNA is not registered the individual will be taken into custody until such time as DNA and relevant checks have been carried out. Any crimes that are discovered, linked to the individuals DNA, will immediately be referred to the Justice and Social Behaviour System.

#### THE JUSTICE SYSTEM

Adults committing criminal acts in the UK, or any other country, will be subject to set punishments. Individuals committing acts of violence against another human being will, on sentencing, be incarcerated; tag-implanted; castrated and deported. Once an individual has been deported, to an undisclosed destination, s/he will not be permitted re-entry to the UK or any other WPPL country. Forbidden entry to WPPL countries will be enforced by tag-implants, activating Country Parameters and notifying Enforcement Patrols.

If visitors are travelling from a non-WPPL country entry will not be permitted until samples are registered on the UK WPPL Database. This will be done on entry to the country and will only need to be carried out once.

*Extract from WPPL's UK Citizens' Handbook 2030 - Edition 1*

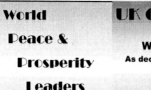

**World Peace & Prosperity Leaders**

# UK CITIZENS' HANDBOOK

### With effect fromJanuary 2030
**As decreed by the UK Marital Referendum 2023**

## MARITAL STATUS
**Eligibility · Applications Process · Benefits**

## ELIGIBILITY

- MARRIAGE OPPORTUNITIES ARE OPEN TO:
- Only individuals whose DNA and other personal data is included on the Government Database
- Individuals aged between 21- 50
- Single sex and both sexes couples
- Three individuals of any sex
- Individuals where there is no evidence of adverse criminal history within the last three generations

### Marriage opportunities are *not* open to:

- Those aged under 21 or over 50
- Anyone where there is evidence of a criminal history within the last three generations of their families
- To any individual who has applied for a marriage certificate previously and was proven to be dishonest in their previous application

*Living with a partner/s without a marriage licence is an acceptable and respected state to both the UK and WPPL.*

*However, contraceptive devices with not be deactivated and marriage privileges will not apply to those without a marriage licence*

## APPLICATION PROCESSES

- Marriage Application Packs can be collected in person from the Marriage Process Facilitator at their local Magistrates Courts and Township Offices
- All applicants must be present when collecting their pack and each party must provide iris and fingerprint images before an application will be allocated to them
- Any applicant found to be providing false information, at any stage during the application process, will incur a set penalty and will receive a lifetime ban from marriage

*Provisional Applications*

- All applicants must be present when applications packs are collected. Before an application pack is released all parties must give iris and fingerprint images and their DNA and other personal data must be shown to be held on the Government Database
- Applications must be completed in the prescribed formats and submitted in person, with all parties present, to the Marriage Process Facilitator at their local Magistrates Courts and Township Offices
- If the completed application form meets with ali set criteria research into the applicant's medical and criminal records, over the past three generations, will be investigated
- If the generation researches meet set criteria, for each party all applicants will be invited for interviews

*All interviews will be held on the same day*
- ◆ At interview stage each applicant will be interviewed separately by two panels. Applicants will not be allowed to communicate between interviews. *Any violation of this ruling will result in the application being claimed null and void*
- ◆ The final interview will be held with all applicants and both panels meeting together where discussions will take place regarding any areas that have caused concern.
- ◆ A decision will be made and given at the end of the day. If successful the applicants will be granted a two year provisional marriage certificate. Unsuccessful applicants will be free to re-apply for a licence, with the existing or an alternate partner, only two years from the date of refusal

### MARRIAGE STATUS CERTIFICATES
- ◆ Couples will be offered the following marital options:
  - ▪ Five year marriage certificate - *renewable*
  - ▪ Ten year marriage certificate - *renewable*
  - ▪ Twenty-five year marriage certificate }    *only those granted the Twenty-five year or life long certificate will have*
  - ▪ Life long marriage certificate    }    *their contraceptive devices deactivated*
- ◆ Applicants are advised to aim for the highest level of marriage certificate they think suitable for themselves. Whilst a panel can downgrade an application they cannot allocate higher grades than have been applied for

*The panels decision as to the level of marriage certificate granted is final and cannot at any time be contested*

### BENEFITS

**5 year marriage certificate** - *will be allocated a Marital Status Government House; will receive 5% discount on rent; will be allocated 5% of the property value for each year of marriage. Contraceptive devices will **not** be deactivated*

**10 year marriage certificate** - *will be allocated a Marital Status Government House; will receive 5% discount on rent; will be allocated 5% of the property value for each year of marriage. Contraceptive devices will **not** be deactivated*

**25 year marriage certificate** - *will be allocated a Marital Status Government House; will receive 5% discount on rent; will be allocated 5% of the property value for each year of marriage, coming under full ownership of the marriage after 20 years. Contraceptive devices will be deactivated and any medical assistance given to aid in the conception of any children. If a couple is unable to carry a child to full term they will be allocated a surrogate mother to carry a child on their behalf, or will be entitled to adopt. Two pregnancies, with healthy offspring will be allowed*

**Life-Long marriage certificate**- *will be allocated a Marital Status Government House; will receive 5% discount on rent; will be allocated 5% of the property value for each year of marriage, coming under full ownership of the marriage after 20 years. Contraceptive devices will be deactivated and full and unlimited medical assistance will be given to aid in the conception and pregnancy duration. All children of a Life-Long Marriage must be of the mother's womb., couples of a life long marriage will not be entitled to a full surrogate baby, be eligible to adopt, or have any child conceived and full term delivered on their behalf. Breach of these rules will deem the marriage null and void and benefits halted with immediate effect. Two pregnancies, with healthy offspring will be allowed.*

*Extract from WPPL's UK Citizens' Handbook 2030 - Edition 1*

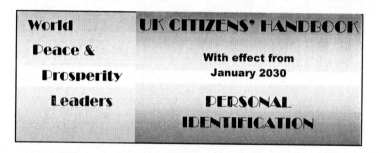

**World Peace & Prosperity Leaders**

**UK CITIZENS' HANDBOOK**

With effect from
January 2030

**PERSONAL IDENTIFICATION**

### THE GOVERNMENT DNA DATABASE

The role of DNA plays a vital role in the solving of crimes in the UK. For this reason the Government has the ownership of any individual's DNA and for all those resident in or visiting the UK. Non-compliance of this regulation will result in a withdrawal of an individual's rights and may lead to prosecution and may incur expulsion from the UK.

#### DNA AT BIRTH

Within the first 12 hours of birth all newborn infants will have digit and ear imprints taken, iris recognition will be recorded and DNA samples taken for inclusion on the Government DNA Database. In addition all infants will have Communileashes embedded and female infants will have contraceptive devices implanted.

### THE INDIVIDUAL'S & MEDICS RESPONSIBILITY

#### THE INDIVIDUALS RESPONSIBILITY

It is the individual's responsibility to ensure that his/her DNA and other identification requirements are included on the Government DNA Database. Samples will be taken automatically when visiting a Medic, Doctor, Dentist or Hospital if records show a patient's details are not listed. However, failure to ensure details are included will result in a withdrawal of citizen rights and may lead to prosecution.

#### THE MEDICAL SECTORS RESPONSIBILITY

It is the Medical Sectors responsibility to ensure that any patients treated have DNA samples included on the Government Database. Any patient treated, whose samples are not registered, must have samples extracted *before* treatment. Non compliance with this will result in unpaid suspension and may result in prosecution. These samples must be forwarded to the appropriate authorities immediately.

*ANY INDIVIDUAL SEEKING ILLEGAL MEDICAL ASSISTANCE AND ANY MEDICAL PERSONNEL PROVIDING ILLEGAL*
*OR UNAUTHORISED MEDICAL TREATMENT WILL BE SUBJECT TO PROSECUTION*
*THAT MAY RESULT IN THE INDIVIUDALS CONCERNED BEING EXCLUDED FROM THE UK.*

#### DNA & ARREST

It is the Government's and local Government's right to arrest any individual whose DNA is not registered. The arrested individual will be detained, without rights, until such time as samples have been processed and matched against the Crime Database.

Any individual arrested on suspicion of a misdemeanour will have DNA samples extracted to match against those registered on the Government DNA Database and Crime Register.

**DNA & DEATH**

All deceased individuals will have DNA samples extracted before disposal. Samples will be matched against registered DNA and the crime Database. Results will be kept indefinitely on file for inclusion in the Three-Generation Crimedical Data and any other purposes, as the Government deems appropriate.

**DNA and VISITORS to the UK**

No individual will be admitted to the UK without evidence of their DNA on the Global WPPL Database. If visitors are travelling from a non-WPPL country entry will not be permitted until samples are registered on the UK WPPL Database. This will be done on entry to the country and will only need to be carried out once.

*Extract from WPPL's UK Citizens' Handbook 2030 - Edition 1*

Excerpt from the sequel to this book

# ANOMALIES

by Meg Plummer

## 1st January 2033

The eerie blue light gave neither darkness nor light and cast no shadow. The only mechanical sound was the low pitched hum of the electronically controlled spy-eye and room conditioning; even that could only be heard if carefully listened for. Living in a world without definition was the torture it was meant to be, and left the occupants with nothing but their own thoughts for company.

In this desolate milieu, a cubic space of just eight feet square, the anguished howls of a soul in torment could be heard. Sobs of self-pity and loss wracked Daryl who, dishevelled and distraught, was crouched in a balled-up heap of human despair, rocking mindlessly as he wailed.

He'd been in these quarters less than three weeks, and with each day his despair had deepened and confusion multiplied. Christmas had been and gone without any relief from the almost inhumane conditions he was kept in. The only reason he knew it was New Year's Day was because, oddly, his food pearls had been delivered by a guard, who'd informed him of the date. 'Informed' though wasn't really the right word, 'mocking' would have been more accurate. It was the guard's mockery that had set off the current paroxysm of despair. When the door had opened Daryl thought he'd a visitor. Someone to tell him how his baby was, what was happening in the world, or just if his mam was alright. He'd had none of those things, only the sneering, mocking tones of contempt from the guard, who'd held his stun gun at the ready as Daryl had pleaded for information.

So what did the New Year hold for him? Whatever it was terrified him. Kept in his bare cell, which consisted of only a sleeping bench, upright chair and hygiene facilities, he was rarely allowed out. Once a day he was allowed an hour to walk in fresh air and to shower afterwards. With the security beams, set up around the prison, he not only had no chance of escape but the beams totally soundproofed the area. The conditions prisoners were kept in verged on being barbaric.

Daryl was allowed no contact with any other inmate and food, liquids and any medications needed were delivered robotically. No entertainment of any description was permitted; no written or writing materials allowed and the cells were devoid of any natural or recorded sound. Disorientating him further was the blue light, whose constant mundane glow prohibited any definition between night and day, with the exception of his daily dose of fresh air.

Trips out into the yard were guarded and monitored by the silent, but deadly, security beams, and the soundproofed cells precluded any sound from fellow prisoners en route. Convicts never associated with any other human being, except for their weekly crimedical examination. This meant that Daryl was subjected to twenty-four hours of his own company. Twenty-four hours of consciousness and sleep-bidden nightmares that tormented him relentlessly.

Daryl spent a lot of the time thinking about his baby. He so wanted to see it, hold it and cradle it. His whole being yearned for physical contact with it and, if he couldn't be granted that, then he just wanted to know it was faring ok. But even thoughts of the baby furthered his confusion. *How had he become pregnant – him a man? And what a bitch that Lucy was, to have leave him in this predicament, the callous cow. What right had she to do that to him, and left him labelled as not only a rapist but a freak too?* It was at times like this that he paced the tiny space of his cell. Barely able to take three strides before he needed to turn and stride back, the almost spiralling movement compounded his confused thoughts.

When he'd first been brought to his cell he'd been frightened to move much at all, scared his healing wound would hurt or reopen. The Skzips they'd repaired him with had finally given up smarting, as had the glued sections of the other incisions. The Skzips scared him most, though, as he knew they were only used when they expected to reopen the wound. The thought that he'd be experimented on and treated like an exhibit for the medical world terrified him just as much as the nation being given the right to decide his future for him. The nation, he knew, held his life in the palm of its hand.

Daryl had sat like a crying baby when he'd been informed of his lack of rights, and what was being instigated in the outside world. He was horrified that a public referendum was being held to decide his fate. He didn't know which terrified him most, the thought of being castrated and deported or kept in the UK to become a guinea pig. With tears and snot running freely down his face, he'd pleaded to be able to speak for himself at the onset of the referendum. He thought it grossly unfair Lucy would be allowed to give her opinion, along with a number of other individuals, speaking for and against each outcome, when he was the victim here. They wouldn't even tell him when the referendum would be or when he'd get to know the outcome. They told him nothing.

*Why should Lucy be allowed to speak when he wasn't and all this was her fault anyway? Why was she being given such privileged treatment? After all it was her who'd made him pregnant. He just hoped the sour-faced cow never got to see the baby. After all why should she when he wasn't allowed to? She wasn't fit to see him.*

He railed constantly against the unjustness of his situation. *He was the victim here. Not her. Why couldn't he see the baby? Why shouldn't he? After all it was his baby wasn't it?* He wondered how his little lad was getting on. *He'd never seen his son or been shown any pictures, let alone been allowed to hold him. His baby had just been whisked away. He could so love the baby. Love it like he'd never been loved, but had wanted to be. He'd teach it to play football and all about cars, he'd make him toys to play with and invent new games to play together. He'd teach him how easy it was to move about without being seen and how he could get round Big Brother's watchful eyes without being detected. There were so many things he could teach him and so much fun they could have together.*

His thoughts would meander off, creating little scenarios of father and son unity and then suddenly turn and become twisted.

*Where could we live? I don't want him to have anything to do with that evil old witch of a mother of mine. She'd sell him. Sell his soul and his right to privacy to line her fucking pockets. She never cared about me. I was just a means to an end. A reason for her not to go out to work. What did she do to me to make me like I am? A bloody woman disguised as a man. What the fuck have I done to deserve all this? I've done nothing. Nothing at all It's her fault. All her fault. She's evil. Twisted. I hope she rots in fucking hell. I hope they throw her in a cell like this one and throw away the key. Feed her food pearls like she always fed me. I hate her. Hate her. Hate her.*

By this time Daryl would be shouting his thoughts out loud in the silent room. No-one came in to comfort him, warn him to take control or console him in any way. The only external contact was the spy-eye recording every movement, word and subliminal thought. Every subconscious thought and picture was being transmitted through to the subliminal voyeur, through the Communileash they'd implanted in his back. Not that he knew it was there. Daryl knew nothing, and would be told even less.

Even though Melanie and Alan had become a couple, their Christmas had not been as they'd planned or expected. The arrangements, surprises and times they'd intended to spend together had all gone haywire. All in all the festive period had been quite bizarre. It had barely happened, but paled into significance against everything else going on.

The pandemonium that ensued the announcement of male birthing, had not subsided. Initially it had been anticipated it would be a one-day wonder. Nothing could have been further from the truth. Things continued to escalate, gaining momentum as more and more men came forward either actually expecting or thinking themselves pregnant. The strategies Melanie had implemented, to increase the number of people registering their DNA, appeared to have been unnecessary. Men in droves, or so it seemed, had been rushing to their doctors convinced they were pregnant or wanting to know what the chances of them getting pregnant were. Many had been unregistered DNAers, with a high majority found to have misdemeanours listed against their DNA.

With the resultant glut of samples and cross-referencing required against the Government DNA database, the Crimedical department was kept busier than it had been in years. It seemed as if criminals were coming out of the woodwork, keeping Melanie's old department on its toes and overstretched. The government ruled for all departments to act on these findings instantly, so newly identified perpetrators wouldn't have time to avoid arrest. From the resultant arrests Christmas 2032 saw UK prisons at more than fifty percent capacity for the first time in almost two decades.

The severity of some of the cases was quite mind-boggling, with some interesting charges being levied. Cases which had defied detection and intrigued the UK for years were now being solved and, as a consequence, drawing higher bonuses. This phase of crime solving was not only creating higher earnings, but regaining much needed credence and respect for the UK within the WPPL. It was also enabling the Crimedical department to identify avoidance tactics and uncover underground factions, as well as closing loopholes. It was a catalyst of events never before seen in the UK, or any other country.

Whilst Melanie's old team was stretched to capacity, her new one was equally busy developing and implementing systems for the ever-growing number of pregnant men. Melanie suspected there was at least one missing link to male pregnancies, and was determined to unearth it as soon as possible. She also knew there must have been some type of intervention, either a natural occurrence or manually manipulated, to have triggered the phenomenon. These were things that would take time no Christmas at all. As it was Melanie, Helen and a small group of medical experts had quickly got together to set up an interim support group, to tide them over this initial period. Whilst it was barely adequate for the present moment it would have to do, but the future would demand much more intense and expert specialists, if male pregnancy was an ongoing evolution of man.

The issue that had taken most of Melanie's time though, which had come as no surprise but had still shocked everyone, was the rapist's baby. Initially it had been thought the child was normal, and had been born without any anomalies. Nothing though could have been further from the truth. Within forty-eight hours of its birth it had become apparent the child was not normal. Whilst in general it seemed to be thriving conventionally, it was quite extraordinary, and becoming more so with every test result. There had been a great deal of concern and controversy raised, within the small circle of medical and scientific staff allowed any information on the child. As examinations had been run and results calculated the child had been passed from pillar to post for one tranche of tests after another, with still further experiments planned and to be developed. The more information gathered and assimilated the more concern was generated over the child's normality and future.

to discover, but if anyone had the stamina to solve the mystery it was Melanie.

In addition to everything else going on in the UK there was a worldwide hunt on for prophylactic manufacturing machines. With the advance in medical intervention it was more than twenty years since they'd been a need to use condoms. Now, with men getting pregnant, it seemed they were the only possible solution guaranteed to keep men safe from pregnancy, apart from abstinence. The problem was that they were now obsolete, along with any functioning machinery. Locating plant equipment had not been a problem; there had been several located throughout the world, but none in England. With the UK's tendency to import as many goods from abroad as possible, there weren't even any manufacturing machines in the museums. However securing one from another country was a different matter. The scarcity of the machinery, in the wake of the UK's experience, led to every country being set on protecting their menfolk and holding onto their now treasured machinery, no matter how derelict or obsolete it seemed. Once machinery could be secured, the problem would then be setting up a manufacturing plant and acquiring the necessary materials, labour and knowledge to commence production. An easy concept in theory, but totally different in reality. Added to that negotiations so far had not been favourable and the government had found it necessary for WPPL to step in on the UK's behalf. So far there was no resolution forthcoming.

Melanie had also had to deal with several issues and crises from the men she'd interviewed before Christmas, who were pregnant. After a distraught and urgent call from Chloe, following Jack's catastrophe, it had been necessary to set up urgent trauma support for the distraught couple. In addition she'd been called in to deal with problems regarding Jed, their youngest expectant male to date. There were profound problems between him and his parents, who were not coping at all well with the situation. All the problems these men were facing, along with their partners and families, had never arisen before, so consequently there were no provisions set up to deal with them. There was no-one in the country, or world for that matter, trained or experienced in any of the predicaments arising from this new situation. The worst thing Melanie could do was provide inadequate support, but the problems had to be addressed immediately, as per government and WPPL rulings. The only saving grace on that score, so far, was the mother of one of the other expectant men, Liam. Liam's mother, Helen, who'd been involved in the initial set up of the government's Parenting Skills scheme was a godsend. Had it not been for her Melanie would have had